SHADES OF GREY

A Selection of Recent Titles by Clea Simon

CATTERY ROW
CRIES AND WHISKERS
MEW IS FOR MURDER

SHADES OF GREY

Clea Simon

This first world edition published 2009
in Great Britain and in the USA by
SEVERN HOUSE PUBLISHERS LTD of
9–15 High Street, Sutton, Surrey, England, SM1 1DF.
Trade paperback edition published
in Great Britain and the USA 2009 by
SEVERN HOUSE PUBLISHERS LTD

British Library Cataloguing in Publication Data

Simon, Clea.
Shades of Grey
1. Women graduate students – Fiction 2. Animal
Ghosts – Fiction 3. Gothic novels – Fiction
4. Murder – Fiction 5. Detective and mystery stories
I. Title
813.6-dc22

ISBN-13: 978-0-7278-6781-0 (cased)
ISBN-13: 978-1-84751-153-9 (trade paper)

All Severn House titles are printed on acid-free paper.

Typeset by Palimpsest Book Production Ltd.,
Grangemouth, Stirlingshire, Scotland.
Printed and bound in Great Britain by
MPG Books Ltd., Bodmin, Cornwall.

For Jon

Acknowledgments

Many people had a hand in helping Dulcie Schwartz into the world. For their assistance with this new series, as well as with many previous projects, I would like to thank my readers Naomi Yang, Caroline Leavitt, Brett Milano, Chris Mesarch, Lisa Susser, Vicki Croke, Karen Schlosberg, and Michelle Jaeger. Ann Porter, Iris Simon, Frank Garelick, Lisa Jones, and Sophie Garelick have been tireless cheerleaders, and Colleen Mohyde of the Doe Coover Agency is everything one could want in an agent. Thanks, of course, to Amanda Stewart and the staff at Severn House, for recognizing Dulcie's charms and helping to polish them. Jon S. Garelick has read this manuscript more times than I thought possible, and improved it every time. Thank you, love. Thank you, all.

One

'The carving knife was the last straw.'

Stomping along the steaming sidewalk, her mood matching the thunder clouds overhead, Dulcie knew that the sentence made no logical sense. How could a knife be a straw? She could hear herself asking her students such a question, her usual wry smile softening the criticism as she urged them back on the metaphorical track.

But as she trudged toward the apartment she shared for the summer, increasingly unwillingly, with Tim, she couldn't stop the grammatical train wreck of her thoughts.

She sighed and paused for a moment, looking around at the other drones on the street. How did they do it, day after day? A man in a suit passed her. At least he'd been able to shed his jacket, which now hung over his shoulder. No such relief for Dulcie. Pantyhose in July ought to be illegal. Had last summer been so muggy and dense?

Thirty minutes ago she'd been shivering, trapped in the recycled cold of the overly air-conditioned Priority Insurance office, like a bug in some global version of 'contrast and compare'. She shouldn't be temping; shouldn't have been in that soulless place at all. Insurance. Bah! It was all numbers juggling, all about profits and odds; nothing that actually affected people. She should have been in the pleasingly cool depths of Widener Library, lost in the fogs of the northern moors. Or perhaps on a night voyage across the Carpathians in a horse-drawn carriage. At the very least, she should have her thesis topic by now. According to the terms of her biggest grant, she should be writing already. But right before the holiday break, she'd heard that summer school enrollment was down. And that meant that her teaching section was canceled. No 'Nightmare Imagery in the Early British Novel', and by then it was too late to grab a section of the basic required survey course, English 10, the bane of freshmen and the salvation of starving grad students. It was too late to back out of the summer sublet that had allowed Tim into her home. And although she hadn't known it at the time, it was too late for Mr Grey.

Thoughts of her late, great cat made her stop again in the street. Mr Grey had been a stray, full-grown and sleek, when she'd found him during her freshman year. He'd been so skinny at the end, though, right after Memorial Day, the ribs obvious beneath his silky grey fur. Even before the vet told her, she knew it was the end of the line for the big cat. Still, she'd tried everything. And now, even though the vet was being super sweet about the bills, she was hundreds of dollars in debt, with no real job, and a roommate who teased her about her still-raw grief.

That was bad enough, but then Tim had taken her knife. One of her few good cooking utensils, along with a cast-iron pan and a two-quart pot that always cleaned up well, no matter how burned, the knife had been her mother's second best. She'd found it, just as she'd found her Wheeler Latin grammar, her new iPod earbuds, and most of her vintage soul collection, in Suze's room – Tim's room as it would be until Labor Day. She'd gone in to close the window during one of the summer's many thunderstorms and found it on the carpet, coated with some dried-on grime, its edge knicked and the point slightly bent. When he'd gotten in, hours after the rain had come and gone, Tim had given her some vague excuse. Something about the window screen getting stuck and how the insulation she and Suze had put in the winter before was really a health hazard. In other words, he had implied the whole thing was her fault. It was after two by then, and Dulcie had been half asleep – and too distracted thinking about what use he'd made of her Barry White CDs to listen to details. There'd been no point. Timothy S. Worthington was a walking entitlement – the 'S' standing for yet another Harvard building funded by one of his ancestors – and she knew she'd never get a straight answer out of him. The knife was damaged, possibly ruined. It *had* been the last straw.

A car honked, swinging around the corner as if driven by demons, and Dulcie jumped back. How she missed Mr Grey! He'd always seemed to understand her moods, coming up with a catnip mouse when she needed distraction; sleeping quietly by her feet when she was reading or grading papers. She'd called Suze almost every night those last few weeks, and even though her friend was starting her internship with a hotshot judge, Suze had listened. Only after the latest bill came, and her mother confided in her usual dithering way that she needed a loan to keep her own power on, had Dulcie cut back. And now she was stranded, alone, and temping in downtown insurance offices until September.

The knife, as Tim would never understand, was more than a utensil. When poor old Lucy Schwartz had packed up her daughter to send her back East, she'd been at a loss as to what practical things Dulcie would need. She had spent too many years on the commune, as Dulcie still thought of the arts colony, and perhaps there had also been too many psychedelic mind excursions as well. But along with an oversized quilt, eight sweaters all hand-knitted into various shapes, and her own Riverside Shakespeare, the one-time hippie had pulled the second best of everything from her small kitchen. 'Give me a penny for luck, dear,' she'd insisted as she'd wrapped the long knife in newspaper for packing. 'If you don't "buy" it from me, it may end up hurting you.'

So Dulcie had given her mother a penny, and hadn't looked back. Leaving the Oregon forests for the university-centered metropolis, she had found she loved the city's bustle and diversity. Everything was businesslike here. Even her reading now had order, strengthened by the discipline of academia. And when Dulcie had discovered Gothic literature, which set its wildest imaginings against the strict conventions of the eighteenth-century novel, she knew she'd found her niche. It wouldn't hurt if her dissertation was on something that might actually get her a teaching gig, something hot like 'Conventions of Morality in Nineteenth-Century Clerical Verse' or 'Beyond the Metaphor: Physics and Metaphysics in Science Fiction's Golden Age'. But she'd worry about the job market later. What she really needed – and soon – was a topic; that, and a few good friends, her cat, and some decent kitchenware.

Instead, she had Tim. Rounding the corner, at last, on to her block, she felt the first drop of rain. Great. But maybe if it really poured, the heat would break. Another drop. She sped up – increasing the pain of those God-awful heels. Maybe she'd treat herself to a good cry. Tim was rarely home in the early evening; the habits that had him sleeping in while she got ready for work and out by the time she arrived home were her favorite of his traits. A third drop hit her face. She definitely needed a good cry. She knew she wasn't up to any more teasing. One more 'it's just a cat' comment would lay her out. But if Tim were true to form, she would have the apartment to herself. She could collapse on to her bed in her tiny room, at the back of the top floor, that she thought of as her garret. The weather was certainly cooperating. But as she crossed the street, she was startled to see a cat on the front stoop leading up to her front door. A long-haired grey who looked startlingly like Mr Grey.

I wouldn't go in, if I were you. Dulcie spun around. The voice had seemed to be immediately behind her, calm and deep and right by her ear. But as she peered down the street, she couldn't see anybody there.

I know it's about to pour, but why don't you hit that coffee place with the good muffins instead? There was nobody behind her. The street was deserted. Was she hearing voices now?

Just good advice. That's all. The cat on the middle step was washing its face, carefully licking its left paw and then running it over each ear in turn.

'Mr Grey?' It made no sense. The cat kept washing, straining sideways now to get its tongue into the thick grey ruff.

Dulcie closed her eyes. The heat, grief, and these damned pantyhose.

She was losing it. When she dared to look again, the cat was gone. Undoubtedly, it was a neighborhood cat, a lovely grey she'd never noticed before. Undoubtedly, it had fled the rain. Climbing the stairs, she reached for the key and noticed that the white front door was ajar.

'Good work, Tim.' At least, she no longer had to worry about Mr Grey getting out. She pushed the door further open and started up the steep stairs that led from the pint-sized entryway up to her second-floor living room. God, she was wiped. For a moment, she paused and thought again of Mr Grey. He'd always met her at the front door, his plume of a tail leading the way in.

'Mr Grey, I miss you,' she couldn't resist saying out loud. Immediately, she regretted it. What would her jerk room-mate say if he'd heard?

'Tim, are you there?' She hiked up the stairs, desperate to shed the pantyhose. If Suze had still been living with her, or any woman for that matter, Dulcie would have started to peel them off as soon as she walked in the door.

Over the top stair, she could see a large dark spot on the industrial tan rug, reaching from behind the sofa into the middle of the carpet. Great. Dulcie and Suze had lived in this apartment close to four years, but only in the past two months with Tim had the place begun to show its age. She closed her eyes. 'Tim?' She was going to have to say something. Not that it would do any good. '*Tim*!'

With that yell, she made it up the last two stairs and looked around. The spot was huge, a wet-looking stain that seemed to be spreading still. And inside the dark spot was something white, like a fleshy spider. Something that looked very much like a hand. Taking two steps forward, she peeked behind the sofa's raised and padded side, to see that the fleshy spider was indeed a hand, and that it was attached to an arm that extended out of a familiar 'Beer Good!' T-shirt. Dulcie blinked, not believing what was before her. Cat or no cat, pantyhose or not, Tim was beyond teasing her now. Instead, he was lying on his back by the sofa on the living room rug, with her mother's second-best carving knife in his chest.

Two

Dulcie couldn't move. For several long moments the day, the heat, even her pantyhose were forgotten as she stood there staring. The blade, still shiny in spots, and the black wooden handle, always a bitch to clean, held her like a magnet. The edges of the room began to dim.

Then, suddenly, to her right, she saw a flash of movement – of grey fur – and she turned. That cat! How had it gotten by her? She took a step toward the kitchen, the spell broken.

'Kitty! Where are you?' Was she speaking? No, though she had half formed the words, meaning to chase the stray down the steps, the voice she'd heard was in her own head. Still, had she heard something?

Dulcie, please, go back outside. Go outside and call 911. She was losing it; that much was clear. *I did try to warn you, you know.* Stepping back, her eyes averted from the still, lifeless form on the living room floor, she hastily descended the stairs and closed the door behind her. The rain had begun in earnest, big fat drops that kicked up the dust on the sidewalk and street. The wet felt good, soaking through her thin summer dress.

She should call the police. She should notify someone. But when she reached for her bag, she realized she'd dropped it, inside. She looked up at her own front door. No, she didn't need any eerie voices to tell her not to go back into the apartment. Her neighbors, though, they were an option. As thunder began to rumble she ran down her stoop and began banging on the door of the first-floor apartment. Helene, still in her nurse's uniform, answered.

'Dulcie, what's wrong?' Helene's broad, dark face immediately assumed a look of professional concern, and Dulcie realized that the wet on her cheeks came from tears as well as rain.

'It's Tim.' Dulcie gasped for breath.

Helene ran a hand over her short, cropped curls and rolled her eyes.

'That full-of-himself frat boy done something again?'

'He's not— He wasn't—' The sky rumbled and Helene reached out to pull the younger woman inside. Dulcie shook her off. 'It's— He's—' A crack of thunder burst the air and both of them jumped. Dulcie was crying in earnest now, desperate to get the words out.

Helene was staring at her, puzzled, maybe a little annoyed. She'd have worked a long day, too. Dulcie closed her eyes and saw a pair of feline green eyes staring back. Focus was the key. She took a breath.

'It is Tim, Helene.' She opened her eyes, her mind clearing. 'But not what you think. I came home and the door was open, and Tim was just lying there, Helene. He's lying on my living room carpet, and I'm pretty sure he's dead.'

Two hours later, Dulcie was sipping sweet, hot tea liberally laced with rum. It wasn't a cocktail she'd ever have thought of, but sitting on Helene's sofa, wrapped in a blanket, it surely hit the spot.

The police had taken over her apartment, she remembered that. After the sudden storm, she and Helene and a growing crowd of neighbors had waited outside as the lights flashed and uniforms scurried about. They'd had plenty of questions for her, too, particularly the portly older detective who seemed to be in charge. What had she seen? Had she touched anything? Dulcie had been over and over her horrible home-coming so many times, she could no longer tell what had actually happened: the man she had seen on the street – he'd probably been walking from the T, same as her; the car that had sped by; the voice she was sure she'd heard – no, that bit she kept to herself. No need to have any of them thinking she was nuttier than she was. But she did tell the stout detective that the door had been open, and that she must have dropped her bag.

'You saw your room-mate lying on the floor, and you continued into the apartment?' He ran his hand back through what remained of greasy black hair. 'Toward the kitchen?'

'Well, no. Not really.' She remembered turning away from the body, but not what she'd been planning to do. Had she been going to proceed through the kitchen and upstairs to her room? Ignore the body in the living room? That's when it hit her: she'd seen the cat again, the grey long-hair who must have followed her in. She'd turned toward the running cat, and he'd told her to get out of the apartment. She was sure of it. She'd tried to explain to the detective then; tried to tell the older man about the strange voice she was hearing – a voice she'd never heard before but that seemed to be coming from the cat. She'd told him that she'd seen it pass by her, and that its movement – a blur of silver fur – had broken her out of her stupor, finally gotten her to move. He'd tut-tutted and 'there there'd' her. Clearly, he thought she was nuts. Ah, well, at least at that point, he'd decided to release her into Helene's care.

'A grey long-hair, you say? Oh, she had a cat like that,' she had heard her neighbor explaining. 'Silky like a Persian, only without that ugly pushed-in face. She had to have it put down, poor girl. She was that upset – and her room-mate? He didn't understand. He used to tease her.'

The detective had looked over at her again at this point, his eyes narrowing under heavy black brows, and Dulcie didn't think it was with sympathy. But she'd been at work whenever – *it* – had happened. Hadn't she? Dulcie recalled her slow trudge up Suffolk Street and how she had paused when she'd seen that beautiful grey cat. She thought of the open door – and the spreading puddle around Tim's body.

Her teeth were chattering now, and the booze in the tea sloshed around in her belly. Huddling in the blanket, she turned toward the back of the sofa. If only she could stop thinking about that puddle, the darkness that had looked almost black on the dingy carpet. If only her stomach would settle down. Were the police still in her apartment upstairs? Had her landlord started to clean it? Helene had called the emergency number for her.

'You're paying rent on that place, child. And he sure has insurance to cover a new carpet!' Dulcie shivered and pressed her head between the sofa cushions. Almost, she thought, she could hear a vacuum cleaner, or maybe one of those carpet shampoo machines, in the apartment above, the low hum coming through the ceiling and her protective cocoon of upholstery. Whirr, whirr . . . the sound was strangely relaxing, rhythmic and even. Whirr, whirr . . . just a little, she thought, like a cat's purr; like when Mr Grey would jump up on the bed as she drifted into sleep. Whirr . . . whirr . . . and she was out.

Three

The funeral was a mistake. Dulcie had known that from the moment she'd walked into the chapel and realized that her long, black Indian skirt was completely wrong for the day, being neither tailored nor linen. She shouldn't be here. She didn't fit. She'd wanted to skip the whole thing, forget that Tim had ever happened, and spend the day curled up with her books. But Suze had insisted that she go.

'You were his room-mate, Dulce. It's only polite.' Although Suze was a couple of hundred miles away, Dulcie could picture her room-mate clearly: tall and lean, her no-nonsense dark hair cut short and chic as well as cool. She'd said it was sweltering in DC, so she'd probably be wearing her old Harvard swim team T-shirt and shorts. 'You've got to go.'

'He's not going to care, Suze.' Dulcie settled in for a long comfort talk, stretching out her own shorter and significantly softer legs on to the sofa. 'I mean, his family doesn't know me from Eve.' It was Friday. Dulcie was back in her own place by then. She'd rearranged the furniture in a desperate attempt to reclaim the space, and had dragged the sofa over toward the window so she wouldn't have to see the spot where Tim had lain. Not that there was any actual spot by then. The stained brown carpet had been replaced with a strange green shag that looked like it belonged on the bottom of an aquarium. It was probably all that the landlord could get in a hurry, but Dulcie was grateful for the distraction. 'Did I tell you about this new carpet?'

'Three times, Dulcie, but I understand it's weird. And, yeah, you've got to go. It doesn't matter if his family acknowledges you. You were his room-mate. Besides, don't you want the cops to think you're mourning?'

Dulcie had grunted. What did she care what the cops thought? They couldn't suspect her, could they? She considered her toenails. Should she stick with the neon-blue polish? She had already changed the color twice. But her attempt to distract herself failed; Suze's comment on protocol had hit home. That was the kind of thing she'd never learned, growing up in a series of cooperative yurts. Lucy – Dulcie never called her 'Mom' – had taught her about compost, sure. But Emily Post? No way. Coming to Cambridge from the social equivalent of Mars, Dulcie relied on Suze for anything approaching etiquette. A law student from a comparatively normal suburban upbringing, Suze could talk about social dos and don'ts with a bit of wry distance, but at least she knew what the rules were.

'Wear something dark,' she had said, and Dulcie wondered just how well her friend remembered how limited her wardrobe was. 'Black's really just for the family.'

Once they'd signed off, Dulcie had gone through her closet, pushing aside both the budget-conscious rayon dresses that served for work and her favorite colorful cottons. Despite Suze's warning, the skirt she'd settled on had seemed perfect; cascading black tiers and long enough so that she could get away with bare legs as the steamy heat of July continued. Paired with a black scoop-neck T-shirt, it looked summery as well as appropriate. She'd even been grateful, just a little, for an excuse to leave the apartment she'd once considered so homey. Until she walked into St Paul's on the Hill, that is. The moment she had entered that bastion of high WASP worship, Dulcie had realized that once again she was the hippie's kid; too messy, too casual, too . . . well, too Dulcie for this crowd.

The cool, dim chapel could have been the staging area for a J. Crew photo shoot. People were mulling, there was no other word for it, in perfect refinement: their conversation soft, their appearances flawless; their hair not captive to the swelling humidity. Dulcie recognized a few of Tim's drinking buddies, preppie-looking ex-jocks, their smooth tans almost hiding where they were beginning to develop double chins. Even with the extra poundage, they looked pedigreed, the show dogs to her stray cat. Short, rounded, with an unruly mop of brown curls that the sun had only lightened to copper, Dulcie tried to ignore the feeling that she didn't fit, though the occasional cool glance directed at her didn't help. In response, she turned away and scanned the rest of the crowd, hoping for anything like a friendly face.

'Alana!' Never before had she considered the tall blonde a welcome sight. But right now she was grateful to spy Tim's girlfriend in the small cluster of equally wispy beauties who had gathered by the side of the chapel. At least the featherweight blonde in the navy linen sheath was someone she had met. 'I'm so sorry.'

The perfect oval face that turned toward her could have come off the cover of a magazine, with flawless skin untouched by lines or worry and a rosebud mouth delicately tinted peach. Dulcie looked into her wide-set hazel eyes, rimmed with a touch of turquoise. Girls like her must know the secret to run-proof mascara. 'How are you doing?'

Alana blinked twice, so slowly that Dulcie could see her thoughts processing. Another girl glanced over.

'I'm Dulcie – Tim's room-mate?' The perfectly shaped eyebrows arched a little higher. Dulcie turned to the rest of the group. 'Tim's subletting my room-mate's room in my duplex,' she explained. 'He was, anyway.'

'Oh, yes. Daisy. Thank you for coming.' As if remembering her role, Alana's pretty mouth pouted a bit. 'I still can't believe he's gone. I keep waiting for him to text me.'

'It must be awful. I'm so sorry. You must be devastated.' The blonde blinked again at that, her smooth face blank with incomprehension. An image of a cow flashed across Dulcie's mind, and immediately she could have kicked herself. The girl must be in shock. She should cut a grieving girlfriend some slack.

'You're the *room-mate*?' One of Alana's buddies turned to Dulcie. 'You're the one who *found* him?' At that, they all perked up. Suddenly, she was interesting.

'Uh, yeah. When I came home from work.' A soft murmur, like the lowing of cattle, went up from the four friends, all blondes, except for one dark-haired beauty who probably styled herself as 'exotic'. Dulcie felt weirder than ever, a ladybug about to be gobbled up from the grass. 'It was pretty awful.'

As if she had just realized that her friends' attention had drifted, Alana suddenly sobbed. Immediately, the crew turned back toward her. The brunette shot Dulcie a look, lifting a dark-berry upper lip in a sneer. Clearly, this was all her fault. 'Honey, are you going to be all right?' Another of the friends put her arm around Alana's perfectly tanned shoulder, turning her away from the offending sight of Dulcie. Suddenly a tall man stepped over, his back wide enough to block Alana from Dulcie's view.

'Hey, babe, come with me. We're all sitting over by the windows.' The cooing increased, as he steered the blonde behind the pews and away from Dulcie. Her flock followed, hovering, and Dulcie found herself alone again. To top everything off, the black T-shirt was warmer than she'd remembered. She could feel sweat trickling down her back.

Tim's parents, his mother veiled, passed by and paused. Surely, they remembered her from the day they had moved their son in, supervising as some freelance dorm crew members had carried up his trunk, suitcases, and the guitars with their amps that he never seemed to play. Dulcie nodded, and Tim's father nodded back. His mother just turned away. It was the skirt, she was certain.

Everyone was taking a seat. Should she bolt? She wasn't sure. The huddle of large boys – she recognized at least one of them, a burly dude called Chuck, as one of Tim's B-school buddies – were looking her way. There was something wolflike about them – maybe it was all those big, perfect teeth – and she was acutely aware of being a woman alone. She looked down at her T-shirt, trying to pull at it so that it didn't stick quite so closely to her ample curves.

That's when she noticed the hair. About three inches long, silvery grey against the black cotton, it could only have come from one place, from one beloved pet. Had she not worn this shirt since Mr Grey had died? She plucked off the hair and smiled, twirling it in her fingers. She wasn't alone, not really, and with that encouraging thought, Dulcie slid into the second-to-last pew, next to another lone female. Dulcie saw that her neighbor had had the sense to wear dark blue. In truth her outfit seemed to fit her no better than Dulcie's. But while Dulcie's overdyed black T was now clinging uncomfortably, this stranger's jacket hung on her slim shoulders like a shower curtain. From the slight sheen, visible even in the dull church light, Dulcie figured it for polyester. It must have felt like hot plastic in this heat.

'We must be the pew of fashion misfits,' Dulcie muttered to herself, and thought of making a joke of it to her seatmate when she noticed the girl was crying. Although her dark hair hung over her face, Dulcie recognized the shaking of her shoulders as genuine, and when a small honk emerged from under an unfashionable cascade of curls, Dulcie passed her a tissue. The face that looked up was red and blotchy. 'Thanks,' the girl mouthed silently. Dulcie smiled and nodded. At least someone here seemed to be truly mourning the dead man.

Who was this crying girl? That quick glance under the hair had shown a face devoid of make-up, though that could have been the result of the tears. Taking in the ersatz clothes, the untamed hair, and the apparently real grief, Dulcie felt a kinship and decided to speak. But just then a white-haired gentleman who looked like TV's perfect Dad from central casting began to talk, so Dulcie tucked her feet under the pew and tried to listen. When another couple of late arrivals, a heavy-set woman and a tall, skinny man, squeezed by to slide into the pew, she spared them a glance. They both nodded to Dulcie and turned to face the front. For a moment, she felt better. The woman's suit was wool. It had to be scratchy and even Dulcie knew it was at least five years out of date. The man's tie looked clean enough, but the neck it rode up on was already red. She wasn't the worst-dressed person here, even if she looked awkward enough for these latecomers to feel comfortable taking seats right next to her.

The white-haired minister had begun to drone, and suddenly it hit her: there was a very good reason the odd couple were so poorly dressed, just as there was a very good reason why they had moved into her pew. Dulcie sat up straighter as a cold chill ran down her back. They were cops.

Was it just protocol that had drawn them here, or were they looking for her? A shudder ran through Dulcie as she thought back to the evening, four days ago now, when she had found Tim. 'We might want to talk again,' one young cop had told her. He'd given her his card, too, 'in case you remember anything.' What else was there to remember? She'd come home, Tim had been . . . well, no sense in going over that again.

Speaking of which, where was the body? Dulcie hadn't been to many funerals, but shouldn't there be a casket somewhere? She looked around, trying not to be too obvious. No, there was no casket. Perhaps it would have been considered gauche. No matter, Tim's death had been real enough for her. She closed her eyes for a moment as that weird dizziness hit her again, and when she reopened them, everyone around her was standing. Dulcie scrambled to her feet. Was the service over? No, they were all muttering some sort of prayer. For a moment, Dulcie's mind flashed back to the commune. Lucy never stuck with any one religion for long, but Dulcie had been to her share of prayer meetings and Wiccan circles. Her mother had even, for a while, gone regularly to a sky-clad outdoor service that Dulcie, then eleven and extremely self-conscious, had refused point-blank to return to, once she realized that all of her mom's friends would happily strip as soon as they entered their sacred grove. At any rate, her mother's spiritual quests had taught Dulcie how to blend in, and now she dutifully bent her head.

'We commend you. Amen.' Ten minutes later, the silver-topped speaker seemed to be done, and Dulcie looked around. No, nobody was kissing anyone else, but that seemed to be it. The two cops shuffled past her, and Dulcie looked to stall a moment.

'Hi, I'm Dulcie.' She turned to the curly-haired girl to her left. The eyes that looked up at her were a striking green, set against light-brown skin. The girl was stunning; exotic-looking, but with a wide-eyed innocence. 'Are you OK?'

'Yes, I am. Thank you.' A slight accent, nothing Dulcie could place, gave a sing-song lilt to her words. 'I just – I hate these things.'

'Me, too.' Dulcie smiled, despite the setting, and when the girl smiled back, Dulcie was struck again by her beauty – and her age. She couldn't be more than sixteen. But when she stood up, Dulcie found herself facing a body like a porn star's. OK, maybe she was eighteen. And after a moment of staring, Dulcie got up too, turning sideways to exit the pew.

The mismatched pair of latecomers were standing by the aisle, and she stepped past them.

'Miss Estrella? Luisa Estrella?' Dulcie looked back and saw that the duo had stopped the buxom girl.

'Yes, that's me.'

'We have some questions for you, Miss Estrella.' The large woman reached to take the girl's arm. 'Would you accompany us out to our car, please?'

'But she's the only one who's crying.' The phrase formed on Dulcie's lips, but she let it drop. What did she know? Instead, she stepped back and let the cops escort the curly-haired beauty out of the chapel. Around her, the buzz grew louder, and she glanced toward the front of the chapel. Everyone was looking at the doors, where the young woman was framed between the two larger cops as they disappeared into the sun. Some of the men frankly leered. Alana, dry-eyed and still perfectly composed, was among the watchers. Dulcie couldn't be sure, but she thought that the girlfriend's beautiful face looked ugly for a moment, frozen in a stare of pure hate.

Four

Dulcie hadn't drunk at all after the funeral; hadn't been invited back to wherever the Worthington clan had gathered, and hadn't regretted the opportunity to socialize further with his family, if truth be told. Still, she felt hung-over when the doorbell rang early the next morning. Part of that was lack of sleep. She'd stayed up late, reading; returning to a blighted castle in Umbria where a distraught heroine was holding out under siege. The nightmares hadn't helped either. No matter how often she told herself that this was *her* apartment, *her* home, she couldn't shake off the dreadful knowledge that someone had died here, violently.

Damn Tim! He was a worse room-mate in death than he'd been in life. Why couldn't Suze be here? Thoughts of her old friend had comforted her, and at around three a.m. she had been able to settle down a little, making herself a cup of sugar-free cocoa, using the mugs she and Suze had discovered together at a yard sale. Then fatigue had finally kicked in, and she had found herself thinking of her other former room-mate, the grey cat she had so loved. Maybe it was silly to imagine that she had seen him; that he had warned her to be careful. Maybe it was worse – crazy, unhinged – but she liked thinking of him, of his wise green eyes and warm presence. Maybe she had seen him, just maybe . . .

Rousing herself from a dream in which Mr Grey had been curled, purring, on the end of her bed, Dulcie grabbed her threadbare chenille robe and looked around for her slippers. The doorbell rang again, and she gave up.

'Coming!' she yelled, and took her time descending the stairs from her bedroom and then from the apartment's main floor back down to the front door. Who would come by first thing on a Sunday?

A peek through the door's peephole showed Tim's square block of a face, complete with tow-blond head.

Drawing in a quick breath, she opened the door before her brain had fully engaged.

'Oh, hi. You must be Dulcie?' Face to face, the man on her doorstep was taller and slimmer than Tim, his hair a little lighter and a little longer. But in her half-asleep state, the resemblance was still close enough to be unnerving. She tucked her robe a little tighter around herself and blinked up at him. 'I'm sorry. I'm Luke, Tim's brother.'

She nodded, still not understanding, and stepped back to let the tall stranger in. Between the cops, the funeral director's staff, and various concerned (or nosy) neighbors, she was getting used to this.

'I didn't get in until late last night, so for penance Mater and Pater sent me to clean out Tim's apartment.'

'Upstairs, two floors. His room is above the kitchen. The room that was his, I mean . . .' Dulcie left the door open and climbed back up the stairs, the new carpet feeling thick and spongy under her bare feet. Luke followed behind her. 'Up one more. On the right.' Without turning, she pointed to the remaining stairs, then realized how brusque she sounded. 'Would you like some coffee?'

'I'd love some, thanks.' He stood there, looking awkward, dirty-blond bangs falling into his eyes. 'I'm sorry to barge in. My folks had a hell of a time reaching me, and then both my flights were delayed. That's why I missed the funeral. The family seem to think it was a lapse of manners on my part.'

Dulcie counted out an extra two spoons of dark roast and started the machine. 'Where did you fly in from?'

'Jakarta, by way of Palo Alto. I'm finishing up at Stanford Law.'

'My room-mate almost went there.' She paused. The lack of caffeine was definitely affecting her. 'I mean, my permanent room-mate – and Stanford. She's doing an internship in DC this summer, so Tim . . .'

'Yeah, I know. He was supposed to be studying for some make-up exams. They'd asked me to keep an eye on him. I was scheduled to take a seminar here next month anyway, and I gather there was some doubt about whether he'd be going back to the B-school at all. He was on academic probation at Christmas, so by spring – well, I don't even know if he was officially enrolled anymore.'

Dulcie rummaged for mugs. All of this was news, though she wasn't too surprised to learn of Tim slacking off. As she poured, she looked up at her room-mate's big brother. 'So, one in business, one in law? Is this a family thing?'

Luke had the grace to smile. It was a nice smile, crinkling up his face in a friendly way. 'Looks that way, right? Prepping to run the foundation? Actually, I took three years off.' He waved off the milk carton. 'I bummed around Asia for a year, then finally ended up working for a social action group in Indonesia. I go back and help out when I can. They made me realize that international law would be right for me. Give me the tools I'd need to get things done.' Dulcie nodded. This was how Suze talked. 'Plus, I'd run out of money.'

'Oh?' She hadn't meant to sound quite so skeptical. It had just popped out.

'I know, with my family . . .' Luke chuckled. 'But they keep us kids on a tight leash.' He saw her look. 'Well, moderately tight. I know they'd pretty near cut Tim off.'

Dulcie swallowed, hard. 'I hope they don't want his security deposit back. I mean, he'd committed through August.'

Luke waved her fears away. 'Don't worry about it. I mean, I won't mention it, and Mater and Pater aren't thinking that way. They don't want to think about Tim anymore than they must.'

That sounded harsh. 'I'm sorry,' said Dulcie. 'It must be hard for them.'

Luke shrugged. 'They don't like mess. I mean, have they even been over here?'

'Not since Tim moved in.' Dulcie thought back. 'They had someone from the funeral home come by to pick up a couple of suits.'

'Tim in a suit.' Luke was smiling more softly now, a wistful look on his face. 'That poor little screw-up.'

Dulcie didn't know what to say to that and, instead, reached for the coffee pot. But Luke put his empty mug on the counter. 'Thanks, anyway. I should get started.'

'OK, come on up.' Abandoning her own half-finished mug, she led Luke up the stairs and opened Tim's door. Clothes were everywhere, CDs and a few books joined them on the floor. 'I'm sorry, the cops have been through here.' In truth, it looked neater than Dulcie remembered.

'Don't worry about it. I grew up with him, you know?'

She nodded. 'Hey, have you heard anything?' She'd been so out of it, she didn't remember if anyone at the funeral had said anything about . . . resolution. The word 'murder' still made her pause. 'Was it, you know, random? Did someone follow him in from the street?' She could still picture the open front door. He'd probably not even made it up to his own room.

'Nothing. I know they've been talking to a lot of his friends, though.'

'Right.' Dulcie hugged her robe closer. 'Hey, did you know this one girl, Luisa? She was at the funeral.' She was the only person there who seemed really upset, Dulcie didn't add. Luke looked puzzled. 'Dark hair? Really pretty?'

'Friend of the blonde's, what's-her-name? Alana?'

'No, I don't think so.' He must be thinking of the sneering brunette. She was a looker, too; dark, in contrast to the blonde Alana, but still with that perfect smile. Whereas, Dulcie suddenly realized, she herself had brushed neither teeth nor hair. 'Um, would you excuse me?'

'Sure thing. I should get to work here anyway.'

Even with the door closed, Dulcie didn't feel quite right jumping into the shower. The half mug of coffee she'd had must be kicking in; she was acutely conscious of Luke right on the other side of the wall, but she washed her face and dabbed at her armpits, too. The July humidity made it difficult to get a comb through her light-brown curls, but a pick worked to fluff them up nicely and after she had brushed her teeth, she could smile at herself without grimacing. She prepared to bolt for her bedroom, already thinking about what to wear, when her own thoughts stopped her. What was she doing? Flirting with her dead room-mate's brother?

It must be the sleep deprivation. But, truth be told, it had been a while. Jonah had taken the NYU teaching gig last September, grateful for anything that might possibly lead to a tenure track position in film. They'd had some nice weekends through the fall; he came up for foliage and for the Cassavetes retrospective. She'd presented a paper at the ALA conference in January: 'Public Perception and the Role of Increasing Female Readership on the Early Gothic Novel'. But by then more than the weather had cooled. The paper had been well received, but Dulcie had not been surprised when Jonah had begun taking longer and longer to return her calls. Not that it hadn't hurt when he'd told her about Summer, the camera woman on his ongoing project. Dulcie remembered lying on the sofa, with Mr Grey curled on her belly, wondering if she could just hang up. That was in March. Had she been so resilient, so recently? Where had her backbone gone? Unable to answer either question, Dulcie gave a last tug to her curls, neatened her robe and prepared to open the bathroom door and return to Tim's room.

'Damn! Where is it?'

So much for a grand entrance. Luke was under the bed, and Dulcie couldn't help noticing how long his legs were in his faded jeans.

'Where's what? If you've found old pizza under there . . .'

'No, not quite.' Luke slid toward her. Dulcie stepped back and felt something soft give way beneath her bare foot. 'I meant his stash.'

Dulcie leaned against the door-frame, trying to be subtle about wiping her foot on the rug. 'I'm trying to remember Tim doing anything other than drinking.' She couldn't. 'You mean drugs, right?'

'I'm his brother, remember? I know Tim.' Luke slid out from under the bed and started rooting around the closet, knocking on the floorboards. 'And I know he was not getting any cash from the folks.'

'Wait a minute.' Dulcie stood up. 'You're not talking about a little personal weed, are you? You think he was dealing?'

'I'd put money on it. And, believe me, we'd all rather I find his stash than that the cops do.' He pulled a chair over and climbed on to it, the better to start pushing at the ceiling of the walk-in closet, the tiny room's best feature according to Suze. 'If they haven't already.' He was tapping on the closet walls. 'My folks aren't as brittle as they look, but still I'd rather spare them.'

'God, this is just great.' Dulcie allowed herself to collapse on the unmade bed, reflecting that anything living in it would have moved out by now, surely. 'He was rude, crude, a slob – and a dealer.' She put her head in her hands, the mess that was her life overwhelming her. When she looked up, Luke was staring at her.

'I'm sorry.' She felt the flush rising. 'I didn't mean to sound so selfish. He was your brother, and what happened was horrible. Unthinkable.' Her cheeks were burning. 'It's just—'

'No, I know.' Luke sat down beside her. 'He was a mess. And I hope I'm wrong but, well, that's what he did all through high school whenever the folks cut him off. I was hoping . . .'

He let the thought slide into the air, and Dulcie found herself biting her lower lip. She hadn't even considered how he must feel. His baby brother – murdered. As an only child, she had no idea how he must be hurting. She thought of Mr Grey and how much she missed him, the physical warmth of him just being there. The pain must be similar. Worse, even. But Mr Grey had been innocent. Tim had been dealing drugs. Here, in her home. He'd been so stupid, so rude; a typical preppie, acting like he owned the world even here, off campus, in the big city.

'Wait a minute.' She grabbed Luke's arm. 'That could be it.' He stared at her, not understanding. 'Tim's used to – what? Peddling a few joints at his prep school? Supplying the local party boys with their nose candy?' Luke shrugged. 'Didn't he realize that he was living in a city now? Luke, I don't want to jump to conclusions, but Tim was not particularly smart – I mean, street smart.

'What if he was doing his little bit of dealing on somebody else's territory? Somebody else who was serious about it? And that's what got him killed?'

'Oh, hell.' The tall, lean stranger seemed to collapse on himself. What she'd said made perfect sense. For a moment, Dulcie really wished it didn't. What she wouldn't give to go back just two months, when she had a roommate she liked and trusted, a pet she adored, and an apartment that wasn't a crime scene.

'Are you out of your mind? I mean, are you, like, *disturbed* or something?' Trying out her theory on Alana two hours later, Dulcie got an entirely different reaction. 'Tim went to Andover!'

'Yeah, where he sold drugs for pocket money.' Dulcie's patience was shot. Luke had spent another hour in her place and together they'd tapped on every board in the bedroom. Dulcie had been happy to help, once she'd gotten dressed; the inch-by-inch search felt like penance for her earlier thoughtless words, and as they'd crawled around, an easy camaraderie had developed. Both their backs were aching by the time they finally gave up, and Luke was overdue at his parents'. He'd taken the amp and guitars, one bag, and Tim's laptop, asking if he could return sometime soon to pack up the rest of his brother's belongings. Despite the kink in her neck, Dulcie had been sorry to see him go.

Alana had barged in less than an hour later, a friend in tow, and demanded access to Tim's room. Figuring that as Tim's girlfriend, Alana had been there often enough, and, besides, everyone else had been up there, Dulcie had just stood back while the blank-faced blonde swept by, her dark-haired friend right behind, like a matched set of models on their way to film a shampoo commercial.

'Someone has been in here!'

With a sigh, Dulcie had put down the Sunday books section once again. It wasn't a question, but the pretty blonde was expecting an answer. Maybe if Alana had sounded sad, with even a touch of the mournful note Dulcie had heard in Luke's voice, she would have gotten up. But the supposedly grieving girlfriend had been all business since she'd marched in, her placid face unmarked by tears or sleeplessness. Dulcie wasn't going to yell up the stairs. Alana could come down.

'*Someone* has been in Tim's room!' Dulcie waited. From the resulting thumps as the peeved, if not bereaved, girlfriend stalked down the stairs, Dulcie figured that her failure to respond immediately had aggravated the insult.

'Who has been in there?' Alana looked flushed, and a flash of amusement passed through Dulcie's mind. What had there been to find? Lingerie? Love letters? Sex toys?

'Where do you want to start?' It had been a long five days. 'The cops came over a few times, and they had all their crime scene people in here, too. I stayed next door for the first two nights, so I don't know how often any of them were in the apartment. And the landlord's people were here, replacing the carpet. I don't think they went upstairs, but who knows? And Luke, Tim's brother, dropped by earlier this morning to pack up Tim's belongings.'

'Luke? What's *he* doing back in town? And what gave him the right to go through Tim's personal belongings?'

'He's family, Alana. He was doing charity work in Asia, and I guess he missed the funeral. He was here because Tim's parents wanted his stuff back.' She paused and watched Alana's face knot up. If she'd left it there, the pretty blonde would have had to accept it. She couldn't be that dense; Tim had said she was enrolled in that upscale finishing school nearby, the one she and Suze had nicknamed 'Mischief Manor'. But the past five days had been trying, and Dulcie's temper had worn paper thin. She couldn't resist. 'If you're looking for his stash, Alana, I can't help you. Luke said it was already gone.'

That's when Alana had exploded, displaying a vocabulary that Dulcie was sure they didn't teach at finishing school.

'You little bitch!' The volume of Alana's diatribe had snapped Dulcie's head back. 'How can you be so *stupid*?'

Dulcie closed the book review, ready for a fight. 'Hey, I don't know what they teach you at Mischief—'

'It's Miss *Chivers*, stupid. It's *British*!' Alana had advanced, leaning over the kitchen table. For a moment, Dulcie wondered if she'd gone too far. The other girl was thin, but had the longer reach. Would a rolled-up newspaper work, as it did for dogs? But just then Alana's friend appeared at the foot of the stairs. 'Alana? Dulcie? Aren't things getting a bit out of hand, here?'

Alana whirled around. 'Stacia! She thinks Tim was selling *drugs*.'

'Maybe it's what *she's* used to.' So the other woman wasn't going to be a peacemaker. Dulcie started to object, but the dark-haired one – Stacia – held up her hand. 'Come on, everybody. Let's be sensible here. Everyone's a bit tense.'

She must have had experience with animals. Alana slumped into a chair. 'Now, Dulcie – it is Dulcie, right? I'm Stacia.' She smiled a lovely smile, her deep tan setting off perfect teeth. Dulcie didn't trust it for a minute. 'Everyone is touchy right now. Alana is grieving. She and Tim were going to announce their engagement soon.' As if on cue, Alana sobbed once. Dulcie looked for tears, but Alana had covered her face with her hands. 'So Alana is understandably distraught.' Her smile grew by a millimeter, making Dulcie trust it less.

'What we came here to retrieve were certain letters. Personal notes and correspondence, including some plans that Tim and Alana had drawn up.'

'And those are missing?' Dulcie wasn't going to let herself be lulled, but she was curious.

'No, no – we haven't finished looking yet. It was just the shock. The violation. Seeing the state of his room like that.'

'It didn't look that different when he was alive.' OK, that wasn't smart, but it was true. And neither of her visitors had seen the real violation, the husk of the room's brief occupant. Maybe something in her tone carried that message. Maybe it was just Dulcie.

With a quick intake of breath, Alana started crying again. Stacia's eyes narrowed, and Dulcie thought she was going to spit. Instead, the sleek brunette wrapped her arms around her friend and shot Dulcie a look.

'Can you make her some tea or something? You're not helping here.'

'Yeah, you're right.' The lack of sleep, the whole horror of the past few days was making Dulcie forget what manners she once had. 'Sorry.' Dulcie stood up and went to check out her cabinet. Suze was the tea person, and the sight of the familiar boxes made her sigh. 'Earl Grey or peppermint?' Talk about a violation.

'Peppermint.' From under the cascade of shiny hair came a sniff, followed by a little voice. 'With Splenda, if you have it.'

'Coming right up.' Suze was a honey girl, but Dulcie was always dieting. She reached for the kettle and paused. 'Stacia, you want some, too?' A truce would just take less energy.

'No. Thanks.' Despite the pause between the words, Dulcie figured the offering had been accepted. Stacia was still patting Alana, but everyone seemed to have calmed down. The dark-haired girl leaned down toward her friend. 'Why don't I just run upstairs, see if I can put a few things together while you catch your breath?'

Alana nodded, and Dulcie didn't bother to point out that this was still her apartment. As she'd noted earlier, everyone and his brother had already been through it. The kettle whistled and Dulcie filled the small teapot. Grabbing one of Tim's mugs – she checked it was clean – she set them on the table. As she turned to get the sweetener, and honey, just in case, she heard Alana's voice, not at all nasal or tearful.

'She's really been a rock, you know. Stacia's so smart. At first I was worried that Tim liked her better, but they were more buddies. They even studied together.'

Tim studied? Dulcie managed a non-committal grunt and refilled her own coffee.

'I mean, Stacia's not at the B-school or anything. But Miss Chivers does have a management program. Systems and all.'

'Well, she is great at conflict resolution.' Dulcie tried a smile. Much to her surprise, Alana smiled back, slowly at first, but that only made it seem more real. 'I am sorry, Alana. I hadn't realized you two were so serious.' No point in bringing up all of Tim's extra-curriculars now.

'Thanks, Dulcie. You know, he really admired you.'

'He did?' She sipped from her mug to hide her shock. She was absurdly pleased.

Alana nodded and blew on the hot tea. Now that the fit of pique had passed, her voice sounded younger and more girlish. 'He said he was really impressed at how you could work so hard for something. He never had the patience.'

He must not have realized how far adrift she was in her quest for a thesis. Clearly, he didn't have to worry about grants running out. Still, to hear that she was thought about at all was a pleasant surprise. 'I'm sure he would have buckled down and finished business school with flying colors, Alana.' What harm could a little white lie do?

'His grades were coming up you know.' Dulcie looked up at her. She sounded like she believed what she was saying. 'He told me not to worry. And once he was off academic probation, we were going to announce our engagement.'

Dulcie nodded. Both options were safely off the table now. And before she had to respond further, she heard Stacia coming down the stairs, her tread noticeably lighter than Alana's despite the milk crate she carried.

'Alana, are you feeling better now? I've found some things.' She put the crate on the floor and bent over it, picking through a pile of papers and plastic. 'Some of your letters and some CDs that I think are yours. Also, some of his school notes. You don't mind if I take them, do you?'

She turned to Dulcie with an embarrassed look. 'I'm taking a summer course at Harvard Extension and I'm so behind.' A slight blush darkened her cheeks further. Of course, the added color only made her prettier. 'I guess I could be working harder. But my own stats teacher was such a dunderhead!'

She went back to rooting through the box and when she looked up, she was smiling again. 'Most important, I found this.' She stood up and held out the unmistakable black velvet dome of a jewelry box. Alana gasped. So did Dulcie, but for a different reason. Tim buying jewelry for a woman? Any woman?

'Oh, Stacia! He didn't!' Alana was all aflutter. Dulcie was rapidly running through memories, trying to recall Tim springing for anything other than a beer. And that was on a good day.

'He did, sweetie.' Her friend handed her the box and stood behind her. 'He asked me for advice.'

Alana flipped open the box and cooed. Dulcie leaned forward, and in the new spirit of sisterhood, Alana turned the box around to let her see what was inside: a square-cut diamond framed by two small sapphires. 'So he really was going to propose.' She sobbed in earnest now, and tears ran down her perfect cheeks.

'Of course he was, sweetie.' Stacia patted her friend's back, her voice low and calming. 'You know he loved you.'

Dulcie sat back, stunned. If that ring was real, and she rather suspected that Stacia and Alana knew the good stuff, it easily cost more than Tim's summer rent. Alana's earlier objections dissolved in the face of more pressing questions. Had Tim been dealing that much dope – out of her apartment? And, if that ring had been up in his room, why hadn't Luke found it – and asked her how his goofball little brother could afford such a stunning rock?

Five

It was a dark and stormy night. No, it wasn't really, but 'hot and humid afternoon' didn't have the same ring to it. And once Dulcie had the apartment to herself again, she grabbed a book and threw herself on to the sofa, ready to return to her favorite haunts. It was dark and stormy in the mountains of Italy, at least.

The Ravages of Umbria might not be great art; most scholars didn't even consider it in the same league as *The Castle of Otranto*, and that popular thriller had been ridiculed as trash even in 1764, when it was first published. Dulcie didn't care.

Although only sixty pages of *The Ravages* remained, the surviving fragments told of an impoverished young noblewoman, an orphan, who lived alone in a ruined castle with only the company of her faithful attendant. The castle was set high on a rocky peak, the likes of which didn't exist in that particular area of Italy, but the 'daunted cliffs' made for a good plot device, keeping both the heroine's high-born suitor and a stout-hearted young knight errant from having too easy access. However, the craggy mountain didn't seem to do much to deter a mad monk who had designs on either the heroine's person or her property. But why argue with geography when the unknown author took such liberties with the rest of nature, Italian or otherwise? Magic abounded in *The Ravages of Umbria*. Although the first fragment, nearly fifty pages of high drama, ended before everything was revealed, there were plenty of hints that ghosts, both benevolent and otherwise, were involved. This was everything that Dulcie loved.

> Hermetria had been visited since infancy by such spirits as were wont to haunt her ruin'd abode. One such shade kept close, calling to mind her father's loyal and aged servant who had tended the lofty retreat, poised as it were, like a cloud atop the mighty precipice. That retainer, guardian of the young orphan'd girl, recalled further the amiable happiness that had once accompanied Hermetria's family, the Baron and his Lady, jewels of conjugal felicity and parental duty.

Ghosts – kindly or not, at the thought of such things, a chill ran up Dulcie's spine and she found herself twisting to look at the carpet, to look at that spot again. No – better not go there.

She turned back to the book and started flipping pages. 'That jealous spirit too great a portion of ambition had, too high for its station and thus designed upon another's'. In this later section, the author hinted that something was up with the ghosts – that the spirits were not all benevolent. The few scholars who had written about *The Ravages* suspected treachery. From the surviving fragments it was unclear what the ghost had done. Probably robbed Hermetria, and perhaps killed her family, Gothic ghosts being able to take on corporeal form when necessary. The second fragment, just ten pages, implied a resolution.

The last pages almost read like a confession: 'Spells most potent for their proximity have robbed you of your patrimony. Beware the jealous spirit of—'

That was all. The fragment ended mid-sentence, the ultimate cliffhanger, although the phrase 'jealous spirits' ran throughout the story. The academics who'd bothered to take up the question basically agreed that the evil monk had been in on it too, with or without another ghostly accomplice. But Dulcie wasn't so sure. Ghosts were tricky things.

She shivered. Maybe this wasn't the book to be reading now. Better to think again of the lovely grey cat she'd seen the other day. Could it have been . . .? That sighting had been the one high point in an otherwise horrible day, but it wouldn't do to get carried away. It had just been *a* cat. A *different* cat, not Mr Grey. Still, when she'd asked Helene and Bob, her neighbor on the other side, neither could recall any cat in the neighborhood that had looked just like that – long silver fur, a face more Siamese than Persian, the slanted eyes giving the feline an intelligent and inquisitive look.

'Didn't you have a cat like that?' Bob had remembered Mr Grey all right. He'd been the one to spot her pet the night Tim had let him out. 'Nice-looking animal. Whatever happened to him?'

She'd replied briefly, not wanting to relive his last days in detail. And, no, nobody else had seen a long-haired grey cat in the area, not recently. Shaking her head, Dulcie readjusted the cushions behind her. Propped up in this way, she had little choice but to look at her book or out over the back porch. The tree outside wasn't that interesting, and so she reopened her much marked-up paperback, and started again with the opening scene.

> Alone but for her companion Demetria, a noblewoman of good family, whose fortunes had fallen prey to evil times, she would gaze over the majestic peaks, whose summits, veiled with clouds, revealed at times their jagged teeth . . .

Dulcie punched the cushion. Talk about rock-like. Usually by the end of the first page, she'd be oblivious to her surroundings, lost in the fictional principality and its family drama. She kicked at the afghan throw she'd automatically pulled off the couch's back, another present from her mother.

'. . . two suitors, despite her poverty . . .'

No, something else was wrong. She sat up, stretching out her legs. It wasn't even Tim anymore, or hardly. The new rug, the rearranged furniture – her apartment was beginning to feel like her own again; all her own. Maybe that was it. It was the couch; she had too much room because Mr Grey wasn't there. It had always been his habit to 'study' with her. She remembered his clairvoyance now with a pang. If she was on the phone or getting ready to watch TV, the grey cat would go about his own business. But whenever she settled in for a good read, he'd be there within thirty seconds. She'd open the cover of a book and feel the gentle thud as he jumped to the foot of the sofa, curling up for a nap as she read. She'd tuck her feet up so as not to disturb him, and they'd stay like that for hours. Now she'd tucked her feet up out of habit, but without that 'thud', without the warmth of a coiled, sleeping cat, the sofa just wasn't as comfortable.

'Alone, but for her companion . . .' Could Demetria have been a cat?

That way madness lies, she told herself, and pulled herself upright. It was Sunday; her last afternoon before the tedium of a mindless work week. She had to be able to relax and read somewhere. Down by the river? Outside the window, clouds gathered. That rainy feeling wasn't only in her head. An iced mocha and one of those muffins she loved would do the trick. With a sigh, she heaved herself to her feet, slipping her book into her bag as she headed for the door.

The sky was rumbling by the time Dulcie reached the coffee-house. But as she pushed open the heavy door a string of brass bells jangled merrily, and she realized she was smiling again. The little shop was packed; the roar of its air-conditioning providing the explanation for its popularity. Dulcie looked around and found herself focusing on a new addition: a small, round fish-bowl set up high, where the coffee-house kept its flavored syrups. It must have been the movement that caught her eye. The bowl's sole occupant, a fire-engine-red Siamese fighting fish, darted back and forth inside, its flowing fins and glittery body reflected large on the bowl's sides.

'Hey, is that new?' She nodded toward the bowl.

'Nemo? He's been with us a while,' the barista called back. He grabbed two empties and retreated, but Dulcie kept staring. Ever since she'd lost Mr Grey, she'd been like this – mesmerized by any animal she ran across: another cat, a sparrow hopping along the sidewalk, and now a fish. If she didn't watch herself, soon she'd be trying to pet a spider. She pulled out her book and within minutes was back on that mountain top.

'Dulcie?' The sound of her name broke the spell and she looked along the bar, crowded with laptops and latte mugs. It was the girl from the funeral. She had a nearly empty glass of iced tea in her hand, and if her swollen eyes were any indication, she'd been crying.

'Hi. It's Luisa, right?' Dulcie patted the stool next to her, and the younger woman squeezed in. The tears as much as the almost-black curls helped Dulcie to place her.

'Uh-huh.' The newcomer nodded and sniffed, taking a last, noisy draw on the straw. 'You remember me.' She tried to smile, but a stray tear escaped. With the back of her hand, she wiped it away – and then pulled on one long, black curl in an awkward attempt to hide the motion.

'Of course, I do.' Dulcie bit her lip, unsure of what else to say. 'You were at the funeral.'

At the mention of the funeral Luisa put her hands over her face, sobbing in earnest again. Maybe that hadn't been the most sensitive thing to say, Dulcie realized. Suze, even Mr Grey, would be better in this kind of situation. 'Luisa, it's OK. I mean, you don't have to be embarrassed.'

Trying to summon the spirit of her room-mate, if not her former cat, Dulcie reached out to pet the young girl's back. Luisa was wearing a thin rayon shell, warm to the touch, and Dulcie could feel her trembling. 'There, there,' she said, feeling extremely ineffective. She looked up at the fish for a clue. The fish continued to swim.

'Yeah?' The barista, bored by the drama, was waiting for her order.

'Large iced latte. And can you bring another iced tea for my friend?'

The barista shrugged, but within a minute plopped down two pint glasses rattling with ice. 'That'll be four-fifty.'

Dulcie fumbled with her wallet, and by the time she'd sent the server off, Luisa had calmed herself.

'Thanks.' She was all but whispering, barely audible as she sipped at the cold drink. 'I'm sorry about that.'

'No need.' Dulcie took a moment to study the younger woman. Despite her swollen eyes and a nose that was definitely red, Luisa was worth the perusal. With dark-tan skin, lustrous curls, and the kind of eyebrows that in novels would be described as raven-winged, Luisa was definitely a looker. But not, Dulcie knew – from both her clothing and her demeanor – one of Tim's usual types. Curiosity was pricking at Dulcie like little cats' claws. The girl was more truly bereft than Tim's supposed fiancée, unless something else was causing the waterworks today. Odds were, she wasn't an orphaned heiress, but she certainly seemed haunted. 'Do you mind if I ask what's wrong?' Luisa looked up, her eyes welling. 'Is it Tim?' A nod and a sniff. 'Were you a close friend of Tim's?'

Luisa sighed and nodded, and then sighed again. Dulcie waited, and after a few more sighs, the younger woman started to talk. 'We met through the Bureau of Study Council. I was helping Tim with statistics.'

Dulcie sipped her iced latte. This wasn't study-partner grief. Sure enough, the story came out.

'And, to thank me, he started taking me out. I didn't want to go at first. I mean, he was paying me, too, to tutor him. But he kept saying that if he had to work so hard, he wanted to enjoy a good meal after; that it was really for him, and that it would help him remember our lesson if I'd talk with him afterward. And, well, we started seeing each other. Sort of.'

Sort of? Dulcie raised her eyebrows.

'I mean, I'm sort of seeing someone else, and I know he has a girlfriend. But I don't know how serious that is. Was.' She gave another sniff, and Dulcie jumped in before the sobs could start again.

'So you were seeing each other casually, right? That sounds fine.' Dulcie thought of the ring, but decided to keep her mouth shut. To Luisa, this might have been the beginning of a real romance. To Dulcie, it sounded like Tim being Tim, hitting on a girl because she was pretty and vulnerable. Besides, she didn't know who that ring was intended for.

'It *was* fun. Tim wasn't like anyone else I'd ever gone out with.' Luisa's face brightened as she told Dulcie about lunches at Sonsie, evenings at Rialto, the late-night sushi place. None of these were Dulcie's usual haunts, but if Tim had been spending so much time with this girl, wouldn't he have mentioned her or brought her home?

'I'm amazed we never ran into each other,' Dulcie said, fishing. 'I mean, at the apartment.'

Luisa had the grace to blush, looking down at the bar so that her heavy hair fell over her face. 'We hadn't gotten that far yet. I mean, I'm not like that. And he was going to break up with his girlfriend first.'

By hitting her over the head with a Tiffany rock? Dulcie had to keep herself from grabbing the younger girl's bare, tanned wrist. 'Luisa, are you sure Alana didn't know about you, too?' It was hard to imagine Alana getting worked up over anything, but still, Tim was hers. And jealousy was a hell of a motive.

But Luisa shook her head. 'Yeah, I'm pretty sure. That's what the cops were asking me about yesterday.'

'The cops? Luisa, if you—' Dulcie wanted to ask more, to find out if the dark-haired girl was a suspect. But just then she felt her empty glass whisked out of her hand.

'Would you ladies care for anything else today?' The moment was broken. Luisa pushed herself off her stool and reached for the bag that had been resting at her feet.

'Here you go.' She fished through the bulky knit bag for her wallet.

'Luisa, if you want to talk—'

'I should get back home. I've got a study group at six. It was just so good to see you. To see someone who knew Tim.' With a smile and a wave, she was gone. Dulcie looked back at the counter, just in time to see the dollar bill before the barista grabbed it. Only someone who had worked in a service job would tip that much for an iced tea. With a sigh, she slid off her own stool and looked up to see that the Siamese fighting fish was no longer circling. Its little 'o' of a mouth still opened and closed rhythmically, but it held to the edge of the bowl, its black button eyes staring straight past her. Brass bells jangled and Dulcie glanced over her shoulder in time to see Luisa slip through the front door. Straightening up again, she saw that the fish's banner of a dorsal was extended to its full height. The fish had been staring at the door – and if that fin was any indication, the bright red fighter was either angry or scared.

'Dulcie, I'm really beginning to worry about you.' She'd told Suze about the cat earlier, and her friend had made sympathetic noises. Suze knew that most of Dulcie's waking hours were spent in a fictional world where ghosts were part of the furniture, at least in the upper reaches of ruined castles. An intelligent fish, however, was going too far.

'Look, I'm not saying that the fish knew something.' Dulcie was lying on the sofa, feet tucked behind a pillow. The pillow didn't fill the space where Mr Grey used to curl, but it was close. 'Still, something spooked it.'

'Like, maybe, being stuck in a tiny bowl in a busy coffee shop?'

Dulcie could hear the fatigue in Suze's voice.

'Dulcie, I think you've been spending too much time in that *Umbria* book, only you're not locked up – you're choosing to stay inside, alone. It's not healthy. I mean, Dulce, we're talking about a creature with a brain the size of a split pea at best.'

'Yeah, I know.' Suze was working hard and the Washington summer was even hotter and muggier than New England. Still, Dulcie couldn't resist. 'And at times I do feel like Hermetria, or at least Demetria, the faithful attendant. But, Suze, I know what I saw. And, well, it's possible, right? I mean, animals are sensitive in ways that we aren't. And first that cat—'

'Dulcie!' Suze's temper was fraying. 'Get a hold of yourself! Your roommate was murdered and you've just had coffee with a person of interest, and you're thinking a fish was freaked?'

'What do you mean, "a person of interest"?' Dulcie sat up.

'Well, think about it. The cops brought her in. She was involved with the deceased, probably sneaking around with him, and it sounds like maybe she wanted more. Wouldn't be too much of a stretch to think she had something to do with Tim's murder.'

Dulcie paused. She had wanted to ask Luisa about the police, but she'd looked so innocent and stricken. She kicked the pillow. 'They let her go.' She was playing devil's advocate. But Suze was a real advocate in training.

'Come on, kiddo.' She could hear Suze sitting up, getting serious. 'That only means they haven't charged her. But Tim was just playing around with her, right? Wouldn't that be motive?'

'If she knew about it. She seemed to think that Tim really cared for her. I was thinking that Alana had more reason to be jealous. A woman scorned, and all that.' In Dulcie's mind, the younger girl was way more attractive, her story more romantic. Maybe she'd have won out in the end. Not that Tim was much of a prize.

'You're forgetting about the ring. If you were a young girl, wined, dined and seduced, and then you found out your knight in shining armor was about to propose to someone else, wouldn't that make you mad?'

'Yeah, but . . .' Dulcie couldn't really see either woman resorting to anything stronger than a good slap. Suze had a good case, in theory. But Suze hadn't seen the blood. 'Well, I don't see it. She seems . . . innocent. Like a young novice who had the bad luck to be seduced by a caddish lordling.' She heard Suze snort. Suze was not a fan of Gothic lit. 'I like her.'

'You feel *protective* of her.'

Suze had a point.

'And you spend much of your time reading books in which innocent women are preyed upon by evil men. But you're not her lawyer, and this isn't a storybook. If you want to help this girl, next time you see her, don't buy her coffee. Send her to legal aid.'

'I didn't buy her coffee.' It was iced tea. 'But I didn't get a bad vibe off her, either.'

'No, the fish did.'

Only after they hung up did Dulcie realize she hadn't told Suze about the biggest potential break in the case: Tim's dealing. With a stab of conscience, she realized why. Between Alana and her buddy coming by and Dulcie's own desire to get out of the house, she hadn't told anyone – not even the cops. And if her legal-minded friend would have said anything about Luke's revelation, it would be that Dulcie should immediately inform the police. Well, it was Sunday night. Tomorrow, during her lunch break, she'd call the detective who had given her his card.

With a slight stab of guilt – she knew Suze was right – she settled in again. What was Sunday night for, if not a good book?

> Two suitors, despite her poverty, laid claim upon her hand. One, a noble lord of great pastoral lands, gay with the song of running water, and fragrant groves of lemon trees and olives, stretching beyond sight. The other, a young knight, who had travel'd far, of haunted visage . . .

Six

What if the chill were the wind? A cold, mountain gale sweeping up into the mountains, where she, Dulcie, was held captive? What if the wind presaged the ghost of the heroine's long-dead fiancé, Rabinovitz?

It was no good. The chill was the air-conditioning vent, blowing straight down on her cubicle, presaging nothing more than goosebumps. Dulcie shivered in her thin cotton dress. Three days away from her desk, and somebody had nicked her office sweater. It had been one of Lucy's better efforts, too, only slightly lumpy, knitted from unbleached wool that she'd carded and spun herself. Best of all, it had been warm.

To add to Dulcie's troubles, the temp agency hadn't bothered to inform her supervisor at the insurance company about why she hadn't been at work since last Tuesday, with the result that everybody seemed to regard her as a slacker. The agency would probably find her another mindless drone job if this one canned her. But it seemed that the powers-that-be at Priority Insurance were so desperate for help that instead they'd been piling up folders since Wednesday morning, only nobody could understand why she was so far behind.

Rabinovitz, Jacob R. Backspacing over a typo, she tried once more to concentrate on what she was doing. Accident reports, all of which came in scrawled in nearly illegible handwriting, and most of which, she suspected, would never amount to anything for the poor claimants.

Date of accident: March third. The day Jonah had told her about Summer, his new camera-toting love. She shook that memory off and looked at the claimant code. It was a 342, a motor vehicle accident. And the poor guy had been waiting more than four months already. With a twinge of guilt, Dulcie picked up another form.

Rabinovitz, Jacob S. Also a 342, as were the next five forms. The guilt was fading. The company could have assigned these forms to a regular employee or brought in temp help earlier. She'd only been out since last week.

Rabinovitz, Jacopo. That opened her eyes but, hey, she was Dulcie Schwartz, full name Dulcinea, thanks to Lucy's half-remembered role in a college production of *Man of La Mancha*. And who was Dulcinea Schwartz to question Jacopo Rabinovitz? Another code 342. Dulcie shivered, both from the arctic air and the eerie sense of *déjà vu* that kept creeping up on her. Maybe it was that date, with its personal memories, but she feared code 342 would haunt her dreams. She stood up and stretched, trying to see into the other cubicles. Maybe whoever had 'borrowed' her sweater still had it here. She looked over to where the office manager, Lily, sat. Something about her nubbly beige top looked familiar. Of course, Lily was a nubbly beige woman. But still . . .

Then it hit her. Jacopo Rabinovitz? March third? Not a date or a name she was likely to forget. Hadn't she typed his form in last Monday? Could there really be two Jacopo Rabinovitzes who'd had fender benders during the last ice storm of the spring, the night Summer had eclipsed Dulcie?

Dulcie raised her voice slightly. 'Hey, Joanie?'

The kohl-rimmed eyes of the other temp poked around the grey cubicle wall. 'She speaks!' Black lips broke into a smile. 'Hey, you wanna take a break? I'm dying for a ciggie.'

From the way she was bobbing, Dulcie could see that the modern-day Goth girl was jonesing. 'In five. But first, what's with these claim forms? I swear I've typed some of these in before.'

'Shh! C'mere.' Joanie beckoned with nails polished to match her lips. Dulcie slid her chair closer to the partition. 'We *are* retyping them, a whole bunch. I don't know the whole story, but last week, during one of those thunderstorms, I was in the smoking room with Ricky. You know, the cute redhead with the freckles, over in Accounting?'

Dulcie couldn't imagine anyone here being cute, but nodded anyway.

'Anyway, he said something about a bug.'

Without thinking, Dulcie lifted her feet off the grimy carpet.

'A computer bug, silly. But he said it's all hush-hush for some reason. Anyway, I'm happy; I wasn't supposed to be here this week. Though, I guess with you out – hey!' Her grey eyes lit up, wide and innocent despite all the warpaint. 'Did you really, you know, find a body?'

'Yeah, my room-mate.' Dulcie was heartily sick of talking about it. But Joanie was as close to a friend as she had here. 'He'd been stabbed.'

'Gross!' Joanie beamed. 'I mean, I'm sorry.'

'Don't be. He was an ass.' It felt good to say it. 'A total preppie creep.'

'I know the type.' Joanie was nodding. 'I went to Milton. So, wanna take a break?'

Fifteen minutes later, Dulcie was sweating and ready to return to the chilled office. Besides, she really shouldn't push her supervisor. Joanie, however, had other plans.

'Let me finish this butt, then I've gotta go to the corner for another pack and a Red Bull. I was at this party last night—'

'I'll catch you inside.' Dulcie waved off her raven-haired colleague and leaned into the glass revolving doors. The cool was lovely here in the lobby, not blasting, just the perfect corporate chill.

'Excuse me.' It sounded like a command, and Dulcie stumbled forward as a woman brushed past, her heels clicking on the polished lobby floor.

'Hey!' Dulcie had paused right inside the doors, but that was no reason for such rudeness.

'Yes?' It was Mrs Putnam, the human resources manager – Sally Ann Putnam, if Joanie was to be believed. It was a name that belonged on a farm girl, although the tart-tongued Goth girl preferred to call her 'the Snake'. And as was true every time she appeared, since that morning she'd first given Dulcie the once-over and then a company log-on, the HR boss was a vision in perfectly polished and undoubtedly expensive neutrals. Maybe it was the coloring, the way her frosted bob was just a shade lighter than her deeply tanned skin, or maybe it was her cold, flat eyes, but something about her did in fact remind Dulcie of a copperhead snake she'd seen once, sunning on a rock. Maybe it was the job; thinking of people as 'resources' could not be good for the soul.

'Um, excuse me? Mrs Putnam?' Whatever she thought of the HR head, Dulcie needed the gig and made herself blink away the image of the reptile. The opportunity, however, was too good to waste. 'I was wondering about the data we're working on now? A lot of the forms have been entered before. I'm sure of it.' A perfectly manicured eyebrow arched, and Dulcie remembered Joanie's warning. 'I mean, maybe there was an announcement while I was out?'

'There was no announcement to any of the clerical staff. Not even to our *regular* staff,' sniffed the older woman, tossing back her head. Her hair didn't move, and Dulcie half expected a slim dark tongue to flash out. Instead, the older woman kept on hissing. 'You're being well paid for your labors. I'd advise you to concentrate more on the quality of your work, and less on details that don't concern you.'

With that Mrs Putnam spun on one slick leather toe and click-clacked off to the elevators, her posture, like her unbleached linen suit, perfect. It was only as she paused for the small crowd at the elevator to part for her that Dulcie noticed what was on her arm. Over the leather strap of a simple fawn handbag was a neatly folded sweater. It looked like raw wool, it was nubbly, and it was hers.

Not until Joanie slammed her desk drawer shut did Dulcie realize it was five p.m. Another day gone. Joanie was already shoving her iPod into her bag as Dulcie stood and stretched.

'I don't know how you can work and listen to music.' She shook her head to clear it and realized how long her curls were getting. 'I'd end up typing lyrics.'

'I don't know how you keep your sanity without it.' Joanie shouldered her black and green messenger bag, and stood, waiting for Dulcie. 'I mean, I know you're quiet and all.'

'I just sort of drift. I daydream, I guess.' She'd been trying to think about her reading, about Hermetria locked in her forlorn castle with only Demetria, who, to be honest, seemed a bit of a drip. But as the day had dragged on, she'd found herself thinking of Luke instead.

'Not Ricky over in Accounting?' Joanie must have seen something in her face.

'Don't worry.' Dulcie grabbed her own bag and followed the black-clad girl toward the elevators. 'My room-mate's brother, actually.'

'The dead guy's brother?' Joanie looked at her with new respect as they squeezed into the crowded elevator. 'Cool!'

'Oh!' That's when it hit her. She'd been so annoyed about the sweater and then so caught up in work and, to be honest, thoughts of Luke, that she'd never called the cops.

'What?' Joanie was bouncing with eagerness, but Dulcie waited till they were down in the lobby.

'I've got to call the cops,' she whispered. 'The detective in charge gave me his card and I found out something.'

'You found out something?' Sally Putnam was behind her. She must have been further back in the elevator, or coiled under a nearby rock. 'Have you been prying into the system?' Next to her stood two men in suits that looked out of place on their block-like bodies.

'Mrs Putnam!' Dulcie took a step back. 'I was meaning to talk to you.' She'd been trying to get up her nerve to ask about the sweater all day.

'I see, and now you think you'll just sidestep the corporate chain of command? Go directly to the police?'

None of this made sense. 'But the detectives said—'

'If Priority has had a breach of protocol, Priority executives will handle it themselves. Securely.' The sibilant hissed between her thin lips. 'So if you have any desire to continue working here, you will respect our rules.' She stared down at Dulcie without blinking.

Dulcie stood there, mouth open, while for the second time that day the executive spun on her toe and marched away.

'Hey, Dulce.'

She'd forgotten Joanie standing beside her.

'Isn't that your sweater?'

* * *

It wasn't until she was about to descend into the Government Center T that Dulcie got through to someone at the Cambridge Police.

'No, it's not an emergency,' she repeated for the tenth time and expected to be put on hold again.

'I gather,' said an amused voice on the other end. 'But you were calling for Detective Scavetti?'

Feeling a little foolish, Dulcie explained what had happened. Standing on a busy sidewalk, surrounded by tired office workers, it sounded weak. Yes, her room-mate had been murdered. And, yes, the detective had told her to call if she remembered anything else. But was a high school memory from the dead room-mate's brother really anything? Well, she was on the phone now, trying to explain.

'So, the victim's brother told you that the victim had sold a little pot while he was in high school?'

'Yes, while he was at prep school at Andover.' She could almost feel the detective sigh. So, Tim wasn't a major league drug lord. He was a spoiled rich kid. Maybe that would have made him more vulnerable. 'His brother said he could usually figure out where Tim had hidden his stash, and he'd looked. So maybe he was in over his head, you know, dealing here in the city, and he got killed for it?' It was a weak theory, but someone had killed her room-mate. 'Isn't that a possibility?'

The voice on the other end of the phone sounded tired. 'Yes, it is a possibility, and I will pass along your theory to Detective Scavetti. But I wouldn't lose any sleep over it. This doesn't look like a gang killing, and frankly, gangs control the drug traffic in this town.'

'But that's just it.' She couldn't let go. 'I mean, what if this one upstart was—'

'Selling a little pot to his friends? Frankly, they wouldn't care.'

But what if he hadn't paid his wholesaler? What if he'd tried to rip someone off? It was too late. 'Thank you very much for calling in, Ms Schwartz.' The line went dead – and then immediately hummed back to life.

'Yes?' She clicked on without looking. Her idea had made sense!

'Dulcie?' The female voice on the other end was familiar, but she couldn't place it. 'Dulcie Schwartz?'

'Speaking.' If this was a telemarketer, she'd just shut the phone. She was still being jostled by brain-dead commuters seeking the T, and the late afternoon had baked the city like a casserole.

'This is Alana – you know, Tim's fiancée?'

Dulcie noted the elevation in status and toyed with the idea of descending into the cool shadow of the subway stop. Maybe Alana wouldn't even notice that she'd lost the signal.

'Anyway, I'm calling because I'm having a little get-together on Thursday,' Alana continued. 'It's just been such a horrible, horrible week, and Stacia and I thought it would do everyone good.'

Dulcie couldn't tell which thought was making her speechless: that Alana would have a party a week after her boyfriend's murder, or that she'd think to invite Dulcie. 'A party?' She managed not to stutter.

'Just drinks. Just to cheer everyone up.'

Dulcie found herself staring at a T map like a lost tourist, noticing for the first time how the lines of color spread out like trickles of blood and bile against the white. What was Alana thinking of? She closed her eyes and once again saw the hand, the puddle. Alana was still talking, and Dulcie made herself focus. Alana hadn't seen Tim the way she had – so bloody, so still. Nobody had, except for the police. To Alana and her friends, Tim was just gone – his absence rather like an inconvenient holiday, as if he'd gone off-trail skiing in Aspen. She swallowed hard and felt her stomach begin to settle.

Alana hadn't missed a beat. 'I mean, Tim would be the first one to tell us that life goes on. Especially in summer! My folks have a shade up over most of the roof deck, and they're going away for the weekend.'

Aha, thought Dulcie, the truth was out.

'So, would you care to drop by?'

Would I care to swim with sharks? Even well-dressed sharks? Dulcie paused before answering. It couldn't be simple kindness that had prompted Alana to invite her. Stupid as she seemed, the willowy blonde had to have an ulterior motive. And, Dulcie had to admit to herself, she was a bit curious. Curious enough to give up a night of reading?

'Um, well, thank you, Alana. I'll have to check my calendar.' Dulcie was rather proud of her stalling technique. 'But why don't I take down your info?'

Alana didn't seem to notice her bluff and gave her the address of a Beacon Hill town house. The invitation was for cocktails at seven. 'We really would love for you to come.'

Dulcie was touched, despite her misgivings. 'Thanks, Alana. And, hey—' She could throw the girl a bone. 'Thought I'd let you know. I talked to the cops about what Luke said and they didn't buy it.' She heard a puzzled noise. 'They don't think that Tim was a dealer.'

'Well, of course not!' Dulcie could hear the refined sniff of disapproval, as if Alana had smelled something distasteful. Maybe this party wouldn't be such a good idea after all.

'Well, uh, thought you should know. See you.' That didn't commit her, did it?

* * *

'You're going to that party!' Suze had perked right up when Dulcie had told her about it later that night. 'One of us should have a social life!'

Suze wasn't exactly in a bad patch, just a slow one. Dulcie had been hearing about it for weeks. Suze loved research, and had finished a master's in philosophy before turning toward the law. But being someone else's researcher was strenuous, the Washington summer stifling, and the long hours were getting to her. Plus, as she'd just told Dulcie, Tom – the really cute guy from Justice – had turned out to be gay.

'Suze, don't you think it's ghoulish, though? I mean, really?' No matter how Dulcie tried to see Alana's planned party as a wake, as a commemoration, the image just wouldn't come. Even Hermetria wouldn't have jumped right into party mode, would she?

'Yeah, that Alana is a piece of work all right.' She heard Suze grunt as she slipped off her running shoes. She'd needed the exercise, she told Dulcie, after the stresses of work, coupled with the romantic disappointment. 'But that's not your problem. There will be *other* people there.'

'Well, with that hostess, they aren't likely to be my kind of people.' Dulcie kicked back on the sofa.

'They don't have fur, you mean?' Suze had grown fond of Mr Grey. How could she not? But beyond referring to the silvery feline as 'our third room-mate', Dulcie suspected that her friend wasn't really a cat person.

'They don't have *brains*. I mean, did you ever meet Alana? I don't think she's ever read a book for pleasure in her life.'

'So much the better for you, Dulce.' She could hear her friend settling into her own easy chair. 'Some men like brains.'

At that, Dulcie had to pause. It was true that she didn't have a great social record. When she had been with Jonah, it hadn't mattered. They had hung out with his friends and seen movies. When he had moved away, she had tended to work on weekends – the better to avoid temptation. Or to avoid noticing that there was no temptation. And then Mr Grey had started on his decline, and she hadn't wanted to leave the house at all. This was a chance to get out. Plus, if she was totally honest with herself, she wouldn't mind seeing Luke again. Would he be there? Judging from Alana's comments, probably not. But there was a chance . . .

'Ah, am I hearing some wheels turning?' Suze always had been attuned to Dulcie's moods. 'Is there a possibility here?'

'Probably not.' She was smiling as she said it.

'So there *is*!'

Dulcie remained silent, despite several entreaties, and finally Suze relented.

'But you'll go, right?'

'Yeah. Unless something else comes up, I'll go.'

The idea of seeing Luke again did have a certain appeal, Dulcie admitted. He'd said he was taking a seminar in Cambridge next month, so maybe he had hung around. For now, though, what she really wanted to do was return to the library.

Dulcie had called Suze after two stolen hours in the Widener stacks, and that had been just long enough to remind her of how much she missed it. Deep in the book-friendly 68-degrees air of the library's innards, Dulcie had begun to feel like herself again. As she padded down to Level A, the third of ten that descended deep below Harvard Yard, her soft flip-flops barely made a sound. The building, home to three and a half million books, hummed softly, like a giant purring beast, and as she had edged down one narrow aisle, books shelved on either side, she'd begun to shed the all-around weirdness of the day. Never mind the data entry, mind numbing as it was, but why was she repeating it? And to think that her boss, a woman who probably could pay Dulcie's loans with a personal check, had stolen her sweater . . . it was all just too odd.

Twenty minutes chasing down a half-remembered quote, and she'd felt like a scholar again. Flipping past the marbleized paper frontispiece, she'd ended up taking the relatively 'modern' anthology – dating from 1890 – over to a study carrel and rereading both of the existing bits of *The Ravages of Umbria*, as well as an essay on the book's possible authorship. Dulcie knew she should be spending her time on something more valuable. Her own adviser scoffed whenever she brought up *The Ravages*, and Dulcie knew he had reason. To remind herself of why, she made herself focus on one of the story's weakest scenes, when Hermetria confides in her attendant about her romantic and financial dilemmas, and Demetria responds with a long-winded and hackneyed speech, largely in verse. It was lousy writing, Dulcie admitted. But something in it drew her. While Hermetria's part was quite touching, the attendant – more of a companion than a maid – replies with rote sympathy:

> I do swear upon my heart, my friend belov'd!
> Whatever rough winds blow from fate, I'll not be mov'd.

The woman was always tearing up with some 'sublime emotion' or other. Maybe it was all the dramatic scenery.

'Maybe she simply meant to go back and rework that part,' Dulcie thought, flipping ahead. Dulcie always imagined the author of *The Ravages* to be a woman, one of the so-called 'She-Authors' who had made their mark with this kind of popular fiction. Perhaps this was what drew her, a sisterly sympathy for any author whose work was either unfinished or lost to time. Had the unknown author abandoned the work; published a first volume, hoping for readers who never came? Legitimate thesis topic or not, *The Ravages of Umbria* had drama built right into every part of it. Dulcie put her feet up and kept on reading. Returning once again to an imaginary Italy and the real peace of Widener – the low whirr of the library breathing – had given her room to think again, to be herself.

Sure, even on a summer evening, the library wasn't empty. The coveted offices that bookended the long, metal aisles down here were largely locked up, the pebbled-glass windows dark in the wooden doors. Tenured professors did tend to abandon the city in summer, preferring to compose their scholarly articles from the deep, shaded porches of their houses on Nantucket or the Cape. And Dulcie had had her pick of the bare-bones study carrels, even though the molded desk-and-shelf units were usually reserved for scholars far more advanced through their theses or post-doc research. She shuffled a bit in the hard plastic seat and then, from memory, froze. Counting the seconds, she remembered other nights down here, long-ago evenings when she and Jonah would wait to see how long it would be before the motion-sensor lights went dark, their private game leading as often to giggles as to romance. Ten seconds; no, fifteen. Or was it twenty?

But Dulcie wasn't entirely alone down here this evening. She'd heard the occasional footstep, the squelched sneeze, and these small signs of life made the peace sweeter. It was a respectful peace, a shared quiet. And even the odd shock – when someone peered into her aisle, causing another row of overhead fluorescents to click on – was part of the polite scholarly world.

'Sorry, sorry,' an impossibly skinny, balding man had whispered, as he retreated.

'No problem,' she'd whispered back. But he'd kept walking, the echo of his sneakers on the metal frame floor fading. At the far end of the hall, a hinged door squealed. He must be one of those special few who could get into the 'cages', the locked sections cordoned off by floor-to-ceiling chain-link fence, where rare and particularly fragile texts were kept. She heard the creak of the door closing, a click, and then silence again.

Dulcie had spent an idyllic two hours there, reading and rereading the 'disputed pages', as the later fragments of *The Ravages* were called. These read like an epilogue, telling of one particular 'jealous spirit, worn lean with longing'. That was the last legible line before 'spells most potent for their proximity had robbed you of your patrimony. Beware the jealous spirit of —'

Who was that 'jealous spirit'? Dulcie had mulled that one over until a librarian came around to chase them all out, lighting up each aisle without apology. Did it refer to the ghost of the old retainer, or some other spirit who'd gotten lost in the missing pages? Dulcie underlined the phrase in her notebook and added a question mark. Perhaps— But just then a voice interrupted: 'The stacks will be closing in fifteen minutes. Please gather up your materials.'

Her train of thought derailed, Dulcie made one last note: 'Which ghost?' Gothic novels were full of such spirits, though the authors tended to debunk their own tales, explaining their phantoms away by the story's end. The author of *The Ravages* had never gotten that far; had not even had a chance to show whether the spectre was good or evil.

'Time, people.'

Dulcie waited till the attendant had passed before reshelving the leather-bound volume. Library rules mandated that staff – not students – take charge of this task, preferring the extra labor to the risk of misshelved books. But Dulcie knew this area well enough to make sure the book went back where it was supposed to be, and, standing on tiptoes, patted it even with its neighbors. She couldn't really say why she'd wanted to reread those segments today. She'd just wanted to check, make sure they were still there. And that she could re-enter the labyrinthine world she knew and loved.

So maybe that was why she was in a mellower mood, willing to be swayed by Suze's enthusiasm for Alana's party. She'd even taken some notes on what to wear from her better socialized friend, on the odd chance that she might actually go.

But they hadn't talked about shoes. So when the phone had rung again almost immediately after they'd hung up, Dulcie wasn't completely surprised. Suze might be falling-down tired, but she was also Dulcie's best friend. Maybe she'd get the OK to wear flip-flops. Maybe there was even hope about the guy from Justice. Much to her surprise it was her mom, Lucy, making a rare long-distance call from the community center.

'Dulcie, is everything all right?'

Somewhere in the background a door closed. Dulcie imagined her mother taking the phone into the communal kitchen for privacy. Without waiting for a response, Lucy kept talking.

'I'm asking for a reason, darling. I've had a serious sense of something not being in balance.'

Dulcie rolled her eyes. Out of balance probably had more to do with her mother's digestive system than any weird waves in the atmosphere. 'Why, are you not feeling well?'

'I'm fine. And I'm serious, dear.'

'Well, it has been a bad week.' Dulcie wasn't the sort to confide in her mother. She had Suze for that. But this had been a truly awful week, and a mother, even a mother like Lucy, was supposed to listen, after all. And so she told her. 'And I was the one who found him. I mean, Lucy, there was so much blood!' Just thinking about it gave her shivers.

'Good riddance to bad rubbish.'

'*Mom*!'

'Seriously, Dulcinea, he had bad karma. I could sense it from here. There was something wrong with that boy and I'm glad he's out of your house. At least, I hope he is.'

Dulcie waited, wondering what was going to come next.

'Sage sticks – that's what you need. I'll send you some smudge sticks for purification. Sage, and maybe some sweetgrass for inner harmony. When you get them, start one burning immediately. Burn them in sequence for three days straight, dear. Promise me you will. You don't want any ghosts hanging around your space.'

Dulcie made a noise she hoped would be taken for assent, but her mother's words had brought up another thought. 'There's one other thing,' she said, choosing her words carefully. Anyone else would think she was odd, but the supernatural was one element Lucy Schwartz knew well. 'I think – well, I think I'm already seeing a ghost.'

'You are? Have you seen its aura? I may have to convene a circle to dispel—'

'No, no, it's not a bad ghost.' How could she explain? 'I mean, I'm not really sure what I saw – or heard. But before I came in that day – the day I found Tim – I thought I saw Mr Grey, and he was telling me not to go into the house.'

There was a rare moment of silence on the phone. Dulcie wondered for a second if she had finally succeeded in out-weirding her mom. But when Lucy spoke again, her voice was confident, calm and completely unfazed.

'This is marvelous news, Dulcie. That's not a ghost you're seeing, you've got a spirit guide. Spirit guides often take animal shapes. I've always wanted one. Now, a cat – what would that be? I know I've got a book on them somewhere . . .'

Dulcie knew the call was costing her mom more than she could afford. 'Why don't you just look it up and write me about it?' She paused. Had the cat been a spirit guide? 'But maybe don't send the sage. I mean, just in case this is the ghost of Mr Grey, I don't want to get rid of it – of him.'

'Oh, sage won't disperse guardian spirits, don't worry about that. And do keep in mind, that young man had lousy karma. Now, have you noticed anything missing? Sometimes an unsettled spirit will try anything to climb back in.'

'Just my sweater, but I know who took that.' If Dulcie didn't talk fast enough, Lucy would have the entire Pacific Northwest chanting for her. 'That was Mrs Putnam, one of my bosses.'

'Your boss took your sweater?'

'Well, I think so.' She quickly told her mother how she had taken three days off work and when she returned, the sweater she'd left in her cubicle to keep warm against the air-conditioning had disappeared. 'I mean, the one she had with her looked like mine.'

'That city is an evil place, Dulcie. I'm not sure I like you being there.'

It had been a bad week, but Dulcie wouldn't go back to Oregon for anything. 'Well, it was only a sweater.'

'A woman who will steal a sweater has bad *qi*. There's no telling what else she'll do.'

Dulcie couldn't argue with that. It was an insurance office, after all. And she hadn't even told her mother how reptilian the manager could be. 'Well, it's just a temp job. And maybe I'll ask her about it. Maybe it was a mistake.' Yeah, right.

'You be careful, Dulcinea. And if your spirit guide comes back, would you . . .?' Her mother paused.

'I'll put in a word for you, Mom. Don't worry.'

'Thank you, dear. Remember, I've always been partial to wolves.'

Seven

She hadn't meant to be late for work but somehow, in the grand scheme of things, Priority Insurance no longer rated very high. After talking with her mother, Dulcie had stayed up way too late reading the arts and literature grad students' journal, *Notes from Tintype Abbey*, and then simply had to write up some thoughts about setting as metaphor before going to sleep. She'd been dreaming of a haunted castle, one that seemed to be up two flights of stairs from the street, and an avenging knight who had suspiciously long whiskers emerging from his visor, when she'd been woken up – not by her alarm, which she'd forgotten to set, but by Helene downstairs, shouting.

'I *know* you're allergic, Duane. *Duane*!' Ah, it was her neighbor's boyfriend who had provoked the normally unshakeable nurse. Dulcie had never liked the pumped-up little muscle builder Helene had met at the hospital. He'd glared at Dulcie for having the temerity to live in the upstairs apartment, and he didn't seem to respect Helene for the light and airy ground-floor place she'd paid for and furnished either. Dulcie had even seen him kick at a cat once, out on the street. The feline had dodged the little man easily enough, but Dulcie had been glad to hear her hiss. 'Of *course* I care about your health, Duane. Don't you know that by now?'

Dulcie couldn't hear a response and wondered if Helene was expending all that energy on a phone call or if Duane's asthma had finally silenced him – if he had asthma at all. Dulcie suspected that the little bully just wanted an excuse to take steroids. 'I wouldn't, Duane. Never. Why would I have a cat in my apartment? It must have been something else! *Duane*.'

Dulcie heard a positively feral growl of frustration and, yes, what sounded like a receiver being banged down. That's when she noticed the time and jumped up. At least she didn't have to wait for the shower anymore. Though, as she balanced on one foot to shave her leg, while simultaneously trying to rinse the shampoo out of her hair, she had to wonder: had a cat been in Helene's apartment? Could this be the ghost of Mr Grey, watching over both of them? As she rubbed a towel over her curls, she could have sworn she felt the soft press of fur, the familiar figure eight of a feline wrapping around her legs. She could almost hear the purr. But when she looked down, all she saw were her own bare feet, the toenail polish beginning to chip.

Between the usual T delays and the absolutely necessary stop for a jumbo Dunkin' iced, she was nearly half an hour late when she ducked into her cubicle. Strangely, nobody seemed to notice.

'Psst.' Joanie's jet-black eyes blinked at her over the cubicle wall. 'You missed all the excitement.'

'Why, what happened?' Dulcie couldn't figure out why they both were whispering, until she realized the office was awfully quiet. 'I overslept.'

'Not to worry. I'll swear you were here if anyone asks. But I doubt they will.' Joanie paused for effect. 'I don't know who will even be left when they're done!'

Dulcie thought of her sweater. Maybe something else had been stolen. 'Come on, Joanie. Spill.'

Joanie leaned farther over the carpeted cubicle wall, savoring her moment of drama. 'Well, first thing, when I got in, all the bigwigs were in the lobby, buzzing like someone had stepped on their ant's nest.' Dulcie blinked away the rather confused image that came to mind. 'Then they all wheeled around and took off. For about ten minutes, there were no supervisors around. None. So I figured I'd take an early break. Anyway, I was just outside when I saw two big guys come in – real bruisers – and when they came out, about five minutes later, they had one of the guys from Accounting with them – in handcuffs!'

'*Handcuffs?*' Dulcie couldn't keep the skepticism from her voice. Joanie was a drama queen.

But the other girl nodded vigorously. 'Handcuffs! Real ones.' She sounded like she knew the difference. 'I cannot wait to grill Ricky on this. Oh, and everyone from IT is in a meeting, too. I was trying to download some music and thought I'd froze the system. Nobody home. This is big. Whatever it is.'

Now that was curious. Whatever was going on didn't get Dulcie's sweater back, but it did add a certain spice to the day. Around eleven, when Dulcie took her first break, she decided to poke around a bit. Maybe she would see her sweater on the back of a chair. Maybe she could 'liberate' it. What she found instead was an office humming with rumor, and very few managers in evidence. The temptation to find out more was too great. Joanie had her source, Ricky, in Accounting. So Dulcie headed over to IT, where at least the staff members could be assumed to be reasonably intelligent.

But when she pushed open the glass-fronted door to their section, she saw what Joanie had been talking about. The place, usually a hive of activity, was deserted. The Guitar Hero posters looked down on empty cubicles. One screen, however, was still glowing, and Dulcie walked toward it.

'What are you doing here?' Dulcie spun around to find herself facing a very tall, very skinny, and very angry geek.

'I'm Dulcie. A temp.'

'I didn't ask who you were, I asked what you were doing here.' He pushed past her and, leaning over the keyboard, quickly typed in something that made the screen go black. In his wake, she got a whiff of nervous sweat. 'This area is off limits.' He turned back to her and she saw how two purple blotches in his cheeks clashed with his acne.

'It was unlocked. I didn't know.' Dulcie could feel her own face growing hot with color, but the programmer turned away to grab a chair. 'I just wanted to know what happened.'

'You and everyone else.' He wheeled the chair toward his desk. 'Forty-eight hours at least we've been working on this.'

'I came in late and everything was in an uproar.' Dulcie wasn't good at this feminine wiles stuff, but how hard could it be? She pulled a nearby chair close and sat on the edge, trying to look demure. She lowered her voice. 'I figured you folks here might know.'

He turned to stare at her. He didn't look taken in. 'And you just happened to be Little Miss Curious? You didn't happen to input a little program while you were just kicking around?'

'I have no idea what you are talking about.' She sat up straight in her chair, realizing too late that this meant sticking out her chest. The pale-faced geek goggled for a second, but then turned away.

'Somebody does. And I don't think it was Accounting. We have to recreate records from the last several months of raw data. There's a ghost in the machine.'

Interesting choice of words, but before Dulcie could say anything, the computer geek turned back to her. 'Now, do you mind?' She was dismissed.

Joanie was gone when Dulcie got back, but within a half-hour the kohl-eyed Goth was once again leaning over Dulcie's cubicle.

'Lunchtime – and I've got the goods.' Joanie looked around. There was still no supervisor to be seen.

'So do I!' Dulcie felt a surge of pride. 'Deli Haus?'

Over serious corned beef sandwiches, they pooled their info. From Dulcie's geek, it was clear that a bug of some sort had been used to infiltrate the Priority data banks. Ricky, who by the sound of things was looking to ingratiate himself with Joanie, had been able to explain why. Premiums, thousands of them, had been jacked up slightly – some by only fractions of a penny a month – but that extra money had been siphoned off, and deposited off-site. Payments, too, possibly, though Ricky wasn't sure about those. Altogether, it explained the meetings and the air of panic, and certainly the accountant who had been taken out in cuffs. It also made sense of what Dulcie had considered dummy work. If the files were corrupted, well, someone would have to type them all back in.

'But how could someone do that?' Joanie was picking her teeth with one of the wooden toothpicks the deli provided. Dulcie toyed with the last dill pickle spear.

'It sounds fairly sophisticated, but there has to be a precedent.' Something on the edge of her memory was making this all sound familiar. 'Someone has done this before.'

'Can you go back to IT later? Maybe flirt with that guy a little?' Joanie was a skinny little thing, but she knew how to work what she had. Dulcie, who had more, shook her head.

'No way. Not until he's had a shower, at least. But I've got some ideas. Believe it or not,' she popped the last of the pickle into her mouth, 'in my real life, I'm considered pretty good at research.'

Back at the office, she started a few searches, humming to herself as Google and Yahoo did their work. But just as she was about to log on to Lexis Nexis, using her academic account, she froze. Management was on a witch-hunt, the geek had warned her. Nobody knew who had fed the worm into the system. Right now every non-mandated keystroke would be a target, the data – and the user – observed and analyzed. Backspacing to erase her password, Dulcie cursed her own stupidity. Being scholarly wasn't the same as being practical.

'There are some interesting legal issues in hacking.' Suze had called her the next night, while Dulcie was stripping the blue polish off her toenails. Dulcie had continued her research on her home computer, but when nothing interesting had turned up, she'd left a message requesting Suze's aid, too. 'Privacy, intellectual property, corporate security . . .'

'Purple or pink?' Something about the array of colored bottles made her living room more like home again. Corporate piracy seemed very far away.

'Purple.' Suze might come from a conventional background, but she wasn't stodgy. 'But what you've described sounds more like electronic embezzlement.'

'Guess so.' Dulcie held one foot up toward the desk lamp. The iridescent purple shimmered like the inside of a seashell. 'I just kept thinking it reminded me of something.'

'A new way to pay your bills?' Suze could be cavalier about her mountain of debt. She had folks who could help with her loans – and a degree that would translate into a major corporate pay check.

'No.' Dulcie fanned her toes. 'Something with the university? Something else about a computer virus.'

'The admissions hackers!' Suze was excited now. 'Not at Harvard, though. Some southern school – Duke? A bunch of prospective students got into the admissions systems. They only wanted to see if they were getting accepted, but when the school found out, they considered it such a breach of ethics that anyone who looked was automatically rejected.'

Dulcie shook her head and the bottle of polish. 'No, that wasn't it. Something like that, though.' Maybe it was that comment about a 'ghost in the machine'. The geek had probably lifted it from a sci-fi novel, but Dulcie remembered it from philosophy: mind–body dualism and all. But there was something else, too. She started on her left foot, splaying her toes the way Mr Grey would when he washed. God, she missed that cat. But Suze was talking.

'There've been a bunch of cases involving smart, competitive types who will do anything for an edge. A virus that feeds out money – or information – is just a step up from peeking at the grading curve. Some of it's theft, some just high-tech cheating; not illegal, *per se*, but is it ethical? Or does it show that the students are indeed the best and the brightest? Like I said, interesting law.'

Dulcie stretched out her foot again and for a split second she thought she saw something – something grey – on the couch beyond. Just as quickly, it was gone. 'Suze?' She needed a reality check. 'Would you think it was really just too weird if I told you that sometimes I think I see something? Or that, right before I go to sleep, I feel like I can sense Mr Grey? Like, I feel him jump on to the bed and start purring?'

For a rare moment, her room-mate was quiet. 'I would understand where you're coming from, Dulce.' Her voice was softer now. 'But, well, it would make me worry a bit. I mean, I don't want to sound rude here. But have you thought about maybe adopting another cat? A cute little kitten?'

'No.' She put the top back on the polish and screwed it tight with a vengeance. 'Not yet,' she added, her tone softening. 'Not ever' was what she meant.

'I don't mean to replace Mr Grey.' Suze spoke quickly. 'I know you can't do that. It's just that you've been through a lot this summer, and the company might do you good.'

Dulcie closed her eyes, fighting back the tears that had suddenly welled up. 'Uh-huh.' She couldn't manage more without revealing her sudden mood swing.

'Oh, sweetie, I'm so sorry.'

With her friend on the line, Dulcie found herself crying again. 'I should go.' She sniffed. 'This is costing you a fortune.'

'You sure you'll be OK?'

Dulcie wasn't, but she could hear Suze's relief. Long-distance comfort, for the nth time in as many weeks, would try anyone's patience. 'Yeah,' she hiccuped, 'I feel better now anyway. Thanks.' She was telling Suze the truth, or at least part of it. What she wasn't saying was that as soon as she'd started crying, she'd been aware of something: at the base of the sofa, near her feet, she'd felt the warm, soft touch of Mr Grey's fur.

Eight

Weird was the new normal at work, and in a way Dulcie liked it. Sure, the first time a uniformed rent-a-cop poked through her bag on her way into the Priority office, it was a bit unnerving. But that was the routine at the university libraries, too, so by her second break she was opening her bag without thinking. The occasional slowdown of the computer systems did make her wonder if somewhere in the building, some poor IT guy was rewriting code – or rewiring the system. For a brief moment, she considered the possibility that, in fact, some shadow program was reporting on her every keystroke. But what she was typing in was so dull that she felt less outrage than pity for whoever might have that job. And the place was decidedly quieter. Maybe for the upper-ups and those who planned on spending their working life here that would be bad – a little more paranoia to ratchet up the corporate tension. But as a temp, the strange, new hush that hung over the office just seemed more peaceful.

'Must be all that time you spend in the library,' Joanie had said, when Dulcie had commented favorably on the new quiet. They'd been on their mid-morning break, and Joanie had been a bit miffed at what she'd called the guard's 'pawing' through her stuff.

'Maybe.' Dulcie chewed on a muffin. 'But isn't it better than having everyone talking constantly and looking over your shoulder?'

'If you like morgues,' Joanie said, and then brightened. 'But you're right. We haven't had to sit through one of those stupid efficiency meetings since last Tuesday.'

Dulcie nodded and broke off another piece of the toasted sweetbread muffin. She'd also found a killer Portuguese bakery around the corner. The summer was looking up.

'You think they'll ever find out who put the worm in the system?' Dulcie blotted up the last few crumbs.

'Who cares, as long as they keep us on the payroll till September?'

Things were so strangely quiet that nobody even questioned Dulcie when she began to pack up a little before five. Joanie found her in the bathroom ten minutes later.

'Hey, I sent a message from your computer, just in case anyone is still looking at what time we log off.'

Dulcie was trying to get her eyeliner straight as Joanie ducked into a stall. 'What did it say?' How come she couldn't put on eye make-up with her mouth closed? 'And who was it to?'

'To admin. Want your money? No, just kidding. I just had you email me asking if we had the new files yet. Nice dress. You going out or something?'

'Or something.' Dulcie had even ironed the Indian cotton print. She couldn't believe she was making this much effort. 'This woman I dislike has invited me to an after-work drinks thing. She's really preppy. Always done up, you know.' She paused; may as well be honest. 'But there's a guy who might be there.'

She heard a flush. 'Well, if he's not, you can always come over to Foley's.' Joanie washed her hands and checked her own mascara. Dulcie noticed the younger girl opening her mouth, too. 'You know, I've been trying to get you to come out with us. At least we're human.'

'Thanks, Joanie.' Had she really been ignoring invitations all summer?

'No prob. But, hey—' Joanie licked her finger and leaned over to dab at Dulcie's cheek. 'You might try the liquid eyeliner. You're wearing more of this stuff on your cheeks than your eyes.'

While that comment did little for her confidence, Dulcie was at least reasonably sure that she was speckle free by the time she arrived at Alana's Beacon Hill address. Fifteen minutes later, she realized she might as well be covered in leopard spots. Nobody would notice.

'The rich really are different from you and me,' she muttered to herself, looking around the roof deck. Under a striped awning, a bartender whipped up frothy drinks, the growl of the blender almost drowned out by the volume of the reggae blasting from an unseen sound system.

'Margarita?' She turned to see the bartender looking her way. He seemed vaguely familiar.

'Dulcie – Dulcie Schwartz.' Had they had a class together?

'No, I mean, would you like a drink?' He smiled, and they both laughed.

'Oh, sorry! Yes, please.' He gave the almost-full blender a quick spin and poured a light-green concoction into a wide-brimmed glass. 'Thank you.' She took a sip. Sweet, but strong. 'Can you tell me, is Alana around?'

He shook his head and reached for more glasses. 'I'm not sure. It was a summer school student who hired me. Stacia Something?' Student bartender, then. He dipped four more glasses in a wide bowl of salt. This was a crowd that wanted its drinks ready fast. 'You might try over by the lilies.'

Dulcie turned and saw the huge flower display next to – was that a fountain? She whistled softly. Beyond the low, white railing the golden dome of the State House glowed like the setting sun itself. The bartender chuckled. 'Not exactly tar beach, huh?'

'I'll say.' There was no use pretending she belonged here. Maybe she should put the oversized drink down and sneak out. She took another sip. Or she could finish it back here with the bartender, and then sneak out.

'Dulcie!' Her plan was interrupted by Alana's squeal. 'You made it!' The blonde looked happy to see her. 'And here you are, all by yourself. Come on over and meet everybody.' With a last look back at the bartender, Dulcie allowed herself to be led out from the shade and toward the small crowd by the fountain. An unnaturally pink dolphin seemed about to buck off an overweight cherub. 'Do you like it? I rented it for the night. It just seemed like fun.'

'It is . . . very summery,' Dulcie managed to say. Over the spray from the cherub's head she could see Luke. He was talking to a dark-haired woman. Yes, it was Stacia. But almost as if he could feel her gaze, he turned. Their eyes met – and then Stacia turned, too.

'Dulcie, so glad you could make it.' Her voice sounded friendlier than her eyes looked, but before Dulcie could get away, the sleek beauty had skirted the fountain and reached her. Taking her by the arm, as if to examine the stacked bangles on her wrist, Stacia walked her away from the cheery cherub and from Luke. '*Great* idea, Dulcie.' She held Dulcie's arm tight, but her words were gentle. 'I told Alana you were artistic. Do you want to be introduced around? You know Luke, obviously.'

Before she could do any more than nod at Tim's brother, Dulcie found herself led around the roof deck. 'Dulcie, you must know Jack and Bruce, of course.' Two of the beefy boys from the funeral nodded in her direction and went back to drinking. 'And Jessica; and this is our other Jessica, Jessica Todd. And Whitman . . .' Must be a family name, Dulcie thought, with a flash of sympathy for the freckled blonde. 'She was just the total heroine of our field hockey team.'

Dulcie smiled until her cheeks began to ache with the strain. Why was she here? 'I should bring this back to the bar.' She raised her empty glass, happy for an excuse to retreat.

'Nonsense.' Stacia whipped the glass from her and deposited it on the white railing. 'That's why we have help.'

Dulcie peered over the railing. 'I hope that doesn't fall.' Stacia wasn't listening, and seemed intent on steering Dulcie into an almost quiet corner. What did this woman want from her anyway? Was she about to be warned off Luke?

'Dulcie, now, I feel horrible asking you this. Just horrible.' It *was* about Luke. Dulcie braced herself, searching for some wonderfully cutting remark. 'I mean, I know you and Tim weren't the best of friends, but he talked about you a bit.' Something cutting and yet suave would fit the bill. All those hours watching classic films must be worth something. 'But Alana is my best friend in the entire world, and she's just a little fragile right now.'

Katharine Hepburn, she mused, or maybe Lauren Bacall.

'And that's why I was wondering if Tim had said something to you.'

'*Tim?*' That wasn't what she'd expected.

'Well, of course.' Stacia's eyes were so wide that Dulcie knew she was lying. Still . . .

'What would Tim have said anything to me about?'

'Oh, you know how boys are. I mean, don't let Alana know.' She lowered her voice and leaned in closer. 'But Tim wasn't always the best boyfriend.'

'Well, yeah.' Dulcie thought of Luisa. 'But, really, Stacia, does it matter now?'

'It matters how she feels. He *was* going to propose to her, you know.' Dulcie wasn't convinced, but nodded anyway. 'But there was other stuff, too; private stuff – on his computer. Alana had told me that he'd wanted something, you know, just for him. I didn't like the idea, but what could I say? And now, well, I don't want to bring it up again. But I don't like the idea of that – material – being out there.'

Porn? Did Tim have compromising photos of his blonde honey? Dulcie's ears pricked up. 'Well, you know Luke took his brother's laptop home.'

Stacia nodded. 'I've already spoken to Luke. But, I was wondering, you know, if Tim ever used your computer?'

Dulcie shuddered. The idea of her late ex-room-mate in her room, not to mention messing with her computer, appalled her. All her notes were on that computer. And her journal, along with about a dozen photos of Mr Grey. 'It's actually an old machine, and I don't think—' He'd borrowed everything else she had though, hadn't he? 'I mean, I hadn't thought. But I'll go through my hard drive tonight.'

'Thanks, Dulcie.' The smile seemed real now, warming up Stacia's dark eyes. 'I really appreciate it.' She reached forward to give the shorter woman a quick hug. 'But please, if you find anything, don't open it. Just delete it, or put it on a disk for me, will you?'

'Sure, Stacia.' Another half hug, and the other woman was gone, a look of genuine relief on her pretty face. Dulcie watched her retreating back and thought about friendship. Suze would go out of her way to get rid of embarrassing files for her, wouldn't she? At any rate, she hadn't been attacked – or warned off Luke. Who, she realized, was heading her way, two margaritas in hand.

'Hey, Dulcie, I didn't think I'd find you still here.' He handed her one of the wide, green drinks. 'In fact,' he leaned closer and dropped his voice to a conspiratorial whisper, 'I figured we'd both have fled this scene long before.'

Dulcie sipped the margarita. It tasted as good as the first. 'I didn't think

I'd last either, but Stacia sort of made me her project.' She slipped him a look. He didn't seem particularly interested.

'Yeah, she's like that. I got to know her a bit last Christmas, when Tim brought her and Alana around. She's the one who invited me, actually.'

That was interesting. 'I think she masterminded this party. I guess she wanted to cheer Alana up.'

'The grieving girlfriend? Hardly.' They both looked over: the supposedly bereaved blonde was illustrating some story with wide gestures that had already doused one onlooker – Jack? Bruce? – in margarita. Luke coughed. 'Oh, I'm sorry.' Dulcie felt her cheeks redden. 'I know, he was your brother. I'm so—'

'Don't apologize. It's OK. It's – these people. I mean, I agree, none of them seem to have really noticed that he's gone. It's almost as if he's just out getting more limes or something.'

'They're not the deepest crew. And it is a shock.' Dulcie didn't know why she was making excuses. 'Maybe this is just their way of dealing with it?'

Luke nodded, his mouth set in a grim line. 'Yeah, I guess. They certainly seem to have moved on.'

'Speaking of moving on.' Dulcie wasn't sure how to broach the subject. Certainly, Luke would want to know that everything was being done to find his brother's killer, wouldn't he? 'I spoke with the police again.'

'Oh?' Luke was staring off at the horizon. The setting sun had burnished the State House to a warm gold.

'I know they're investigating, but I thought they might want to know what you told me. About how Tim had done a little dealing and—'

'You *what*?' Dulcie had his attention now. Luke's grey eyes looked hard as stone.

'Luke, I know he was small time, just selling to friends or whatever. But this is a big city. And I don't know how streetwise Tim was.'

'I can't believe you talked to the cops about this!' Luke was fairly spitting. 'That was told to you in confidence.'

'Luke, all we can do for him now is try to get him some justice.' Dulcie couldn't understand where this anger was coming from. 'Tim is beyond anyone hurting him.'

'But my family isn't. My *parents* aren't! If this gets out – if their friends hear . . .'

Dulcie stepped back. She hadn't thought about his family. Unlike hers, they were in the same city. And unlike her family, they probably cared about things like propriety and reputation. Could she be any clumsier? 'I'm . . . I'm sorry, Luke. I didn't think. I can't imagine the police will make any of this common knowledge.'

'You didn't think is right.' He stormed off.

'Whoa, what was that about?'

Dulcie turned, surprised to find one of the beefy boys right behind her.

'Are you OK?'

'Yes, I think so.' Dulcie heard the shakiness in her own voice. 'Bill?'

'Bruce, we met earlier.' He was another tall one, towering over her like Luke had. His muscles had made him look shorter from a distance, but when he took her hand, his grip was gentle. As was his voice. 'You sure you're OK? Would you like another margarita?'

'Yes – I mean, no. Thank you.' Bruce had blue eyes. Sky blue. 'I think I've had enough.'

'Probably wise. I think a lot of folks here have had enough.' They shared a smile. He had dimples, too. 'But I was meaning to come talk to you anyway.'

She raised her eyebrows, not entirely trusting herself to speak.

'I wanted to thank you for standing up for Luisa.' She blanked. 'You remember – the Spanish girl?'

'Latina.' She was getting flustered. 'I mean, you're welcome. She seems very nice.'

'She is, I know.' His grin turned sheepish. 'She was very gentle with me when I was failing statistics, just like Tim promised she'd be. But this crowd . . .' He shook his head and his grin faded as he looked around. Dulcie followed his gaze. Silhouetted against the reddening sky, the scene looked like a TV ad for summer. But the noise level was getting louder. 'They can be, well, tough, if you're not born on the Hill; or a linebacker – for the right school.' He chuckled softly and leaned in. 'Some of us get by on brawn. But Luisa isn't one of them, and a lot of people here wouldn't give her the time of day because of that. You must know what I mean, right? I see it in you, too. It's just so rare that you get to meet someone who is genuine.'

Dulcie felt her cheeks flushing and hoped she'd simply blend in against the sunset. She hadn't expected this: gallantry – and blue eyes. Even Bruce's bulk seemed more toned close up. 'Well, we all have some part of us that's not for general consumption.' She was babbling, and she knew it. 'I mean, we all want that.'

He leaned closer still. Maybe she'd made sense? Maybe he didn't care. 'In fact, Dulcie, that's what I was hoping to talk to you about—'

They were interrupted by a musical tone. 'Excuse me, please.' He held up a sausage-like finger. 'I've been waiting for this call.' He turned away from her to answer and she found herself looking around again. She could see the attraction of living like this. Up here, the slight breeze kept things cool, and she hadn't heard the buzz of a single mosquito. Maybe things were getting better, finally.

'Dulcie?' She turned back to find that Bruce had pocketed his cell. 'I'm sorry, but I've got to run.' He paused, on the brink of saying something else. 'I look forward to seeing you again.'

'See you,' she said, but he was already halfway to the roof door. He hadn't asked for her number, but he knew how to find her. Maybe these people weren't so bad. She licked the salt off her lips and thought about another drink. The sound of laughter caught her ear and she turned toward it. Luke was standing off by the railing, the golden dome of the State House still glowing behind him, and Stacia was by his side.

'So, it wasn't so bad after all.' Suze deserved to gloat a little bit, and Dulcie was feeding her all the details. Luke might have a screw loose, but now there was blue-eyed Bruce in the picture, a muscle-man with dimples. And Stacia's news had been a bit of a bombshell. Dirty pictures of the All-American Alana?

'No, it was actually pretty fun.' Dulcie had called Suze as soon as she'd gotten off the T. 'Those people weren't all half bad.' She waited. Nothing. 'Oh, all right. Susan Laurel Rubenstein, you were right.' The silence on the line made Dulcie wonder for a moment if her cell service had dropped out. More likely, Suze was multitasking – they both tended to do that – and had been distracted by an email. 'Suze?'

'Sorry, Dulce. That was just the strangest thing.' Suze sounded disturbed. Maybe she'd lost something on her computer?

'What?' Dulcie stopped. She was half a block away from her building, but she didn't want to risk losing reception again.

'I don't know. Maybe it was another network. It just sounded . . . creepy.'

Suze was freaking her out now. What made matters worse was that she could see her own front stoop. On it, just as on the night when Tim had been killed, was a long-haired grey cat. He was staring straight at her.

Please be careful, Dulcie. Trust, like faith, can weave spells.

She heard the voice in her head, calm and warm, but with an overtone of urgency. 'Trust can weave spells,' she repeated.

'That's it! That's what I heard just now. Did you hear it, too?' Suze was talking, but her voice barely registered. What did that mean anyway?

The cat on the steps had flicked its tail once, blinked its green eyes, and disappeared.

Nine

'Hangover? Must have been a good party, then.' Joanie's voice sounded unnaturally loud in Dulcie's cubicle. But despite the throbbing headache, Dulcie wasn't complaining.

'Margaritas,' she said as explanation, both to her office mate, who today had traded her customary black for a virulent purple, and to herself. Better the odd apparition should have been alcohol induced. *Please be careful*. The words came back to her. Who had she trusted? Why did cats have to be so enigmatic? She'd flirted with Bruce, sure. But that was it. She hadn't even given him her number.

Still muzzy-headed as the office day wound to a close, she decided to go directly to the library from Priority. Not that she'd get much work done in this state, but maybe the air-conditioning would clear away the fog.

But once she'd climbed out of the T and hiked across the Yard, she began to have second thoughts. The broad stone steps up to the library entrance seemed particularly steep this evening, the marble foyer somehow chilling. It was better than going home, particularly after another sweatbox day, but the familiar comfort was lacking. As she swiped her student ID through the entrance turnstile, she found herself thinking about that feline vision once again. Was she losing her mind? Last night's apparition had been disturbing, rather than comforting, appearing with a warning and then gone in a flash. And Mr Grey, no matter how much she missed him, was dead and gone. She had held his still body herself.

She shook her head to clear it. That didn't help the headache, but as she rummaged through her bag for yet another dose of aspirin, she realized the obvious. Dulcie Schwartz specialized in research. Why not look into what was bugging her? She'd given up the other day at work, but she was on her own turf now – and Widener was research central.

A quick detour to the water fountain and she fairly bounced up the steps to the reading room, the huge, hushed heart of the library. Unlike the stacks, the reading room was never even close to empty. With its high, arched ceiling and skylights, the long hall felt like a cathedral, and here in its nave supplicants were always ready to worship. Passing by the great wooden tables, where summer school students had spread out their books and papers, she made her way to one of the computer terminals set against the paneled walls.

'Paranormal, ghosts, sightings'. As she typed the words into the library database, she chuckled. She'd entered these very words before, only then she'd been looking for iterations in eighteenth-century fiction. Skimming through the listings, she also had to wonder, if she was going to be haunted, why would it be by her cat? Weren't most ghosts supposed to be of those who had met a violent or untimely end? That question was at the core of *The Ravages,* provoking scholars to wonder whether that kindly old family retainer had met a bad end – or whether there were other spirits hanging around the mortal coil.

Could the same rules hold true in her current situation? Much as Dulcie had loved Mr Grey, and as hard as it had been to let him go, she knew the grey cat had lived a good, long life. Tim, on the other hand, had barely begun his. If anyone was going to haunt her, it should have been her obnoxious room-mate, shouldn't it?

The thought was chilling. But as the counter passed 2,000 hits without anything interesting, she gave up and moved the mouse to click 'Exit'. She might be a research wizard, but the ultra-modern Widener reading room was no place to search for ghosts. Instead, she pulled the ergonometric keyboard toward her and started typing in more earthly terms: 'Crime, Cambridge, City of'. Now that might get her somewhere. Maybe Tim's murder was part of a series. Maybe it was drug related, and some crime lord had set out to make Central Square his own.

But if that was the case, the HOLLIS catalog had no word of it. Even when Dulcie clicked over to the library's extensive periodicals section, the pickings were slim: a sexual assault down by the river; a rash of purse snatchings near the Porter Square mall; a mugging that had left the young victim without the twenty in his wallet or his new leather jacket ('black, described as "biker style"') according to the police report. The big, bad city just wasn't that bad.

Strange that Tim's murder hadn't made the news. Dulcie pushed her chair back from the carrel and looked around the reading room. Like the rest of the library, it had been renovated recently, the college's deep pockets paying for not only these new computers but also the restored paneling that glowed with polish, the glare-free lighting over the communal work tables, and that wonderful air-conditioning that kept both temperature and humidity at constant, book-friendly levels. Come to think of it, maybe the lack of any news stories wasn't that strange. Tim's family was old Crimson. From what Luke had said, they'd prefer a low profile in this community, and they could afford it.

But that didn't mean that they were bad people. They just wanted privacy. After all, not all preppies were evil. Maybe it was the hangover, but Dulcie found her thoughts wandering to Bruce. He might belong to that crowd but he had seemed nice, and not just because he'd seemed interested in her. Dulcie gave herself a reality check; the big guy liked her at least in part because she'd befriended Luisa, an outsider. And that thought led Dulcie back to Tim again. He'd at least recommended the pretty Latina as a tutor, and something about Bruce's tone of voice suggested that Tim had said more about her, too. Perhaps Tim had been serious about Luisa. Despite Alana's confidence, there had been no evidence that the ring was for her. And actually, if Tim had been planning to dump Alana *and* he had compromising photos of her, well, that might be motive for some kind of violence, mightn't it?

She'd check her computer when she got home. Not that she wanted to see photos of Alana, but it was a point worth pursuing, and, besides, she'd promised Stacia. For now, she might as well try to get some work done. Thinking of work, Dulcie pulled herself back to the terminal. Nobody could watch her keystrokes here, and she typed in 'Priority Insurance' and 'embezzle'. Nothing. She erased the second word and substituted 'fraud'. Just then, the gentle hush of the reading room was broken by the jarring ring of a cell phone. All through the hall, heads bobbed up.

'*Shhh!*' They were all staring at her. One older man with a goatee was positively scowling, and Dulcie realized that the galling noise was coming from her phone. She reached into her bag and, with a quick fumble, turned it off. She shrugged and smiled; the silent version of an apology. The goatee guy shot her a look.

Two minutes later, a quick glance around the room showed only a dozen bald pates, five scruffy hairy ones, and one woman who seemed to be sleeping. Dulcie snuck the offending phone out of her bag and into her lap. The missed call had come from the Cambridge Police. Well, good. She had been hoping they would follow up on the drug angle. And now she might have more to tell them: about Alana and Luisa, about the ring, and the possibility that blue-blood Tim might have had compromising material on a Beacon Hill deb. Should she call them back now? The terminal in front of her had finished its search. More than two dozen citations linked her daytime employer and the word 'fraud'. Most of them seemed to be news stories, the kind of reports that quoted insurance executives justifying their premiums by blaming consumer fraud. But one or two looked like they might go deeper. She hit 'print' and by the time she had gathered herself together and wandered over to the library's print center, the sleek and silent machine had already spat out the pages. Stuffing them into her bag, she headed for the door.

'Hello, this is Dulcie Schwartz. I'm returning Detective Scavetti's call.'

There'd been a short queue at the exit as it was so close to closing time, and by the time the guard had checked Dulcie's bag and let her through another fifteen minutes had passed. Dulcie stood on the Widener steps, looking up at the clouds.

'Ms Schwartz? This is Detective Forrester. I'm afraid Detective Scavetti is gone for the day.'

Dulcie sighed. Maybe Tim's case wasn't that high priority after all. She'd left the quiet cool of the library for nothing. Even though the summer twilight was fading, the humidity remained oppressive.

'But I do know he would like to speak with you. Could you come in tomorrow at ten?'

'Of course.' Tomorrow was Saturday and she'd have preferred to sleep in but at least she was getting somewhere. Maybe Scavetti would prove to be her knight errant, righting wrongs around him. 'Did he get my message about the drugs? Something else has come up, too. There's something about Tim's old girlfriend—'

The voice on the other end cut her off. 'I'm sure you can explain all that to Detective Scavetti. I don't have his notes here. I just know that he is very insistent that you come in as soon as possible for questioning.'

'*Questioning*?' Dulcie straightened up. 'Me?' But the line was dead.

As if on cue, the clouds cracked open and it started to rain.

Ten

Dulcie was still standing there, holding the open phone and staring at the torrent pouring down from the edge of the library portico, when the little machine came back to life.

'Hello?' She heard the quaver in her own voice. Right now all news seemed like bad news.

'Dulcie! I'm so glad I've caught you.' It was her mom, breathless as usual. Life was a continual wonder, and a continual crisis, for Lucy Schwartz. 'You weren't at home and I was worried.'

'I was in the library, Lucy. And you could have left a message. I'd have called you back.' She glanced up at the sky. The rain didn't look ready to stop any time soon. 'What's up?'

'I've had a vision, Dulcie. And you were in it.'

Dulcie closed her eyes and leaned back against the cool stone of the library. A vision could mean a dream, or it could mean her mother and her buddy Nirvana had been hitting the peyote again. For purely mind-expanding purposes, Lucy would say, but over the years, Dulcie had been regaled with enough of her mother's fantastical visions to make even *The Ravages of Umbria* seem tame. Inspired by her psychedelic experiences, Nirvana had been ordained as a priestess of some sort about a decade ago, but since the mail-order certificate listed her given name, Shirley, most of Nirvana's religious experiences remained private.

'A vision, Dulcie!' Lucy repeated.

'Yes?' Dulcie drew out the one syllable. She didn't want to encourage her mom's craziness, but she knew she was going to hear it whether she asked or not.

'You never believe in my visions, do you?' Blessedly, Lucy didn't wait for an answer. 'But this one was different – very clear. And vitally important.'

Of course; it was always something major – someone who meant to do her harm or some secret that would lead to great treasure. Lucy never called her daughter with a vision that told her to take an umbrella, and Dulcie suspected that the calls had more to do with empty-nest syndrome than with any real psychic ability. Still, Lucy was her mother.

'Uh-huh?' Even without the prompt, Dulcie knew her mother would elaborate. She was just stretching out the drama.

'There's been an intruder in your house!'

Dulcie choked back a laugh. 'Lucy, my room-mate was murdered in my apartment. Don't you think this vision is coming a bit late?' Tim's death wasn't a joke, she knew well. But a week and a half later, it was beginning to seem like history, and her mother's visions – well, she shouldn't get started on those. 'And shouldn't your warning have been for him?'

'And how do you know he was the intended victim?'

Lucy's words made Dulcie stand up straight. But with only a second's pause, she answered, 'Because he was a womanizing pig; because he may have been dealing drugs; because he was a spoiled kid who didn't know how to take care of himself; and, I don't know, maybe he was flashing a wad of cash on the street? Because it might have been a totally random thing.' She wished she had more reasons to give. 'Because the police don't seem worried about my safety.'

'The cops!' Lucy made a noise that was half laugh, half dismissive snort. 'As if they care about my baby like I do.'

Now she was back on familiar territory. 'So, what would you have me do, Lucy? I got the sage smudges.' She hadn't burned them yet, but her mother didn't need to know that.

'I'm not sure, dear. That's what really worries me. I see something with falling water.' She probably heard the torrent over the phone, Dulcie told herself. Even standing back against the wall, she was getting splashed by raindrops bouncing back off the granite steps. 'And I knew I had to tell you to look across it. Look across the water.'

'So, there's an intruder waiting for me across the water? Like the Atlantic? Or maybe the Charles River?' The rain was letting up, and Dulcie realized she was hungry. 'Any idea what he looks like? Or is he—' She paused, trying to recall her mother's Tarot deck. 'A dark man, clad in motley?' That was often a favorite.

'Oh dear, I wish this had been clearer, Dulcie. I'm afraid I'm letting you down again. But I think the motley is wrong, dear. And I don't really understand about the water. I just know I'm supposed to tell you this. Oh – and, dear?' Dulcie waited, unwilling to encourage her mother to go on. 'It's not a man at all. The intruder is a woman.'

The sound of another incoming call helped Dulcie get her mother off the phone then, but not before she had promised to be careful – and to burn the first sage smudge that very evening. As a result, she missed the other call which, she was pleased to see, was not from some mysterious woman at all. It was from a Bruce Patchett.

'Hi, Dulcie, this is Bruce – from the party? Would you give me a call back?' Indeed she would, thought Dulcie, snapping the phone shut. But not here on the steps of Widener, where strange females might intrude. Lighter at heart than she'd been in ages, she started down the steps – and nearly wiped out. Her old flip-flops had long ago lost whatever treads they might have once had, and the wet stone was slick.

'Watch your step, dear.' Her mother's closing words came back to her. Well, maybe Lucy knew some things after all, thought Dulcie, removing her flip-flops to walk barefoot down the cool grey steps.

By the time she'd gotten her customary post-library dinner – hot and sour soup and the yu shiang eggplant special from the Hong Kong – it seemed too late to call Bruce back. Just as well. Suze would approve of a little reticence. If it weren't for the echo of her mother's warnings, Dulcie would have been feeling quite smug as she unlocked her front door.

'Honey, I'm home!' She yelled into the empty air. This was her home, a place of comfort she'd created with Suze and with Mr Grey. 'I'm here!' Of course, anyone watching would know that she lived alone now. But, hey, maybe somewhere, somehow, Mr Grey would hear her and know that she'd resumed her old habits. She imagined how he would come running, chirping, at her voice. Ah, well. At least, it would amuse Helene.

Once again, Dulcie stayed up reading. The printouts on Priority proved worthless; their management seemed as efficient at covering up crime as Tim's family. With a groan of disgust, she tossed thirty pages into the recycling bin. 'Innovations in Fraud Protection', indeed! But although Dulcie knew she should keep at it, or maybe get to sleep at a reasonable hour, the temptation to reward herself was simply too great. She deserved a little 'Dulcie' time, didn't she? And one book in particular beckoned.

Two hours later, even her preferred subject was proving frustrating. There were only so many pages for Dulcie to go through, and these were maddeningly vague. So she went from rereading *The Ravages* to an essay and then to another book, which confused the issue more – and kept her up until past three.

Thus, it was nearly ten the next morning before she dashed out of the apartment, into decidedly un-mountain-like humidity. No time to call Bruce, Dulcie was already late for Detective Scavetti, and she'd only downed about a third of the large iced coffee she'd bought by the time she reached the police headquarters on Western Avenue. Toss or not? These were questions Hermetria never had to answer. But that girl was decisive, too, somehow managing to straighten out both her own finances and her personal crises, and so Dulcie took a long pull before tossing the plastic cup into the trash. She wouldn't bring a beverage into a library, after all.

'Ms Schwartz, thanks for coming in!' The portly Detective Scavetti came forward to greet her even before she could give her name at the front desk. 'Coffee?'

'Oh! Sure.' Following the large man off to a private office, Dulcie decided this wasn't going to be that bad. Of course, the coffee – when it came – was thin and bitter. And Detective Scavetti looked way too stout to fit into knight's armor, not to mention too close to bald. But he had been nice to offer.

'Let's go somewhere private, so we can really talk,' he said, leading her into a small room with a table and a few plastic chairs. 'Detective Forrester said you had something to tell me?'

'Well, yes.' Dulcie had a moment of confusion. 'But you wanted to ask me some questions, too?'

He nodded, tossing a manila folder of papers casually down on the desk. 'Paperwork, mostly. It can wait. Why don't we start by talking about Tim Worthington?'

'Tim.' She took a breath. It was hard to conjure up her temporary room-mate as he had been. All she could think about was the last time she'd seen him. 'It was so horrible. He was so still. It was like he wasn't real anymore. But the blood . . .' She closed her eyes. The bitter coffee had been a mistake.

'I understand, Ms Schwartz. But why don't we think about what he was like before.' He paused, but she was stuck in her memory: the hand on the rug; the blood. 'Ms Schwartz?'

'I'm sorry.' She forced herself to focus. 'You had a question?'

'Actually, you called us. You said you had something to tell us. Something about Mr Worthington and his girlfriend?'

'Girlfriend?' The room came back into focus. '*Girlfriends* is more like it.' Thinking about the women she had met helped her see Tim as he had been. She breathed again, and then she could talk. She leaned forward, eager to share what she knew. 'I don't know what you'd call motive exactly. But it turns out Tim had been seeing at least one other woman behind his girlfriend's back. And one of her friends told me that he might have had some compromising photos of her.' She realized then that she'd forgotten to check her computer. A pity, it would have been nice to give something to the detective.

'So, your room-mate was a real hound?'

She'd drifted for a moment. Say nothing but good of the dead, and all that. But the detective brought her back.

'Ms Schwartz?'

'Yeah, I guess he was.' Dulcie swallowed. 'Alana – that's the girlfriend – thought they were serious. I mean, she's now saying they were going to get married. But she can't be *that* dumb.'

'And you knew him much better, of course.'

Dulcie sipped at her coffee. It was pretty foul, but it was caffeine. 'Well, I *was* his room-mate.'

'And?'

She put her cup down. The fake cream had left a chalky taste in her mouth. 'And what?'

'Well, you're young, single.' He ran one hand over his thinning hair. 'Tim was by all accounts an attractive guy.'

'What? No.' The thought – and the non-dairy creamer – made her mouth pucker. 'We were not – repeat, *not* – romantically involved.'

'Oh, that's right.' Scavetti pulled the folder back and opened it with one hand. He flipped through a few pages and seemed to settle on one. 'I'd forgotten. Sorry. You two didn't get along, right?'

'Well . . .' It was true, but it would be bad karma to spell out what a jerk Tim had been.

'Your neighbor, Helene Duvoisier? She said he was pretty mean to you. Used to tease you about your pet cat?'

'Yeah.' The weight of the last few days hit her and she sighed. 'Mr Grey.'

'You still miss him.' For a big guy, his voice was gentle.

'Yeah, I do.' Oh, God, was she going to cry?

'That wasn't very nice of your room-mate, then, was it?'

She shook her head and reached into her pocket for a tissue. Detective Scavetti leaned back and retrieved a box for her. 'Thank you.' She blew her nose.

'That must have made you so mad.' He kept talking, politely ignoring her distress. 'And you come home from work, after a long, hot day. And here's this rich kid, who doesn't have to work, and he teases you about your cat?'

'Wait a minute.' Dulcie sat up. 'Am I a suspect here?'

'We're just talking.' The big man leaned back to give her more space and put his hands up in a gesture of surrender. Something about it looked like a practiced move. 'About your old cat – now, you said something to the officer on the scene about seeing the cat that day?'

'I saw a cat that looked like Mr Grey. I'm fully aware that he's not around anymore.'

'That's not what you told Officer Priz—'

'I was very upset that day. I'd just come home to find my room-mate dead. Killed. In my apartment.' She was a doctoral candidate, at the most prestigious university in the country; she should be able to make herself clear. 'Yes, I thought I'd seen a cat that looked like my old cat. But clearly it could not have been him.'

'Uh-huh.' Detective Scavetti was nodding, looking at the blank window behind her. 'And this cat spoke to you. And you must have been tired, and so angry with Tim—'

'I don't think I want to talk with you anymore.' Dulcie pushed her chair back and stood up. 'I don't believe you can keep me here, and I know you haven't read me any rights.'

'Now, I didn't mean to upset you, Ms Schwartz.'

'I'm not upset.' She was furious, but better he shouldn't see her temper. 'I simply came in this morning to tell you what I'd found out about Tim. If you choose to ignore that perfectly good information, well, I have other things to do.'

'Of course, of course.' He rose too and walked quickly to the door. For a moment, Dulcie held her breath. Was he going to prove an evil monk, intent on imprisoning her? But after a moment's pause, he pulled the heavy door open and gestured her through. 'Thank you for coming in, Ms Schwartz.' He walked her to the end of the hall. She could see the building's main lobby and, outside, a bright Saturday morning, as brilliant and beckoning as the Umbrian plains. 'We'll be in touch.'

'I'm sure you will.' It was as cutting a remark as she'd dared to make. When she got home, she promised herself, she'd start burning that sage.

But first, she needed to call Suze. She not only needed a friend, she needed some legal advice.

Suze was not encouraging. 'You did *what?* You talked to the police about a homicide – without a lawyer?'

'Why would I need a lawyer, Suze? I didn't do anything.' The groan that came back over the line didn't help Dulcie's mood. She'd been pacing as she recited the events of the morning, but now she pulled up a chair and grabbed a pen and a notepad. Maybe Suze would have some practical suggestions. 'I'm serious, Suze. I never thought they were, well, investigating me or anything. I mean, I'm the one who found the body. Why would I have called them if I'd just killed him?'

'If it were a crime of passion. Annoying room-mate pushes you over the edge. If you were mentally unstable and had scared yourself. If you felt you weren't really responsible because some ghost cat had made you do it—'

'Suze! You're scaring me.' Everything her old friend was saying made sense. Dulcie started doodling nervously.

'I'm sorry, sweetie, but you should be scared. The number one thing we always tell everyone at legal aid is "keep your mouth shut". Never – and I mean, never – talk to the police without counsel.'

'But I didn't realize I was being questioned.' Dulcie went over the session in her head. She should have been taking notes then. How had things gone so wrong so quickly? 'He seemed really nice at first, like he was really interested in what I had to say.'

'Yeah, it's a common technique. He was building rapport. First they develop trust, and then they start suggesting ways that the crime might have occurred. They make it sound only logical, like you *had* to kill him.'

Oh, man, all that stuff about how Tim was a jerk. Well, he *was* a jerk. But that hadn't made Dulcie kill him. And she wasn't going to be talked into confessing, either. 'They didn't read me my rights.'

'Doesn't matter.' Suze sounded depressingly confident. 'They don't have to do that until they bring you in and charge you.'

'Great.' Dulcie dug her pen into the paper, working out her frustration in a series of darkening crosshatches. 'But why would they think it was *me*? I mean, especially if he was dealing?'

'Because he probably knew the killer.'

Suze's reasoning was disheartening.

'The door was open, right?'

'But maybe he knew his supplier, or his customer or something. And, besides, Tim always left the door unlocked. It was one of the things I hated about him! Like, he expected "the staff" to take care of it.'

'You're not sounding particularly sympathetic, Dulcie. That's motive.'

'Great.' Dulcie knew she was muttering. 'Tim – the room mate who keeps on giving.'

'It's not all bleak.' Dulcie heard rustling on the other end of the line. Maybe Suze was making notes, too. 'I mean, if they had anything solid, they'd have arrested you by now.'

The crosshatches became darker. The paper rippled beneath Dulcie's pen. 'I can't believe this!' She knew she was whining, but Suze would understand. 'I mean, why me? OK, I know why me. But, well, you make it sound like I'm definitely a suspect.' The lack of an answer drove the point home. 'What if they never catch who really did it? How am I going to know when I'm cleared? Will they let me know?'

'Not likely.' Suze could get sort of lawyer-y at times. 'But, you know, every day that they don't arrest you is another day you're free.' Dulcie groaned. The sound must have broken through Suze's legal fog. 'I'm going to look for some names for you. Get you someone to go with you if they bring you in again.'

'You think they're going to question me again?' She drew a big question mark and underlined it, then started filling it in with more crosshatching.

'I hope not, kiddo. But if I were them, I think I might.'

Sometimes Suze sounded more like a mother than Dulcie's real mother.

'That's great, just great.' All she wanted was to be writing. Or reading.

'So, are you getting any work done?'

Suze wasn't psychic. Dulcie knew her old friend was only trying to cheer her up, but it was the worst question at the worst time.

'Oh, Suze.' She could hear the despair in her own voice. 'That's not working either! I'm not getting anywhere. I just keep going back to the same old fragments of *The Ravages of Umbria*. And there's nothing there. If there were, it would've been written already.' Suze had heard plenty about the unfinished manuscript. She could probably compose her own chapbook on it, but she wisely remained silent. 'I'm not going to find anything. I'm not going to be able to renew my grant. I'm going to have to drop out.' She sighed. 'Maybe I'm not a scholar, Suze. Maybe I just want comfort reads, and stories that I can write my own endings to.' She twirled the pen and then started doodling again. 'There's nothing new to say about *The Ravages*. Nobody's cared about this story for more than two hundred years.'

'Dulce, you've had a hell of a week. Cut yourself some slack.'

Dulcie snorted. This from the woman who'd just told her to be on her guard and call a lawyer?

'I mean, in terms of your thesis. I guess I shouldn't have asked. But, hey, maybe you are getting work done – on the back-burner, so to speak. Maybe your subconscious sees something in that old story that your conscious mind just hasn't acknowledged yet.'

'You mean, maybe I'm getting a message from beyond?'

'I wouldn't go that far, Dulcie. One ghost is enough.'

Dulcie looked down at the paper. Her nerves had resulted in some dark scribblings and one stylized dagger. Just what the cops would want to see. She ripped the page off the pad and crumpled it up. On the page below was a picture of a cat, drawn in her own hand, and it was smiling.

'Mr Grey, if you are here still, please help me.' She'd lit the sage finally, placing the fragrant fist-sized bundle of twigs in a cereal bowl, for lack of a better receptacle. 'Mr Grey, are you here?' Following her mother's instructions, she walked around, fanning the smoke into various corners. 'Mr Grey?' With luck, the smoke alarm wouldn't go off.

There was no answer. Of course, when did a cat ever come when called? Still, maybe she hadn't seen the spirit of her pet at all. Maybe she was losing it. With that thought, and for fear of the alarm, she doused the smoldering bundle in the sink and soon found herself lying on the sofa, eyes closed. What a day, and it wasn't even noon. In an ideal world, she'd go back to sleep and wake up on Sunday, but the interrogation and the bad coffee wouldn't let her relax that much. Maybe she should head back to Widener: the question of the 'jealous spirit' was nagging at her. Was that spirit the same as the retainer's ghost? Were multiple spectres haunting the old castle? Or were they all simply manifestations of Hermetria's own over-heated brain? The girl was under a lot of stress. By the end of the first fragment, the castle was crumbling, the mad monk was hovering, and things looked pretty grim. At least she had two suitors. This thought reminded Dulcie that she hadn't called Bruce. Maybe the day was salvageable yet.

She didn't really need more coffee; her stomach told her that. But she could use something that tasted the way coffee was supposed to – and the company of normal, living human beings – before she made that call. Plus, she could check out Nemo, see if the little fish had returned to normal. But as she was entering the coffee-house, her cell rang. Bruce. Maybe she *was* psychic.

'Oh, hey, Dulcie. Glad I got you.' The big guy sounded flustered. She told him she'd been meaning to call him back, but she couldn't tell if he believed her. 'I've been wanting to talk to you since that party. I still can't get over you showing up.' Not the opener she'd expected, and she excused herself for a moment to order a tall iced. 'That crowd can be pretty insular.' He laughed, but his humor quickly faded. 'What am I saying? They can be a bunch of awful snobs. I know it, and I think it's worse for girls. I mean, women.'

He was trying; Dulcie had to give him that. And if one of his goals was to set himself apart from his cliquish crew, he was succeeding. 'I was sort of surprised to be invited,' she admitted as the barista brought over the frosted pint glass. 'I guess Alana felt comfortable with me because I was Tim's room-mate.' Not that the bland blonde had spent any time with her.

'Tim, yeah. Tim.' The pause was so long that Dulcie checked her phone. Still connected. Down the bar, a stool opened up and she slid into it. She was facing the high shelf, but when she looked up the little bowl with the Siamese fighting fish wasn't there.

'Nemo's gone home.' She spoke without thinking, but it served to get Bruce's attention back.

'Sorry?'

'The fish. They've been keeping a fish behind the counter at my local coffee place.' Even though he'd been the one to drop the conversational ball, she felt embarrassed and talked more to cover it up. 'One of those Siamese fighting fish? They named him Nemo.' To herself, she murmured, 'I hope he's OK.'

He hadn't heard that. 'I get it. That's sweet,' he said, his voice sounding warm again. 'I'm sorry, Dulcie. I had wanted to talk to you about Tim, about our stupid friends. My so-called friends, that is.'

Dulcie leaned over her pint glass, cradling the phone, and waited. Bruce had more promise than a surrogate pet fish. The silence dragged on. 'Were you and Tim close?' she asked him, finally.

'Tim? No! I mean, at one point we were, but not by the end. What I wanted to ask you, though—' As if on cue, the signal beeped. 'Sorry, Dulcie, I've got to take this. Do you mind?'

'Not at all.' He couldn't see that she was rolling her eyes. 'Bye.' She sipped her drink. Why should she suppose that life would ever change in her particular fishbowl?

'Excuse me?' She waved. The barista looked up, flustered. The frozen mocha machine seemed to be on the fritz. 'What happened to the fish?'

'Oh, Nemo?' Dulcie nodded as the barista got the blender-like contraption working. With a roar, it filled two large cups to go in quick succession. 'Yeah, Ringo had to take him home. He was freaking out.'

Dulcie thought of the last time she'd been in here. The little fish had been on full alert then, his red dorsal fin erect. 'What was it? The noise? The air-conditioning?'

'Who knows?' The barista shrugged and reached to clear an empty. 'It all started when this one chick was in here – dark-haired girl, cute. But Nemo didn't like her. He was ramming against the bowl so hard, we all thought he was sushi.'

Eleven

After her last few social interactions, an evening out was not high on Dulcie's list of priorities. Still, she found herself scrambling for excuses when Trista reached her at home later. She and Trista had been undergrads together, bonding over 'Introduction to Anglo-Saxon', which was difficult at any hour but particularly at eight a.m. Trista, too, was in the throes of a thesis, though at least she had started writing. Yes, she'd heard about Tim. All the more reason, said the voice on the phone, for them all to blow off some steam. Take a little time. Have a few beers. These were her friends, not Tim's, but still it sounded a little too much like Alana's party for Dulcie to warm to the idea.

'I can't,' said Dulcie finally. 'I've got some reading I've been putting off for days, and I'm just wiped.' It was partly a lie, but even as Dulcie said it, she had a thought. 'I'm re-examining a novel fragment. There might be something in the setting I can work with, pathetic fallacy and all that.'

Trista groaned. With her bleached blonde shag, she might look post-modern, but academically, the tiny scholar was all Victorian – and by then readers had stopped searching for emotional cues in the landscape. 'OK, weatherbird, I'll leave you to your dramatic fogs and whatnot. But if you change your mind, we'll be at the People's Republik.' The Cambridgeport pub was one of the few that still sold discounted pitchers, making it a prime grad student hang. 'Speaking of emotional peaks and valleys, you know we all miss you.'

Dulcie sighed. What with all that had happened, she barely felt a part of the grad school gang anymore. How could she concentrate with what had happened to Tim? But if she didn't, she'd lose her grant and be out by the New Year.

'I don't know, Tris. I'll try and come, if I can get some work done.' Somewhere behind Trista, she could hear her petite colleague's boyfriend beginning to chant: 'One of us! One of us! One of us!' She caught the reference – *Freaks*, 1932 – but, for a change, the film reference made her smile. Maybe she was getting over Jonah finally. 'Better go feed Jerry, Tris. Sounds like he's getting restless.'

'OK, Dulcie. But I hope to see you later. And, either way, remember – softball tomorrow at one.'

'I don't—'

'Don't say it, kid. We're all nerds, remember? We can take turns in the outfield.'

Cheered by the brief interaction, Dulcie returned to her computer with more energy than she'd felt thus far. She wouldn't be lying if she actually did some research. A few keystrokes and she was back into a file she'd abandoned weeks before, a survey of critical papers on one of the most popular Gothics, *The Italian*. That novel was rife with the kind of imagery she and Trista had been talking about. Too much so, really. If Dulcie had to read one more reference to 'tumultuous skies' or a veil as a metaphor for concealment of just about anything, she'd be sick. Maybe that explained the appeal of *The Ravages*. For all its supernatural elements and improbable plot points – didn't readers know right from the start that Hermetria would eventually regain her wealth? – it was, in some ways, underwritten. Well, maybe not Demetria's overwrought speeches. But those weren't what drew her, were they?

Dulcie closed the file and turned her mind to more contemporary concerns. She'd promised to look for phantom files on her computer. What Stacia had said had rung true; Tim had no sense of personal boundaries. Even though his sleek laptop was years younger and more powerful than her little budget system, if his was busy downloading some pirated Hong Kong flick, he'd have had no qualms about invading her space. She could easily picture him barging into her room – and her cyberspace. The idea that he might have done more than use her system; that he might have left something on her computer, like the dishes he routinely left on the table – or the rug – was both aggravating and vaguely creepy. The ghost of sleazy presence, she thought.

But where would such a file be? She'd flipped open her little laptop half an hour ago, and had already run a couple of 'find' functions, searching for anything under the name 'Alana', 'nude', and 'hot'. When Trista had called she'd been browsing through the various photos in her computer, mostly opening up file after file of Mr Grey. God, she'd forgotten how cute he was, the way his green eyes seemed to see right into you. He could play the clown as well. She'd found several of the grey cat with his head twisted upside down, white chin up and wide ears flattened out on the carpet. 'Yes, you look the same from this angle,' he appeared to be saying. 'You're still my Dulcie, always will be.'

Truth was, she'd spent so much time with those photos, she could have gone down to the bar with Trista and had a beer. But it had been a day. Maybe she'd reconsider the softball game tomorrow. For now, she'd move on past the cat photos. Stacia had said that whatever Tim had gotten was embarrassing, but that didn't mean it was a photo. She opened up her documents file, and was pleased to recognize all the labels; nothing untoward here. She went down the list, looking at stuff dated six months ago, a year. 'Smollett notes'. Now, why hadn't she done her thesis on the earlier, humorous writer? She opened the file and started reading: 'Narrative experiments, the beginning of character-driven fiction'.

That started her thinking. Unlike her attendant Demetria, Hermetria was a great character. Even alone and broke she spoke her mind, standing up to the nobleman who came to woo her and to the various villains – the evil monk and that ambiguous ghost – who braved her mountain home. And she did it all with just one sketchily drawn sidekick.

Maybe it was time to take a larger perspective – the role of the heroine and all that. Mary Wollstonecraft's *Vindication of the Rights of Women* had been published in 1792, a year or two before *The Ravages of Umbria*. Was the unknown author of *The Ravages* making a statement about women helping women? Someone had written about all of this, she vaguely recalled, and dug around till she found it. But the paper, written by a doctoral candidate in California, failed to ignite Dulcie's own feelings of sisterhood.

'How could someone write about sexual imagery and be so dull?' Dulcie skimmed a few pages: characterization and the questioning of noble traits. She shook her head; maybe she was just a jealous spirit. If she'd written on this topic . . . well, if she had, she'd be halfway through her thesis, with no more worries about time – or money – running out. But maybe there'd be a loose end that Dulcie could grab on to; a stray thought that would unravel, giving Dulcie enough yarn to knit her own thesis – a study of the relationship between Hermetria and Demetria, for example. After her eyes had started to close for the fourth time she was ready to call it quits.

'Enough,' Dulcie muttered. If this kept up, she'd be seeing the weather as a manifestation of her own mood. With another shake of her curls to wake herself up, she maneuvered the mouse. A bigger page would be easier to read. But just as she clicked down to grab it, something else caught her eye: a file, right by the edge of the desktop, almost buried beneath the icon for the trash.

Dulcie clicked on it and waited for it to open. Was this going to be something from Tim; a compromising photo of Alana or some heavy-metal blog post? Or was it something she herself had meant to discard? Just as in life, sometimes one didn't hit the basket. But no, it was another picture of Mr Grey, and a glorious one at that. As the pixels resolved, she saw him as he'd been in his prime, posed as if for a formal portrait, sitting up and staring straight at the camera. His silver-grey ruff looked freshly brushed, his long whiskers spread wide. Between the alert, upright pose of his ears and the intense stare of his green eyes, the cat appeared to be staring straight at Dulcie; willing her to concentrate.

'How could I have meant to trash this?' She clicked to enlarge. With no room-mate around to make fun of her, she could make this her screen saver; a portrait to remember. But what could that stare be trying to tell her? She shook off the fancy, and was struck by another: what else was poking around the edges of her desktop?

Although the portrait now filled most of her screen, she wiggled the cursor underneath it, next to the trash and the icon that linked her through to the university library. Yes, there was another file. She clicked twice and suddenly her screen flashed. Blank – and then, as she held her breath in a moment's agony – on again. She let herself breathe again, and then bit her lip. Had anything been lost?

This was a corrupted file. It was damaged somehow, or improperly stored – she'd dealt with those often enough to recognize the garbled icons at its top. If Tim had put it there, he'd probably not bothered to look to see if her aging computer could handle it, or even if her small share of software had the right tools to make it work. She scrolled down its margin. It was some kind of a spreadsheet; once the initial nonsense coding was past, its page split into neat little boxes. Two pages in, she was ready to give up. Whatever the file had held originally, it was worthless now.

Then she saw something, far over on the right. Dulcie shifted the margin and there was a series of numbers. They looked like phone numbers, although some had extra digits. If Tim had been selling drugs, maybe he'd been more organized about his business than he had been about his personal life. But no, if these were phone numbers, the area codes were wrong. He couldn't have been selling to 718, could he? Or 919. Wasn't that in North Carolina? Several more columns stretched to the right. Some were blank, but most had been filled out with long strings of numbers and letters. Tim had been taking statistics. Could this be a project? A homework assignment that Luisa had given him, and that they had shared – here, in her room?

The thought repulsed her. That pretty young woman and – *Tim.* She turned and looked at her bed. *Ick.* Swinging back around, she went to close the file. But she must have been moving, the swing of her chair carrying over to her right hand, because whatever she had clicked – something wasn't right. Instead of that one file closing, everything flashed again, blank, and then back on. But this time, the desktop looked different.

'Hell, hell, hell.' The enlarged portrait of Mr Grey was gone. 'What'd I do?'

She found the oddly named file and clicked on it. 'ERROR', the screen read. 'CORRUPTED FILE/UNABLE TO OPEN'.

'I *know* it's corrupted,' she yelled at the screen as she clicked again. The same message flashed before her. 'But you opened before . . . Come on!' She had started talking to machinery; Dulcie knew she was losing it.

'Calm down, girl.' She sat back, put her hands in her lap. Tim's old file – if that's what it was – was no loss. But could she somehow salvage that lovely portrait of Mr Grey? Dulcie had been working on her old iBook long enough to know its quirks. Picking up the mouse again, she started sliding the cursor around the edges of her desktop.

Something flashed. There! Tentatively, she dragged the icon out from behind the trash. It *looked* like the cat jpeg. She realized she was holding her breath as she clicked it open.

'Damn!' What had only minutes before been a glorious photo was now – another spreadsheet. Somehow, that accursed corrupted file had gotten into the only other file she'd had open on her desktop. 'Damn, damn, damn. Damn you, Tim.' A flash of guilt ran through Dulcie as she remembered how, in fact, Tim had come to his end. But if he'd been fooling around on her computer, if he was responsible for her losing material – losing a gorgeous photo of Mr Grey in particular – almost, almost he deserved it.

'Bother.' Dulcie was feeling a little embarrassed now. Maybe she was overattached to her late pet. Still . . . she scrolled down through the file. How could that beautiful image be gone? Her cursor was flying but all she was seeing were those little rectangular boxes, waiting for data. Three, maybe four pages in, some gibberish started to show up and she slowed her search. Maybe, somewhere in here, she'd find a version of that image.

)#$¶•••¶host_1™¢¢¢achi)(••§¢¢™¢¡¡atcho_(ªºæ¬

Were those words? She slowed further and tried to make out the fragments.

©.østint•ªºmac_(§¶Dul•ªª

There! What was that? Was someone spelling out her name? A wave of irritation swept over her. Tim! Wasn't it enough that his document had somehow gotten into her photo? Had he been gossiping about her, too?

She moved the cursor to the far right, exposing more long strings of gibberish. There was nothing here. Thanks to Tim, the photo of her pet was gone. Even from beyond the grave, he was—

Wait . . . she slowed further. There it was, the 'Dul' again; the beginning of her name. Had she been a topic of conversation between Tim and Luisa? Between Tim and who knew who else? She opened the window to its limit, dragging the file to its far edges. The letters kept repeating and then, right as the file reached its end, buried in nonsense, she saw it: lkª8g*(&•¶ghos¡)*i@#he*machi&. 'Ghost in the machine?' A literary term showing up in something Tim had written? Maybe he'd learned it from a sci-fi book or something. But there it was again: (•ª¶ghost¶•uuintheººº¶achine. Hadn't someone else used that expression recently?

She was thinking it through, trying to trace back the reference, when she stopped cold. Two lines later, there it was: •™£§DULCIEWATCHOUT)°∞.

'Dulce, honey, you've had a really stressful day.' She'd had no choice but to call Suze back, even though by this time, she knew her studious friend would be in bed. 'I mean, come on, messages in your computer?'

'I'm not imagining what I read, Suze. I can email it to you, if you like.'

'No, no, thanks.' Suze grunted to clear her head. 'I don't need a corrupted file messing up my system, too.'

'But that's just it, Suze. This file wasn't corrupted at first. It was a photo of Mr Grey. And then I thought that somehow Tim's file had gotten into it. But what if that's not it? I mean, what if this is a warning?'

She could hear Suze yawn and pictured her running her hand through her short, thick hair. 'A warning from – oh, you mean, from Mr Grey? Your ghost cat version of Mr Grey?'

'You don't believe me, I know, Suze. But—' She was about to argue. She'd seen the file; Suze hadn't.

'No, no, Dulcie. I believe that *you* believe. And, hey, cats always do seem a little like they're in their own alternative universe anyway. I'm just, well, I'm worried about you. Like, why are you home on the computer on a Saturday? Doesn't your department hang out at the People's Republik anymore?'

'Yeah, Trista called a while ago. I just thought I'd do some work instead. I'm thinking that maybe I can do something with female friendships in *The Ravages of Umbria*.' Suze had minored in women's studies.

'Are you telling me I'm not being supportive?' There was a touch of humor in her voice. 'The spirit of sisterhood and all that?'

'No, Suze, I just wish – well, did I tell you about the fish? The fish was gone today. It had become too frantic, they said. And it was just yesterday that my mom said something about "crossing water", and I was wondering—'

'Dulcie!' Suze interrupted her, speaking loudly to be heard. 'Dulcie, stop it! Listen to yourself. Or, no, even better – do me a favor, will you, hon? Turn off your computer, Dulcie. I think you're seeing things. I think you're making connections where there aren't any, and I think your mother's craziness is creeping into the spaces where sleep should be. It's stress, Dulcie. You've been through a lot. Now's not the time to do more work. Go to sleep – and please try to get out of the house tomorrow. Go somewhere there are people – live people. Have some fun.'

Suze didn't believe her. But what else could Dulcie say? Here she was, reading about friendship and yet in real life she was alienating her closest buddy with all this talk about magic and ghosts. 'OK, Suze, I'll try.' The pause was awkward. Dulcie thought she heard a soft snore. 'Sorry to have woken you. Go back to sleep, Suze. And, thank you.' There was a mumble and then the line went dead. Dulcie was alone, once more, with a mystery she couldn't begin to interpret.

Twelve

Dulcie woke close to noon the next day to find not much had changed. For starters, she was still wearing the T-shirt she'd had on the night before. From the fuzzy feeling in her mouth, she hadn't brushed her teeth either, whenever it was that she'd finally given up on her computer and crawled beneath the sheets. Several more hours of searching through her lost file folders had failed to turn up that beautiful portrait of Mr Grey – or any other mystery documents. And her computer still sat there, unmindful of the trouble it had caused her as she'd cursed and hunted deep into the night. Unmindful of anything, she reminded herself. Between the visions of cats and Lucy's phone calls, she had enough non-human consciousness in her life right now.

But how unmindful was it? Pulling on her gym shorts, Dulcie made her way over to the lifeless machine. The sun didn't seem to have risen much either, and she flicked on the overhead light just in time to hear a peal of thunder. No wonder it was so dark. She pulled back the shade to see a sky roiling with grey and black. Better to leave the computer off, then. At some dark hour of the morning, she'd had the realization that, possibly, neither Tim's intrusions nor ghostly intruders had caused the corrupted files. Her little laptop was old enough to qualify as an antique in the cyber world. Without the means of replacing it, she should treat it carefully, and that meant not risking anything during a thunderstorm.

Still feeling dopey from her late night, Dulcie found herself staring out of the window. The gathering storm was fascinating, in a dark way. She could see why so many novelists fell prey to the old saw of using the weather to reflect inner turmoil. For her, it was a welcome distraction. How could she think about death and destruction with that one black cloud moving so swiftly?

The shrill telephone bell scared her more than another crack of thunder, and she jumped to answer.

'Dulcie?' It was Trista. If she was calling to say the grad students were still playing softball, she was more of an optimist than Dulcie thought.

'The game?' A low rumble came through the phone and Dulcie heard it outside her own window a split second later.

'Yeah, we're calling it. Why drag all the equipment out just in time to get drenched? Besides, the law school always whups our butts, anyway.'

'We were playing the law school?' Dulcie liked to think she'd stayed up on the social calendar, but obviously she'd let a few things slide. 'Since when?'

'Since the grad school league started up in June.' Silence. Dulcie hadn't realized it had been that long. 'But that doesn't mean you're getting off this easy. We're all going back to the People's Republik instead. It's 10-cent hot dog day.'

Dulcie laughed. 'I doubt the future lawyers of America need the discounted food.' Still, she thought of Luke. Would he be there? Did she care? 'We ladies of literature, however . . .'

'That's the spirit, Dulce. We all miss you. It's been too long.' Trista sounded like she meant it. More important, her words echoed what Suze had said. Maybe Dulcie was going a little nuts, locked up here alone with her computer and her memories.

'OK, Tris, I'll try. What time are you gathering?' At the very least, she'd see her own colleagues and maybe some of Suze's, too.

'Same time, one o'clock. Sun will be over the yardarm by then – if it comes out at all.'

Forty minutes later, Dulcie was still staring at the sky. Even two mugs of coffee later, it was fascinating. And it beat looking in the mirror. While working on her curls, she'd realized that the past two weeks had taken a toll on her. Not only was she pale, but dark rings were shadowing her eyes, threatening them like the storm clouds outside.

'Well, who cares, right?' She'd said it out loud, but even alone, her voice wasn't quite convincing. 'It's just a bunch of folks at a pub, right?' Without another thought, she reached above the sink for her limited cache of make-up. A little paint couldn't hurt.

Two beers in and the Red Sox had almost been exhausted as a topic of conversation. Trista's boyfriend Jerry had an explanation for why all the pitchers did what they did and soon the tall towhead had everybody agreeing that the annual team dive was due to start any day soon. Two World Series championships didn't stop a curse, he'd explained with mathematical certainty.

'And they say that academics don't care about sports,' Trista yelled over to Dulcie, rolling her eyes as Jerry spouted numbers, his pale face turning red with excitement. Somebody had put ZZ Top on the jukebox – again. 'All this talk about curses – sounds like one of your stories!' Trista's Victorians were long-winded, but decidedly mortal.

'This isn't sports,' said Jerry, shouting to make himself heard. 'This is *statistics.*' Just then, the song ended and the friendly math nerd realized he'd been yelling. 'Sorry, folks, the Sox get me worked up.'

'No need to apologize, bro,' his room-mate Chris did something with computers, 'not in any bar in this state, anyway.'

What was it about statistics that rang a bell? Dulcie had a pleasant buzz on. Luke hadn't shown up, but she found she was enjoying the company of her more bookish compadres. Trista had even pulled her aside to tell her she looked great. She was feeling mellow. Still, what Jerry had said reminded her of something: that file . . .

'Hey, Jerry, Chris, do either of you know if this weather could be making my computer wonky? I had some kind of corrupted file on my computer last night, and then when I went to open up a photo, it had turned into some kind of spreadsheet thing.'

'Ouch!' Trista bit her lip in sympathy. Jerry looked interested, but it was Chris who spoke up.

'A spreadsheet? Are you sure?' He pushed his wire frames up on his nose and brushed his dark bangs back, a sure sign he was thinking.

'No,' admitted Dulcie. 'I mean, it became like a form, with lots of rectangular boxes. Some of them had text in them, but most of it was gibberish.' Even with a few beers in her, she wasn't going to mention any ghostly messages. 'But, if this helps, it was the same kind of form that I'd just opened. And I'm pretty sure that was some kind of spreadsheet.'

'I didn't know you did any accounting.' Jerry refilled her glass and signaled for another pitcher.

'I don't.' Dulcie took a sip and pushed the glass away. She'd hit her limit. 'In fact, I never saw this file before. I thought that it was something my room-mate had done on my computer.'

'Suze?' Trista looked surprised.

'No, my summer room-mate. A guy named Tim—'

'Oh, the dead guy,' Jerry blurted out, before he caught himself. 'Sorry. You found him, right?' Dulcie nodded – and took a drink. 'Pretty awful, huh?'

She nodded again. They'd all heard the story. But Chris was still thinking. 'And why did you think it was a spreadsheet, exactly?'

'Well, it wasn't any of my files. Ghosts and haunted castles are scary enough on their own. But my late – well, Tim – he was studying statistics. And one of his friends suggested that he might have been working on my computer, using it when I was out. So . . .' She let it hang.

'Yeah, but that's an odd thing to have happen, although I've heard of stranger. But what's more likely is some kind of virus.' He looked excited by the idea. 'You're on the university system, right?'

'Yeah, but I never open attachments from people I don't know.'

'Doesn't matter.' Chris took a pen out of his pocket and began drawing on a napkin. 'You get your email through the university server. You go into university sites, like the libraries, right?' Chris pushed the napkin over to her. Between the wet spots on the bar and the rough surface of the paper napkin, the drawing wasn't too clear. What Dulcie could see, however, was a simplified drawing of a house – her house – with arrows going two ways, both into a bigger building fronted with columns – she figured that was Widener – and coming out toward her private computer.

'But, there are firewalls, right? I mean, I have to type in a password whenever I go into the library.' She tried to make more sense of the drawing.

'Let me guess.' Chris was looking right at her, the strain of suppressing a smile showing in small dimples. 'You have your passwords set on some kind of automatic system so as soon as you go to a site, it 'recognizes' you, am I right?'

'Uh-huh.' This was sounding worse and worse.

'And you're probably set up to get all kinds of news, automatic updates, whatever the university server sends out, right?' The dimples were getting deeper.

'Yeah.' She drew the word out, unwilling to accept what she was hearing.

'Well, I'm sorry, kiddo. But you left the door, well, not wide open, but off the latch.' He threw up his big hands and laughed; a graveyard kind of laugh. 'I can't tell without looking, but this sounds pretty classic. Someone's been poking through your system.'

'I can't believe it.' Dulcie started to push back from the bar and remembered, just in time, that she was on a stool. 'First Priority, and now this.'

'Huh?' All three of her friends were looking at her now.

'Priority. It's a big insurance firm where I've been temping.'

Jerry made a face and Dulcie started to laugh despite herself.

'Hey, I didn't get my sections this summer and my grants don't pick up again until September. And I can type.' She wiggled her fingers in the air. 'Anyway, there's been a big brouhaha over there. Someone definitely tapped into their system – and made off with some funds.'

'Electronic embezzlement – cool!' Despite his theatrics, Jerry didn't seem to be too upset.

'Actually, it's a very interesting field.' Chris looked like he was about to launch into an explanation, but Dulcie cut him off.

'That's what Suze said when I told her.' Suze had some surprising similarities to the bespectacled geek.

'Really?' He smiled again, his pale face lighting up.

Maybe he'd noticed the commonalities, too. She'd have to throw them together come fall.

'I wouldn't worry too much about it, though,' he continued. 'I mean, you have backups of all your important files, don't you?'

Dulcie blanched.

'You don't?'

'Well, I've been sending copies of my work to my adviser pretty regularly. Not that he's crazy about anything I'm doing. And during the school year, I got in the habit of printing everything out. The department has a super-fast laser printer.' It sounded lame, even to her.

Chris had heard it all before. 'And do you really want to have to retype everything? I can look into some backup systems for you, something that will keep your files in cyberspace. But in the meantime, you should get one of those portable thumb drives. They're tiny and relatively cheap.'

Relative was relative, Dulcie wanted to say. They were all grad students, but she doubted if any of her colleagues was on quite as tight a budget as she was. Something must have showed in her face.

'Or email. You can email yourself your files as a way of saving them.' He paused for a moment, a thoughtful look lighting up his pale face. 'Hey, have you emailed yourself at work or emailed your home address from that office? Maybe that's what happened to your system. Maybe you infected yourself.'

'Oh, great, just what I need.' It was possible, certainly. Dulcie hadn't been at the job that long, but she did get bored there. 'Is there something I should do? Somewhere I should look?'

'Check your emails, both at home and at that job. If you find you sent yourself anything that now looks strange or has an attachment you don't recognize, let me know. I'll come over and I'll bring my bug spray.'

'Thanks, Chris.' He was a good guy. 'And I'll tell Suze you said "hi", too.'

By the time Dulcie left the bar, her buzz had faded but the warm feeling remained, surviving a reprisal of the earlier thunderstorm that caught her yards from the T. She really did need to get out more, she told herself, even if the short walk home had left her drenched to the skin. As a bonus, her answering machine was blinking.

'Hi, Dulcie.' It was Luke. 'I wanted to apologize for not coming back and finishing the clean-up of Tim's room. I thought maybe if you were around today, I'd come by. Maybe I could even treat you to dinner by way of an apology?' He left his cell number, noting that he was still staying at his folks' place, and a promise to try her again soon.

Dulcie fairly purred with contentment as she stripped off her wet clothes. Maybe Luke was still an option. It was still early, not yet six, and her first instinct was to reach for the phone. But a little voice that she recognized as her own stopped her. It didn't take a ghost cat to remind her that, first, she might still be a little loose from the beer; and, second, reticence was better than catnip. No, she was content to let Luke wait a bit. He'd said he'd call her again, anyway. She grabbed a dry T-shirt and jeans. And, who knew? Maybe she'd hear from Bruce again, too.

Still, the evening was young – and dime hot dogs weren't exactly dinner. She finished toweling off her hair. No, she would do better to think about what had happened to her computer. Had it been infected by something that came through the university system? No matter what Chris said, Dulcie found it hard to believe that the university firewalls would allow anything to get into their system.

'That's just the point.' His words echoed through her head. '*They* didn't. They just let someone get through to you. *You're* the one allowing free access.'

More likely, she'd emailed herself from work, some note, a phone number or a reminder to pick something up – and sent a bug packing along with it. Unless the original contaminant had been something Tim had downloaded into her machine. Tim's laptop! Luke had taken it with him on that first visit. Now she had a legit reason to call him.

Or did she? Lucy would say there were no coincidences. Of course, Dulcie had spent much of her life disagreeing with her mother. She reached for the phone.

'Dulcie! How are you? I'm so sorry I've let things slide. I meant to get back to you at that party the other day, but you took off before I got the chance.' Luke had picked up on the first ring. From the sounds around him, he was at a bar or restaurant. Could he have shown up, late, at the grad student gathering? 'Thanks for calling me back.'

'No problem. I just got in.' Was he going to repeat his offer of dinner? 'Actually, I wanted to ask you about Tim's laptop—' She didn't get a chance to finish.

'What is it with my brother's friends and that computer? Stacia wanted to take a peek at it, too.'

Of course she did – for the same reason that she'd asked Dulcie to check her computer. 'Yeah, she said something to me.' Why embarrass Alana? The sooner those photos were destroyed, the better. 'But I think there may be a bigger problem.'

'Oh?' He sounded happy, rather than concerned. He was definitely at a bar.

'Yeah, I have a bad feeling that there's some kind of virus in Tim's computer. I think he may have sent me a file or typed something into my computer that's making it act up.'

'Sounds like Tim. I'm sorry.' At least he had the grace to apologize. 'And you think it might help to look at Tim's laptop?'

'It might.' Not that she could make any sense out of it, but maybe Chris or one of his buddies could.

'I could bring it by tomorrow, if that would work. Or if you're free now, you could come out. We're having dinner but I could pick it up after, and Stacia and I would love your company.'

Ouch. Suddenly those dime hot dogs were lead in her stomach. 'No, thanks, Luke.' How should she put this? 'I'm just back from a day out with friends and the weather isn't encouraging.'

'Suit yourself. But what if I swing by tomorrow evening? I'll call first.'

'Sure, that would be fine.' Feeling anything but, Dulcie collapsed on the sofa. Outside, the rain poured down.

Thirteen

Dulcie had one thing in mind on Monday as she marched to her cubicle. All the way through the now-normal gauntlet of guards and along the hall by the newly hushed coffee room, the only thing she could think of was her email. 'Look for strange codings,' Chris had explained. 'Particularly the extensions.' It had taken Dulcie a few moments to realize that what Chris meant was what she'd always termed the suffix. But he'd made it clear: if she found an .exe, .cmd, or .bat at the end of an email, she'd have a rational explanation for what had happened to her computer at home. She'd been loose enough to ask if there might be a 'cat' extension, but he only smiled and told her that it stood for catalog – and went on to warn her that if she saw a .vbs extension, she should call him right away.

'That may as well stand for "very bad shit",' he'd said. 'And that could explain a lot of your woes.'

She'd kept the list in her mind – and taken his cell number. Maybe something would surface here at her work email. Maybe Priority would be liable, if there was permanent damage to her laptop. It seemed unlikely that a company that worked so hard at not paying out claims would reimburse her for damage, but if she could prove to them that something from the office had followed her home, so to speak, she'd at least ask. If along the way she shed some light on Priority's problems that would be nice – Dulcie had a brief image of herself being lauded by her obnoxious boss – but that was not, well, a priority.

And so, with barely a grunt of hello to Joanie, Dulcie slid into her seat and booted up her computer. 'Come on, come on!' She urged the system. She didn't care right now if some electronic hall monitor was counting her keystrokes. What she wanted was the window that let her email in and out.

After a few more moments digesting her name and password, the system brightened up. Before she could delve further, however, an internal memo popped up on her screen.

'Priority Employees,' ran its bold header. 'As of August 1, Priority Insurance will be refocusing its network security operations to further secure its corporate identity. As of this date, the network usage and data of all hourly employees, as well as salaried staff, will be subject to increased monitoring and security applications. New intrusion detection systems are currently being uploaded and may cause temporary activity declines in the Priority systems. Be assured that these changes are in everyone's best interests.'

'So that's what the slowdown is,' Dulcie muttered to herself. She itched to edit the memo: so brief, and yet so pompous. 'A bit like closing the barn door after someone stole the horses.'

'You say something?' Joanie's head popped around the corner. She must have had a wild weekend; her hair was green.

'Whoa!' Dulcie looked up and realized that she'd been particularly anti-social – and to the one person here she liked. 'Great hair. That was just – I just saw the security memo.'

'Oh, yeah, the new programs. Great, huh? Just make sure you back up all your work.'

'I will.' Dulcie rolled her chair to the edge of the cubicle. 'But what I'm really worried about is my home computer. Something went off on me this weekend and I'm wondering if a virus could have followed me home.'

Joanie rolled her eyes. 'Don't tell me, you've been emailing attachments to yourself at home?'

'Yeah,' Dulcie felt foolish admitting it. 'I do it all the time. I mean, this stuff doesn't exactly take all my concentration, and I've got real deadlines – grant deadlines – breathing down my neck. So when I have a thought about my thesis I type it up.'

'And you're wireless at home?' Dulcie nodded. Joanie made a face. 'It could be. I'm sorry. But you know, unless you've got good firewalls at home' – the blank look on Dulcie's face answered the implied question – 'well, it could have been any number of hackers. But, hey, did you check the server?'

'No, I thought I'd just check my own "Sent" box.'

Joanie dismissed that notion with a clucking sound and rolled her chair over to Dulcie's desk. A fast spate of typing, and Dulcie found herself looking at a huge 'Sent' file full of old emails. 'Don't tell anyone, but I figured out how to get into the server,' she said. 'The password was so stupid – "PRIORITY123".'

'Wow.' Dulcie was impressed. No wonder Joanie seemed to keep herself busy. 'Can I read everything everyone in the company has sent out?'

'Not without their passwords you can't, at least not any high-level stuff. This is as far as I got before the ax came down on us all.' She smiled. 'But peons like you and me, you know, our emails aren't encrypted. I confess, I was following a flirtation between Bart in graphics and Penny upstairs.' Dulcie looked at Joanie, but the younger woman wouldn't meet her gaze. 'After a while I started to feel a little, I don't know, sticky. Anyway, check through these. At the very least, you'll be able to find your own emails – or anything that was sent to you. Maybe some spambot picked up your address and hit you with something.'

Spambot? The language never stood still, did it? 'Thanks,' was all Dulcie said, and with a quick glance around – they were on the clock, after all – she got to work.

Three hundred emails in, she was ready to give up. How many times had she sent herself the link to that cat cartoon? And why had she thought that her ramblings on the symbolism of cloud formations would add anything to her research? It was almost a relief to get back to her paying work. The names and addresses she was typing in no longer seemed to repeat. Could it be that they'd finally re-entered all the old data? Or was her brain just mush?

'Maybe I've got a virus in my brain.' She hit return on yet another file.

'Ms Shorts?'

Dulcie started. The voice came from so close behind her that for a moment she thought perhaps a program in her head had come to life.

'Ms Dulcie Shorts?'

'Schwartz,' she said, spinning her chair around to face a dark-blue jacket, with a matching tie. She looked up. A tall, clean-cut suit stood in front of her. The man inside seemed to have no personality, so still was his face. Behind him stood his clone, different only in that his tie was striped. 'It's Schwartz. Dulcie Schwartz.'

Dulcie couldn't tell if either of them got the Bond reference, although the second suit blinked. 'Come with us, please, Ms Schwart,' said the first suit. Well, that was closer to her name. But the whole twin thing was disconcerting.

'Why? What do you want with me?' Dulcie heard her syntax changing. This was too weird. The suit closest to her reached for her upper arm. 'Unhand me, sir!' After this many years of literature studies, the phrasing was automatic.

'Hey, what are you doing?' It was Joanie. Dulcie's tone of voice, if not her words, had alerted her colleague. Down the aisle three other sets of eyes peered her way.

'The computer security officer needs to see you,' said the clone. Dulcie reached under the desk to get her bag, and found her chair pulled swiftly back. 'We will retrieve any of your belongings for you. Please get up now without touching anything.'

Speechless, finally, she did and watched as the second suit – he was ever-so-slightly blonder – reached for her bag. He opened it up and began to look through it; something the security guard did every day, twice a day, but this felt different.

'Hey, that's private.'

He didn't even look up. The darker suit took her by her upper arm and propelled her down the narrow aisle. 'You gave up any right to privacy as part of your agreement of employment here at Priority.' He looked down at her. 'If it was personal, you should've left it at home.'

'If it *were,* asshole,' Dulcie muttered under her breath. It was her last bit of resistance, and with a glance at Joanie, she let the two virtual robots escort her to the elevator bank.

'What is this about? Where are you taking me?'

'I'm sorry, ma'am. Please just come along,' said the blonder guard.

'Why?' It seemed a reasonable question to Dulcie, but neither of her escorts answered. By the time they deposited her in a conference room, she was bursting with questions. 'Do you even have any right to have me marched about like this?'

'You are on our property, young lady. We have the right to do anything we please.' Dulcie spun around and found herself facing Sally Putnam. The snakelike manager didn't look pleased, and her dark eyes pinned Dulcie in place. 'And I'd watch my tone of voice in this office.'

She didn't strike, she didn't hiss. Dulcie got her breath back.

'What is going on here, anyway?' Now that Dulcie was calming down, she realized she was curious.

'As you may already know,' the perfectly coiffed boss put an emphasis on the last word, 'we've been experiencing some security mishaps.'

Dulcie nodded, noting the woman's coy choice of words.

'We are in the process or rooting out the culprits and making sure they will be punished to the full extent of the law.'

Dulcie waited. What did this have to do with her looking for her own email? Was wasting company time a dismissible offense? 'And I'm here because . . .?'

'We know full well that you were on the company server, in clear violation of company regulations—'

'Regulations I was never informed about.' Dulcie cut her off. If she was going to lose her job, she wasn't going down without a fight. 'I'm a temp, remember? All I was ever told was, "Sit here and type what we give you".'

'Ignorance of the rules is not a legal defense.' Dulcie was surprised to hear one of Suze's oft-repeated lines coming from that tight little mouth. Sally Putnam must have been well briefed; as the head of human resources she was probably being held responsible for hiring a thief. But then the woman's words kicked in: why would Dulcie need a legal defense?

'Are you considering firing me?' She might as well face the worst option. 'I mean, officially, I'm an employee of TempLive, not Priority.'

'Terminating your contract is the least of your worries, Miss Schwartz.'

Dulcie bridled. That 'Miss' was an intentional insult, and the hissing sound made the phrase more ominous still.

But Sally Putnam wasn't done. 'We're considering having you arrested.'

Fourteen

'That . . . that *sweater thief* threatened me!' Several hours later, she was at Foley's with Joanie and a few more of the office's friendlier faces. Her boss had kept her in the conference room until closing time, but after her brief interrogation, had pretty much left her alone. Several times, one or the other of the security clones had come in, and despite Dulcie's best efforts she'd been unable to hear much of their whispered conversations. The blonder clone had taken over babysitting finally, and although he had looked like he was on the brink of speaking several times, Dulcie had been unable to engage him. Finally, his partner had showed up to let her go, holding out her bag with the ominous words, 'We'll be in touch.'

'They detained me. Is that even legal?' Back out in the free world, she was finally getting angry.

'Was the door locked?' Joanie seemed to take the question seriously.

'I didn't check.' Dulcie was embarrassed, but it was the truth. Joanie looked disappointed. If it had been her, Dulcie was sure, she'd have shimmied out of the fourteenth-floor window and up to the roof.

Right now, Dulcie just wanted to let off steam. She had managed to call Suze once she got her phone back, but had only reached her voicemail. She had been about to call Trista, too, just to have someone to spout off to, when Joanie had grabbed her outside on the sidewalk. 'She was going to have me arrested!'

'She still might.' Ricky, Joanie's friend, had the grace to look unhappy at the prospect. 'I mean, they've got IT guys tearing apart your desktop now.'

'Great.' Dulcie slumped in her seat. Joanie had bought her a beer and a shot, but she needed a clear head to think through what had just happened. 'Not that they're going to find anything.' A horrible thought hit her. 'Unless, well, you don't think that the virus on my home computer could be the one that hit Priority, do you? I mean, by accident?'

Neither of her drinking companions had an answer, but Joanie's face lit up with a sly smile. 'Hey, Dulcie, tell me the truth. *Did* you have something to do with it?'

The thought was appealing, but truth will out. 'No,' she acknowledged with a sigh. 'I wish.' Joanie kept looking at her. 'I mean, if I'd managed to embezzle from Priority, would I still be working there? As a *temp*?'

'It would be the perfect cover.' Joanie had a point, but the thought of money had moved Dulcie from righteous anger to simple depression.

'No, I'm innocent. Innocent and broke. And jobless.'

'You're not coming back?' Joanie looked a little surprised.

'I don't think they'd let me in the building. And I can't imagine the temp agency will want to place me someplace else after this.' At least she had Tim's half of the rent. But where was she going to come up with the rest? She still owed close to a grand to the vet, not to mention phone, food, and the all-important caffeine fixes.

'But that's so unfair! They don't know anything.'

Dulcie nodded. 'I know. And they told me that they would be in touch. But I'm not holding my breath.' Mr Grey. Tim. Luke and Stacia. And now this. Didn't she deserve a break? As if on cue, her cell phone rang.

'Yes?' She knew her voice sounded tentative, but at this point, she dreaded news. She turned away and put a finger in her ear, the better to hear the latest bombshell.

'Dulcie? This is Bruce. I was so sorry to be so out of it the other day. A friend was, well, having some troubles and I was distracted. I was wondering if you'd give me another chance to explain. Maybe you'd want to get some dinner?'

She knew her reaction must have been obvious by the way Joanie was looking at her. 'Are you cleared? Are you coming back?' Joanie was bouncing off her stool.

'Even better.' Dulcie could feel the smile spreading across her face. 'I've got a date.'

Although she and Bruce had agreed to meet at the Vietnamese place in Harvard Square, Dulcie still wanted to stop by her apartment first. There was no way a day like this wouldn't show in her face, if not her hair. But maybe the anger had been energizing. The face that stared back from the mirror had more color in it than she'd expected. And her hair was unruly, but not in a bad way.

'I look positively rock and roll,' she said, and immediately regretted it. Not that long ago, Mr Grey would have been sitting on the counter beside her. He rarely responded when she spoke, but she could remember the way he'd flick his tail in acknowledgment. If she kept looking straight into the mirror, she could almost imagine him in the corner of her eye. With his silky fur and flag of a tail, he always looked good. Even his eyes, green with a hint of gold, shone, set off by a natural dark rim like kohl against his silver fur.

Mascara. Without it, her own hazel eyes almost disappeared in her face, and Dulcie reached for the tube, knocking it into the sink.

'This isn't mine.' Startled out of her self-contemplation, she rescued the black and gold container before the constant drip from the faucet could damage it. Unscrewing the applicator, she saw that her usual soft brown had been replaced by a darker shade. A quick swipe on her wrist showed traces of gold glitter, too. No wonder everyone at the pub had thought she'd dressed up. It was a nice color – but not one she had purchased. The maker – she checked the bottom of the tube – was a fancy brand that was decidedly out of her budget.

How had it gotten into her bathroom? Had one of Tim's girlfriends left it there? In a moment of revulsion, she dropped the tube with a shudder. Already, her eyes were itching. Did she really want Alana's cooties? But, well, she'd been using this same mascara since . . . since when? At any rate, she knew she had used it before without having her eyes fall out. Picking up the slim tube, Dulcie turned it over in her hands. It was expensive, certainly pricier than her usual drugstore brand. And, yes, very flattering – especially on her fair lashes. Carefully unscrewing the brush again, she sighed and took a breath, and then dabbed the curved brush at her long, but light lashes.

Why hadn't she noticed the strange tube before? It must have been left here recently, maybe not long before Tim's death. And why hadn't the cops seen it when they'd been searching her house? Well, why should they? She answered her own question as she moved on to the other eye, her mouth open. They wouldn't know if it were her mascara or belonged to someone else. They didn't know she could only afford the cheapest drugstore paints and brushes.

'Men are clueless.' She leaned back and blinked, looking for smudges. This was good-quality mascara, all right. It all stayed on her lashes, rather than migrating to her cheeks. Which of Tim's women had left it? In her mind's eye, she imagined Mr Grey looking up at her, his own unblinking eyes gorgeous and green. He seemed to be prompting her, urging her to take her thoughts one step further. 'Is it possible that what we have here,' she closed the sleek tube, 'is what we call a clue?'

As she waited for the T, she mulled over the mystery of the mascara. Alana was the obvious owner. But would anyone with hair that light, whether it was real or bleach, really be using a color this dark? Dulcie closed her eyes to visualize the bovine beauty, but all she could think of was her blank stare – and a hint of turquoise. Did Alana's eyes bulge ever so slightly, or was that her memory getting creative?

The rush of cool air alerted Dulcie that a train was approaching the station and, as she shook her head slightly to clear her mind of the image, she felt her curls bob. Her hair was behaving well today. As she turned her head, she saw another great hairdo: long, glossy curls so dark they were almost black. Now that woman could wear dark mascara – if she needed it – with a touch of gold. Dulcie strained to get a look at the woman's face, but just then the train arrived, and a door opened right in front of her.

The car air-conditioning was even working. Maybe her luck had turned. One stop was long enough to completely perk her up and she bounded up the stairs to meet Bruce with more spring than she'd felt in days.

'Dulcie!' She turned as a woman's voice called her name.

'Luisa.' It was the dark-haired woman from the T, looking fantastic, sleek and glossy as a seal. Dulcie realized that she'd never seen Luisa when the younger girl hadn't been crying. 'You look great.'

'Thank you.' The younger woman fell into step with her and looked up, a smile on her face. 'My boyfriend and I have patched things up.'

'That's great.' One good side effect of Tim no longer being around. Dulcie imagined Luisa with an earnest undergrad, perhaps another tutor holding down multiple jobs to make ends meet. 'I'm really happy for you.'

Maybe Luisa's luck would rub off, she thought as she turned into the converted parking garage. It had been remodeled into a mall years ago, but still kept the curling up-ramp. Luisa kept pace with her.

'Are you going to Pho House, by any chance?' The budget soup joint was popular, but this could be awkward. In response, Luisa only smiled and nodded in the direction of the open glass front. Bruce was standing there, a look of anticipation on his broad and open face.

'Bruce,' Dulcie called. He looked up, his wide face breaking into a grin. Dulcie's heart leaped as she saw those dimples.

And plummeted as those blue eyes looked past her to Luisa. As Dulcie stood, frozen to the spot, the bouncy little brunette ran up to the big jock, who wrapped one large arm around her. Together they turned toward Dulcie.

'Ah, so *this* is the mystery boyfriend!' Dulcie felt her cheeks stiffening around her own smile. 'I should have guessed, when Bruce said he wanted to talk with me.' No wonder he had been so grateful to her for defending Luisa. It wasn't that he appreciated her kindness or warm spirit. It was that she'd stood up for the pretty outsider when he'd lacked the courage to do so.

'You found out! I knew you were smart.' Luisa was blushing, her tan cheeks darkening with an appealing glow that only served to make her look more beautiful. 'Bruce and I – he's my real knight in shining armor.'

A knight who let me speak up for you, Dulcie thought. At least Bruce seemed aware of her role in their lives. 'I can't thank you enough, Dulcie.'

Bruce was glowing now, too. 'You've been so great, so when we decided to go public, we wanted you to be the first to know.'

As the two lovers turned toward each other, Dulcie used the opportunity to relax her frozen face. So that's why Bruce had wanted to talk to her about his clique's prejudices, about Tim. Dulcie had been casting herself in the romantic heroine role, the impoverished noblewoman courted by a young noble. Only she'd misjudged her part. She wasn't the heroine, she was some minor character – maybe the faithful attendant. Luisa, with her angelic looks, was the young Hermetria.

Except that Luisa was no angel. She'd been introduced to Bruce as Tim's tutor, and she'd been stepping out with both her students. Was it possible that Bruce knew that his girlfriend was two-timing him? Was she the 'friend in trouble' he'd been trying to help out? Suddenly Dulcie realized that Bruce, as much as Alana, had reason for jealousy – and more strength to put behind a killing rage. Maybe he'd come by to visit Tim and found his little Luisa there. Maybe . . .

Maybe Dulcie was simply green with envy. By the time the happy couple had finished rubbing noses and giggling, she'd gotten herself under control. She was even able to eat a little, though she had never thought that the rich house pho with the spicy sliced peppers and thick noodles would taste so much like paste.

Declining dessert, Dulcie pled fatigue as an excuse to duck out. By then, the two lovebirds were pretty much oblivious to her, anyway. 'Great to see you . . . both!' With one last half-hearted smile, she managed to get herself out of the pho house and on to the street, where the reality of her situation hit her.

She leaned back against one of Cambridge's omnipresent brick walls and covered her face with her hands. First the debacle at Priority, now this date that had turned out not to be a date. 'Could my life get any worse?'

Count your blessings, Dulcie. The voice jerked her upright. *Better to see people as they are.* 'Mr Grey?' She said the words aloud. An elderly man, dapper in a summer suit and straw hat, turned toward her and quickly away again. 'Oh, great. Now everyone thinks I'm losing it.' A couple in shorts and Red Sox T-shirts stopped short on the sidewalk and darted across the street.

Question the relationships. Well, that message has come a little late, she snapped back – mentally and silently. From now on, when a man asked her to dinner, she'd assume he wanted her to meet his girlfriend. *Dulcie* . . . She could swear the voice had become peevish, and suddenly visualized Mr Grey lashing his tale, always a warning signal. *Speaking of warnings* . . .

I know, she thought, I'm too trusting. Not anymore, though. Now she had another suspect for Tim's murder. Bruce seemed to truly treasure Luisa. If he'd known his friend was hitting on her and, worse, probably just looking to seduce her for a bit of fun, he'd have a fine motive for murder. Of course, how Dulcie was going to let the cops know about it was another problem. She wasn't sure what they thought of her, or if she was still a suspect. But then, if she brought them one more viable option . . . It was all too much. She rubbed her face, not remembering till a second too late that she'd put on full warpaint for her supposed date. A quick glance at her hand confirmed the damage: black and gold streaks tiger-striped her knuckles. 'I must look like Alice Cooper,' she muttered.

And then it hit her. Warnings – the latest warning she'd received hadn't been Mr Grey's general words of advice or comfort. It had come from her mother. Lucy might be daft, but she had called with a specific message – something about a female intruder crossing the water. Well, this mascara had been evidence of another woman in her bathroom, hadn't it? And she'd had to reach across the sink to get at it. No, that couldn't be. Dulcie shook her head. Across the *tap* water?

That was insane. She was getting into *Ravages* territory here, with everything blamed on magic or a ghost. But when Dulcie thought about it, the connection began to make sense. Mascara this dark and dramatic would certainly look better on a brunette like Luisa than a blonde like Alana. Luisa had said that nothing much had happened with Tim, but she'd been awfully upset by his death. What if it wasn't only Tim who was making moves? What if Luisa had been looking to trade up, to leave Bruce for his richer, taller buddy? What if she had been fooling around with Dulcie's room-mate behind her boyfriend's back – only she had found out that Tim had no intention of making her Girl Number 1? Dulcie could imagine the scene: an afternoon tryst. Maybe Luisa had said something about going public, about telling Bruce and Alana. Maybe she'd thought that ring was for her. Tim was never one for tact; he might have laughed in her pretty face. And if she'd just freshened up and reapplied that fancy mascara before meeting him downstairs, well, Dulcie's chopping block was right out on the kitchen counter. Suze had warned her that the young brunette was a 'person of interest' to the police, and Dulcie herself knew the sting of jealousy. 'Hell hath no fury like a woman scorned'. She didn't need her late cat's voice inside her head to explain how that could have played out.

Fifteen

By the time Dulcie got home, Suze had called – four times – and Luke had left a message, too. 'Love to come by and finish up but today's just gotten crazy,' his voicemail said. 'May I have a rain check? I'd love to get together when we could really talk.' His voice was warm and inviting, but odds were good he just wanted to pump her for information about Stacia. And as much as Dulcie wanted to get Tim's laptop, she didn't think she was up to more romantic rejection. What she really wanted to do was crawl into a book, ideally *The Ravages*, and pull the cover closed behind her. However, if she was facing prosecution at Priority, she really needed Suze's expertise a.s.a.p., not to mention a shoulder to cry on. With a small sigh, Dulcie hit 'delete', erasing the message from Luke, and dialed Suze.

'So you really think I might be able to sue them for illegal dismissal?' Forty minutes later, Dulcie's mood had done a neat 180, thanks to Suze's aggressive and affronted reaction to Priority. 'And I might have a civil liberties case, too?'

'Well, they kept you imprisoned, didn't they? That's kidnapping.'

'I'm not actually sure they had locked the door.' This was the best: righteous indignation, with the possibility of money at the other end. But it was probably too good to be true. Suze had jumped right in with a counter-offensive that had lifted Dulcie's mood out of the cellar Bruce and Luisa had dug. But, truth be told, she was willing to let bygones be bygones, especially if she could get her stupid job – or any job – back. Dulcie was too tired to fight; she'd taken too many blows today. And besides, Suze had become tantalizingly evasive when Dulcie had asked where she'd disappeared to for the past forty-eight hours.

'Never mind my dull old routine,' she'd said, before giving Dulcie a vague reply; something about research and a colleague from Duke. 'We've got to figure out your life first.'

Dulcie knew Suze would spill eventually, if there was anything to spill. So she let herself be comforted, moving on to the spotlight that Priority had focused on her. 'I mean, they told me to sit there. And like a fool, I just sat.'

'Doesn't matter.' Suze tended to clip her sentences when she was angry.

As a lawyer who would one day charge by the quarter hour, this habit would save her clients plenty. 'The point is – countersue. We're fighting back. If they pursue, it *will* cost them.'

Dulcie's mood dropped a notch. 'If they *pursue* it? But I thought you said their case was groundless.'

'Probably is. But they can argue circumstantial. You were on the server without permission.'

Another notch.

'They don't have much, but they might pursue it to warn people off, convince their insurance carrier that they're doing something.'

Two notches.

'But I've been keen for you to talk to a lawyer, anyway, due to the whole – ah – Tim thing.'

Three notches, at least. 'Suze, I'm broke.' Dulcie was whispering, her voice gone with her spirit.

'Legal aid, Dulce, legal aid.' Suze must have heard something, because her voice warmed up as her sentences expanded. 'The clinic is open to everybody, free of charge, Dulce. I've been going through my files, trying to figure out who's working there this summer – and who is any good.'

Dulcie whimpered.

'Dulcie, you've got to. Even if you do end up spending a couple of thousand.' She must have heard Dulcie swallow. 'You know I'll lend it to you, but you've got to do this. I mean, being in debt is better than being in jail, isn't it?'

'At this point, Suze, I'm not sure.'

It wasn't Suze's fault. She was only trying to help. Still, Dulcie never expected to be able to get to sleep after that final crushing blow to her sense of self, security, and general all-round worth. She hadn't even had a chance to tell her old friend about Bruce or the mystery of the mascara. But the endless Monday must have simply worn her out. She fell asleep dreaming of a warm, purring animal beside her. In her dreams, Mr Grey appeared on her computer screen again. Only this time, he was able to talk to her, and he was saying something about magic: *Spells most potent for their proximity*. There was more, she remembered watching his whiskers move, the way his tufted ears flicked back and forth for emphasis. But the rest of the dream was confused, computer viruses were created by evil spells and the third-floor bedroom looked out on to a wintry, windswept peak.

The dream had been so compelling that when Dulcie awoke she was surprised to see sunshine, rather than snow, through her open window. A gentle breeze promised a pleasant day. Birds chirped and chattered, and Dulcie snuggled into her pillow, forgetting for a moment that she had moved to the city. Was that a cardinal she heard? From her bed, she could see one fluffy cloud, like a child's drawing, floating across the sky. She yawned and stretched and turned toward her clock.

'Oh, hell, it's eight thirty!' Dulcie jumped out of bed and was halfway into yesterday's skirt before the realization hit her: she had no job anymore; there was nowhere she had to be. Only two months before, on such a beautiful morning as this, that would have been a wonderful realization, money be damned. But today . . . she sank back down on to the bed. All it meant was that she'd have more time alone with her worries. Outside her window, that one puffy cloud must have moved. The bright sun was replaced by shadow.

'Great.' She'd become so used to talking to Mr Grey that speaking her thoughts out loud had become second nature. But as she heard her own voice, she felt again the one-two punch. Mr Grey was gone. And Tim, who used to tease her, had been stabbed to death in her own living room. For a brief moment, she contemplated crawling back under the covers. Maybe she could sleep until the cops came for her or everybody just went away.

Dulcie . . . Talking to yourself and your deceased cat was one thing; hearing your cat respond was too much. Dulcie sat back up. She'd been letting herself drift into some fantasy-fueled dreamland for too long. No wonder the police had doubted her sanity. No wonder no man was interested in her. If she wasn't careful, she could end up just like Lucy.

Dulcie shuddered. That thought got her out of bed. If she was losing it, slipping into some kind of heat- or grief-induced dementia, she could at least fight it; assert some kind of control, make some kind of discipline for herself, to slow the inevitable decline. A shower and a proper breakfast would be a start. And then she would go right down to the law school's legal aid office and begin dealing with her problems. That's rational, Dulcie told herself, that's behaving in a reasonable, adult manner. Still, as she lathered up her thick brown curls, Dulcie couldn't fight the feeling that, sitting right outside the shower, in his usual post on the top of the toilet seat, a large grey cat was watching her, purring, his tail coiled neatly around his front paws.

A bagel with low-fat veggie cream cheese and two large iced lattes later, Dulcie had mustered the courage to proceed with her plan. Taking the T into Harvard Square, she made her stride brisk and purposeful as she marched the remaining four blocks to the legal aid office. Suze had warned her the night before that the office where thirty-odd students and a handful of actual lawyers worked would be easy to miss. But although the small white house blended in nicely with its surrounding neighbors, Dulcie liked the look of it. The neat little colonial was set back from the street behind a small lawn, but its tall, open windows and dark-green shutters looked inviting; less threatening, less corporate than a cool glass-and-steel office.

And far less organized. Although Dulcie had let the brass fox-head door knocker fall on the wooden front door before letting herself in, she was almost run over by a set of boxes with legs. 'Sorry! Sorry!' The front entrance way, built for colonial-era occupants, wasn't made for them both, and Dulcie found herself pressed against a wall of wooden cubbyholes, from which envelopes and flyers poked. As the boxes squeezed past her, a male voice emerged from beneath them. 'Sorry! 'Scuse me.' The boxes were marked with sections of the alphabet: A–F, G–P, T–Z.

'Did you lose a box?' Dulcie couldn't imagine carrying a higher stack, especially if the boxes were even halfway full, but she couldn't help calling after the retreating form.

'Sorry? Oh, no. We don't need those today.' A round face emerged as the boxes leaned briefly against a fax/copier. 'Are you one of the new interns?'

'I'm a supplicant,' she replied. Then, catching the confused look, 'I mean, I need help.'

'Oh, sorry. A client.' He hoisted the boxes back up, and raised his voice to carry over them. 'Go down that hallway to the right. Sorry for the mess. August 1. New interns start today. Everything is crazy.'

'I gather.' But he'd already gone, leaving Dulcie to pick her way over more boxes and into what must once have been a formal dining room. The layout was familiar from other university offices, a good number of which were housed in equally old, quaint, and impractical converted homes. In this building, every available inch had been turned to office use. Cubicle-like desk spaces lined the walls, leaving only a narrow walkway around a central table that was itself covered with papers. Three women were pecking away at laptops, not even bothering to look up as someone – the round-faced young man? – dropped something heavy in the next room. The entire house – admittedly, not particularly big – shook slightly, and the low, muttered sound of cursing filtered through the wall into the room.

'Dulcie!' At the sound of her own name, Dulcie spun around. There, in the open doorway, stood Luke. He was smiling. 'I left a message for you last night.'

'I know, I'm sorry.' She felt flustered and fought it. She would *not* care that this man was handsome and smiling. She would *not*. 'I had just the worst day. Which – well – is why I'm here.' She gestured at the activity going on around her, and realized she was saying more with her hands than with her voice. 'I mean, I ran into some issues yesterday that made it seem like I should get some legal advice.'

'Follow me, then. We can talk back here.' He opened a door she hadn't seen before.

'No, I mean, from legal aid.' She wasn't making herself clear. Luke was a law student, but she wasn't asking him, personally, for help.

'I figured that out.' He was smiling more broadly now. 'I'm working here for the rest of the summer.' He saw her puzzled look. 'I'll be a 3L when I go back to Stanford, my seminar doesn't take that much time, and one of the August interns fell through. So,' he gestured again to the open door, 'would you like to chat?'

It wasn't like she had a choice, she thought to herself, as she walked past him into the back office. Dulcie wasn't sure it could even be called a room. Almost windowless, with one high cut-through that let in some air and the sound of soft chatter, the tiny space must have originally been a pantry or even a large closet. Small as it was, it had been divided into three workstations, each barely big enough for a computer. Bookshelves climbed up the wall and a filing cabinet behind the door kept it from opening entirely. Luke motioned for her to roll one of the chairs toward a lit computer screen, and took a seat beside her. After the bustle out front, this space felt quiet and intimate.

And so Dulcie dived right in. 'Well, Luke, I'm here about two legal problems. The first is criminal. I seem to be under investigation for Tim's murder.'

Luke blanched, but when he spoke his voice was calm. 'I should give you the legal aid spiel, Dulcie. First, we don't actually handle criminal cases. Work, housing, various forms of discrimination – that's it. But, off the record, tell me more.'

Dulcie felt herself flush. Her obnoxious room-mate had been this man's brother, after all. 'I'm sorry, I shouldn't have just dropped that on you. But, well, the police have heard that he and I didn't get along. They brought me in for questioning on Saturday and they implied that I went over the edge.' She didn't want to add that they'd also suggested that she might be jealous. Her lack of a sex life was not Luke's business. She swallowed. 'I want to make it clear, Luke. Tim and I did have our disagreements. But I did *not* – I could never – have killed him.' She paused. That sounded odd. 'I mean, I couldn't kill anyone.'

He smiled. 'I believe you, Dulcie. It's just still hard to get my mind around what happened. But I can't seriously imagine the police are considering you as a suspect. You're too gentle.' He looked away from her, down at the keyboard.

'Thanks.' This was awkward. Why couldn't they be out in that busy front room? 'Suze, my room-mate, says they're probably talking to everyone and that if they don't call me back, I'm in the clear.'

'That sounds reasonable.'

'I just hate waiting.'

He nodded. 'It's like you want them to make a positive declaration of your innocence. You don't want to feel like you escaped.'

He got it. Dulcie breathed a small sigh of relief. 'Anyway, the other problem I'm having really might fall under your jurisdiction.' He raised an eyebrow at her phrasing and they both laughed. 'I mean, maybe you can help me?'

As succinctly as possible, she explained the Priority Insurance situation while he took notes on a yellow legal pad. Although she'd felt embarrassed at first by the very nature of the job – temping in a clerical position! – he put her at ease. Asking simple, direct questions and nodding as he listened to her answers, Luke seemed as much like a counselor as a soon-to-be-attorney, and she found herself warming to him. She even told him about the apparent theft of her sweater.

'So what you're saying, to use a technical term, is that your boss is a bitch?' He looked up at her, pencil poised, face serious. But then he broke into another wide grin and they both laughed.

'Yeah, that about says it all. But seriously, Luke, what can I do? I mean, I need this job – or at least I need to not be totally discredited with the temp agency that sent me there. And I really do *not* need to be accused of embezzlement or computer malfeasance.'

'Computer malfeasance, I like that. Sounds Victorian!' They shared another smile.

'Why me, though? I'm just a temp.'

'That's a good point.' He drummed his pencil on the pad. 'Do you think that could be why you've been accused?'

Dulcie nodded and explained Suze's theory; that perhaps the company was simply looking for a scapegoat, for insurance purposes.

'I'm afraid to say it makes sense, in an awful sort of way. I mean, unless you think someone has it in for you personally.'

Dulcie shuddered. 'God, I hope not. But . . . why?'

'To cover for themselves, obviously.'

Himself – or herself, Dulcie silently corrected him. Grammar aside, Luke's logic made her shiver. Still, she forced herself to focus. It was Joanie who had shown her how to get on to the server, and Joanie definitely had an anti-authority streak. But she was a friend, wasn't she? Or at least a kindred spirit? Dulcie knew her instincts had been off recently, but she liked the kohl-eyed Goth girl and shook her head. 'No, I can't think of anyone.'

'Let's tackle this from another angle, then.' Luke looked down at his notes. 'How are you supposed to have hacked into the system? Does your terminal have a disk drive or even a USB port?'

'I don't think so.' Dulcie grimaced and tried to recall exactly what her workstation looked like. 'I just go in there and type. I mean, I've never noticed. But I think they were accusing me of getting the virus in through the email.'

'That doesn't sound likely.' He bit his lip as he thought it through. 'I mean, I don't know for sure, but doesn't it seem likely that a large corporation, an *insurance* company, would have all sorts of firewalls and virus detection programs at work?'

'You'd think.' Dulcie was feeling better by the moment. And the privacy of the little room had grown much more comfortable, too. 'You know, I never asked them and I should have – I mean, I will. I'm going to confront them about my so-called methodology.'

'Great.' Luke's eyes lit up when he smiled. 'But let's arm you properly for battle. I want to find out a little more about these computer worms and how they work. I want you to be able to march right in there and explain how you couldn't have done whatever they're saying you're falsely accused of.' Dulcie had a brief urge to correct his phrasing, but she was enjoying his enthusiasm – and his attention – too much to give in to it. 'You know who you should talk to about this?' He was rummaging in his canvas briefcase now, obviously looking for a phone book or cell. 'Stacia – Alana's friend.'

Dulcie was grateful that he couldn't see her face fall.

'She may look like an airhead, but she actually knows quite a lot about computers.' He continued rooting around in the bag. 'She's really sharp.'

Great, so she's not only beautiful, she's smart, too, Dulcie thought as she worked on composing her face. By the time Luke had surfaced with his cell phone, she believed she looked cool as a cucumber, or an unencumbered client.

'Here's her number.' He scribbled on the bottom of the page and tore it off. 'Have we covered everything?'

As much as she now hated Stacia, Dulcie remembered her promise to look for the compromising photos. Despite Stacia's movie-star looks, she was human, too; they were both single women, trying to make their way in a rough world – and Stacia was only trying to look out for her friend. 'Actually, there's something else, Luke. I really would like to look at Tim's laptop, if you don't mind. I think he used my computer and messed up a file, and I'd like to take a peek at it.' Considering what might be on it, she didn't want to be any more specific.

'Yeah, sorry, I know you'd mentioned it before. I'll bring it over when

I pick up the rest of Tim's stuff, if that's OK. It's funny, Stacia asking about it was how I found out she's into computers.'

Dulcie almost told him not to bother. If Stacia had already seen the laptop, maybe she had already found – and deleted – any compromising files. But then she remembered her own compromised file – and her lost photo. Maybe there was a virus on Tim's computer that he'd put on hers, and maybe she had sent it to Priority without knowing about it. At least, if she could trace it to her late room-mate's computer, she wouldn't be liable, would she? Was Typhoid Mary ever cleared of evil intent?

Luke was scribbling on a form and seemed unaware of the shift in his erstwhile client's mood. When he looked up, he was still grinning.

'OK, so, forty-five minutes. That'll be $750.'

Dulcie blanched.

'Bad joke! Bad joke, sorry. But you do have to sign, so they know I'm not just sitting in here flirting with you. And, well, you don't have to, but I would like the chance to take you to dinner. Maybe after I finish packing up Tim's stuff?'

'Maybe.' She signed her name and stood to go. Just what she needed, another dinner date with another man who wanted another woman. 'But I've got to take care of this business first. Thanks for this, though. You've really helped me figure out where I stand legally.' And with you, she almost added, as she hurried away.

Sixteen

The day had returned to its first promise: breezy, not too hot, the deep-blue sky holding a hint of autumn to come. The walk back into Harvard Square was a pleasure, the dream summer day. But Dulcie had too much on her mind to enjoy the obvious comparisons. If she wanted her interior landscape to be this beautiful, there was only one place to go. Sliding her ID through the silver gate, she smiled at the guard and ducked into the tiny back entrance of the library. Nothing could get to her here.

The cool hush of the library greeted her like an old friend, as did some of her actual old friends. Mona, at the circulation desk, nodded and smiled as she walked past. Frank, who had been working on his dissertation since the Paleozoic, looked up as her flip-flops slapped softly on the marble steps. In minutes, she was deep in the stacks, descending below ground level to where the British history books were stored. Context, that's what she needed. If she could immerse herself more fully in the time frame of *The Ravages of Umbria*, maybe she would find a clue about why it mattered so to her. How many 'she-authors' were writing then, exactly? How many of their works had been lost to the ravages of time, if not to evil monks and critics? Research, not gut instinct, was the key.

She'd use this time to catch up on her colleagues. Maybe she'd become so involved in her primary sources that she'd lost track of what other scholars were doing, what they were thinking and writing about.

Not that Dulcie wanted anybody else's ideas. This wasn't just Lucy's DIY ethos, ingrained into her daughter through years of making her own everything, from clothes to candles. Coming, as she did, from a decidedly non-traditional background, Dulcie also knew she'd be more open to accusations of plagiarism, if she wrote a line that echoed another, published paper. The spectre of such accusations hovered over the entire department, like its own jealous ghost. Trista had confessed that she had nightmares which Dickens scholars from the past 150 years began pounding on her door, demanding co-bylines. She woke up sweating, she'd told Dulcie, shaking with the uncontrollable urge to footnote everything.

But sometimes reading academic works could snap Dulcie into *thinking* more like an academic. Mr Grey had told her to look carefully at relationships. She recalled that charming photo, cat inverted, one fang exposed. Well, maybe she wasn't looking from the right angle.

But halfway through a journal article, 'Exemplary Characters in the Middle Gothic Novel', Dulcie wanted to throw up her hands. Yes, Demetria, Hermetria's attendant, was a bit too perfect. So what? Did Dulcie care that she was a stereotype, a flat cut-out of a character, particularly compared to the full-blooded Hermetria? She let the book fall flat and shut her eyes. So much of this had been written about, the character types analyzed to death. Yes, the supernatural themes were a reaction to increasing industrialization, valuing emotion over pure intellect. Yes, the Gothic novel was a response to the Enlightenment; the beginning of Romanticism, with all the connotations that entailed. But the work to which she had decided to devote her academic career was more than what she was finding in these papers, wasn't it?

Dulcie thought of all the books she loved and tried to take some notes. It would help if she could figure out *why* she so adored these ghost stories and horror tales. It wasn't just . . . she paused, afraid of continuing. It wasn't just because they were *fun*, was it? Folding her arms on the study carrel in front of her, she let her head sink down. Had she wasted two years of her postgrad life, not to mention all those undergrad semesters, trying to justify a simple diversion?

There had to be more in her attraction to the genre. There had to be. She went back to reading. Two hours later, she was more lost than ever. She was also famished. Breakfast had been a long time ago. But the extra time had paid off, and rather than wait for the elevator she hit the stairwell to mull it over. It was barely a thought, more of a whim. But, some vague, half-starved brainwaves were coming together. As she climbed the stairs, she looked around. The roots of her beloved Widener reached back to the eighteenth century. Libraries weren't public places then, or even well organized. But the books she adored had launched the system she knew so well. Even with the rise of chapbooks, the 1700s' equivalent of mass-market paperbacks, novels were expensive. And so readers, largely women, had gathered to share and circulate the newest adventures. Maybe those gatherings – those early book groups – were the key, the basis for that almost sisterly relationship. Life hadn't been easy in those days, before antibiotics, painkillers, or the widespread use of flush toilets; but then, as today, the thrill of sinking into a good book had offered an escape, and something to share, for those who could read.

And that hadn't included too many people, she admitted to herself, as she faced the final flight of stairs. In some ways, access to literature was as narrow as, well, Widener. Not just in the sense of limited access to the university either. Because of the cavernous library's strange layout only two elevators serviced all ten levels, and Dulcie rarely bothered to wait. She'd forgotten what a drag this could be though, particularly in flip-flops. Ah, well, what she had found had been worth the slog. If she could think of a way to tie in the early Goths to the rise of literacy among the middle classes, or simply among women, she might just have a thesis yet. Could Hermetria be a stand-in for the average reader? Or, more likely, the mealy-mouthed Demetria? Dulcie mulled the idea over as she emerged from the stairwell into the small entrance chamber that separated the stacks from the Circulation room.

Maybe she was too much in the past, she thought as she walked, not taking any notice of the three marble steps that led down to Circulation. Maybe – she caught herself as she began to slip, her flip-flop taking off ahead of her like a small rubber glider. Those marble steps, few as they were, were worn to a concave polish, and they would be the death of her if she wasn't careful. Hoping nobody had noticed, Dulcie slipped the other sandal off and stepped carefully down the remaining slick stones, retrieving the errant flip-flop and donning both again, as she stepped into Circulation. No, nobody had noticed. The big room was a buzz of activity, but all of it focused around the checkout desk where Mona, the queen bee, reigned supreme. Half a dozen people – unusual for a summer day – had clustered around her friend's computer terminal, and even their lowered voices made an audible buzz.

'What's going on?' She turned toward Frank, who was craning his neck to see.

'I'm not sure. Something with the system.' They both turned as one of the hovering men pulled out a cell phone and started talking.

'Wow . . .' Frank was whispering and Dulcie didn't need to ask why: a cell phone in use and nobody challenging it? This must be official, and it must be serious.

'I'm so glad I don't have anything to check out,' Dulcie whispered back. 'But still . . .' She walked up to Mona's desk and waited until she could catch the librarian's eye. 'What's up?'

'I've been invaded!' Mona, a large woman, had a flair for the dramatic. 'By aliens!' Her bright-red lipstick exaggerated her grimace of disgust. Perhaps to show off her bejeweled nails, she also raised both hands in the air in exasperation. 'It's crazy.'

'Bookworms?' Dulcie said with a smile. While the paper-eating pests had been the scourge of libraries in the past, she doubted they'd survive in such a well-kept library.

But Mona opened her mouth with a look of shock and horror. Her voice, when it came back, was appalled. 'What are you talking about?'

'It was a joke. Sorry.' Dulcie tried to explain. 'You know, bookworms in a library?'

'That's not very funny right now.' Mona glared, but then motioned to her friend. 'Come over here.' With a glance at the two officials, the flamboyant librarian walked to the end of the circulation counter unnoticed, gesturing for Dulcie to follow. 'Seriously, Dulcie, do you know anything?'

'About what? What's going on?' This was more baffling by the minute.

'I'm sorry,' Mona said to nobody in particular – and rather more loudly than was usual for a career librarian, 'we cannot check out materials just at present.' She looked back toward her terminal. Nobody was paying attention. 'I can't . . . I'm not supposed to say anything. But what you said . . .'

'What?' Dulcie was bursting.

'We're being hacked, Dulcie. Someone has been trying to feed a bug into the university computer system!'

Mona wouldn't tell Dulcie any more details – 'I can't, Dulcie, I've been told it's worth my job!' – but that didn't stop Dulcie's imagination from filling in the details. Computers were going nuts all over town: at Priority, a computer worm or virus program had allowed someone in the system to embezzle funds; and now this. But what would anyone gain from hacking into the university library? Reduction of overdue fines? Dulcie recalled a scandal from years before. A student had been smuggling out rare books, selling them on eBay for huge amounts. But that had been old-fashioned stealing, involving backpacks with false bottoms, not technical expertise.

She thought again of her own corrupted computer file. Maybe it hadn't come from something Tim had typed in or from Priority. Chris had mentioned that the university had a clear path into her own system. Maybe whatever was eating away at the library computer had messed up her picture of Mr Grey. It seemed unlikely though; her system was still working, after all. But she made a mental note to call Chris as soon as she got home. She couldn't afford to take her laptop to a professional repair place, certainly not until she got another job. But he'd said if she found anything he'd come by.

She could always call Stacia, she thought with a grimace. Luke had seemed truly impressed with the sleek brunette's computer expertise. She rejected the idea immediately. No, that woman and her clique had humiliated Dulcie enough for one summer. Chris it was. She could sweeten the deal with talk about Suze, too. Her old friend was spending too much time in the library, even for a law student. It was only healthy for one of them to have a love life.

The phone was ringing as Dulcie unlocked her front door. By the time she had raced up the stairs, the answering machine had kicked in. The male voice speaking didn't sound like anyone she knew.

'Ms Schwartz, I'm calling from Priority Insurance.' Oh, great. She sank on to the sofa and waited for her fate to be pronounced into a cheap answering machine. 'We'd like you to come into work tomorrow. We need to speak with you first, and would like you to report to Conference Room B at nine a.m. But there is no reason for you not to continue your clerical duties at Priority, and we'd appreciate it if you were able to resume these duties tomorrow, after our meeting.' That was it. No name, no number to call back. No waiting to see if she still *wanted* their stupid job. But then again, she didn't need to threaten them with legal action, either. It was a stupid job, but it sounded like it was *her* stupid job, if she wanted it.

The afternoon in the library had spoiled her. She'd been on the edge of something, some breakthrough. But her classes and her grant would resume in one more month. She'd go back to Priority in the morning.

While she had time, though, Dulcie really wanted to recapture that library buzz. Did she dare start up her own computer? Holding her breath, she flipped the laptop open and, sighing with relief, watched as the screen saver resolved into her regular assortment of folders and pages. OK, so the system was working at least a little. Before she got started on anything, though, she thought of Chris's warning. It was so easy to forget about backing up her files . . .

With a twinge of guilt, she opened an email to Suze. 'Hey, Suze, hang on to these for me, please. Don't open until I give you the all-clear,' she typed, dragging her research folders over to the electronic letter: '*RoU*: Fragment 1'; '*RoU*: Fragment 2'; 'Hermetria speeches'; 'Demetria, Others'; probably all the sidekick deserved. She decided she ought to buy one of those tiny thumb drives, and she would – next pay day. But until then, sending her files to Suze couldn't do any harm, could it?

Dulcie paused, weighing the risk to her friend – and to their friendship. Suze had asked her not to send that weird file. But these were her research notes, the beginnings of what just might become a thesis and might keep her in Cambridge and at school. If there was some kind of virus in her system, Suze would have to open the files to be infected, wouldn't she? And she'd understand. She always had, right? With a silent prayer, Dulcie hit 'send'.

Seventeen

On Wednesday morning, Dulcie walked back into the Priority Insurance building feeling as if she were in another world. Was it only two days ago when she'd last pushed through these revolving doors? On Monday, she'd still thought of Bruce as a prospect – as opposed to a suspect. And she'd pitied Luisa, not envied, let alone suspected, her. Dulcie caught herself up short; the whole mascara thing was weird, but she shouldn't blow it out of proportion. Tim had had some kind of fatal attraction for women, but that didn't make any of those women murderous, did it?

Just because one of his women had left some make-up at her place didn't mean anything. It might have been Alana's; she was wealthy enough, she probably didn't think twice about buying high-end cosmetics, even if the colors were wrong for her. And just because Luisa had succumbed – correction, *might* have succumbed – didn't mean either she or her cute blue-eyed boyfriend had stabbed Dulcie's cheating room-mate. Dulcie was letting her imagination run away with her, and all because her crazy mother had a dream.

'Bag, miss?' Dulcie was woken from her reverie by the guard. The line had been moving slowly and now it was her turn. Had it really only been two days since she'd let him paw through her bag, without giving the new security procedures a second thought?

Automatically she queued up for the elevator along with all the other office drones. 'Fourteen, please,' she said from habit, and then remembered. 'I mean, eight.' Before she could go back to work, she had to meet with human resources, and who knew who else from Priority's upper management. That thought, as much as the sudden start of the elevator, made Dulcie's stomach lurch, and the conference-room floor arrived a little soon for comfort. Dulcie made herself remember what Luke and Suze had told her. She had done nothing wrong. She could be suing these guys, if she wanted. She could be – she opened the door to Conference Room B and walked in.

It was difficult to hold on to her righteous anger, but Dulcie was trying. At the far end of a long oval table, facing the door, sat the unsmiling Sally Putnam. To her right sat a blue-suited man of indeterminate age, and flanking them both were the security guards who had escorted Dulcie out of the building only two days before. Caught in the HR capo's unfriendly glare, Dulcie felt herself pinned, silent and frozen.

'Please be seated,' the suit said. Dulcie slid into the nearest chair. It was the farthest from the Snake, and she mentally kicked herself for choosing it – and for waiting for permission to sit. Didn't she have any spirit left?

'We deeply regret the necessity of the unpleasantness on Monday, Miss Schwartz.' The suit seemed to be in charge, and Dulcie realized with a start that as head of human resources, Sally Putnam was probably considered the employee's representative. 'We were within our rights to act as we did, but new evidence now indicates that perhaps we acted precipitously.'

Dulcie's ears pricked up. The new evidence sounded interesting. Even more important, she realized, the suit was apologizing in his own way. She hadn't been Suze's room-mate for so many years without being able to hear the legal underpinnings of office-speak. He was covering his butt!

'Oh, yeah?' Dulcie spoke before she realized what she was saying. Sally Putnam blinked, slowly. The suit, who had been about to continue, shut his mouth. 'I'm sorry, and you are?'

She didn't know where this attitude was coming from. Cat-itude. She envisioned Mr Grey sitting up tall, his tail wrapped around his front feet, and purring.

'As Mr Olmstead was saying,' the Snake spoke up before the suit could answer, 'we don't believe you were directly culpable in the breach of security. However, there have been indications, several indications, that your workstation was involved. Compromised, shall we say.' She leaned forward ever so slightly, the words hissing between thin lips.

'What do you mean, compromised?' As her fear ebbed, Dulcie realized that she was curious.

'We mean, Miss Schwartz, that someone else may have used your workstation for . . . illicit purposes.' Olmstead, the suit, seemed uncomfortable with the phrase. 'George, please?'

The older of the two security guards took over. 'Basically, we can trace the breach, Miss Schwartz. And it originated at your terminal.'

'And what is it, exactly? A computer virus?' The quartet at the other end of the table exchanged glances. So Joanie's information had been correct. 'Is someone hacking into the Priority computers?'

All eyes were back on her now. 'Never mind that.' Sally Putnam's eyes narrowed, but the blue-suited boss put up one hand.

'We understand that some information may have been leaked. Now, Miss Schwartz, I don't know what you've heard, but I can assure you that it probably isn't accurate, and rumors and half truths do nobody any good. That said, we would rather not go into details. Let it suffice that we at Priority believe strongly in safeguarding the integrity of our systems, and we intend to trace this breach to its source. Which is why we asked you to come in this morning.' He paused.

Here it comes, thought Dulcie. Whatever they mean to do, it will happen now.

'What we need to know, young lady, is who has had access to your terminal during office hours.'

'My terminal?' Dulcie thought of her email, and of the strange disruption in the library system. She'd assumed some cyber attack, something coming in online, not an actual person.

'Yes, your terminal. Your floor is locked after hours, and we haven't seen any ID cards showing up in inappropriate places.' Dulcie flashed for a moment on her own visit to the IT offices. Those doors had been opened. Was she leaving electronic footprints everywhere she went? 'We'd like to know if you've seen anyone else typing, or otherwise' – he paused, searching for the word – '*fiddling* with your terminal.'

'If this is a computer problem, isn't it just as likely that it came in through cyberspace; through email or a hacker?' Curiosity was once again outweighing her fear.

The two bosses exchanged a look. 'We're considering all possibilities,' said Olmstead. 'Please answer the question.'

Dulcie sat back in the chair. The row of cubicles was usually half empty. There was she – and Joanie. Joanie had often arrived earlier than Dulcie, and Joanie had been the one to get her into the server. But, could the little Goth be a cyber hacker? That was awfully like the question Luke had asked. Dulcie bit her lip. In truth, she could imagine her cubicle neighbor doing something destructive – but for fun, not profit.

'No,' she said finally, 'I have never seen anybody working at my cubicle.' The suit looked grim, his face set in stiff lines. Sally Putnam, however, nodded as if she expected as much.

'Never?' She turned her head slightly, as if to focus one cold eye on the younger woman.

'Never.' Dulcie held firm. 'Though I have to say, security doesn't seem that tight up on fourteen. I mean, even before all of this happened, someone stole my sweater.' The eye blinked. 'I mean, during the days I was out, it just disappeared. To be completely honest, Mrs Putnam, I kind of thought, well, maybe I saw you wearing it the other day.'

The manager turned her tanned face fully toward Dulcie. Her eyes, dark and hard, looked as opaque as beach pebbles, though not as pretty. 'Are you accusing me of stealing? A *sweater*?'

Dulcie could have sworn the woman hissed.

'Are you *insane*?'

The man in the blue suit tried to stifle a smile.

'I—' Dulcie started to respond; to defend herself, her perceptions, and the sanctity of her property. But something about the question, or maybe it was the unblinking stare of those dark eyes, stopped the words from coming. Was she, in fact, insane – not in general, but right now, two weeks after the murder of her room-mate; two weeks after she started having visions of her dead pet? She thought of her mother's 'flights of fancy', the latest of which may have turned out to be a psychic warning about second-hand mascara, and wondered about the genetics of mental health. 'I don't think so,' she stammered. It was the best she could do.

'Never mind.' The suit looked at her, vaguely disappointed that no cat fight would be in the offing. When it became clear that Dulcie had nothing more to say, he sighed and placed his hands flat on the table. 'The morning is getting on.' He stood up. 'Thank you for your time, Miss Schwartz. If we have any more questions, we'll be sure to contact you.'

She was dismissed. For a moment, Dulcie thought he would reach out to shake her hand. But then Sally Ann Putnam, senior manager of HR, turned toward him, putting her long, lacquered fingers on his blue sleeve, asserting her dominance in the field of human resources and recalcitrant employees. With only the lightest pressure from that hand, she turned them both away. Dulcie, muttering something she was afraid sounded too much like 'Thank you,' slipped back out of the door.

'What happened? What did they do to you?' Joanie wasn't even trying to hide her excitement as Dulcie took her seat in her cubicle. Her hair had reverted from green to its customary black in Dulcie's absence. 'Did they have the cops there to question you?'

'No, but I probably won't sue them either.' Dulcie couldn't help smiling as she stowed her bag in the bottom drawer of her desk. All in all, she'd come out OK and could afford a bit of swagger. 'They even sort of apologized.'

'Tell!' Joanie rolled her chair around the cubicle divider, and Dulcie did. From that ignominious exit on Monday, when the security men had marched her out, to her return had been less than two days. But telling her workmate about the legal advice she'd gotten from Suze, and from Luke at the clinic, made the whole thing seem more like an adventure. Dulcie paused for a moment while she related her latest meeting with her employers. She didn't necessarily want to reveal to the black-swathed Joanie that she had wondered about her own involvement. Still, it only seemed fair to warn her.

'So, then they asked if anyone else had access to my terminal.' Dulcie studied Joanie's heavily made-up face. The girl didn't blink. 'And I thought of you.'

To her surprise, Joanie's black-lined mouth broke into a big grin. 'Am I a suspect? Cool!'

'I don't think so.' Even the piercings on the girl's nose and eyebrow seemed to fade and lose their sparkle. 'I'm sorry.'

'That's OK. I just liked the idea of striking a blow against the man, and all that. I mean, my stepdad works for Citibank, and my mom's the über-boss of Krall Information Tech.'

Information – the word struck a chord. 'Hey, tell me something, Joanie.' Dulcie leaned in. 'The day I came back to work, you knew about Tim, my room-mate. How?'

'Are you serious?' The sparkle returned. 'Lou Ann in the phone center took the call. *Everyone* knew by lunch!'

'Then why didn't the bosses? It seemed like nobody knew I wasn't going to be in. The files kept piling up.'

Joanie shrugged. 'Maybe someone didn't want to know; didn't want to deal.' They both sat silent for a moment, musing on the inscrutability of the corporate world.

'I guess we should get to work.' Dulcie began to push her chair back toward her terminal, confident once more that the Goth girl had had nothing to do with hacking Priority.

'Are you crazy?' Suze's voice was friendly, but the undercurrent of worry could be heard clear from Washington. 'Dulcie, you don't know this woman at all. And she did help get you into trouble in the first place.'

'All she did was poke around—' The remainder of her work day had been dull, blessedly so. More than anything, Dulcie wanted life to calm down.

'She logged you on to the company server.' From Suze's voice, Dulcie could tell she was sitting up. It was easy to picture her counting off points against Joanie on her fingers. 'She was the first one to tell you about the nature of the hacking. And, unless I'm misremembering, she also tried to send you off to the computer guys to ask questions for her.'

'No, you're not misremembering.' What kind of word was that anyway? Dulcie sank back on to her own cushions. Suze in lawyer mode could be exhausting. 'It's just, to be honest, I don't want to think about it anymore if I don't have to.'

'But—' Dulcie closed her eyes. She really couldn't deal. 'No, you're right. I'm sorry.' When push came to shove, Suze the friend would always win out over Suze the lawyer. 'So, anything else fun happening up there?'

This was her cue, Dulcie knew, to tell Suze about Lucy's dream and the discovery of the mascara. Suze had actually met Lucy, on one of her mother's rare trips East, and she'd heard enough stories so that she didn't need any prepping on Dulcie's mother's various crazy theories. But somehow, Dulcie didn't want that one dismissed just yet. Maybe because it would lead to the whole Bruce thing. The whole Bruce and Luisa embarrassment, to be accurate, and Dulcie didn't want to go there. Suze had warned her about protecting Luisa, in much the same way as she'd warned her about Joanie. But Luisa wasn't a murderer, was she? She was just a more attractive, younger woman.

'I feel old, Suze. Old at twenty-six.' How that slipped out, she wasn't sure. The last few days must have gotten to her.

'You just need to get back to work on your thesis.' At times, Suze really was the voice of reason. 'You've got, what, another six months before all your grants come up again?'

'Five months, Suze. I've been counting. I spent a couple of hours in Widener yesterday and it was a homecoming. I feel like I almost have it.' A soft murmur on the other end of the line meant Suze was listening. 'I think there's a populist angle that I could focus on. Feminist, even, considering that *The Ravages of Umbria* is really about two women against the world.'

'Are you asking me or telling me, Dulcie? And, well, isn't that whole proto-feminist take sort of common knowledge?'

'Yeah, but . . .' Dulcie was surprised. Suze had been listening more than she'd thought. 'But I've got to get working on something. I've got to re-file for grants in September or I'm out.' Panic started to tighten her throat, and she heard her voice rise. 'I'm out, Suze. I'm out!'

'I know, Dulce. And I'm on your side. But you're a real scholar. I know it. And, yeah, I know I was never into those ghost stories. There's a reason I'm studying law, and not just because my mom wants me to make partner in some big firm before I'm thirty. It's just more concrete. For you, though, it's different. Has been for as long as I've known you. It's always been about the writing, the language – the style. You've never looked for a message in these books before. Don't start now.'

Dulcie thought back to Freshman Week, when she'd dragged her Army Surplus duffle into the dorm room to find the upper bunk had already been claimed by a super-serious student with long dark braids and thick glasses. Both the braids and the glasses were history, and Suze had learned to lighten up. What hadn't changed was her laser-like focus. If she thought Dulcie was on the wrong track, maybe she was right.

'I just felt like I'd hit on something – something I could write about.

I mean, just loving the books isn't enough. I want to be serious, not just a fan.'

'You are, kiddo. I mean, you know more about obscure authors and who influenced whom than anyone else I know. Would it help to just read through your notes, maybe some of your old papers?'

She had a point, but Dulcie winced. 'It would – if I weren't worried that my computer was tainted.' The time had come to confess. 'Suze, you haven't checked your email in a while, have you?'

'No, why?' She could hear her friend getting up. She'd probably be walking over to her desk next. It was now or never.

'I know you said not to send you the infected file. But I was worried about losing my work, my real work. So, ah, I sent a backup of all my major papers and stuff as an attachment. Don't open it till I get my machine checked out.'

'Hang on.' Dulcie could hear the soft click of typing. 'Well, it's in my Inbox. Any damage it was going to do, it's done.' She sighed.

'You're not mad?'

'No, though I do wish you'd warned me. I met a computer geek down here, and he's given me some good anti-virus programs. I'm not too worried.'

'Thanks, Suze. I've been meaning to call Chris. He likes you, you know.' A non-committal grunt could have meant that Suze was powering down her computer. 'One of us should have a social life.'

'Look who's talking. Hey, whatever happened with the cute guy you met at the pity party? The big bruiser – Bruce?'

With a bigger sigh than the moment called for, Dulcie flopped back down on the sofa and gave her old friend the whole story. While they were talking, she heard the beep of a call waiting, but she didn't much care.

'That son of a bitch!' Suze was suitably appalled.

'Well, maybe he didn't realize I'd thought he was flirting.' The thought did salve her ego some.

'Bullshit. I hate him. Him and all his preppie friends.' This from the woman who had urged her to go to Alana's party? Dulcie took the sympathy with a grain of salt.

'I've got to admit, Suze, I don't mind losing Bruce that much. Luke was very comforting yesterday.' Somewhere in her narrative she'd told her friend about her visit to the legal clinic. 'He wasn't stuffy at all.' But, she reminded herself silently, he seemed awfully impressed by Stacia. 'Not that I care.'

The 'call waiting' beep sounded again.

'Another preppie. Hey, maybe *you* should give Chris a call.' Suze sounded a little too happy at the idea. 'Have him look at your hard drive, while you're at it.'

'But he's— Never mind.' Poor guy, thought Dulcie. Why are the nice ones so unsexy? As if to goose her off the phone, 'call waiting' beeped again. Suze must have heard the click on the line. 'Someone's hot to trot with you. Anyway, I should go.'

'Big date?'

'Yeah, right.' She laughed, and Dulcie could picture her piling books into her backpack. 'But, hey, while there's life, there's hope.' With a friendly smooch, she hung up.

Dulcie dialed her voicemail. Maybe it was Luke. He did have to finish cleaning out his brother's room, and besides, she owed him an explanation of how things had turned out with Priority. And hadn't he said he was going to look into how computer viruses worked for her? More likely, she sighed, it was Chris. Reliable Chris, who would be just perfect for Suze.

But the voice on the other end of the line was neither male nor totally lucid. Instead, the three messages all came from Luisa – a panicked, breathless Luisa.

'Dulcie, are you there? Oh, God, I hope you're there. I really do. I hope you get this.' In the last one, Luisa sounded tearful. 'I really need to talk to you. You've been so kind and everything. Oh, Dulcie, I hope you're there. Something's happened, Dulcie. I'm scared!'

Eighteen

A tiny, nasty part of Dulcie wanted to ignore the call and simply curl up with a book until she could go to sleep. It had been a long day, and she'd been on the phone with Suze for over an hour before she heard the other girl's panicked plea. It was late. Besides, Luisa wouldn't know that Dulcie had even gotten her messages. Wasn't Suze always telling her not to be so helpful?

Dulcie got up to brush her teeth. She'd gotten as far as squeezing out toothpaste when her inner voice stopped her. Suze kept on at her to be less trusting, not less helpful. And Dulcie *had* gotten Luisa's messages. Resting the toothbrush on the edge of the sink, she went back to the living room. At least Mr Grey wasn't around to knock her toothbrush on to the floor.

'Luisa? It's Dulcie. I just picked up my voicemail.' Dulcie bit her lip after saying that, but in truth she'd only delayed a few minutes. 'What's wrong?'

'Oh, thank you! Dulcie, it's been horrible. I've been getting calls.' Luisa sounded breathless. Dulcie could picture her red eyes; she'd been crying again. 'The police. And these weird hang-ups. And, well, I think from something he said that maybe Bruce figured out about me and Tim. Not that there was really anything going on—'

'Hold on.' Dulcie didn't know if it was her own fatigue, but something wasn't making sense. 'The cops have been hanging up on you?'

'No, no, they're not the ones hanging up. At least, I don't think so. But they had me come in again and asked me all sorts of questions. Really rude questions about me and Tim – and about me and Bruce, too. When I got out, I was so flustered, I don't know what I said – to them or to Bruce.'

So maybe Bruce was only now finding out that he had a romantic rival. Unless he knew all along, and was good at hiding it. At least the cops were finally considering the jealousy angle. Dulcie thought back to her own interrogation. I wonder what other women they've called in? The breathless young beauty was still talking.

'That's the scary part. I mean, if the police were keeping tabs on me, they'd leave messages, right?'

'Sorry.' Dulcie refocused. 'What did you say?'

'The blank messages.' Luisa sniffed, but Dulcie thought she was also making a point. 'The hang-ups! Someone has been calling me and staying on the line long enough for my voicemail to pick up – and then hanging up.'

'And it's not Bruce, right? Do you have caller ID? You said maybe you said some things to him. Did you have a fight?'

'Not a fight, really. He's just acting odd.' Luisa's voice started winding up. 'And, no, I can't afford anything but basic phone service. And I'm scared!' Dulcie closed her eyes, bracing for another round of tears.

'Maybe you have a secret admirer?' Dulcie meant it as a compliment, anything to lighten the mood. But even as she said it, she realized the calls sounded more like a stalker than a suitor. She thought back to the funeral. Luisa might be young, but she was a bombshell, and several of the men there had noticed the ample curves inside the cheap suit. Tim's friends wouldn't care that Luisa didn't wear couture. In their minds, they'd already stripped her bare. 'Um, do Bruce's friends know that you two are a couple? Maybe one of them likes you?' That was putting it gently.

'No, Bruce wants to be "discreet", he always says.' Her voice perked up as she spoke of her beau. How innocent was this girl? 'Bruce says he wanted you to know that he trusts *you*. But that some of his crowd can be really catty and mean, and because I'm not from the same schools as they are and I don't have the money they have, he wants to protect me from all of that.'

'Hmmm.' Bruce had seemed truly smitten with Luisa at that horrible awkward dinner. But still, he had been a friend of Tim's. It would be easy to act loving toward a little hottie like Luisa and still keep his options open while he browsed for a more socially acceptable mate. 'And how do you feel about being kept a secret?'

Luisa sighed. 'Oh, it was fine at first. I mean, I was tutoring Tim and he referred me to Bruce. I didn't know if it would be professional to date one of my students.' Especially if you had your eye on your other student, Dulcie thought. 'But now it just seems silly. I need to finish school, but I want to get married some day and I don't want to be too old to have kids. I mean, you want to have children while you're still young enough to enjoy them, don't you?'

Dulcie rolled her eyes and grunted something she hoped sounded non-committal. Her best theory was falling apart. On the one hand, perhaps Bruce was jealous, and he'd been a fool for keeping his relationship with Luisa hidden. In which case, maybe now he did suspect something of Luisa's relationship with Tim – but he couldn't have known before, and there went his motive for murder. On the other hand, perhaps he didn't care at all, and no jealousy meant no motive. And if Luisa was that worried about losing Bruce, why had she been stepping out with Tim? Maybe neither of them cared, and this was simply the best either could do right now.

No matter which way you sliced it, Luisa hardly sounded panicked enough to justify her calls. And it was too late at night for relationship – or reality – counseling. 'And how can I help with all of this?' She heard the sarcasm creeping into her own voice. 'I'm sorry, I don't mean to be rude, but it's late and I've got work tomorrow. You sounded really scared when you called, so that's why I called you back right away.' The line was silent. 'Is it the calls and hang-ups? Because if you are really worried about them, you can tell the phone company—'

A loud sniff interrupted her. 'If Bruce leaves me, I don't know what I'll do!'

'Luisa, hang on a minute.' Dulcie needed a reality check, even if Luisa didn't. 'Let's back up here. What was really going on with you and Tim? I mean, if you just went out for a few meals, then Bruce doesn't have any reason to be jealous, does he?' She thought of the mascara. A few meals, indeed.

'Well, maybe it was more than that. I mean, maybe it was just in my head.' Dulcie waited. Luisa wasn't going to spill on her own.

'You were sleeping with Tim, weren't you? When you were over here, supposedly tutoring him in statistics, there was more going on, wasn't there?' Silence. 'Luisa, I found your mascara in the bathroom.'

'My what?' As a stalling technique, ignorance was annoying.

'Your mascara. You know, the stuff you put on your lashes to make them darker.'

'I don't wear mascara, Dulcie. I use a little shadow and some concealer sometimes. But my lashes are really dark on their own. I mean, they're almost as thick as my eyebrows, and if I don't pluck them, watch out.'

'Well, never mind the mascara.' Dulcie thought for a moment; the image of someone pulling out eyelashes was pretty disconcerting. 'But you were more involved with Tim than you've said, right?'

More silence. Even the sniffling had stopped. 'Luisa, you want my help, don't you?'

'Uh-huh.' The soft syllables were followed by a hiccup and a small whine. The girl could cry at will. 'But it wasn't like that.'

This was like pulling teeth, Dulcie thought. In *The Ravages*, both women were always launching into long speeches to explain themselves. When did young women grow so silent? Was Luisa so deluded she imagined herself in love? 'Luisa, I don't know how to break it to you, but Tim wasn't always the most considerate person. Is it possible that he hinted something to Bruce? Maybe something he said accidentally that only now is sinking in?' How could she tell this girl that Tim bragged about conquests real and imagined?

'No, I don't think so. I mean, last week everything was *fine* with Bruce.'

The sniffling was starting up in earnest. 'And now, I don't know what to do. The police are being really rude. And these phone calls are creeping me out. And if Bruce— If Bruce—' Loud sobs cut her off.

'Breathe, Luisa.' Dulcie heard a discreet snort over the line. Luisa could even blow her nose in a cute way. 'Look, I can help you with some of this. Do you know about the legal clinic over at Harvard Law?' She gave the younger woman directions. 'Now, officially, they're not supposed to get involved in criminal cases, but ask for Luke. He's Tim's brother, and he's a really nice guy. Maybe he can help you.' As she said the words, Dulcie felt a pang. Here she was, sending a raven-haired looker off to see Luke. What the hell, he was already in thrall to Stacia anyway. He'd probably consider Luisa fat. 'Tell him that I recommended you speak to him. You can tell him everything.' Luke already knew about his kid brother's habits.

'Tim's *brother*?' Amazing what registered.

'Yes, but he's a law student.' And I think he's already taken. Dulcie bit back the words. 'You should also tell him about the strange phone calls. He can probably put you on the right path to having those traced.'

'Well, maybe for the legal advice.' Why was she hesitating? Whatever it was, it soon passed. 'Thanks, Dulcie. I knew you'd be able to help me. You're so smart!'

Dulcie smiled. The faithful attendant. 'We have all got to have something going for us, right? And maybe the phone calls don't mean anything.'

'Maybe.' Luisa sounded calmer. 'I just hope they're not from Bruce.'

'Me, too,' said Dulcie, signing off. At this point, she'd rather think of him as a callow cad than a heartbroken nice guy, stuck with this ditz; or, for that matter, as a killer.

Could Bruce have been faking it? Dulcie climbed back up the stairs, trying to remember every word and gesture from that awful dinner. Had he really been smitten with Luisa, or had it all been an act? Maybe he'd arranged for the three of them to meet so he could show off his 'devotion', when he had really known about Tim all along – and stabbed his rival to death in Dulcie's apartment. Dulcie shuddered and clutched her frayed bathrobe closer. Fighting an urge to run down and double check the doors, she made her way to the bathroom.

'I locked the door. I always lock the door,' she said to her own reflection above the sink. Then she looked down. Her toothbrush was on the floor.

'What are you trying to say to me, Mr Grey?' Dulcie stared at the upended toothbrush for a moment before picking it up. 'Are you trying to warn me about Luisa? I really think she's more innocent than dangerous. But I'll be careful.' She washed off the brush. The smear of toothpaste on the bath mat was going to be a little harder to get out. 'Or was this just some paranormal prank, letting me know you're still my cat?' She held the sticky part of the mat under the faucet and left it hanging over the edge of the tub to dry.

'Is it something else?' Pulling her robe belt tight for courage, Dulcie went back downstairs, turning on every light as she checked the door and windows. 'Not that anyone would want to climb up the fire escape,' she muttered. This was getting silly. Maybe the brush hadn't even been a sign of her dear departed cat. Maybe it had simply fallen, dislodged by her heavy tread on the stairs or . . . well, by something. Dulcie couldn't think of a good reason for a toothbrush to go flying. But if she really put her mind to it, she couldn't think of a good reason for the ghost of her pet to come to her either. When was the last time she had 'seen' Mr Grey anyway? Had those earlier apparitions been the result of shock, some kind of temporary derangement caused by finding her room-mate dead and bloody on the living room floor?

As disgusting as the memory was, she chuckled. Of course, that was it. She'd taken enough psych courses – and she'd read enough ghost stories to provide the basics. Her overstimulated mind had done the rest. Speaking of rest . . . turning out the living room light one more time, she headed toward the stairs, just in time to hear the phone ring.

'At this hour?' She turned toward the phone. 'If it's Luisa again, I'm going to give her a piece of my mind.' Dulcie lifted the receiver.

'Hello? *Hello*?' She heard breathing and waited for a voice. Then a click – and nothing more.

Nineteen

Sleep should have been impossible. But either fatigue got the better of her, or the sense that the spirit of Mr Grey was still hanging around the apartment eventually lulled Dulcie into a deep and dreamless slumber. Much to her surprise, she woke refreshed, even before the alarm clock had a chance to break into its annoying buzz.

One cup of coffee later, she realized she had time for a phone call.

'Luke? Hi, it's Dulcie. Dulcie Schwartz.' It wasn't that she was feeling possessive, Dulcie told herself. If she were, she'd be stalking Stacia. 'I thought I should let you know what happened with Priority.'

'Dulcie! Great to hear from you, whatever the reason. What's happening? You ready to sue?' He yawned, and Dulcie looked at the clock. Not even eight. She should've waited and called him at the clinic.

'Nope. I didn't even need to threaten them.' She told him what had happened the day before, and he sounded honestly pleased. Of course, he had called it: Priority had no legal right either to fire her or detain her. 'So, well, I hope you didn't feel like I wasted your time.'

'Not at all.' From the sound of water running in the background, Dulcie assumed he was either making coffee or running a bath. To keep herself from thinking of him nude, she carried on talking.

'And I haven't heard anything from the Cambridge police. I mean, they haven't called me in for questioning again. So that's got to be good, doesn't it?' She paused for air and the implications of what she'd said hit her. 'I mean, I really hope they find whoever did it.'

'Yeah.' She heard a sigh. 'I don't know if they ever will. We haven't heard anything.' Another pause. Maybe she'd gone too far. But, no, it wasn't her. 'I haven't, I mean. I'm the only one pursuing it. My folks are acting like it was just an unpleasant accident that they'd rather forget. Makes me wonder if they are capable of loving anyone.'

'I'm sure if anything happened to you—' Dulcie didn't like defending the Worthingtons, but she wanted to offer comfort to the man on the phone.

'Yeah, they'd care. But that's just because I'm the "good" son; the one they can trust to carry on the family name.' There wasn't any response to that, but Luke didn't seem to expect one. 'Which reminds me; I should really come by and finish cleaning out Tim's room. It's not fair for you to be left with his junk.'

'That's all right, really. It's not like I'm going to sublet it again for just a month.' A thought struck her. 'But, Luke, if you're going to come by, would you remember to bring Tim's laptop?'

'Sure. You still thinking my baby bro gave you some kind of virus?'

'I don't know.' She thought about Tim being inside her personal space and shuddered. 'There's something funky going on with my laptop. I was making some notes for my thesis the other night and, well, something weird happened.' Dulcie felt oddly reticent about telling Luke about Mr Grey. Maybe he'd think she was too girlish or sentimental. 'Anyway, I'm pretty sure Tim was using it.'

'Sounds like Tim, I'm afraid. Have you talked to Stacia yet?'

Maybe they hadn't been spending much time together. 'No, I have another friend who understands operating systems. I thought it would help if we could trace the bug.'

'Makes sense to me. I'll bring it over. How about tonight?'

'Sure, I get home around six.'

'And may I take you to dinner after?'

A glow that could not be entirely attributable to hot coffee rose up to Dulcie's cheeks. 'I think that might be possible.' Good thing he couldn't see her turning pink.

'Great! And then maybe you and Stacia can slug it out.'

He meant about the computer, she knew that. But the coffee chose just that moment to go down her windpipe and kept her from answering for nearly a minute. By the time she'd recovered her breath, she realized it was time to get ready for work. If she left now, she could pick up an iced latte to make up for what she'd just spat out.

'Now that I have a job again, it doesn't make sense to lose it.'

'See you tonight then.'

She shouldn't be so hard on Stacia, Dulcie knew that – and kept repeating it to herself as she joined the throng of commuters on the Red Line. The woman was only doing the same thing she herself was, she said as she walked up to Priority's revolving glass doors. Trying to get ahead, finish her education, and maybe meet a nice guy. By rights, they should be friends.

'Miss Schwartz?' She'd been so distracted as she opened her bag for the guard that she hadn't even noticed when he finished poking through it. 'Miss Schwartz?' She absently started to hand him her extra-large latte. 'No, Miss Schwartz. Keep your coffee. I have a message here for you.'

She withdrew the proffered cup and looked up.

'You're to report to security before heading up to your workspace.'

'Security?' Dulcie felt her stomach clench up. Suddenly the extra caffeine seemed like a very bad idea. 'Again?' But they'd just cleared her!

'It's the office over to the right.' She could see the door. There was still time to bolt.

'Hi, I'm Dulcie Schwartz.' She hated the way her voice squeaked, but at least the guard seated in the tiny office wasn't one of the two gorillas who had marched her out of her cubicle on Monday. Instead, a tired-looking older man glanced up.

'Oh, yeah, Schwartz. Hang on. You've been reassigned or something. I'm supposed to call when you come in.'

Great. Dulcie leaned back against the wall. Bolting was growing more attractive by the minute. But just when she was ready to slide out of the door, it was blocked by the smaller of the two gorillas.

'Miss Schwartz?' He looked up from a sheet of paper. 'Sorry to inconvenience you. We're relocating your workstation. Would you come with me, please?'

Dulcie started breathing again and followed the large man to the elevators. 'What's going on? Did you find out who was using my computer?'

'From all they've told me,' he looked over at her with what almost seemed like a smile, 'this could be routine maintenance.'

He pressed the elevator for the fourteenth floor. It was not yet ten minutes after nine and they had the car to themselves. 'Did you leave any personal items at your former workspace?'

Dulcie thought of her sweater, now long gone. 'No.'

'OK, then. Follow me, please.' As they exited the elevator, Dulcie looked over toward what she thought of as 'her' cubicle. The walls obscured the computer itself, but nobody was standing near it. Maybe the terminal had already been removed for dissection.

'Miss Schwartz?' Her escort was waiting, already a few steps ahead, and he led her down a long passageway that she'd never noticed. Suddenly, all was light. They were in the front of the building, where actual windows let in actual sunlight. Maybe this wouldn't be so bad after all!

'Ah, work area eleven.' Her escort consulted the paper again, and led her through a maze of grey-carpeted cubicles into an open area. A large round enclosure held six older women, all wearing headsets.

'Priority Insurance, can I help you? Priority, please hold . . .' She was standing by the message center. 'Priority Insurance, can I help you?'

'Here it is.' The large man led her around the circular phone bank and over to a desktop. On it, a computer that looked identical to her old one was lit up with the Priority logo screensaver. On her right, a taller, more solid wall divided the open space. On her left was the call center.

'Where's Joanie sitting?' Behind her was only open space, leading back to those windows. She could see no other cubicles like hers.

'I'm sorry.' He didn't even bother looking at the paper in his hand. 'I don't have any information about other employees.'

'But we worked together—' He started to walk away.

'Please hold, can I help you?'

'It's *may*.' She hadn't meant to say anything. The words had just slipped out, but suddenly the escort stepped closer again.

'Are we going to have some kind of problem here?' He was very tall.

'No, no problem. It's just – the way they're answering the phones—'

'I'm sure you'll get used to it.' She could see that he'd already written off this particular chore as done. 'So, from now on, your computer logon will only work at this station.'

He walked off and Dulcie slumped into her new seat. Even that wasn't as comfortable as her former chair, and she spent the next fifteen minutes trying to ratchet up the base so that she faced the terminal and wasn't straining her neck.

'Who sat here before me? An elf?'

'Priority Insurance, can I help you?'

Not even ten a.m., and she was missing Joanie. The day had not gotten off to an auspicious start.

This wasn't about space. She and Joanie had both commented on the empty cubicles around the other side of the building. This was personal. By noon, Dulcie realized that she was in temp Siberia. They might have said they didn't suspect her, but putting her out here was hardly a sign of trust. Did they want her to quit? Maybe save themselves the legal complications of firing her? Or did they have another reason for isolating her in this noisy corner of the building?

By twelve thirty, when she usually took her lunch break, Dulcie had decided to investigate. With a smile to the message center ladies ('Can I help you?'), Dulcie shrugged her bag on to her shoulder and slowly walked around their large, circular station. If anyone asked, she was simply looking for the ladies' room. She had a right to pee before taking her lunch break, didn't she? She wasn't a prisoner. Yet.

It was only when she arrived at the open area in front of the elevator banks that she realized she didn't have a plan. What was she looking for, anyway? Maybe Joanie would show up and they could confab. Two men in suits walked up and she smiled at them. One fixed her with a dead-eyed stare and looked away. The other didn't even acknowledge her. One elevator opened, going down, and Dulcie watched them step in. The dead-eyed man turned to her. Smile still plastered to her face, she nodded, trying to convey the idea that she was waiting for the up elevator. Three more suits came up next, and this time Dulcie got some glances. She was a car wreck they were passing on the highway, a corporate casualty. She didn't bother to smile back as she watched them get into the next elevator.

She couldn't continue to stand there, waiting for a friend who never came. That was clear. But – wait – what was that? As Dulcie was trying to peer down the short hallway, back toward where she used to sit with Joanie, she was sure she saw something moving, something low to the ground. Could it be? A fluffy tail bent itself back around the cubicle, its grey fur standing out against the dirty carpet. *Dulcie, there's something you should see.*

Not sure at first if she had actually heard the voice, so low and yet so reassuring, she stepped toward the tail. It disappeared around the corner and, with a discreet glance, she followed, hurrying to catch up. There! Up ahead was the plume-like tail, on top of those bouncing white jodhpurs. *Now, Dulcie, this is for your eyes only . . . be careful.* She had heard the voice! She had! But she'd also heard what it – he – had said, and so she ducked down slightly to keep her head below the level of the carpeted dividers as she turned the last corner, toward the warren of cubicles she'd occupied since the middle of June.

The big, maze-like space was quiet. Maybe Priority really was renovating the area? Taking courage from the silence, Dulcie looked around. Mr Grey was nowhere to be seen, but she knew where she was now and she walked up to what had been her area. She could hear typing, the quiet tap-tap-tap of fingers on a computer keyboard. The area hadn't been completely vacated then. So why had they moved her? Water damage? Or – she thought of the phantom feline again – a rodent problem?

She shuddered and moved on until she heard a voice, vaguely familiar. Dulcie was about to call out when she realized she didn't have any rationale for being here. Could she say she was looking for something? Her lost sweater, perhaps?

Armed with that idea, she walked forward. The voices were definitely coming from her former workspace. She held her breath, trying to eavesdrop. This must have been what Mr Grey wanted her to see, right? Did listening count? People tended to forget that the cubicles had no ceilings or doors – and that sound carried. But whoever was talking kept his – or her – voice low, and that made Dulcie's curiosity stronger. Were some Priority minions searching for clues – or, worse, for some trace that would link Dulcie with the virus? She was only a temp!

With a gulp, Dulcie realized how perfect she could seem for this crime. She was an impoverished graduate student, someone with 'higher goals' than a mere corporate job. Someone who was new to Priority, who had arrived right before the problems started – and then disappeared for several days. She'd told them about Tim, about finding his body. But had anyone checked to confirm her reasons for absence? Maybe that would just make her more of a suspect. Maybe they'd wonder if she'd gotten him killed, through drugs or gambling or some other massive debt-related crime.

Dulcie's head was beginning to hurt. The morning's constant noise had taken its toll. The powers that were Priority couldn't know that she was fundamentally honest, a scholar with a sense of honor. They couldn't know that she was used to being poor, that all she really needed was library access and enough to pay the rent. No wonder they were investigating her. Didn't she have a friend anywhere in this cold, corporate world? She closed her eyes and leaned on the grey carpet of a cubicle, shaking the thin wall.

Not ten feet down, a jet-black head of hair popped up and turned. Kohl-rimmed eyes blinked.

'Joanie! I'm so glad to see you!' Dulcie was almost shouting. But before her Goth friend could respond, another face appeared over the grey carpet. Tanned and sleek, Sally Putnam stared back, her basilisk glare fixing Dulcie to the spot.

'Miss Schwartz, I trust you have a reason for entering a work area from which you've been expressly forbidden?' Her dark eyes looked flat and hard. Dulcie felt they could see right through her.

'I . . . I thought maybe my sweater had turned up.' God, that sounded lame, but it was the best she could do under that gaze. The reptilian eyes blinked slowly, her excuse was processed and rejected.

'Your *sweater*?' The recollection of their last conversation must have surfaced, because those snake eyes narrowed. 'You are not going to continue in that ridiculous accusation, I trust. But I must say, it is a convenient excuse for you, allowing you to cast aspersions and to snoop. I'm beginning to wonder if this sweater ever existed.'

The complete effrontery of the words sparked something in Dulcie. 'Well, maybe you didn't take it. But I liked that sweater.' Her courage grew, and the words began to tumble out. 'Joanie, you saw it, too. Right?'

Joanie stared back, mouth open. She was shaking her head slightly.

'My mother knitted it for me, and it did go missing while I was away from my desk and I was hoping—'

'You should be hoping you still have a job here, young lady.' The HR boss was positively hissing now. 'And you should be extremely grateful that we haven't pressed charges. Not that that course of action isn't still under discussion.'

Dulcie stepped back, her train of thought – and her courage – interrupted.

Was this why they had brought her back to work? To keep an eye on her? And why wasn't Joanie saying anything?

'Now, if you know what's good for you, you'll go back to your workspace. Your *proper* workspace. We aren't paying you to snoop, you know.'

Dulcie couldn't think of another rebuttal. The reality of her position here – that they were keeping her, under glass, while they decided what to do – had driven all other thoughts from her mind. She stepped back. Sally Putnam kept staring. And so Dulcie turned and walked swiftly past the elevators, down the long hall, around the message center, and back to her new desk. The encounter had robbed her of any desire for lunch. But as she sat there, staring at the cursor blinking on her screen, waiting for her heart rate to still, another thought came to mind. Mr Grey had told her there was something she had to see. She'd seen her friend, Joanie. She'd asked Joanie for help; Joanie, who had nicknamed Sally Putnam 'the Snake' in the first place. And Joanie had said nothing.

'I can't believe I didn't turn her in,' Dulcie was muttering to herself back at her new desk. The message center was so loud, nobody would hear her anyway. 'I could have told them that *she* had access to my machine.'

The forms were beginning to blur: George Esposito, claimant code 278; George Espossita, claimant code 366. She slammed one form on top of the other and reached for a third. The pile might not have grown during her brief absence, but at this point Dulcie wasn't putting anything past Priority. 'I could have told them that *she* was there sometimes when I wasn't. And she's had that job longer than I did.'

Dulcie stopped typing. Maybe that was it. Here she was, blaming Joanie for some kind of treachery, when maybe she was simply next on the list to be investigated. Why else would Sally Putnam have been down by her old workstation, anyway? The grey maze of cubicles was hardly upper management territory. Kicking herself for jumping to conclusions, she reached for another form. Quiroga, Michael, claimant code 887. Were these forms in any kind of order? Almost without thinking, she looked over at the code key: 887, accident in home. A wave of nausea hit her. Tim. Just when she felt she'd gotten over it – over that awful, awful day – it would come back. She remembered how tired she had felt that day, how hot and depressed. And how the sweat on her back had gone cold when she realized what she was seeing: the hand, the spreading puddle. The horror of it all. She opened her eyes and realized she had crumpled the form in her hand.

What had gotten her through that? Had it been the grey cat, appearing first on her doorstep and then, mysteriously, inside her kitchen? And now she was seeing him, hearing him even, in this corporate hell-hole. Had she in fact been seeing visions, seeing the ghost of her beloved pet? Or had the pressure finally pushed her around the bend? Dulcie found herself thinking about Lucy's 'visions', her mother's so-called psychic moments. For too long now Dulcie had dismissed them as New Age puffery, a lonely middle-aged woman's solace. But was there something else at work here, and was it hereditary?

She smoothed out the form and began to type. She wouldn't find the answers here at Priority. And if there was something unbalanced in her supposed visions, maybe it was passing. She hadn't had a detailed vision just now: she'd only seen a tail. And, well, she had heard a voice. But her ears had been almost ringing with all the noise of the day. It could have been her imagination. Just like the toothbrush. Dulcie sighed. The evidence was mounting. She was developing a mental illness – or she had a spectral pet. Finishing Mr Quiroga's claim, she began on that of a Ms Levinson; a nice normal code 333. Industrial. Maybe before Luke came over tonight, she'd call her mom and try to make some sense of all of this. Maybe they were both just lonely ladies in need of a chat.

But four hours later, she was in no mood to call Lucy. The constant noise and the lack of lunch had given her a throbbing headache. She needed aspirin, a drink, and a good friend. As she queued for the elevators – there was always a crowd at five o'clock – Dulcie looked around for Joanie. Her earlier suspicions now seemed foolish. She would drag the black-clad girl over to Foley's, get the dirt, and still be home in time to meet Luke. But even though she waited for two elevator cars to go past, her eyes strained on the far corridor, the Goth girl never appeared.

'Maybe they've taken her in for questioning.' Dulcie said, without realizing she was talking out loud.

'Excuse me?' She jumped. Next to her, a queen-sized older woman in tiger-striped polyester was staring. 'You said something?'

'Sorry. I've been sitting at a terminal too long.' She tried a smile. 'Talking to myself.'

Tiger-stripes pushed ahead, her wide hips herding Dulcie into the elevator. 'You're the new girl. The one they have seated by the message center.' She said it as a statement of fact, not a question, but Dulcie nodded.

'Yeah. They moved me from the cubicles. Might be for repairs or something.'

Overplucked eyebrows rose up. 'Could be,' she said, her doubt clear, and Dulcie recognized her as one of the phone operators.

'Why, can you tell me anything? Would you tell me what you've heard?' But the elevator had reached the ground floor, and the fat woman had pushed through, leaving Dulcie in her wake. Dulcie stepped into the lobby and looked around. Still no sign of Joanie. Should she head to Foley's? No, she decided. The sky outside looked too threatening to make a walk anywhere feel like fun. Besides, she really needed to talk to someone with some sense. Suze, maybe, if she wasn't tucked away in the library.

Dulcie reached for her phone just as it began to ring.

'Bag, please?' She opened her bag for the guard, retrieved the phone and flipped it open.

'You're all clear.' The noise in the lobby and the guard's voice obscured the line on the other end. Beyond the glass doors, Dulcie saw pedestrians scurry as the clouds opened up.

'Excuse me? I didn't hear you.' Dulcie stepped toward the revolving doors to look at the downpour. Two burly guards, new since that morning, stood on either side, ignoring the soaked pedestrians coming in.

'Dulcie, this is Helene. I found your number. I thought you'd want to know.' Dulcie looked around the lobby. What could be so important that her neighbor would call her twenty minutes before she'd be home? 'The police have been all up and down the block, Dulcie. They talked to Bob next door and he came over right before they rang my bell. I didn't answer, but I thought you should know. They're talking to everyone – and they're asking about you.'

Twenty

Never mind the downpour. Dulcie ran through the rain, desperate to get home and – what? Confront the police? Find out what her neighbors were saying about her?

At least Helene had called, though if her neighbor's intention was to warn her to stay away, it had the opposite effect. Dulcie was sick of being acted upon. As she descended into the T, she realized she wanted to do something, *anything*.

By the time she surfaced at Central Square, the two uniforms were long gone, of course. But at least the rain had ended, and Dulcie was able to fold up her umbrella before knocking on Helene's door.

'They were asking about visitors, friends.' Helene handed Dulcie a towel. Even with the umbrella, she'd gotten soaked. 'Boyfriends – you know.'

'Great.' Dulcie rubbed her hair down, hiding her embarrassment in the fluffy terry. 'Like I have any boyfriends.'

'Well, that's the problem.'

Dulcie looked up. Helene wasn't smiling. 'My stupid ex, Duane? He's been hanging around. I think he's seeing that slut, Marcella. Anyway, Bob says he saw Duane actually run after the cops – and this is when it was raining. They ducked into a doorway, and Bob says Duane talked to them for, like, five minutes. He kept pointing to your door, too.'

'Why would he do that? What does he even have to say about me?'

'I don't know. Men. He's a loser.' Helene made a face and then a decision. 'Truth is, he knew you never liked him. He used to say you were a man-hater; that you were trying to break us up. He even said you planted cat hair in my place so he couldn't stay over, what with his asthma and his allergies and all.'

Dulcie hid her face in the towel and closed her eyes. 'That's crazy.'

'I know, and I figure the cops have enough sense to suss that out. I just thought you should know, too.'

It was all too depressing for words. But just as she was about to hand the towel back, Dulcie felt a familiar warm pressure on her ankle. She looked down to see a small, orange-coloured back. 'Helene? You got a cat?' In her present state, Dulcie wasn't quite sure she was seeing a real feline.

'Yeah, this is Julius. Get it?' She lifted the kitten with a smile, revealing a fluffy white belly. 'I went to the shelter last night, picked out this little fellow and his brother, Murray. Cute, huh?'

'Adorable.' Dulcie reached out to take the kitten, which began kneading in satisfaction. 'By any chance, the brother isn't grey, is he?'

'You're still thinking of your old kitty, aren't you?' Helene smiled. 'No, sorry. He's orange, too, all over, with the cutest pink nose. But striped more, like a tiger.'

Makes sense, thought Dulcie, holding the kitten up to her neck. If this little fellow was so young, and had such a neat, short coat, what were the odds he had a long-haired, full-grown sibling? 'Well, I'm thrilled for you.'

'Thanks. Better two good cats than one bad man. Which reminds me, have you given any thought to getting a new cat in your life? There are a lot of great animals down at the shelter.'

'I know,' said Dulcie, enjoying the warmth of the kitten. 'I'm just not ready yet.' Up close to her face, she could feel the soft vibration as the kitten began to purr.

The brief feline interlude was wonderful, but Dulcie had a visitor coming over. Once back in her own place, the full weight of Helene's words hit her. Kicking off her sodden shoes, she hit 'play' on her answering machine and heard two more call-and-hang-ups. Great. She just managed to dial Suze's number before collapsing on the sofa. The heat was still suffocating, sapping the energy from everything except her out-of-control curls. The rain had failed to break the hold the humidity had on the city. Drained by the subtropical conditions, Dulcie peeled off her pantyhose and propped her bare feet up on the back of the sofa to air dry. What was happening to her life?

'OK, it's not so bad.' She knew she was talking out loud. At this point, she didn't care. 'I mean, maybe the no-messages are just wrong numbers, right? And if the cops really thought I was a suspect, they'd pick me up, right?' There was no answer, and even when she wiggled her toes, she could feel no soft fur, no batting of leather paw pads. Well, maybe the visions of Mr Grey had been just that: flights of fancy when life had gotten too hard to bear. Considering how much time she spent reading about ghosts and beleaguered maidens, it made sense, right? At least she was sane. Nor, despite the silence in her apartment, was she completely alone and friendless. She'd left a semi-frantic message for Suze. And, she remembered, Luke was due any minute. Well, if Suze didn't call back in time, she could always pick his brain for legal advice.

If only he didn't seem sweet on Stacia . . . Dulcie closed her eyes. She might as well wish for the moon; or that she'd never agreed to sublet to Tim; or that she had listened when that eerie voice had told her not to go inside. Dulcie pulled the sofa cushion over her face. She couldn't go there. She couldn't. And, holding on to that resolve, she fell asleep.

She was in such a deep sleep that the doorbell made her jump. On her feet before she thought about it, Dulcie also realized that she was still wearing her drab office dress – and she hadn't so much as washed her face. Well, there was nothing she could do now.

'Hi, Luke. Sorry about this.' She gestured to her hair, sure that it had taken on a life of its own, and probably of an asymmetrical, lopsided kind. 'Got home from work and fell asleep.'

'It's the weather. Not fit for man or beast.' He handed her an empty box and grabbed two others off the stoop. 'But you look fine. We're still on for dinner, right?'

Dulcie smiled, and immediately worried about her breath. 'Thanks, yeah. Uh, do you mind if I wash up while you start?'

'No problem. No reason you should have to deal with Tim's crap, anyway.'

Dulcie led the way up to the top floor and left the box by the closed bedroom door. She could hear him muttering as she splashed cold water on her face, trying to wake up, and found herself staring into the mirror. She was too pale, too . . . Dulcie. But after a moment's hesitation, she rejected the strange mascara. Luke had just seen her without it. If he noticed her wearing some, it would seem too obvious. Instead, she ducked into her own bedroom to change, looking back to see him emptying out the bottom drawer of the old dresser Suze had cleared for her temporary replacement.

'You OK in here?' She peeked around the half-opened door a few minutes later. Although Luke had already taken a carload of stuff, Tim's possessions seemed to have multiplied.

'Yeah, I think I'll take these sweaters directly to the dry cleaner.' He was folding a baby-blue cashmere. 'We'll probably end up donating them anyway.'

Someone will get lucky, thought Dulcie, as she watched Luke pile two identical pullovers – one a soft lemon yellow, the other pale cream – on the first. 'I didn't realize he had so much stuff.'

'That's the Worthingtons. Rich in stuff,' said Luke, bending over for one more sweater. 'At least, clothes. I think Mother had all of Tim's measurements on file at the Andover Shop. She still sends me sweaters occasionally.'

'That's sweet.' Dulcie leaned back against the desk, to be out of his way.

Luke snorted. 'It's all image. *Her* boys wore Pendleton. Besides, she likes to shop. Hey, while you're sitting there . . .' He handed her the remaining empty box. 'Would you look through the desk? I think I grabbed most of his papers last time. But if you see anything there that you think might be his, would you throw it in here?'

'Sure.' She started leafing through the papers on the desk's surface. Suze was not much neater than she was, but she had tried to tidy everything away before she left for the summer. Odds were that anything out here was Tim's. 'These look like course papers.' She found a stack of Xeroxed notes on statistics. Some kind of study guide from Luisa probably.

'Throw 'em in. Who knows? Maybe someone else can use them.'

'Maybe.' Leafing through the notes, Dulcie had the distinct impression that they'd not been touched. Perhaps, she acknowledged, that was just because she couldn't remember Tim ever studying. But then she came across two pages stuck together, as if they'd gone through the printer together. The type that started on one ended on the other. Nobody had even bothered to pull them apart. At least Luisa had been trying to tutor him. Maybe he would have come to care for her. Maybe he had.

Dulcie pulled open the top desk drawer. Suze had made a point of emptying it out completely, not that Tim had much use for a workspace – or for pens and pencils for that matter. She pulled a bunch of loose papers out and reached back into the drawer. All she could find was a box of matches. She thought then of the huge diamond and sapphire ring that Stacia had found up here.

'Luke, do you know about that ring, the one Tim supposedly bought for Alana?'

'How could I help it?' He didn't look up. 'Alana was shoving it under everyone's face at that party of hers.'

'Don't you think it's funny that we didn't find it? I mean, when we were turning this place upside down?' She emptied out the top right-hand drawer. More matches, a package of condoms, and some pens. Including, she noted, one of her favorites: a refillable fountain pen that she'd been missing since July.

He shrugged. 'We weren't looking for it. Neither of us were; we were looking for a plastic bag of weed or a hidden compartment in the floor or the closet.'

'But still, that's a pretty big find.'

He shrugged again, and she was reminded: money meant less to his family than to hers, because they had so much more of it. 'If I'd seen a velvet box, I might have assumed it was his cufflinks or his tuxedo studs.'

The image of Tim in a tuxedo startled Dulcie enough so that she let out a questioning noise. 'Huh?'

'Yup, Tim in a tux. Hard to believe, I know. But that's how we were raised.'

She tried to picture her former room-mate formally dressed. She'd seen his suits – three, all custom tailored – when the funeral home representative had come by to pick them up. But even those had seemed foreign. And a tuxedo? All that came to mind was Luke. She could see him in a shawl-collared tux, looking a bit like James Bond, ready to go to some wonderful event . . .

'Did that bother you?' Dulcie's voice had gone quiet and, for a moment, she thought Luke hadn't heard her. 'I mean, the party? That Alana would have people over so soon after?'

'Yeah,' he said finally. 'But I wasn't surprised. I'd met her last Christmas and, in a way, they were the perfect couple. She didn't seem like the most warm or caring woman, to put it mildly. In fact, I doubt Tim was ever real to Alana. He was a prize. Someone who would propel her to the next stage of life.' He looked up at Dulcie. 'But Tim wasn't any better. I mean, to him Alana was just a blonde – the blonde of the moment. She came from the right background and the right family, so maybe he was planning on marrying her. But that never stopped him from having a brunette on the side. Or a redhead, for that matter.' He looked at her and Dulcie was horrified to realize that she was blushing. Luke either didn't notice or was too polite to comment. 'Even if he had married her, it probably wouldn't have stopped him from chasing after any other woman who caught his eye.' He turned back to his boxes. 'I don't think I ever heard him say he loved her.'

She returned to shuffling papers. Anything to keep busy. 'I didn't know you two talked that much.' Truth was, she had barely been aware that her room-mate had a brother.

'I didn't.' He looked down. 'And I'm sorry that I didn't. Maybe I'd have made a difference. I mean, it's not like Tim learned any different at home.' Folding the last of the sweaters, he avoided Dulcie's eyes. 'My folks were never what you would call nurturing. They didn't really care what we got up to, as long as it didn't embarrass them. We were the classic "heir and a spare". And, well, if we were just status symbols to them, where was Tim going to learn to treat people any differently?'

'But you're not like that!' The words burst out of her. 'I mean, you were just in Asia helping out and now you're doing the legal clinic and everything.' He kept packing. 'And, well, you obviously loved Tim.'

He did meet her eyes then, with a wry smile. 'Maybe that's what saved me. I'm the big brother. I was the one who was there when he fell off his bike. I was the one he ran to when he got picked on. He was a chubby kid, did you know that?' Luke grabbed another box. 'Anyway, for a while there, he would come to me. I liked it, I guess. I liked being responsible, having that connection with somebody.'

Dulcie looked at him, unsure how to ask the obvious next question. 'So, did you two . . . drift?'

'Did we have a falling out, you mean? Not in so many words. I mean, I was still bailing him out when he was prepping. That's how I know about his little side business. But then I went off to "find myself", and he hit his growth spurt, slimmed down, and discovered he could be the big man on campus. I don't know, I think maybe I still saw him as a screwed-up little fat kid, and he could tell that I saw him that way. He didn't want much to do with me the last few years. Spent more time with his school buddies, and pretty soon he'd got an in at finals clubs and eating clubs at every college on the East Coast.' Luke shrugged. 'Maybe I could have tried harder, but he seemed to be doing OK for himself. I mean, until I got the call from the folks that he was flunking out, I thought he had found his level.'

They were quiet then, as Luke continued to fold clothes and Dulcie worked the papers into one big pile. One page stuck out, and she pulled it out for a look. It was better quality paper, more like stationery than printer paper. No wonder it didn't slide neatly in with the others. 'You don't think his tutor would want these back, do you?'

He took a step closer and looked over her shoulder. 'What is that, some kind of computer code?'

'I think it's statistics.' The page Dulcie was holding didn't have much type on it, just a couple of lines of nonsense, maybe shorthand or instant messaging. Maybe it was a tip sheet. 'This looks like it was a first-generation printout, not a copy. Could be his tutor's original.'

'Whatever it is, it's not statistics. I had to take that, too, didn't you?' Dulcie shrugged and shook her head. She had a vague memory of tables and percentages. But any mathematics she'd once known had long ago been pushed out of her mind by author biographies, varieties of typefaces, and the ever-present search for a thesis topic. She looked down at the odd lines, wondering if maybe something there would ring a bell.

```
//use the new Jcode @SmileyMe.frame.pack.
Hellowlow.code =.frame
```

None of it made sense to her. She looked up at Luke. 'Maybe it's gibberish?'

'Maybe.' Luke went back to the clothes. His box was nearly full.

Dulcie kept reading: "sweetheart:))) use //linecode."

If it wasn't homework, maybe it was a love note; some kind of code between Tim and his smitten tutor. She thought of the distraught Luisa. If she saw her again, she'd ask. In the meantime, she folded the page up and slipped it into the pocket of her jeans. Whatever this was, nobody else had to see it.

'That's it, I think.' Luke stood up and looked around. Dulcie handed him the last pile of papers, and he squashed down the clothes to make room for them. Finally, the mess was gone, all somehow contained in the four large boxes that Luke had stacked by the wall. The furniture, once distinctively Suze's and then for a short while covered in her temporary room-mate's clutter, now looked barren and dorm-like. The last of Tim's life had been packed away.

'It wasn't much, was it? Once you'd packed it up, that is.' Dulcie found herself talking softly, as if she were back at the funeral. 'I mean, it's just stuff.'

'But he didn't have much of a life, did he?' Luke's face was set and grim. He grabbed one of the boxes and hoisted it on to his shoulder. 'Let me hump these down to the car. You still up for some dinner?'

'Definitely.' Whatever else was going on with him, this man had just cleaned out his dead brother's room. At the very least, she could keep him company. 'I can even help with these.' The box might contain only clothes but it was still heavy. Nevertheless, Dulcie got it up to waist level and headed into the hall.

'Careful on the stairs!' he yelled up to her. She heard her own front door open

'Watch out for —' Dulcie stopped herself. Would she ever stop asking visitors to watch out for the cat? But Luke was already outside, loading the box into the back of a Mini Cooper. She slipped on her flip-flops and joined him.

Two trips later, the little car was full and she was about to lock the apartment door behind them when she remembered. 'Oh, Luke? Did you bring Tim's laptop?'

'Next best thing.' He leaned back against the cute little car, sweating from the exertion. The night had cooled, but the humidity remained high. 'Tim's old tutor wanted to look at it and came by my folks' place. Said she'd made some notes on testing for him that she needed. Since she wasn't likely to get a recommendation, I figured it was the least I could do. But I told her you had dibs on it. She promised to be done with it by tonight. In fact, she said she'd meet us in the Square.'

Luisa? Dulcie bit her lip in thought. Maybe the tutor did want copies of her test tips. More likely though, she was hoping to destroy any trace of her relationship with Tim before Bruce could find out. If the printout in Dulcie's pocket was any indication, Luisa and Tim had at least exchanged some unscholarly notes. And, based on what Stacia had told her, maybe there was photographic evidence of the relationship as well. Whatever the truth of the matter, it wasn't like Dulcie had any choice.

'Sure, where are we meeting her?'

'I'll give her a call now.' He pulled out his cell and punched in a number while Dulcie finished locking up and tried not to eavesdrop.

'You have access? Oh, sure. Fine. Fifteen minutes then? Great.' Luke closed the phone. 'She's got a dinner date in the Square, too, I guess. Anyway, she's meeting her friend on the Widener steps, so we can pick up the laptop when we get in. Is that OK?' He opened the car door for her.

'That's great. Thanks.' It wasn't really. Something was nagging at Dulcie that she couldn't put her finger on. Of course, driving around in a car packed with her dead room-mate's clothes could be unnerving. But Dulcie couldn't fight the feeling that something was off – something she should be taking note of. Even with the car's powerful air-conditioning and the cool comfort of the leather seats, she was glad when Luke found a space right on Quincy and backed the car neatly into the metered spot.

'You're OK with leaving all this stuff here?' As Dulcie closed the car door, she looked at the boxes piled in the back. How Luke had backed into the space was a mystery.

'Sure.' He beeped the car's alarm on. 'It's just clothes.' Clothes that cost more than anything she owned, thought Dulcie as she waited for Luke to step around and join her on the brick sidewalk. A week night in the middle of summer, and still Harvard Yard was crowded. There were enough summer school students for other teachers' classes, she noticed with a grimace. A pack of Japanese tourists walked by, their eyes fixed on their leader's long-stemmed plastic rose rather than the historic brick buildings around them. Another group, speaking what sounded like German, crossed the yard on a facing path.

'Now this looks like a campus.' As they walked down the path the Japanese tourists had vacated, Luke seemed to relax. 'Old brick, just the right amount of trees.'

'Isn't Stanford like this?' She had to hurry a bit to keep up with his long stride. He noticed and stopped, looking over at Emerson Hall.

'You kidding? For starters, it's all sandstone, not brick. And there are palm trees, if you can believe it. It's all very California.'

'Sounds nice.' As they passed between the two buildings, she pointed to Sever Hall. 'Now that's my favorite building here; H.H. Richardson, Romanesque. It's from 1880, so it's really rather late for my area of interest, but I always think those towers look Gothic. Aren't they great?'

Luke nodded, but Dulcie noticed that he was looking at her, rather than the molded brick. She pointed to the low arch over the building's front entrance. 'Did Tim ever tell you the Sever secret?'

'Nope.' He smiled. 'Are you allowed to tell a Cardinal?'

'Hey, cardinals are red. That's close to Crimson.' She grabbed his hand to pull him along – and immediately dropped it. 'Come with me.'

Together they walked toward the wide stone steps. 'Now, stand here.' She positioned Luke by one end of the arch. 'Lean your head in a bit.' Walking to the other side, she found herself humming. Whatever had been bothering her before had been left outside the Yard gates.

'So, what do you think?' She had turned into the arch to speak, but looked back in time to see him jump and laugh.

'Wow! That's great.' He was speaking into the arch now, the brick curve's acoustics carrying the words right into her ear. 'Can you hear me?' Luke had lowered his voice, but the soft sound came through loud and clear.

'Uh-huh.' She caught the breathiness in her own voice. Somehow, standing a dozen feet away felt more intimate than being alone in her apartment.

'I'm glad, Dulcie. I've been wanting to tell you—'

'Ow!' A sharp nip, not quite a bee sting, made her reach down to grab her foot. In a moment, Luke was by her side.

'What's wrong?'

'Something bit me.' Dulcie examined the top of her foot. No mark or swelling had appeared yet.

'A yellow jacket, maybe? I saw some when we crossed the lawn.'

'I don't know.' She wasn't about to tell him that it had felt like one of Mr Grey's playful nips; the kind he gave her when she wasn't paying proper attention. 'I'm sorry. What were you saying?'

'It can wait.' He looked around; another tour group was crowding into the arch. 'I almost forgot about the laptop, but we should pick it up. That girl will be waiting.'

Damn that cat, Dulcie thought as they both turned toward the library. Or, at least, damn whatever had interrupted Luke; he had seemed about to make a promising confidence. In companionable silence, they walked over toward Widener. The big library's stone steps, still damp from the afternoon's shower, were cluttered with tour groups, each jostling for placement. Next to the bronze statue purporting to be John Harvard, these stone steps were the top photo stop on the Yard tour. Dulcie remembered how slippery they could be, even without the crowds, and took off her flip-flops.

'These steps can be murder,' she explained with a smile as she bent down to pick up the polka-dotted sandals. 'Slippery when wet.'

Then they heard the scream. Screams, really, as half a dozen tourists backed their fanny packs into each other, clearing a space halfway up the wide steps. '*Aiuto*!' A man's voice called for help. As the crowd backed up, Luke stepped forward, grabbing Dulcie's hand and pulling her up the stairs and into the crowd.

There, face down on the wide steps, lay a young woman, her dark curls spread out around her.

'Don't touch her!' Another voice yelled above the rest, but somebody hadn't heard. Hands reached down to flip the woman over, at the same time, pulling down her denim skirt to cover slim, tanned thighs.

A woman – a Southerner from her accent – pushed forward. 'Is she hurt?'

Luke broke through, with Dulcie close behind. 'Oh, my God!' The words burst from Dulcie. 'It's Luisa.' The pretty tutor was lying on her back, a trickle of blood on her mouth and more on her forehead, where she must have hit the stone. Someone reached over to put her purse by her side. But even as the crowd backed up to allow the EMTs through, Dulcie could see that the ground around her was bare. There were no signs of a laptop computer, not even a shard of plastic, anywhere near the fallen girl.

Twenty-One

'Coming through. Watch out.' Luke and Dulcie backed up as the Harvard cop made a pathway through the crowd. Over his blue-uniformed shoulder, Dulcie could see that Luisa was coming to, moving her head and one arm as the EMTs lifted her on to a stretcher.

'These stairs! In winter they put down those wooden risers, but I swear, it's just as bad in the rain.' The voice, a little way behind them, caused Dulcie to turn around. Sure enough, behind a family of khaki-clad tourists, she spied an orange and green tropical print.

'Mona!' Dulcie pushed her way back to the flamboyant librarian. 'Did you see what happened?'

'I just heard the scream. These stairs, I swear.' A large man in a Red Sox T-shirt jostled Dulcie and, for a moment, she had reason to be grateful that she had removed her own flip flops.

'You think it was an accident?' asked Dulcie

'Sure, what else?' But before Dulcie could explain, Luke was by her side again.

'Dulcie, I've got to run. I'm sorry. There's an emergency.' At that word, Dulcie's gaze automatically went over to the ambulance. Luisa was still strapped down, but she seemed to be talking to the EMTs, answering questions and pointing. 'I mean, a different emergency.' Luke had the grace to look shamefaced. 'Nothing so serious, but I've got to run. I'm sorry. Dinner another night?'

'Yeah, sure.' Dulcie couldn't focus on him now. What was Luisa pointing at? She craned to see over the heads of the small crowd, but the EMTs had loaded the injured girl into the ambulance and were driving in the direction of Massachusetts Avenue. The University Health Services probably qualified as the closest emergency room. Even on foot, Dulcie could be there in five minutes. Should she follow? The lack of the laptop could mean anything. Maybe she'd been about to tell Luke that she needed it for another day. Maybe it had hit the ground further up, and some kind soul had already brought it back into the library, to leave at the front desk or at Lost and Found.

Dulcie turned to climb up the stairs. She wouldn't be able to talk to Luisa immediately, anyway. But as she mounted the stairs, Mona grabbed her arm.

'No, Dulcie! You can't go in.' Dulcie looked over and noticed, for the first time, that her friend had bitten off most of her usual thick coat of lipstick.

'Why? What's wrong?' Widener shouldn't be closed for hours yet.

'They're kicking everyone out. Everyone! I was supposed to be on till eight.'

Dulcie turned toward her friend and took her hands. Never had she seen Mona, the implacable mistress of the circulation desk, so flustered. 'What's happening, Mona? Is there a fire? Anthrax?'

'Worse!' Her penciled-in brows rose almost to her hairline in emphasis. 'The hackers have been at it again. The virus is trying different ways to get into our system.'

'Whoa.' Dulcie stepped back. Was this related somehow to the problems with her computer? Could this be linked to Priority? She shook her head. Computer crime was everywhere, but what would electronic embezzling have to do with students trying to change their library records?

'Hey, Mona, since you're off, you want to grab some dinner?' Dulcie felt a serious need to talk this all out.

'Wish I could, Dulcie.' Mona's voice went uncharacteristically soft. 'I've got to be back here within an hour. Security wants us all to bring our laptops in. They say the program will continue to attack our firewall until it gets in, and they're looking everywhere for the source. We're all under suspicion!'

Mona lumbered off, her jungle print swallowed up by the T-shirts of tourists, and Dulcie was left alone, thinking. Granted, Mona thrived on drama. But what she'd said was ringing chimes in Dulcie's head. She thought of Priority, Tim, the cops, and Helene's brutish ex, who seemed to have some grudge against her. And then Luke running off just when it seemed something might be about to happen between them. It was all too much. Dulcie needed a friendly face. But then, she realized, so did Luisa.

Dulcie had to wait a good forty-five minutes before she could find out anything about Luisa's condition. The EMTs had indeed taken the bloodied girl to the University Health Services; Dulcie had a glimpse of her, sitting up in bed and talking to a nurse, before another attendant drew the curtain closed. The fact that she was talking seemed like a good sign, although the bloody lip and hairline had been covered by bandages that wrapped all the way around her head.

'I hope they don't have to shave her head.' Dulcie didn't realize she'd spoken out loud until a young doctor turned and smiled.

'Not to worry. She's just scraped her forehead. Scalp wounds bleed a lot.' The doctor turned to walk off, and Dulcie grabbed his arm.

'Wait, please. Can you tell me anything more about how she's doing?' He blinked. 'She's a friend,' Dulcie added. God, that sounded weak.

But the young doctor – maybe he was still an intern – had pity. 'It's Luisa Estrella, right? Let me check.' He ducked down a hall and, for a moment, Dulcie feared that he'd slipped away. But a moment later, he returned, his smile bigger than before.

'I just grabbed her attending physician. Your friend will be fine.' Dulcie let out a sigh. She hadn't realized how worried she had been. 'But she hit her head, so we're going to keep her for observation. I can even get you in to say "hi" if you want.'

'Could you?' Dulcie didn't know when Luisa had flipped from being a suspect back to being a friend. But she was hurt and in the hospital and Dulcie felt she could probably use a friendly greeting right now.

'Come with me.' He led the way. 'She may be a bit out of it. She got whacked pretty hard.'

'Got it.' The young doctor pulled back the curtain around Luisa's bed and stepped aside as Dulcie walked into the room. Three other beds lay empty, their white sheets folded up to flat pillows. Below the bandages, Luisa's dark hair was still in luxuriant evidence, spread out over an equally flat pillow, but her tawny skin looked almost pale, vaguely green against the hospital white.

'Hey, Luisa. You OK?' Dulcie spoke softly

Dark eyes blinked open. 'Dulcie.' Luisa started to smile, but winced instead. That cut lip must hurt. 'I'm sorry. The laptop.'

'It's fine, Luisa. I'll get it another time.' Dulcie stopped herself from the automatic comforting. 'I mean, you didn't bring it with you, right? You must have left it at home or something?'

'No, I had it.' Luisa tried to shake her head, but the effort made her close her eyes. 'I had it with me.' Her voice was fading. 'I was waiting. You were late. It was crowded. Someone shoved me . . .' Her eyes flashed open, but Dulcie didn't think they were seeing her – or the hospital room. 'Bruce was so angry. And that friend of his . . .' The long, lush lashes slowly closed and the voice faded.

'What friend?' Luisa didn't respond. 'What are you saying? Someone pushed you?'

Those dark lashes fluttered. 'Bruce, and his friend . . .' Dulcie tried to remember the names of Tim's other buddies as Luisa's voice faded further. 'Luke,' she whispered, and fell silent. But into that silence a loud beep-beep-beep broke in, a machine by the side of the bed suddenly flashing a warning red light.

'Excuse me, Miss. Excuse me.' Suddenly the young doctor was by her side and leaning over Luisa. Another pair of hands placed themselves firmly on Dulcie's upper arms and shoved her aside.

'You'll have to leave now, Miss.' With a hiss, the curtain was drawn between her and the silent young girl. The voices of the medical professionals were barely audible, soft and urgent, but they couldn't help to answer any of the questions in her head.

Back out on the street, Dulcie realized that not only was she more confused than before, she was famished. And, despite the negative connotations, the pho place was only half a block away. Within minutes, she had placed an order – chicken, wide noodles – and was checking her voicemail. Where was Suze? Why was she going missing just now, when all hell was breaking loose? Should she, sigh, call Lucy? A hand on her shoulder made her jump.

'Dulcie! Sorry, did I startle you?' It was Trista. With Jerry and Chris in tow, she looked a bit like a diminutive rock star, her nose stud and bleached blonde hair looking incongruous beside her gangly posse.

'Tris. It's good to see you. It's great, actually.' Dulcie put her phone away. 'You wouldn't believe what's been happening.'

'Tell us about it.' The hostess was waiting with menus. 'I left a message for you at home, to join us, but I guess you were already in the Square.'

'I already ordered take-out.' A wave of sadness flooded Dulcie.

'That's OK. We can change it, can't we?' Trista looked over at the hostess, who nodded. Pho House was used to students and their inconstant ways. Not long after the four were seated, Dulcie's pho arrived and, with the urging of her tablemates, she began slurping up the long noodles.

'Sorry, I'm starved.' She paused to wipe her chin. 'I missed lunch today.'

Jerry looked horrified at the thought and began toying with the hot sauce, anxious for his own meal to arrive. Chris, however, seemed concerned. 'Are you still at that McJob? The temp thing?'

Dulcie, her mouth full, nodded.

'How's that going?' He waited for her to swallow.

Dulcie slurped again, while the waitress placed three more large bowls in front of her colleagues along with a plate of spring rolls and another of condiments. As her friends reached for the basil leaves and bean sprouts, she started to explain. 'I'm not sure exactly.' With a little food in her, she could think more clearly. Not that anything about the Priority situation was clear. She sucked a piece of basil from between her teeth and continued. 'I'm pretty sure they're still trying to figure out who hacked the system, but at least I'm back at work. Although they've moved my workstation to this really loud, exposed part of the building.'

'They trying to make you quit?' Jerry looked up from his own bowl and Dulcie remembered: the lanky math genius was the son of auto workers, both long-timers on the assembly line. He'd gone through Harvard on a Teamsters scholarship.

'Maybe.' She saw him start to speak and held up her porcelain spoon. 'But I'm not sure, and I don't think there's anything actionable yet. There is definitely something weird going on, though.'

Jerry continued slurping his soup, but his eyes were questioning.

'I know, Jerry. I won't let them get away with anything. But right now, I just have to wait and see.'

Nobody questioned that. But Chris did point a fresh spring roll at her. 'Hey! Speaking of weird, are you following our own hacking scandal?'

Dulcie reached for another of the cold rolls just as the waitress brought over a plate of chicken sate. 'Just a bit – I know they closed Widener early and that they're supposedly checking staff laptops.'

'Oh, it's better than that.' Chris's dark eyes shone with excitement. Maybe geeky could be cute, thought Dulcie. 'It's completely amateur hour. Totally! I'd say it was a prank if it hadn't gotten so far.'

Jerry held out a hand. 'My room-mate here is getting carried away. The algorithms are not sophisticated, it's true. But they are sufficient unto the day.'

Trista shot him a look.

'Well, they *are*. This is nearly the same bug that was used at Duke and some of the West Coast schools. It's set to keep trying different approaches until one works. It may not be pretty but it does the trick.'

'And the trick is?' Trista obviously hadn't heard the details either.

'It opens a back door. Once in, you do what you want.'

'Or what you have the technical know-how to pull off,' Chris interrupted. 'At Duke, I believe they were checking admissions records. You know, seeing who was going to get in before the announcements? Pretty minor stuff. But at LA Poly they'd gotten as far as altering transcripts before they were caught.'

'Wow.' Dulcie dipped her roll in the pepper sauce and thought about this. 'Do they know if the Harvard hackers did that? I mean, did they change anyone's grades?'

'Didn't get that far.' Chris shook his head, but Jerry corrected him.

'That we know of. You can be sure that forensic techs will be going over everything in the system with a fine-tooth comb.'

Chris made a dismissive sound. 'They won't find anything. These guys might as well have rung the front doorbell to announce their intention. A subtler bug would have gone dormant, but this keeps trying – that's making it pretty easy to trace. I mean, OK, it's taking some time, but that's just legwork. The word on all the boards is that the code is completely inelegant.'

Maybe it was the food finally kicking in, maybe it was the hot sauce, but Dulcie started to pull things together. 'Chris, the other day you said that I had an open door on my computer from the university, that maybe that's how something got into my computer. Is there any chance that the bug in the university system is what's been messing up my little laptop?'

Rather to her surprise, Chris paused to consider it. He and Jerry exchanged glances, and Jerry raised his eyebrows.

'It's unlikely, but possible. You said a file disappeared?'

'Well, it was altered, actually.' It must be the hot sauce; Dulcie felt a flush of blood in her cheeks. 'Wait a minute! That doorway works both ways, right?' Three equally flushed faces nodded back. 'Is it possible that my computer is the source? I mean, that Tim planted the bug? Before he – you know . . . That he was using my computer to hack into the system?' It would be a perfect scam: a lot less dangerous and potentially more profitable than selling drugs. It might explain why neither she nor Luke had found any stash. Plus, he'd never be blamed. *She* would.

The noodles turned to lead in her stomach and she closed her eyes. This time it would be Harvard, the center of her life, that would be turned against her, rather than some shoddy summer job. Her thesis, her grants, her entire academic career were all at risk. But when she opened her eyes, her friends were smiling.

'Dulcie, when I said the programming was easy, I meant for one of us; someone in computer science or "apple" math.' Chris must have seen the fear that had passed through her. 'From what you've told me, your roommate knew as little about applied math or programming as he did about – well, early British novels.'

Reality came back, and with it, Dulcie's appetite. 'You're right.' It was flattering that he remembered her area of expertise. She swirled some bean sprouts around in what was left of the soup. 'I was just thinking that if anyone had a motive for changing grades, Tim did. But, well, he never did get his grades up, did he? And besides, it's been more than two weeks since . . . since he . . .' The bean sprouts lay there, pale as dead things.

Trista pushed the skewered chicken sate toward her friend. 'Enough of that, Dulcie. Eat.'

She did and for a few minutes the only sounds were the munching and slurping of hungry grad students. When the conversation came back, it was of a more mundane variety. Trista had heard that the University of Oregon was going to be expanding its Renaissance program, maybe creating entirely new tenure track positions. From there, the talk moved on to outdoor sports. Jerry expounded on the Sox for a while, and then Chris, much to her surprise, started talking about skiing. He and Suze really would be a good match, Dulcie realized. He was obviously considerate, too.

'Hey, Chris,' she broke in. The bus boy was clearing the table of empty bowls and the few remaining bean sprouts. 'Even if it's not anything earth shattering, or even mildly felonious, would you take a look at my laptop?'

'Sure. After we stop at Herrell's?'

Dulcie wasn't sure she could eat ice cream after all that spicy food, but she was enjoying the company too much to want to go home. 'Yeah, that would be great.'

The four exited the restaurant and waddled – that was the only word Dulcie felt was accurate – over to the ice cream shop. No surprise, considering the weather, there was a line stretching out the door. Chris sidled up to her.

'Hey, Dulcie, I've been meaning to ask you . . .' He paused. No, *please*. Dulcie made sure her prayer was silent. You're for Suze. 'It's just that, what with the cops floating around and all, have you talked to Suze lately?'

She could have laughed with relief. 'I just left a message for her this evening.' A party of six left and Trista and Jerry slid inside the air-conditioned shop. 'I was actually trying to call her again before the whole thing happened at Widener.' It felt like days ago, now.

'You mean, the early closing?'

Had she not told them? 'Yeah, that, and – well, this is really weird. I was trying to borrow my old room-mate's laptop – Tim's, not Suze's. Anyway, Tim's brother had lent it to Tim's old tutor, who I think Tim was fooling around with, too.' Chris raised his eyebrows. Dulcie explained, 'No, really, I think it may be relevant. But the point is that she was going to meet us at Widener and hand over the laptop. But when we got there, well, it's hard to say exactly what had happened. At first everyone was just assuming that she had slipped on those damned stairs. But from what she was able to tell me, it seems that someone grabbed the laptop and pushed her down the stairs.'

His eyes were wider now. 'What do the cops say?'

'I didn't – I don't know.' She'd been so intent on Luisa that she hadn't thought of talking to any authorities. 'An ambulance took her to UHS, and I followed. I wasn't sure what had happened until I talked to her, but then she passed out and they kicked me out of her room. And then I ran into you guys.' It sounded completely lame.

'Well, do you want to go talk to the police now?' He looked down at her intently, his dark eyes serious under his heavy bangs. Inside Herrell's, the line had moved up, but he stood there, waiting for her answer.

'I should. I know I should. It's just . . .' How could she explain? The previous times she'd tried to give the cops leads, she'd been brushed off. In retrospect, her urge to help probably contributed to her being considered a suspect. Now, if she were to report an attack on Luisa, wouldn't she get the same reaction? At best, the cops thought she was a kook; at worst, a killer. And mightn't this just seem like a cover-up; like she'd botched her payback to a rival? Chris was waiting.

'It's just that I guess I'm not their favorite person right now. I think they may even suspect me of Tim's murder. And, well, if I'm going to talk with them, I'd rather have something concrete.' It still sounded lame. 'Besides, when Luisa comes to, she'll probably tell them.' *When*, she told herself. Don't even think about *if*.

Chris said nothing. Peering inside the shop, she could see that Jerry and Trista were at the counter. Trista was getting a taste of ice cream on a small wooden spoon. The scene looked so friendly and normal.

'You're right, Chris. I should go talk to the cops.' He nodded, a smile returning to his lean face. 'At least it's only the university cops, so maybe they'll actually listen to me.'

'Good girl. You want a cone for courage?'

She shook her head. 'Thanks anyway.' She stepped back from the door. 'If I'm going to do this, I need to do it now before I lose my nerve. Hey, can you come by tomorrow, maybe around sixish, instead?'

'Sure thing, Dulcie. I'll bring over some good virus protection programs, too.'

'Thanks, Chris.' She walked back down the stairs, passing the end of a line that hadn't grown any shorter, and headed back toward the health services. First, she'd check on Luisa. Maybe she had already reported the shove – and the theft. If Luisa hadn't told her story to the police, Dulcie would do it, and they could talk to the pretty tutor when she was back on her feet. *When*, Dulcie repeated like a mantra. Not *if*.

Twenty-Two

Half an hour later, Dulcie was home again – without having spoken to the cops, and without any ice cream. She'd meant to do the right thing, and had pushed open the big glass doors to the health services full of determination. But as soon as she'd asked for Luisa at the front desk, things had started to get weird.

'And you are?' the woman at the information desk had asked.

'I'm a friend.' Dulcie didn't mean to be evasive, but something about the woman's stare unnerved her.

'A friend? Want to show me some ID for that?' This was sounding way too much like the police.

'I would, but, um, I left my wallet in my dorm room.' Dulcie realized she was standing on one foot, the other raised nervously behind her, as she always did when she lied. She forced herself to stand straight while the attendant checked her out.

'Yah. You left your ID at home.' Even without the tight-mouthed smirk, not quite a grimace, Dulcie could tell the woman sitting in front of her was being sarcastic. 'Wait right there.' The desk jockey picked up a phone and pressed one button. 'Please,' she tacked on. But it was too late, Dulcie was already backing away. Why hadn't she noticed, when she'd burst through those doors, that two uniformed police were standing on either side? And was that security guard always by the elevator?

'Never mind.' Dulcie salvaged a smile, knowing it looked fake. 'I'll catch up with her later.' The woman was talking on the phone but raised a hand as if to make Dulcie pause. Dulcie ignored her, though, and after taking two more swift steps backward, she turned on her heel and walked quickly back outside, her flip-flops slapping the hard tiled floor in retreat.

None of her neighbors were out, which was a mixed blessing. While a sultry night would have had everyone chatting – and swatting mosquitoes – back at the commune, here in Cambridge, the city retreated behind air-conditioning. But at least she wasn't being interrogated, and no explanations were necessary. Only the whir and drip of window units greeted Dulcie as she climbed the steps to her apartment – and the sound of a phone ringing.

'Hold on!' As if the phone would understand. 'I'm coming!' She dropped her bag and tore up the stairs, just in time to pick up to dead air. Was she still getting those calls, or had she just missed someone? She looked hopefully over to her blinking message light.

'Hey, Suze, where you been?' Two of the calls had been from Suze, one from Lucy, none from Luke. Dulcie had called her room-mate back first, trying to hide her disappointment. 'I've been trying to reach you.' She heard the peevishness in her voice, but couldn't do much to stop it.

'Things have been, well, interesting,' her old friend had replied. 'There's a lot going on.' That was uncharacteristically vague for Suze. Dulcie waited, not wanting to interrupt. She and Suze had been friends for long enough for them to know each other's rhythms. But instead of continuing, Suze countered with her own question. 'What's up with you?'

'The drama never stops here in the People's Republic of Cambridge.' Dulcie tried to make her voice light. She didn't want to start distrusting her best friend. Not now. 'And Lucy's left a message, too. So I'm sure the spirit world is somehow involved.'

'No doubt.' Suze had been blessed by one of Lucy's readings. 'But what's the new drama?'

Dulcie paused. She hated wondering, even for a moment, if something was going on with Suze. It was at times like this when Dulcie really missed Mr Grey. He couldn't contribute much in the way of advice, but just his being there – the solid, warm bulk of him – had been a comfort. Without him, Dulcie feared she was turning into a weepy, whiney mess.

'Dulce? It's not more computer problems, is it?'

'No, not really.' Her fears were groundless. Suze wouldn't get involved in something underhanded.

'I do have your thesis files, now. I've put them on a disk, too, for backup.'

'Thanks, Suze.' Her friend was a rock. Dulcie had to believe that. 'Each time I power up, I'm sort of nervous to see what's going on. But did you hear—'

'That the university has been hacked? Yeah. And I called it, didn't I?'

'You did?' How did Suze know what was happening so fast? 'I remember you talking about the Duke case.'

'Oh, maybe I was talking to someone else. We were talking about systems security and I said, "You watch: Harvard is next".'

Systems security? Suze? 'I didn't know you spoke computer.'

'Well, I've been chatting with some of the systems guys here. I mean, I'm spending so much time in the computer lab anyway . . .'

'You are?' Something was off. 'Well, maybe Chris stands a chance with you, then.'

'I wouldn't go *that* far!' Suze sounded like herself again, and true to form, she followed up. 'So come on, kiddo, what's going on? I hear something in your voice.'

At times, a friend was as good as a cat. Dulcie lay back on the sofa and brought Suze up to date. From her new workstation at Priority to Luisa's tumble down the Widener steps and the missing laptop, it all sounded so melodramatic.

'This is just so crazy, Suze.' She wound up with the face-off at the University Health Services, and her own rapid retreat. 'I mean, what if she's dead? What if someone pushed her? What if someone pushed her *because she was going to meet me?*' Dulcie heard her voice start to rise. 'What if—'

'Dulcie! Take a breath. Think about it. She fell. She hit her head. When you talked to her she was woozy. Confused. And now they have her upstairs, where maybe she's still vulnerable. And you go over late, after ten p.m., and you want to go right up. Of *course* they asked for ID! You could be anyone. You could be going around stealing patients' wallets or something. I think, well, to be honest, I think you're overreacting.'

She was about to protest, but something stopped the words. She'd known Suze for years and always looked to her as the voice of reason. 'Suze?' Her voice was softer now. 'Do you think I'm paranoid?'

'I think you've been under a lot of stress.' Her old friend's voice was measured. 'You have a crappy job. You had a crappy room mate. And then he was murdered and the police called you in for questioning. People are acting all freaked out around you. Someone you know had an accident – an accident, mind you – and now you might lose your job, too. I think it's enough to unbalance anyone.'

'Especially your artsy-fartsy room-mate, right?' Dulcie kicked and a pillow went flying. The pillow that Mr Grey had been most fond of, she noted, with a sinking feeling. She glanced over and saw the red velvet plush on the floor. Against the aquarium-green of the carpet, it looked particularly hideous. She'd only kept it so long because her cat had liked it. Maybe it was time for a change. If only she had money for redecorating; for new cushions, or an entirely new sofa . . .

But she didn't. 'Dulcie?' Suze sounded concerned, but Dulcie sank further back into the old sofa's remaining cushions. 'I didn't mean it like that.'

Dulcie allowed herself the comfort of one more self-indulgent sigh.

'Are you all right?'

'Yeah, I'm OK, Suze.' She was, really, and sat up to prove it to herself. 'It's just that I feel, well, picked on. But, you know what? It's making me mad. I mean, why should I be running and hiding and making excuses? I'm sick of it! I'm not going to hide from my neighbors – or the police – anymore.

'That's my girl. You feeling better now?'

'Yeah, I am. Thanks, Suze. Thanks so much. Tomorrow, I'm going in to talk to my boss at Priority. I won't be a scapegoat.'

Of course, her work situation was the least of her problems, Dulcie thought as she and Suze said goodnight. But she was smart, wasn't she? She was Dulcie Schwartz, survivor of the Oregon forest, possibly psychic grad student, and just a whisper away from finding her thesis topic. Maybe, if she could straighten out her work situation, she could also make some headway on her bigger problems. She would not interfere with the police, though. Dulcie had enough sense not to do that. But, hey, the police seemed to be on the wrong track, whereas she had inside knowledge. She'd tried to pass along leads, but that had only gotten her in trouble. Maybe this time she should follow some of those leads herself. Tim wasn't much of a room-mate, but he deserved justice – and so did she. What was the use of a Harvard education, if it wouldn't help one girl solve a murder?

Twenty-Three

Dulcie woke from a troubled night to the realization that she hadn't called her mother back. In her dream, she'd been watching Mr Grey. He, however, had not been watching her. He'd been faced toward a crack in the siding, a tiny gap between radiator and wall, his entire body tense with anticipation. *The key is to stay close.* Even though he wasn't facing her, she heard that voice in her ear and knew that the concentrating cat was communicating with her. *That's how you get them. Listen!* His large ears twitched. *And be careful.*

The nature of the dream left her dissatisfied and anxious, perhaps because she hadn't been able to see her beloved pet's face. It also left her wanting to go over the kitchen with a flashlight. Now that there wasn't a feline on the premises, mice were a definite possibility.

But first, she should call her mother. She looked over at the clock. Lucy had sounded frantic, not that this was unusual. But even torn up with her own crazy fears, Dulcie doubted her mother would be up at five a.m., West Coast time. She'd just have to call during her lunch break. Which she would take today, come hell or high water.

Rather to her surprise, Dulcie encountered neither on her way in to Priority. The day was bordering on cool, one of those early August surprises that presage fall in New England. The sky was even blue, instead of its usual washed-out summer white, and the security guard smiled at her when she opened her bag. Of course, her desk was still in the office equivalent of Siberia. But Dulcie had come prepared: she'd brought earplugs to block out the noise of the message center.

This must be what most of the country feels like, she told herself, as she settled in, logged on, and started typing up the day's forms. This kind of brainless work was hypnotic, actually, the earplugs magnifying the sound of her breathing. She might be a drone, but she was an effective drone. Her productivity had never been higher.

Two hours and forty-six forms later, Dulcie's outlook had faded a bit. The unrelieved tedium of the codes had progressed from numbing to painful, and the loud rasp of her breathing had begun to make her think of an iron lung. She pushed back from her terminal and popped the earplugs from her ears. Maybe, the thought hit her, her parents had had a good reason to drop out of the corporate rat race.

'Wow, where did that come from?'

Only when she looked up at the large circular desk did she realize she'd spoken out loud. Too many hours in her own head had almost made her forget the phone bank, and now four pairs of eyes turned toward her. 'Sorry!' She waved and smiled at the four women, a mismatched set of two very large and two rather short, but still round, women. 'Just talking to myself!'

Two sets of eyes blinked, but they all turned away. After her hours in relative silence, their voices sounded abnormally loud to Dulcie. And they weren't, she noticed, answering calls.

'*Her*? Are you sure? That little thing?'

'Uh-huh, that's what Billy – the cute guard? – told me he'd heard from Wallace.'

Keeping her face forward, Dulcie leaned slightly toward the message center. Maybe it was just gossip. But maybe she could learn something to salvage her wreck of a week.

'So, are they going to make an arrest?' Time on the switchboard must have made the larger of the big women deaf. Her whisper was as loud as a shout.

'I think so. Maybe even today.' One of the short women drummed her finger on the desk for emphasis.

'Maybe they'll take her out in handcuffs.' The other woman could have been her twin.

'That would be something, wouldn't it?' The big woman wasn't even trying to whisper now. 'Serve her right though. Endangering all of us here.'

Dulcie leaned too far and her chair began to tilt. Reaching out, she caught herself, but not before all the eyes had turned on her again. Who were they talking about? Could it be Joanie? Could it be *her*? She looked up at the message center ladies, but they'd dispersed to their posts. With a few glances between them, they'd resumed their duties, and Dulcie couldn't tell if it was because she'd made them aware that they could be overheard – or because she was the object of their mean-spirited chat.

'Priority. Can I help you? Please hold.'

That was it, Dulcie needed air. Besides, she was entitled to one fifteen-minute break every two hours. The elevator was closing as she heard someone calling, 'Dulcie! Dulcie!' After a moment's hesitation, she hit 'open' and Joanie slammed in.

'Glad I caught you! This place is crazy.' Joanie slumped back against the elevator wall, out of breath. In her black eyeliner, black-lined lips, and tight striped top, she looked like the same Goth girl Dulcie had befriended weeks before. Still, Dulcie waited. 'What?'

'I saw you talking to the Snake.' It sounded so much like an accusation that Dulcie felt embarrassed. 'I mean, back in my old cubicle. And, well, they moved me . . .'

'And you think I'm some kind of corporate spy?' The conclusion was so obvious that all Dulcie could do was shrug. 'Hey, I know they wanted to separate us, but as far as I know, they're looking at me for this, too.'

'Really?' Dulcie wanted to believe her, but too much was at stake. 'Why do you say that?'

'Well, they know that I've been hanging out by the business side of things – Accounting is right next to Computer Services – and I gather they were grilling Ricky, poor boy.' Dulcie remembered the redhead. With his fresh face and freckles, he and Joanie must make quite a couple. 'And, well, I may have said something about breaking through firewalls at some point.'

Her dark lipstick set off a stunning smile. Dulcie found herself smiling back. Just then, the door opened and three men in suits entered, effectively shutting down the conversation. Dulcie was grateful for the break. Joanie sounded reasonable – and the spunky Goth had been her only ally in this corporate prison. But she couldn't deny what she'd seen: Joanie and Sally Putnam talking. And if she wasn't completely bonkers, Mr Grey had meant to show her something. That conversation had to be important.

The elevator opened on to the ground floor, and the two followed the suits out. 'So, what was the Snake talking about?' She had to be proactive. Plus, it was her butt on the line. 'Was she asking about me?'

'Yeah, she was. She wanted to know how often you emailed and whether you were secretive about stuff you were typing; did you use other computers? Stuff like that. I kept telling her it was ridiculous. I mean, you're clueless around computers.' Dulcie opened her mouth to protest, but Joanie was right. And, besides, it was a good defense. The two lined up for the guards.

'Did she believe you?' Dulcie asked, as soon as they were out of the door. And can *I* believe you? she added, silently. They were about ten feet from the main entrance, standing in the sun alongside the opaque glass front of the building. The day had heated up while they'd been chilling inside.

'I can't tell.' Joanie bit her lip. 'I'm sorry. She's an odd duck, all right. She seems to have it in for you.'

'Great.' Dulcie leaned back against the building. The heat bounced her back up, and she turned to look at the wall. Dark glass. Maybe they were watching her, even now, whoever 'they' were.

'Creepy, huh?' She turned and saw that Joanie was staring at the building, too. 'So Darth Vader.'

'Tell me about it. I think they've isolated me for a reason.'

'Why don't you just quit?' Joanie pulled a cigarette from her bag and offered one to Dulcie, who waved it away. 'Oh, yeah, sorry.' She lit up. 'But why don't you? There are other jobs out there.'

Dulcie sighed. Joanie was younger – and a preppie. Her family had money. Maybe to her things were as simple as that. 'I need this job, Joanie. I owe money and I really can't afford to miss even one pay check. If I walk out of this assignment with a cloud over me, the agency is going to want to know why. And besides,' she felt something stir, 'why should I quit? Why should I be hounded out like – like some kind of scapegoat? I didn't do anything.'

'Because they're evil corporate bastards?' Joanie took a deep drag. 'It's a definite possibility.'

The idea was settling in. 'I was thinking that, in a way, I would be an obvious candidate for a suspect.' Her paranoia from the day before now recurred in a new light. 'You know, I'm broke, I'm new, and I'm smart enough to break into their system.' Joanie snorted, and Dulcie held up a hand for silence. 'I mean, theoretically, I'm a great suspect. But what if someone knows that? What if someone chose me as a fall guy? Fall girl.'

Joanie looked at her and exhaled. With the smoke coming from her nostrils and her latest piercing – a nose ring – she looked like a petite and determined bull. 'Or you could just be talking yourself into staying in a shit job.'

'Maybe.' Dulcie had to concede that point. Joanie might be into the Goth look, but Dulcie didn't think she would necessarily believe in a ghost cat leaving her clues. 'I just feel there's something going on that I should look into, you know?'

'Cool.' Joanie ground out the cigarette and popped a Tic Tac, offering Dulcie one. 'I'm your gal.'

The breath mint saved Dulcie from having to respond. I hope so, she thought. I could use a friend here.

'So, where do we start?' If Joanie had noticed Dulcie's hesitation, she didn't let on. Dulcie rolled the mint around in her mouth and tried to think. She imagined Mr Grey stalking a spider – waiting and watching.

'We need more info. Can you talk to Ricky about the investigation? I want to know what the Snake was getting at. If we can find out what exactly she was looking for, maybe we can discover who really planted the bug.'

Joanie's pierced eyebrow went up. 'Wow, you're serious.'

'It's my life, kiddo.' The more Dulcie thought about it, the more determined she felt. 'I've got to be.'

With Mr Grey's unblinking concentration in mind, she marched back to her cubicle. This time, she wasn't going to block out the noise. This time, she was going to listen for anything that might give her a clue.

'Priority, can I help you?' Two hours later, she'd barely gotten through fifteen forms. And all she'd learned was that someone called Guy was having an affair with his sister-in-law's daughter. Fifteen minutes later, a crucial detail followed – Guy and 'that little tramp' were characters in a soap. By then Dulcie was drained and empty, and ready for lunch.

Joanie was nowhere to be found when Dulcie peeked over to her section. Either she was off gathering info, or flirting with Ricky. Or maybe she was filing a report. Either way, Dulcie found herself looking forward to a quiet lunch by herself. If only she didn't have to call Lucy.

'Dulcie! I'm so glad you're OK!' Her mother must have been waiting by the community phone. 'I had another dream!'

'Thanks, Lucy, I'm fine. What's up?' There would be no point in getting her mother more worked up.

'It's the books, Dulcinea!' Her mother sounded breathless. 'You've got to avoid the books!'

Dulcie took a bite of her sandwich. Since her mother's usual demeanor was halfway between panic and drama queen, her current level of alarm didn't seem to be any reason to miss lunch. 'You mean, like accounting?' Maybe her mother had picked up something, albeit retroactively. 'I should be careful around bookkeeping?'

'No! No! It's the library.' Lucy was growing increasingly agitated.

Dulcie rolled her eyes. 'Mom, I've barely been able to get to the library this summer.' How could she explain this to her mother? Lucy had no interest in the 'dead culture of European imperialists' anymore. 'And my adviser is expecting me to come up with something by September. But maybe that's what your dream was – a warning that I have to hit the books more.' She took another bite. It was a possibility.

'Don't you dare, young lady. I know you don't believe in my visions.' With her mouth full, Dulcie could hardly contradict her mother. 'I know in my heart that they're not ordinary dreams,' she was saying. 'And I saw what was happening. It was horrible! You should watch out for your spirit guide – that cat. He's looking out for you, but there's only so much he can do, you know, trapped as he is on the spectral plane. You've got to avoid the library, Dulcie. There's great harm for you in that place.'

Dulcie swallowed and started to explain about the extraordinary security of the Harvard libraries, but her mother cut her off. 'I'm serious. I've seen you, alone in there in the dark. Trapped, like a rat in a maze.'

Ten minutes later, Dulcie had finished both the sandwich and the phone call. She'd been able to calm her mother down only by making the ridiculous promise that she wouldn't study alone. Even her detailed explanation of how the library lighting system worked – that it was impossible to be 'trapped in the dark' when the lights flicked on automatically – had only brought more panicked pleas.

'OK, Lucy. No studying alone after dark. Maybe I can make a career in data entry.' Her mother had huffed and muttered about that. 'And, yes,' promised Dulcie, 'I will look out for that cat.'

Between the aggravation and the increasing humidity, Dulcie ended up returning to her workstation early. Too much air-conditioning wasn't all bad, she decided, knowing full well what her mother would say about such environmentally unfriendly thoughts. And, besides, she did have work to do: not the pile of forms that had grown in her absence, but trying to glean information about the mystery of the Priority virus – or at least her part in it. If Joanie was right – and Dulcie had begun to believe she was – then 'Snake' Putnam had it in for her. Dulcie had to find out what she could in order to fight back.

Shunning the earplugs, Dulcie made another effort to eavesdrop on the message center ladies. It didn't take much; their volume was set on roar. Still, there wasn't much to hear until – yes! – she dropped a form on the floor and leaned toward the center's round desk.

'She's real trouble, that one.' The fat one on the far right lowered her voice to a yell as she shouted over to a skinny, pasty-looking woman who had just come on duty. 'And a B-I-C-H, too! If you know what I mean.'

'Who's a bitch?' An older operator, seated on the opposite side of the pale woman, shouted over.

'Esperanza. You know, on *One Night to Live?*'

Great, they were talking about soaps again. A thought struck her: had they simply been talking about one of their dramas before, when Dulcie had heard about an impending arrest?

'Oh, I love her.' The pale, skinny woman seemed to have woken up. 'She's wicked!'

No, Dulcie decided. Earlier they had mentioned that somebody would 'make trouble for *us*'. Even these women couldn't take their TV programs that seriously.

'And she's carrying his twin brother's bastard, too!' Dulcie sat back and reconsidered the earplugs. Would she learn anything here? How could adult women be captivated by anything so inane? In frustration, she picked up the pile of finished forms and began banging them on the edge of her desk, forcing them into a nice, neat pile. Just like . . . no, could it be? Lucy had never been the kind of mother who cared about neatness. Dulcie had often considered herself lucky to be fed. But her late grandmother – Sarah – had been a stickler for order and all things proper. She was also, Dulcie recalled, carefully replacing the pile on her desk, a terrible snob.

Dulcie knew that some of her own sense of propriety was a direct reaction to her childhood with Lucy. Keeping up to date on bills, for example, meant that the phone stayed connected. But maybe in some way, she resembled her late grandmother. 'Channeling' was the word Lucy would have used, although Dulcie saw it more as the swing of a pendulum.

Was she also a snob? Being at Harvard certainly made that easy. Even in a minor discipline, she could still hold her academic head over the vast majority of her peers. Is that who she wanted to be? The answer came with a shudder, and years of her mother's training kicked in. Don't subscribe to the dominant paradigm; not without examining the facts for yourself. Think globally, but act locally.

Starting with the immediate situation, what, she reasoned, were soap operas anyway but the latest version of her own favorite novels? They were all forms of popular entertainment designed to excite the emotions. Dulcie stopped herself. Wasn't there some artistry involved in the drama of *The Ravages of Umbria*?

She flipped a claim form over and started a list. Soaps had characters and plot aplenty. Well, Gothic novels did, too. Even in its surviving sixty pages, *The Ravages* had two beleaguered women, two possible suitors, a mad monk, and at least one ghost. Plus, they had settings that furthered the plot. Wild landscapes and tumultuous weather supported the stories' themes; Hermetria was always looking out of her chamber window to 'gaze long upon the splendours of clouds twining 'round the jagged peaks.' Dulcie hesitated, pencil point in air. Soaps were often set in luxurious or exotic locations, weren't they? But, no, she gave her books another point. In *The Ravages*, the scenery wasn't simply window dressing. (Dulcie winced at her own phrasing.) Some critics – and most of her colleagues – made fun of how the Gothic authors used their backgrounds. But she always loved the way the weather, a mountain, or even a stand of trees could be used to underline a point or deepen the plot.

'Is it something in the background?' She was talking out loud again, but the women at the message center didn't seem to notice. Was that what Mr Grey had been trying to tell her when he told her to keep watch? Dulcie looked around. Whatever it was, she didn't see it, but Mr Grey's words came back to her more strongly than before.

Stay close, he'd told her. *Listen*. She would have to keep her ears and eyes open. Somewhere out there, Mr Grey had let her know, there was a trap. Her pet was still looking out for her.

Twenty-Four

The rest of the day couldn't have been more frustrating. While Dulcie played mental volleyball, bouncing back and forth the relative merits of books versus television, she kept half an ear open for anything that might pertain to her situation. But not only did she not hear any hints or newsy tidbits, by the end of the day she suspected she was becoming addicted to *One Night to Live*. And when Sally Putnam crept up behind her – in all fairness, it would have been hard to hear anyone's footsteps over the noise – she'd been adding to her list, rather than typing in the claims forms.

'It doesn't seem like you're getting much work done here, today.' The reptilian boss blinked at her slowly, sizing her up. Her gaze shifted to the two piles on Dulcie's desk. 'Perhaps you don't want this job as much as you led us to believe.'

'No, I do. I'm sorry.' Dulcie hated to hear herself apologize, but this time her boss was right. 'I've been distracted.' She saw an opportunity. 'This area is really loud, you know. It's hard to concentrate.'

'Smart of you to bring in these, then.' One long lacquered nail, only a tad darker than the finger it extended, pointed to Dulcie's earplugs, still in their case. 'I knew you were a smart girl.' The way she hissed the words indicated that this wasn't a compliment, and Dulcie found herself scrambling for a response as the impeccably dressed woman spun on her heel and click-clacked across the room. Concentrating after that was near impossible; even the message ladies' volume seemed toned down a notch. With TV on the brain, Dulcie thought of a nature program: the monkeys hushed in the presence of a python. Her train of thought irrevocably derailed, she applied herself to a dozen more claims and logged off the moment her watch said five o'clock. It was Friday, she deserved a little time off.

'Brrr!' Dulcie didn't shiver exactly as she stepped out of the overcooled building and into another sultry late afternoon. But something about that place had gotten under her skin. It was hard to act in charge when you felt like prey, and she knew Mr Grey wouldn't approve of that. And so, shaking off the day, she strode purposefully toward the T. Dulcie Schwartz was a woman in charge of her own life. It was time to act on her resolutions, to stop being so scared. She'd visit Luisa and see what the battered girl could tell her, security guards or not.

But Mr Grey's warnings came back to her as she approached the glass doors of the university health services. *Stay close*, he'd said. *And be careful.* Tossing back her curls and feigning courage that wasn't quite genuine, Dulcie reached for the door.

'Oh, excuse me!' It swung open and she was nearly pushed aside by a tall form, walking fast. She saw brown hair, glasses. 'Chris?'

'Oh, Dulcie, hey.' The striding figure looked up just long enough to push his glasses up on his nose.

'Is everything OK?' Dulcie was the one who'd almost been run over, but it was Chris who seemed uneasy.

'What? Oh, you mean 'cause I'm here?Yeah, everything's fine.' He looked down at his feet. 'So, uh, do you still want me to look at your computer?'

'Yeah, if you could.' She paused; something was wrong. 'I mean, it would be great. I'm on Suffolk, you know?'

'Yeah, I was at that party you and Suze threw last winter.' Dulcie vaguely recalled him showing up at their holiday open house. Maybe his crush on Suze had lured him in – and left him in the corner. 'Anyway, well, I've got some stuff to do first. See you soon.'

'Bye.' Dulcie watched him lope away, long limbs moving swiftly, dark head down. Was it merely a coincidence that he'd been here?

'May I help you?'

Dulcie realized she was holding the door open, air-conditioning the open mall in front of the building.

'Sorry.' She smiled at the receptionist. 'I'm here to see a patient, Luisa Estrella? I'm a friend.'

The woman turned to her computer and typed something in. For a moment, Dulcie panicked. Her eyes darted around the room, but she could see no uniforms.

'Room 304.'

'Excuse me?' Dulcie had been scanning the reception area, braced for someone to come rushing out.

'Your friend. She's in room 304. Visiting hours end at six, though, so you'd better hurry. Elevators are over to your left.'

'Thanks.' So maybe it had just been the hour that had mandated increased security the night before. But, still, shouldn't someone be checking ID? It had been so easy to just walk in. There was nobody else in the elevator, either, and as she walked down the third-floor hallway to Luisa's room all she saw were two orderlies, and they were busy dispensing foul-smelling dinner trays.

'Get a grip,' she muttered to herself. The only thing suspicious here was the broccoli. 'Hey, Luisa!' She entered room 304 to find the dark-haired girl sitting up in bed, bandages on her chin and forehead. 'How're you doing?'

'Hi, Dulcie! Thanks for coming by.' No chipped teeth showed in that smile. 'I'm feeling fine. I guess they just want to keep me in for observation one more night, because of this.' She pointed to her forehead. 'They tell me I have a concussion at least.'

'I believe it. Do you remember talking to me after? You said you were pushed?'

'I did?' She put a hand up as if she were going to touch the bandage and pushed her hair back instead. 'I was pretty loopy back then, for a while.'

'You did. You said somebody grabbed Tim's laptop and pushed you.' Luisa shook her head slowly and shrugged. Dulcie went to sit in the one chair by the bed, but as she did, she saw Luisa look up.

'Thanks, sweetie.'

It was Bruce, who came into the room holding a white paper bag. 'Veggie Reuben with cheese. Just what the doctor ordered.'

Dulcie stood aside as he pulled a styrofoam take-out container and a pile of napkins from the bag.

'Hi, Dulcie. You're here to see our girl?'

She smiled and nodded.

'I figured hospital food wasn't doing her any good.'

'That's awfully sweet,' Dulcie said. 'I actually wanted to ask Luisa about what happened. I mean, right after they took her here she said something about someone pushing her.'

'She hit her head pretty hard.' Bruce took the seat and slid it closer to the bed. Was he intentionally putting himself between Dulcie and Luisa? Or merely being affectionate? 'I think the whole thing was fairly traumatic for her.'

'That's OK, baby.' Luisa put a hand on his arm. 'I already told her I was pretty looped there for a while after. I don't know what I was saying. And I don't remember what happened to the laptop.' She smiled. 'Sorry.'

There wasn't much more to say after that, and nothing to take to the police. So Dulcie stayed long enough to be polite and left when the two began to baby talk. Maybe Luisa truly didn't remember anything, but Dulcie couldn't help wondering. The wounded girl had a ditzy side, for sure, but she also had secrets she kept from her boyfriend. Maybe she knew more than she was letting on. Maybe he did, too.

What those other secrets could be occupied Dulcie's mind as she walked home, skipping the T to stretch her legs – and her mind. There was a lot to process, even without *The Ravages*. She wasn't so preoccupied, however, that she didn't notice the two kittens playing outside as she rounded the corner on to her own block. Both orange, one with a white chest, they were lolling about the top of the steps that led down to Helene's apartment, toying with a rather slow beetle. Dulcie looked around; her neighbor didn't seem to be anywhere nearby. She couldn't have been so foolish as to let two small kittens out alone on a city street, could she? They were still so tiny and uncoordinated. As she watched, one little orange bundle overreached and flopped down a step. Had Helene's new pets gotten out without her noticing?

'Hey, little guys.' She stepped down into the entranceway and knelt by one of the kittens. 'Julius, right? Or are you Murray?' In response the orange fur ball reared up and boxed at her outstretched finger. He was all orange: Murray. Dulcie extended her other hand to the slightly lighter tiger-striped kitten by his side. 'And this must be your brother, Julius?' The other kitten flopped on its side, revealing a snow-white tum. 'Now, what are you youngsters doing out at this hour?' Murray began to wash.

Don't worry, Dulcie, I'm here. At the sound of the voice, Dulcie's head jerked up. 'Mr Grey? Where are you?' Ignoring the kittens, she stood and turned around. *I'm keeping watch.* The long-haired grey was nowhere to be seen. And yet, she'd heard that voice, so close. She turned. And saw the bulky figure of Duane, Helene's ex, lumbering up the street. Hadn't Helene said that he was seeing someone else on their block? Whatever his romantic complications, he looked angry, his thick arms pumping up his sides as he came up the middle of the empty roadway.

The kittens, Dulcie. She didn't need a spectral voice to remind her: Duane was a cat hater. With one hand, she scooped up the protesting babies and ran down the remaining steps to pound on Helene's door.

'Helene! Helene! It's Dulcie! Let me in!'

A moment later, she heard her neighbor's heavy footsteps and the door swung open. 'Oh, my goodness, how did they get out?' Before Dulcie could answer, Helene looked past her and saw her ex. He'd reached the sidewalk in front of the apartment. 'Duane Rigardi! Don't even *think* about coming down these steps!'

Dulcie thought of Duane as a big, scary guy, but Helene was no lightweight either. In her nurse's uniform, she cut an imposing figure.

'You threw out my Pats mugs! You—' Duane's shouted protest was cut short as he gasped for breath. 'Marcella said—'

'I put all that *junk* out on the sidewalk. I told you, Duane, that you could pick it up. And you didn't!' With her hands on her hips, the big woman nearly filled the door.

'Oh, honey, I just thought that maybe if you and I—'

Dulcie, still holding the kittens, peeked out from behind her neighbor.

Duane was having trouble catching his breath. But even bent over, big mitts on his knees, he made a threatening presence.

'Forget it, asshole. Tell it to your new girlfriend! We're through.' Duane was audibly wheezing as Helene delivered the decisive blow. 'I've got *cats*!' With that declaration, she slammed the door.

Dulcie could feel the frame of the house shake. Not wanting things to get any worse, she snuck a glimpse out of the side window. Duane was slowly walking back down the block, the way he had come. One hand was on his chest, but Dulcie figured if he was walking, he was breathing.

'You OK, child?' A small but firm push made Dulcie realize she was still holding the squirming kittens.

'Yeah, sorry. That was something.' She put the kittens down and Helene knelt to check them out, her former ferocity gone. 'I know how Duane feels about cats, so when I saw him charging up the block—'

'You did right, Dulcie. Thanks.' She picked up Julius, and Murray scampered off to the back of the apartment. 'End of the week, he has the bad habit of drinking his pay check. But how did these little guys get out? I've been home for an hour now, and I swear I just fed them.'

Dulcie shrugged. In a way it didn't matter; Mr Grey had said he was looking out for them. 'Has anyone been by?'

Helene shook her head, and suddenly Dulcie's brain started working again. 'I'm sorry, I've got to run. I'm meeting someone at my place.' She turned to let herself out. 'Pet the kittens for me,' she called as she bolted up the stairs. But as she looked up and turned toward her own stoop, she saw that her front door was ajar.

'Not again.' There was nobody in there anymore. No pet, no roommate. Nobody who could be lost or hurt, but the memory still started Dulcie's heart beating like mad. Her throat tightening up, she ascended the first step. 'Hello?' Her voice came out in a croak. 'Chris?' No answer. 'Anybody there?' She should go back to Helene's. She should call the cops. But the open door drew her up the remaining stairs of the stoop. 'Hello?'

There was no sound as she swung the front door open. Memories flooded back as she climbed the stairs. 'Is anyone there?'

Nobody was. But somebody had been. Her chair lay on its side. Somebody had used it to smash the back window. Shattered glass sparkled like glitter on the green rug and the fire escape outside. The TV, old as it was, was still on the table; the little stereo, too. The noise out front must have startled whoever it was, caused the intruder to flee before Dulcie came in. Dulcie remembered those words: *I'm here, I'm keeping watch.* Had Mr Grey been guarding the kittens – or her? Had he arranged to distract her, to keep her from walking in during a burglary? Had he chased the intruders off before they could steal—? Ignoring the glass shards that seemed to have flown everywhere, Dulcie raced upstairs to her bedroom – to her desk. Her laptop was gone.

This wasn't like the other time. There was no body. No blood. Everybody was OK. Dulcie kept repeating these facts to herself as she stepped carefully back down the stairs. 'I'm breathing. I'm OK.' Saying it out loud made it real, and slowly the panic ebbed, until she was down her own front stairs, out the door, and back out on the street.

Then she lost it. 'No!' Her scream had the frustrating breathiness of a nightmare, all gasp and little volume. But it was loud enough to cause Helene to wrench open her front door again – and to alert Chris, who had just turned the corner, and who now started running up the street.

'Dulcie! Dulcie! What is it?' Chris got to her first and reached for her, but she shook off his grip.

'Where were you just now? Why couldn't you look at me?' She whirled to face her pale classmate, who blinked behind his glasses, mouth gaping open. 'Have you been calling me?'

'What's up, honey? What's wrong?' Helene had the sense not to touch Dulcie, but she inserted her considerable bulk between the girl and the speechless Chris. 'What's happened?'

Dulcie took a breath, and realized that she had been holding it. She put her hands up to her face. 'Somebody broke in.'

'Again? Come with me.' Helene put her arm around Dulcie and pulled her back toward the sidewalk. 'You, too.' Chris followed dutifully behind.

Soon Dulcie was holding yet another mug of tea laced with rum, while the police went through her apartment once again. 'And you are?' Helene was predisposed to suspect any man these days, and Dulcie's attack on Chris hadn't made her trust the lanky computer whiz any more.

'I'm Dulcie's friend. I mean, I'm a classmate. I was going to help her with her computer,' he stammered, his lean cheeks turning pink. His fluster must have looked authentic, because Helene nodded, and fixed him a mug of her special brew, too.

'Dulcie? What was all that about between you two earlier?' Helene asked the question that must have been on Chris's mind. Clearly, he was too afraid. 'Why did you yell at this boy?'

'I'm sorry.' Sitting on Helene's sofa, inhaling the warm, sweet drink, Dulcie had begun to relax. 'I just thought, I don't know, that maybe he'd been in my house.'

'Me?' His voice almost squeaked as he jerked to his feet. 'But I just got to your place. You saw me in the Square like a half-hour ago!'

'I know.' Dulcie looked up at the lanky young man. 'I'm sorry.' He relaxed again enough to sit. 'But I thought you were acting weird, you know? At the health services.'

'Yeah, well.' It was his turn to look away. 'I didn't expect to see anyone just then.'

Dulcie sipped and waited. Helene hovered. The kittens wrestled on the floor.

'I'm in counseling. I see a shrink. Ever since my mom got sick again, I've been . . . I don't know. It's been hard.' Chris's dark bangs still hid his face, but his voice was clear.

'I'm sorry, I didn't know.' Dulcie felt like a heel.

'Well, you haven't been around much, you know?' His voice had gone soft, but Dulcie heard the rebuke in it and grimaced. That was what Trista had been telling her. What else had she missed?

'I guess I've been stuck in my own head these last few months.'

He reached out his hand and one of the kittens – Murray – began batting at his finger. 'You're not the only one.' He looked up. 'In fact, that's what my shrink has been talking to me about. She's been pushing me to go out, be with my friends. Be with—' His face fell, but he finished the sentence. 'Healthy people.'

'Oh, Chris, I'm so sorry.' She reached over but he'd withdrawn again, face down, long hands back in his lap, clamped around his mug. She found herself holding on to his forearm. 'And here I was, wondering if you were, I don't know, using my laptop as part of the Harvard hacking.'

He looked up again, this time with a weak smile. 'Actually, the virus has been a great thing for me. A bunch of us in apple math are helping track it, break it down. I like the distraction!'

'Well, if my laptop shows up, I'll have more distraction for you.' She smiled back and leaned forward. Just in time for Helene to clear her throat.

''Scuse me, folks, but, Dulcie? The officer would like to speak with you again.'

Forty minutes later, Dulcie felt more drained than her empty mug. The officer had asked a lot of questions, but hadn't provided any information in return. Was this random? Was it related to Tim's murder? Dulcie had told the cop one more time about all the calls with nobody on the line, but whenever she tried to ask a question, the young officer steered her back to his own.

'He kept asking me if I could've left the door unlocked, and he wouldn't say anything about all the hang-ups. He wouldn't even tell me if there were similar robberies in the area.' Dulcie was back on Helene's sofa. At least the police had allowed the landlord's handyman to come in, and she could hear the hammering as he nailed a board over the broken window.

'You should get caller ID, child, and a police lock. That damn latch is just too easy to jimmy. I'm just hoping that this time, they got what they wanted.' Helene was walking back into the kitchen, and Dulcie wasn't sure she'd heard her.

'What?' Chris, sitting beside her, shook his head. He didn't know what she was talking about, either.

'I mean, maybe this will be it.' Helene came back out with the tea kettle and the bottle of rum. Dulcie shook off the rum, but accepted more hot water. 'Whatever they were looking for when Tim got in the way, maybe now they have it and they won't bother you anymore.'

'You think Tim interrupted a robbery, and that's what got him killed?' Dulcie, warmed by the previous servings of rum, mulled the idea over. 'You think he was just in the wrong place at the wrong time?'

Helene shrugged. 'Makes sense to me.'

'But I'd been thinking it was personal, with all his girlfriends and everything.' Helene and Chris both turned to stare, and Dulcie realized that only Suze had heard all her theorizing. 'He was kind of a dog. He had a girlfriend and at least one other on the side. I'm pretty sure one of his women was in a relationship, so I thought, maybe it was a jealous boyfriend.' Chris seemed to consider this, but Helene only shook her head.

'If that was the case, why did they come back?'

'So you don't think this – today – was random?'

Helene shot her a look.

'But all they took was my laptop.' Dulcie's head was spinning.

'That laptop might mean something.' Chris spoke up. 'We're looking at Harvard-connected laptops as the path through which the hackers are attacking the firewall.' Dulcie thought of Mona, dashing off to get her own machine, as Chris explained the situation to Helene. 'The head of my department is leading the task force. He thinks the virus was probably inserted into the system through a student computer, maybe even camouflaged in an anti-virus or anti-spyware program. That might be it, Dulcie. Your laptop might be evidence.'

The pieces began to fall into place. 'Maybe someone did come for my laptop before – and Tim had left the door open again.' Dulcie was barely aware that she was speaking aloud. 'I should look into that.'

'Don't you think that's a job for the police?' Helene was looking at her strangely, like maybe she'd given the girl too much rum. 'I mean, don't you think they've figured that out, too?'

Dulcie felt her thought processes slowed by the rum. 'I don't know.' She tried to picture her own place in the city, the tensions that always spring up between a wealthy university and its urban neighbors. 'I don't know how well coordinated the Cambridge cops are with the university police. Town–gown problems and all.'

'Well, you could *tell* them about the linkage,' her neighbor said. Chris nodded, backing up Helene's advice.

'Like they'd believe me . . .' Dulcie reflected on her previous attempts to make suggestions to the police. 'I don't think I'm exactly their favorite person right now.' And besides, she said to herself, they don't have Mr Grey helping them.

Twenty-Five

When her cell rang, Dulcie nearly jumped out of her skin. Between Helene's heady tea, the cops' questions, and the maintenance crew's noisy progress, she'd felt her head start to spin once again, and she'd retreated to the stoop to think things through. It had truly been the week from hell. She'd sent Chris home a half-hour before, with many thanks and apologies – and promises to catch up once life settled down. Helene kept sticking her head out, offering more boozy tea, but what Dulcie really needed was a little time alone to piece together all that had happened. As she sat, slumped against the steps, none of it was fitting together.

Was there a reason that two computer crimes were converging on her fairly computer-illiterate life right now? Could the Harvard bug be the reason why Tim's laptop had been taken? Did it explain why her own place had been burgled? The roar of an industrial vacuum cleaner added to the chaos in her head. If all this did have something to do with Tim's laptop, was that why Luisa had been attacked? For that matter, what was Luisa's role in all this? Did the pretty tutor really not remember being pushed, or was she covering for Bruce? Or was it all an elaborate ruse to keep Bruce from finding out about her past with Tim?

Dulcie was trying to find reasons to dismiss the obvious – such as, that perhaps Luisa fell by accident – when the shrill ringtone broke through her daze.

'Hello? What's going on?' The receding buzz was making her cranky.

'Dulcie, what's up?' It was Luke. 'Hey, I'm sorry for running out on you yesterday. I had to get over to the clinic.'

'The clinic?' She hadn't seen him when she'd visited Luisa, but maybe there was more violence than she'd imagined.

'The legal clinic. The university is confiscating computers and we've got a ton of client files, confidential material, on ours.' Dulcie sat up and took a deep breath to clear her head. Of course. 'My boss put out an emergency SOS and since I was already in the Yard, he asked me to get over there a.s.a.p. I've been printing and deleting files pretty much nonstop. But I've been thinking about you. Can I make up for running out on you? I was wondering about dinner this weekend, if you're not too busy.'

Dulcie's head whirled, but not from the tea. One little mystery had been solved – and a date offered. Maybe even a real date this time. 'I'm sorry,

Luke, I'm just all discombobulated right now. You wouldn't believe the day I just had.' She looked around the empty street. The kittens were nowhere to be seen, of course. Helene had been properly spooked. She'd be keeping them inside from now on. And Mr Grey? She felt tired just thinking about it all. 'Someone broke into my place. Someone stole my laptop.'

'*What?* Dulcie, are you OK?'

'Yeah, yeah. I almost interrupted them – him, whoever – but I was distracted.' She sat up straighter, trying to make herself sober up. It wouldn't do to start telling Luke ghost stories. 'And, well, the good news is I'd backed up all my thesis material. I'd emailed all my notes to my old roommate Suze just last week.'

'Oh, man. Still, that's terrible. I'm so sorry. Is there anything I can do?'

Just then, her stomach rumbled. Maybe she was waking up. 'Actually, I wouldn't mind a little dinner company right now.' Chris had suggested getting some food earlier, and she felt a stab of guilt for sending him off. What the hell, Luke would be more appetizing company anyway. 'I'm famished.'

'Um, sure.' There was something wrong, she could hear it.

'If you're busy, Luke, forget it. I just have to get something to eat and, well, I don't think I can do take-out right now.' The roar of the vacuum had subsided, but Dulcie knew from experience how long it would take to clean up the oily, dark fingerprint powder.

'No, no, I'm sorry. I'd love to see you. It's just that everyone here was planning on going out. We're all pretty wiped. But you could join us. We're going to Burrito Heaven.'

'That sounds perfect.' Right now, a beef and bean special, with plenty of hot sauce, would be balm for the soul. 'I can be there in fifteen.'

'OK.' He was laughing. 'We're actually right around the corner. But I'll order you a Corona and try to keep these guys from scarfing down all the chips before you arrive.'

The walk back into Harvard Square did Dulcie good, clearing her head of everything that had happened. By the time she hit Burrito Heaven, she felt almost human again – a little less freaked out, a lot more awake. But when she stepped into the crowded, noisy Mexican joint, she was in for a surprise.

'Dulcie! I thought you'd be in for the night.' Chris was standing in line to order take-out. The look behind his thick glasses was startled, rather than hurt, but Dulcie still felt like a heel.

'Yeah, I thought so, too. But the cleaners are still working in my apartment and I realized I was starving so—'

'Dulcie, over here!' In the back, Luke stood up and waved. Dulcie looked from her skinny friend to the tanned figure who gestured to her from the back of the room. 'And so, when this guy I know called, I figured . . .' She could feel her face growing red.

'Yeah, I can see.' Chris's dark eyes flashed an intensity his words lacked.

'Dulcie, we're in the back. We've got a table.' Luke had pushed his way up through the crowd. 'Hi, I'm Luke.'

'My friend Chris.' Dulcie tried to make the introductions casual. 'He was going to help me with my computer – before it got ripped off.'

'Chris, good to meet you.' Luke seemed unfazed. Then again, he was a few years older. And blonder and more muscular. 'You want to join us?'

Dulcie held her breath. 'Yeah, sure. Why not?' Chris motioned for Dulcie to take the lead, and together they threaded their way through the crowd.

'Chris, Dulcie, this is Andy, Rose, Dylan, Matt, Cy . . .' The noise level drowned out most of the introductions, and Dulcie settled on a hearty general 'hi' as Luke pressed a clear bottle into her hand. 'As promised, Ma'am, your Corona.' She turned to thank him, but he was already yelling across the table at a skinny black man – Dylan? Matt? – and so she took a long pull of the beer instead. She hadn't thought it was a date; it certainly wasn't going to turn into one.

After the craziness of the day, the beer tasted good. More chips arrived, hot and salty, and the volume rose even higher. Between the salt, the shouting, and a killer guacamole, Dulcie found herself ordering another.

'What?' She cocked her head as Chris said something to her. He had found a chair just one over from her, but she still had trouble hearing him.

'A loaner!' He was shouting at her. 'I said I could probably get you a loaner computer to work on.'

'Thanks.' Chris really was a sweet guy. Suze should definitely reconsider. 'Sorry?'

'Backing up! I was asking what kind of backup you had.'

'The old-fashioned kind. I sent everything to Suze!' The arrival of the waitress had quietened down the table, and Dulcie found herself yelling into relative silence. 'Sorry.' She modulated her voice. 'I sent copies of everything to Suze about a week ago. I figured I'd just ask her to send it all back. And, uh, I'll have the burrito grande special, with extra hot sauce.'

'And another round!' Luke, to her left, seemed to be ordering for the group, so Dulcie took the moment to sneak behind him on her way to the bathroom. As always, on a crowded Friday, there was a line.

'Another Corona?' Luke held a bottle up to greet her as she squeezed back behind him and plopped heavily into her seat.

'Thanks, yeah. It's not like I'm going to be getting any work done tonight.'

'So how are you?' The noise level had climbed again, and he leaned toward her to be heard.

'A little shaken,' she confessed, and took a sip of beer. Was this her second or third? 'But I think it'll be fine. Suze insisted we get tenants' insurance, and Chris is going to loan me another computer until I get that all straightened out.'

'But didn't you lose a lot of work?'

Mouth full of foam, she shook her head. 'Nuh-uh.' She swallowed. No sense explaining that everything she had for her thesis was pure conjecture. At this point, it was going to remain as unfinished as *The Ravages of Umbria*. 'I sent everything by email to my old room-mate. Not a very sophisticated backup, but there it is. I guess I should figure out a better system next time around.'

'You know who you should talk to?' Dulcie had a sneaking feeling, but Luke didn't even wait. 'Stacia! She's been coming down to the clinic, helping us out. I thought she was going to join us tonight.' He craned his head around.

'So that's—' Dulcie stopped herself. She wasn't that drunk. But it all suddenly made sense: Luke's invitation to dinner – on some other night. She was a buddy or, at best, a safety. She felt vaguely sick. 'I think I've got to go home.'

Dulcie meant to push her chair back, but it fell over with a crash. 'Sorry, sorry everyone! I've just had too big a day. I think I'm gonna book.'

Just then the waitress showed up. 'Wait a minute.' She turned. Chris was standing beside her. 'I'll get them to wrap our food to go.'

Dulcie opened her mouth, and then shut it again. Too much booze and too little food were what had gotten her into this mess. 'Thanks, Chris.' She knew her whisper wasn't audible.

'Wait, Dulcie!' Luke was standing on her other side; he'd already righted her chair. 'I'm sorry. I feel like I said the wrong thing.'

'No, no.' She waved him off, her body swaying. 'I'm just fried. Here.' She pulled out her wallet.

'Put that away.' Luke pushed her hand down and held it. 'I'm treating everyone tonight. My way of saying thanks. Otherwise, I'd see you home.'

'I'll take care of her.' Chris had two foil-wrapped packages in his hand and was sliding them both into a paper bag. 'Come on, Dulcie.'

The walk that had been so refreshing less than an hour before seemed impossible now, but Chris hailed a cab – and woke her when they reached her apartment.

'Are you going to be OK, Dulce? Do you want me to come in?'

'No, I'm fine. I really just need to lie down.'

Chris looked at her for a moment, his eyes dark and serious. She realized her own were closing. 'Well, OK, then,' he said finally. 'Here's your dinner.' He pulled one of the foil packages out and handed her the bag. 'Try to eat something. You'll feel better in the morning. I'll put together a loaner over the weekend, I promise.'

'Thanks, Chris.' She took the food and slid over to the door. Standing was going to be difficult. 'Thanks for everything.' She pulled herself to her feet and held on to the cab.

'You lock yourself in, OK? I won't take off till I see your kitchen light go on.'

She smiled. Walking up both flights of stairs was going to take all her energy. But by pushing herself off the top of the yellow cab, she was able to navigate her own stoop, the door, and the steps inside. As tempting as the sofa was, she made herself walk over to the kitchen window. Chris was looking up from the taxi, his pale face clear in the dark. She waved, and the cab drove off.

Grabbing a fork, Dulcie made her way back to the living room. She managed to get the foil open and was stuffing her mouth with black beans when Suze's voicemail picked up. 'Hey, kiddo, it happened again. Well, almost. We've had another break-in. Can you believe it? They got my laptop. Oops, sorry!' Melted cheese draped over the phone. 'Call me?'

Hanging up, she turned her full attention to the food, which was none the worse for wear. It wasn't until the burrito was history, the last of its cheese used to pick up a few remaining grains of rice, that Dulcie really began to notice her surroundings. The shag rug looked as good as it ever had, thanks to the cleaning crew's powerful vacuum cleaner, and she risked walking barefoot into the kitchen for some juice. Powerfully thirsty, she drank directly from the container.

'If I'm going to live alone for a while, I might as well enjoy it.' Maybe it was the sound of her words in the silent apartment. Maybe it was the way her temples had begun to throb. Maybe it was that finally, with her appetite sated, she could focus on something other than her belly, but suddenly it hit Dulcie. She looked up at the big living room window, now covered with plywood. Someone had broken in, had been in her space. She turned her back to the defaced window, but that was worse. An intruder had been right behind her; had come right into her home. She could have been here.

'Get a grip, Dulcie.' She walked back into the kitchen, flipping on the light in the short hallway and the bathroom, too, as she passed by. 'If they'd wanted to get you, they could have. Those calls were probably checking to see if you were home.'

But that didn't make it better, and Dulcie found herself standing with her back against the kitchen stove, her heart now matching the pounding in her head. 'I'm fine. This is my home. I'm fine.'

A quick fumble through the kitchen drawer revealed a mean-looking carving fork and a dinner knife. With one in each hand, she crept back into the living room and down the front stairs. Yes, the front door was double locked, with the chain on for good measure. Back up in the living room, she pulled at the plywood. It was nailed firm. The kitchen window was open but it was small – and the kitchen was two floors up. Dulcie looked through the screen and sighed. It was too hot to close it and, besides, here she was, armed for steak.

This was silliness. 'Put the cutlery on the table.' She was trying for humor, but this time, her voice just sounded hollow. And so, toting the utensils, she climbed the stairs. Tim's door – would she ever think of it as Suze's again? – remained closed, and Dulcie turned away. And kicked herself. She'd never be able to sleep. Taking a deep breath, she yanked the door open, the pointy kitchenware raised, and saw . . . nothing. Strangely, since Luke had finished emptying it out, the front bedroom looked smaller than it had when full. Suze's desk, now cleared, sat against one wall, waiting patiently for its real owner. The striped mattress looked bare in the dim light filtering through the clouds. Even the big, shadowy closet seemed innocent. Finally exhaling, Dulcie left, closing the door behind her, to collapse, exhausted, on her own bed.

'Oh, Mr Grey! I hate this. I hate being afraid of everything.'

Dulcie didn't know why she was still talking out loud. The sound did nothing to fill the space. And Mr Grey, if he was out there, certainly heard even her most private thoughts. Flipping on to her belly, she buried her face in the pillow. 'I hate being lonely.'

I can't help you with that, Dulcie. But you know you're not alone.

'Mr Grey?' The voice was so clear that she sat up and looked around the room. 'Are you there?' The lights from the floor below filtered up the stairs, casting shadows in her bedroom. But – there! – was that a movement?

I'm here, Dulcie. I'm always here. The voice was accompanied by a soft thud on the foot of her bed.

'Mr Grey?' She pulled her feet up automatically, to make room. That sound, accompanied by the soft pressure on the bed, was what she used to hear every night as she drifted off to sleep and Mr Grey jumped up to join her. 'Is it really you?' She peered at the rumpled blankets. In the shadow, she thought she saw the outline of a cat, but when she stared, it disappeared.

I'm here, but not here. Dulcie felt a rhythmic pulse, like a cat kneading, near her feet. *With you, but not with you.*

'I drank too much tonight, Mr Grey. I don't understand.' Dulcie wrapped her arms around her knees and lowered her head. 'I don't understand anything that's going on.'

You will, Dulcie. You're learning to listen; you'll hear it when you're ready.

'Hear what?' She looked up again. Were those green eyes, glinting in the dim light?

It's in the voices. A warm bulk leaned on her feet.

'I don't get it, Mr Grey. I'm sorry, but it's just been too hard a week. Can't you be any clearer?'

Like a dog, Dulcie? She thought there was a note of humor in his voice. Could cats laugh?

'No, I'm sorry. I just—' She sighed.

There are good forces looking out for you. Others, besides me. Don't underestimate the power of love, Dulcie. Keep your ears open. Keep your heart open. You'll hear the difference. But now, Dulcie, you've got to get some rest. You've got work to do.

'You sound like Mom – like Lucy.' She did feel her eyes getting heavy, and lay back down. 'But she's been telling me to stay away from the books.' Her mind began to wander. 'She told me not to go back to the library.'

She wants you to keep your senses sharp. She knows how worlds can overlap, how the same forces apply for us all. Dulcie felt the pressure of a paw on the inside of her arm; one, then another, kneading her. *We need you to be alert*. Her eyes closed now, she couldn't check to see if indeed her cat had lain down in the crook of her arm. But she felt, she was sure, the warmth of his body nestled against her. *So, for now* . . . the voice was softer now, more purr than sound . . . *we need you to sleep.*

'Why should I be surprised?' The half-formed question didn't even make it to her lips. 'Mom got it wrong again.'

Sleep, Dulcie.

And she did.

Twenty-Six

Dulcie's hangover the next morning wasn't improved by the nagging feeling that she was planning on doing exactly what her mother had warned her against. But even though Lucy had sounded as panicked as ever, the truth was, Dulcie needed to get back to *The Ravages of Umbria*. There was something in that book for her, she knew it. And without a thesis topic, she might as well give up and look for a permanent job with Priority. Besides, although her memory of the night before was decidedly fuzzy, it seemed like the ghost of Mr Grey had been encouraging her to do more research.

'Why can't cats be more straightforward?' She voiced the question aloud, while waiting for her triple-shot skim latte. The barista smiled, but remained silent. Even on a Saturday, he seemed to know most people didn't make sense before their coffee.

Dulcie began to wake up as she climbed the steps up to Widener. 'Maybe the air is clearer up here.' She smiled at her fancy, and startled the guard with a happy 'Glad to!' when he asked her to open her bag.

'Lucy is such a worrywart.' Dulcie looked around the marble lobby. Electronic gates opened only with a valid ID, and there were two guards on duty. The place was as safe as a courthouse. Safer, probably, since scholars rather than criminals came in to try their cases.

'Which brings me to Exhibit A.' Dulcie had the elevator to herself, and so the trip down to level A was fast. Most people might find a dim library basement a dull place to spend a sunny summer weekend, but to Dulcie this was heaven. Besides, she reminded herself as she unloaded her pad and pens on to an empty carrel, fair-haired girls sunburned easily. 'Let Alana and her crew hit the beach. They'll envy me when they hit forty.'

A gentle cough from behind the nearest bookshelf reminded her that others sought the same sanctuary. 'Sorry,' she whispered, and got down to work.

Two hours later, the carrel was piled high. Dulcie had been pulling books from the tall, metal shelves and toting them back to her seat like a restless squirrel, preparing for autumn. First she brought the novels – some of the lesser ones that she didn't know by heart – but also other critical works. *Not* duplicating somebody else's thesis was as important as writing your own, and with a school of literature more than two hundred years old, many of the available topics had been well covered.

'Thank God for scholarly trends!' Dulcie was careful to keep her voice low. With her feet up on the corner of the carrel, she could cradle one book open in her lap and still refer to a second, open on the desktop to her right. This was the way to study. Just to keep everything in perspective, she started with *The Italian,* the Gothic equivalent of a best-seller. A real potboiler, the Ann Radcliffe novel was never one of her favorites. The heroine, Ellena, was such a wimp – tossed back and forth between her noble lover and yet another mad monk. She was nothing like Hermetria, who took on all the odds by herself. Dulcie flipped the pages ahead to check, and looked over at the critical study open on the desktop. There was nothing about gender roles, just someone going on about the use of veil imagery. Maybe there was a connection.

'No. Been done.' Dulcie dismissed the idea before it had even fully formed, as she had dismissed so many others over the past year. 'Veil Imagery in Late Eighteenth-Century Gothic Novels': even the title bored her. What about the difference in heroines? 'Hermetria and Ellena: A Study in Contrasts'. Yawn.

But there was something here, a flicker of an idea. Were these novels a genuine reflection of sex and social roles, or just more fantasy? And if they were geared primarily toward women readers the chick lit of their day – were the heroines supposed to be role models? There must have been some reaction, some anger among the authors when they were dismissed by critics as 'housewives' and 'She-Authors'. It wasn't that far from being referred to as 'just a girl'. Dulcie sighed and closed the book on her lap, sending up a waft of dusty air. She feared that was what she was destined to be: 'ABD – all but dissertation', a struggling grad student, for ever. It was enough to make her envy Hermetria. At least she probably got to marry her prince. Or nobleman. Or knight. Dulcie slumped in her seat. It was all the same, and crushingly dull. As dull and conventional as Demetria's speeches.

Suddenly, Dulcie straightened up. Maybe she was coming at it wrong. Sniffing aside the incipient sneeze, she reached for her yellow legal pad. Maybe slumping over had finally gotten some blood to her brain. She began to outline the rude germ of an idea. The unknown author of *The Ravages* could write. Those great scenes on the mountain peak, with Hermetria declaring her independence, proved that. But she really fell down on the job with Demetria. It was like going from a three-dimensional character to a flat cartoon.

'Could that be the point? Was the author making this secondary character less interesting on purpose?' She jotted down the idea and underlined it – twice. 'Well,' she asked herself, keeping her voice soft, 'could it?' These last few months, she'd been so involved in reading for entertainment that she hadn't paid attention to where her books took her. She'd needed the escape. First there had been the loss of Jonah, then Mr Grey – not to mention all the craziness of the summer. But the reason it had worked was that the books were good. She'd fallen for Gothic lit, for *The Ravages* in particular, *because* it was lively and well written. Even Suze had commented on that – had noted that Dulcie was a scholar because she looked at the writing, the characterization. Therefore, if one character was particularly flat, maybe there was a reason. Maybe the author was trying to give her a clue.

Listen to the voices, Dulcie. Is that what Mr Grey had been trying to tell her all along? Not to eavesdrop on the switchboard women – but to pay attention to the voices in the text. The voices – the author – was trying to tell her something. But what?

Dropping *The Italian* with a thud, she raced back to the shelves for her favorite edition of *The Ravages.* Here it was, the passage that had always stayed in her mind:

> I do swear upon my heart, my friend belov'd!
> Whatever rough winds blow from fate, I'll not be mov'd.

What was it Shakespeare had said, 'The lady doth protest too much'? Well, the author of *The Ravages* would certainly know her *Hamlet*. Dulcie flipped ahead to check the details. Yes, much had been made of the attendant's loyalty. She herself had been 'of noble birth', though clearly her circumstances were reduced if she had become, essentially, a paid companion. So the author wasn't trying to denote a class difference, or make the lesser character appear badly educated, just down on her luck. So why the cheesy speeches?

What if – Dulcie held her breath while the idea came together – the ghost of the old retainer wasn't the malicious spirit? What if the old retainer had hovered around Hermetria trying to warn her? Could Demetria be the 'jealous spirit'? The one close enough to have cast 'spells most potent'?

She started writing. It made sense. 'Spirit', from the Latin, had both connotations by the eighteenth century – 'ghost' and 'soul' – and the author of *The Ravages* might have enjoyed stirring up some confusion. Sure, there were details missing. Motive, for one, and also the mystery of the missing riches: if Demetria had ripped off Hermetria's 'patrimony', then why was she still hanging around? But Dulcie would have months to explore possible clues and hints. She might never know the whole truth. But she had a new interpretation of *The Ravages of Umbria*. She had, maybe, possibly, her thesis topic.

'"Jealous Spirits": A New Reading of *The Ravages of Umbria*.' Dulcie could see it now – or at least that title, in gold, embossed on a leather book cover. Then it hit her. If she was going to make this work, she had a ton of research to do. For starters, there were several versions of the remaining text. Little things – word choices, even the spellings of names – might trip her up. Or give her more fuel for her argument. Wasn't there another Demetria in some other book from that decade? Dulcie grabbed her pencil to make a note. She'd have to look it up, make herself familiar with every repetition of the name. Everything was fair game now, and she was dying to dive in.

How could no one have thought of this before? Even as the question formed in her head, Dulcie knew the answer. Serious readers, even the critics from those very first days, had lambasted the Gothic novels, in particular, the 'She-Authors' who wrote so many of them. Radcliffe, the author of six hugely successful multi-volume novels, had been called 'just a housewife'.

'Talk about "jealous spirits",' Dulcie muttered and jotted another note: 'AR – "housewife"?! Hysterical women?'

Looking at her own writing, Dulcie sat back and chewed on her pen. Housewives, soaps . . . Should she draw the connection with chick lit or was that going too far? Better she should focus on the character of Demetria. Motive – that was the big weak spot. If the gal Friday was the villain, what had she gained? And why did she stay with Hermetria?

Listen to the voices. She could hear that one voice as clearly in her memory as she had heard it in her head. She looked over her notes, but they were silent. Maybe that was because her stomach was now growling loud enough to drown them out. She wanted to keep going, to track down every version of the text and start comparing speeches, but that was going to be the work of months. For now, she had to be content with a lead, a clue; the beginning of a thesis. The rest would come. 'Thank you, Mr Grey,' she whispered as she tucked her notebook into her bag. Man, she was hungry!

Fifteen minutes later, Dulcie was at the counter at Lala's, a good quarter of a three-bean burger in her mouth. Lala's was a student hangout of the best kind, serving up healthy fare that still tasted good. Sure, the travel posters – framed shots of the Acropolis and the Marrakech souk – might be tacky, but the servings were large, the prices low, and Lala herself was known to work the grill on weekends.

Dulcie chewed contentedly. All around her, the Saturday lunch crowd had bellied up for bean burgers, couscous, and salads piled high in blue plastic bowls. She should have gone for one of those salads, she knew. The waistband of her jeans had been growing increasingly tight, but she was too hungry – and too close to a breakthrough – to risk depriving herself of crucial nourishment. She glanced around. Despite the boisterous crowd, nobody looked familiar, and Dulcie let herself indulge in the pure pleasure of a big bite. Something about the spicing, or maybe it was the house-made pickles . . . A stray drip of Lala's hot sauce made its way out of the bun and Dulcie reached for a napkin, happily chewing.

'Dulcie!' Mouth half open, she looked up and quickly shut it, wiping at the streak of sauce with the back of her hand. Stacia, whose even tan was probably never augmented by hot sauce, was standing right beside her.

'Lup?' It was the best Dulcie could manage, as she choked down her mouthful. 'What brings you here?'

'The three-bean burgers, of course!' As luck would have it, the bearded professor type at the next stool stood up, taking his check over to Lala's register, and Stacia slid into the empty seat. 'Especially when Lala is at the grill.'

Dulcie took a smaller, more ladylike nibble and chewed carefully while Stacia ordered. 'I haven't seen you here before.' Was all her turf going to be invaded?

But the smile Stacia gave back was wide, warm – and apparently natural. 'Best thing about summer school. Well, that and getting to help out at the legal clinic.'

And spend time with Luke? Dulcie took a sip of her Diet Coke as she digested the thought. But something – and she didn't think it was Lala's hot sauce – wasn't sitting right. It wasn't the pickle's fault either, it was her own thoughts. What had Mr Grey said about the same forces functioning in different worlds? If Stacia had been a beleaguered noblewoman, Dulcie wouldn't be the jealous Demetria, would she? The thought was enough to put her off her food.

'Luke mentioned something about you working there.' That sounded possessive, like she was marking her territory. Swallowing, she tried again. 'It sounds like you're really helping out.' Dulcie did her best to give the compliment with a smile.

'Oh, I don't know that much.' Stacia had the grace to look abashed, staring down at the napkin and silverware that had appeared on the counter before her. 'I'm just grateful that they're willing to let a summer student sit in.'

'Oh come on!' Dulcie was warming to her theme. 'Luke says you're the computer mastermind down there.'

Stacia was shaking her head as she took her plate from the counter woman. 'Oh, I wish! I'd be doing a lot better in my classes if that were the case.' She took a gratifyingly large bite out of her own burger.

'Luke really has been raving about your expertise.' Dulcie dragged a fry through the small pool of hot sauce and popped it into her mouth. 'In fact, he was suggesting I ask you to look at my laptop.'

'Your laptop?' Stacia dabbed at her own lips. How did she get her lipstick to stay on? 'I think he's just being kind to me. You know, because I've been taking care of Alana and all.'

'I don't think so.' Dulcie reached for her wallet and noticed that her cell was buzzing. With all the bustle in the little luncheonette, she hadn't heard it. She flipped the phone open: Cambridge Police Department. 'Do you mind?'

Stacia waved her hand, her mouth too full to talk. Maybe she was human after all.

'Hello, Dulcie Schwartz.' She could hear the nerves in her voice.

'Ms Schwartz, this is Officer Ron Pipkin in Property. You lost a laptop?'

'My laptop was *stolen*.' Dulcie didn't dare hope.

'Well, we've found it. You can come pick it up anytime. But we'd like to talk with you when you do. Do you know where we're located?'

'Uh-huh.' She listened as the officer gave her directions anyway, and hung up, feeling completely restored.

'They found my laptop!' She bounced off her seat. 'I'm off to get it now! And I've got to call Suze.'

'That's great, I guess.' Stacia looked happy for her, if confused, and Dulcie realized she hadn't told her what had happened. 'Who's Sooz?'

'My old room-mate; I sent her everything as backup just last week, thank God! So I've got to call her and get her to send it all back right away.' Her earlier enthusiasm welled back up. 'You wouldn't believe what I'm on to!'

'Oh?' Stacia took another bite, waiting. But it was such a long story.

'I can explain it some other time. Anyway, I've got to run.' Dulcie flung her bag over her shoulder. 'See you around!'

Stacia raised her hand in a half wave. She still looked confused, though it could have been the hot sauce. It did tend to build up. Or maybe, thought Dulcie, the pretty brunette just wasn't that sharp after all.

Fifteen minutes later, Dulcie was bounding up the stairs of police headquarters. The mix of inspiration, good food, and an insight into the vulnerability of a rival had combined to lift her mood still further. 'Sure, she's pretty. But she's human. And Luke's a thinker . . . Oh, excuse me! I'm looking for Officer Pipkin?'

The woman at the desk just nodded and pointed off to the right.

'Hi! I'm Dulcie Schwartz!' Dulcie swung the Property door open in a grand entrance. The three men who looked up didn't seem impressed.

But one, who had been standing by a file cabinet, motioned for her to approach.

'Ms Schwartz. I'm Officer Pipkin. Would you have a seat?'

Probably forms to fill out, Dulcie thought, sliding into an empty plastic chair.

'You called the police yesterday evening? To report a break-in?'

'Yes, yes, I did.' He sat down at his desk, the deep grooves around his mouth weighing down his drooping lips.

He probably looks like a hound no matter what his mood, Dulcie thought. 'Did you catch someone? Is that how you got my laptop back?'

He leaned back. 'Ms Schwartz, you've been under a lot of stress lately. I'm aware of the murder of your room-mate, and the circumstances surrounding that investigation.'

'Circumstances? If you mean finding Tim, well, yes, that was pretty awful.' They couldn't still consider her a suspect for Tim's murder, could they? She'd never been called back in. 'In fact, my neighbor and I were wondering if the break-in was connected. Like, the murderers had come back for something—'

'Ms Schwartz.' Hangdog or not, Pipkin's voice had a certain authority, particularly when he was interrupting her. 'We're prepared to be lenient here. We're not entirely without human feelings, you know. I myself have a daughter of approximately your age.'

'Yes?' This seemed to be leading somewhere.

'But if you persist in your story, there will be consequences. We are not prepared to take false reports lightly. The waste of resources, of manpower, of a major metropolitan police squad—'

'Wait a minute.' It was Dulcie's turn to interrupt. This dog-faced fellow was accusing her of . . . what? 'Do you think I faked the robbery? Stole my own laptop?'

'The door hadn't been forced, and the one so-called missing item, your laptop, was found during a follow-up visit, right behind your building.' Pipkin reached back for a clipboard. 'Yes, under your own window, behind some foundation planting. In a black plastic bag much like the ones you have in your own kitchen cabinet.' He checked the board again. 'In the bottom drawer, next to the refrigerator.'

'This is ridiculous!' Dulcie stood up. 'This is *crazy*! Next, you'll be saying I stabbed Tim.'

Dogface raised his heavy eyebrows. The rest of his face remained unmoved. 'Do you have something you want to tell us, Ms Schwartz?'

'No. Not what you're asking, anyway. I didn't kill my room-mate. I didn't like him, but I'm not a murderer.' Why was she explaining herself? Perhaps there was something about that sad, long face. 'And I didn't fake that break-in. Why would I do that? Smash my own window? No, never mind.' He'd looked like he was about to speak. 'Can I just get my laptop back?'

'Well, there's a complication.' Pipkin picked through some other papers. 'You see, if you persist in your claim, then we'll have to hang on to it for a while longer. Check it for evidence, and all that.'

'Fine!' Dulcie had grabbed her bag. She was ready to put all this craziness behind her.

'We're going to have to let the forensic techs go over it as well. It looks like someone tried to wipe it clean, but that won't bother our guys.' Pipkin kept his eyes on his papers, but Dulcie felt sure he wanted her to listen. 'After all, we are coordinating with the university. They're very interested in any suspicious computers.'

'*Suspicious*? It's my computer! It's got all my work on it. Personal stuff and photos, too.' Dulcie knew she was shouting; she couldn't help it.

'Well, then, maybe it's just as well that we're going to have it for a while.' Pipkin looked up at her, his large brown eyes staring into her own. 'If it's here, then you know it will be safe.'

Twenty-Seven

When her cell rang again, Dulcie was tempted to throw it at a tree. She'd stormed out of the brick building, infuriated. How could they? The entire interview – all twenty minutes of it – had been strangely humiliating. It wasn't just that they wouldn't give Dulcie her own computer back. It was that sad sack's attitude: he was acting like she was a child. Deranged. Like she was a *hysterical female*! God, two hundred plus years, and nothing had changed.

Still, the number was vaguely familiar and when she answered, she was relieved to hear a friendly voice.

'Hey, Dulcie, what's up?'

Luke appreciated some smarts in a woman, right? 'Hi, Luke. I've just had an . . . odd experience.' Standing in the sunlight, it all seemed too crazy to explain.

'You don't lead a settled life, do you?' Before she could protest, he continued. 'But would you want to tell me about it over dinner? I owe you one.'

Before she really knew what she was doing, Dulcie found herself agreeing to be picked up at eight. If she could shake off the encounter with Cambridge's finest, she thought, she might enjoy herself. And if she could reach Suze before then, she could tell her about the germ of a thesis idea – and also get some feedback on what she should wear.

'Suze? Bother. Well, life continues to be interesting.' Back in her own apartment, Dulcie found herself facing the boarded window and fuming. How *dare* the cops think she had done that to her own place? How dare they accuse her of faking it? 'Call me.' Suze's voicemail wasn't satisfying and Dulcie's immediate urge – to give more detail in an email – was stymied by the realization, once again, that her trusty laptop was gone.

'At least, it's not *gone* gone.' Dulcie heard her own command of the language disappearing. 'I mean, I'll get it back at some point.'

With several hours to kill, she could be reading. But she needed to vent. It was *her* computer! Didn't they get that?

'Hey, Chris.' He'd cared enough to help out, hadn't he? And she ought to update him, anyway. 'I don't know if I'm going to need that loaner.' Wasn't anyone at home? 'The cops found my laptop. They're holding it – long story – but I think I'll get it back soon. Anyway, uh, thanks for being there.'

She was about to hang up when she heard someone pick up. 'Dulcie?' So he was home after all. 'I just got in. So you've got your laptop back?'

Dulcie sighed. She'd said it all in the message. But he'd been so generous. 'Well, I'm going to.' She settled back on to the sofa. 'And maybe soon I'll actually need it again.' She just couldn't resist. 'I think I finally have my thesis topic.'

'Oh?' His voice rose in a question. 'I thought Trista said you'd taken your comprehensives together. Isn't she already into hers?'

'She's ahead of me – in every sense.' For once, Dulcie could say that and not feel the grip of fear. 'My concentration is about a century before hers, and until today I wasn't sure what to write about. But I think I'm going to be focusing on this one book – well, *part* of a book – from the late 1700s, *The Ravages of Umbria*.'

Chris made an interested noise, and Dulcie warmed to her topic. 'Novel serialization began pretty early in the eighteenth century,' she began. 'Newspapers carried them, and printers made cheap copies, printing out a bunch of pages at a time as little chapbooks. It made books affordable and really popular – but not very durable. So we don't know if most of *The Ravages* is lost, or just never got written. But I think I found something today.' She quickly related the plot – what there was of it – and her theory. 'You could say, these books were more or less about the readers, about seemingly ordinary women who go through amazing trials of their personal character and convictions. So making jealousy a motive might not be too far-fetched.'

'Fascinating.' He seemed to mull over what she'd said, and when he responded it wasn't what she expected. 'It must be difficult,' his voice sounded thoughtful, 'to be championing something based on emotions in our era of logic.'

'Spoken like a computer sciences guy!' He meant well, she knew it. But she couldn't resist the tease.

'No, really.' He pushed on. 'I mean, Harvard is all about logic, about proof. This place can make it very hard to trust your instincts, to trust yourself.'

'Well . . .' she began, pausing to think about it. Was this era any different than two hundred-odd years ago, when the books were written? 'Things haven't changed that much. Even back in the 1780s, some of the authors tried to pass their novels off as real. They were always framed as "true" stories. Some of the authors even made up elaborate fake documents to back them up.'

'No wonder the critics hated them.' Chris was chuckling now. 'And no wonder you stick up for them.'

That caught her attention. 'What?'

'Well, it sounds like being a grad student. I mean, we're involved in uncovering truth. And we spend half our lives checking documentation. But, really, isn't being a grad student kind of romantic – pursuing knowledge for its own sake? Isn't that the ultimate expression of humanity? Dreaming the impossible dream, and all that?'

'That's Cervantes. He was Spanish. But some do say that *Don Quixote* was the first novel—'

'OK, OK!' He was laughing outright. 'Excuse a computer nerd's ignorance. But go on – if you have a theory you must have an idea about the ending, right?'

'These books always turn out the same way.' She sighed; it was all so predictable. 'The villain is uncovered and punished, the heroine triumphs and finds true love. Pretty conventional, really.'

'So, what's the problem?'

Did Chris actually care? In a way, it didn't matter. Dulcie knew she had to talk this out. 'Well, if my theory holds, I know who the villain is.' That part still sounded good to her. 'But, I don't know *why* really.' There; she'd hit the crux of it. 'I love the whole idea that the author hid Demetria's villainy in a stereotype, sort of like linguistic camouflage. In so many ways it makes sense with the text. But then it just starts to fall apart. If Demetria is the villain, why isn't she wealthy? Why is she still hanging around her victim? She doesn't seem to profit from her evil deeds.'

'Would she have to?'

'Yeah, I think so. These books were a reaction against the so-called Age of Reason. They were a celebration of emotion, of the heart, of human nature. In some ways, the beginning of Romanticism, maybe even of feminism! So her crime is valuing something over loyalty and friendship. But what?'

'Everybody has secrets, Dulcie.' He paused and she remembered him coming out of the health services. 'Everybody – and didn't you say these books celebrate human nature? Maybe there was a guy they fought over in that missing part. Maybe she was driven by love?'

'Who knows?' It was no good. Even though Dulcie herself had wondered about Demetria's suitors, the dearth of evidence was getting to her. Plus, she was beginning to get the nagging feeling that Chris – Suze's intended – was flirting with her. 'I'm just hoping I can make my case about the author's use of characterization.' What had seemed like a slam dunk only a few hours before was slipping out of reach.

'You should trust yourself, Dulcie,' Chris said, sounding surprisingly like Mr Grey. 'Trust what you've found. Faint heart never fair thesis won, and all that. Or is Gilbert and Sullivan too modern for you?'

They both laughed, and Dulcie felt herself cheered. 'Maybe that'll make its way into my thesis.'

'Glad to be of help, milady.'

After they hung up, Dulcie walked into the kitchen. The boarded-up window had been preying on her nerves, and at least from the kitchen she could look out at the street. Late summer, and the afternoon sun was just beginning to fade. Shadows stretched from the trees and street lights, and Dulcie stood there long enough to feel them approaching. She knew she could go for a walk, even see what was up with Helene and the kittens. But everything seemed like too much work. Times like this were when you needed a room-mate, someone to just sit with you when you needed company. Someone you could talk with, who would understand what made you tick.

Sort of like Chris did? The thought broke into her consciousness so unexpectedly that she turned around, looking for Mr Grey. But no, this one came from her own mind. Chris really had been there for her yesterday, too, first offering to help with her computer, then accompanying her home when she needed an escort. She shook her head. Two hours till Luke would pick her up for a real date. A Saturday night dinner. And here she was, thinking of Chris?

And why not? Her own thoughts had begun to take on a Mr Grey-like opposition; phantom pet as devil's advocate. Just because he's not involved with someone else? 'But I didn't know Bruce was seeing Luisa.' She spoke aloud. Or interested in anyone else? 'I don't know for sure if Luke likes Stacia.' The voice ignored her. He's tall. He's smart. He's not bad looking. 'But he's Suze's. And I don't want to be the Demetria in this drama.' Saying it out loud didn't help. She knew the truth: Suze didn't want him.

So, does that decrease his value? God, she was back to that again. She was 'just a girl, a grad student, and ABD'. And Chris was just a . . . what? 'A really nice guy, who's smart and kind'. She envisioned his broad mouth – the way it wrinkled back up to his eyes when he smiled – and his thick, dark hair, the bangs that always fell into his face. 'And, yeah, he's cute, too.'

This time, she was sure she heard a purr.

It was with great confusion, therefore, that she heard the doorbell two hours later. She'd settled, finally and with no help from Suze, on a sundress that showed off her shoulders, but was still undecided between a jacket or a more informal wrap – one of Lucy's knit jobs – in case of heavy air-conditioning. The bell rang again, and Dulcie grabbed the wrap. It wasn't one of Lucy's best, she'd run out of the cream wool halfway through and switched to a dark purple. But Dulcie felt defiant. 'Some men seem to like me just as I am!' With one last tug at her curls, she descended to the front door to meet her date.

An hour later, she was confused all over again, but not unhappy. Luke was, as he always had been, charming. He'd chosen the perfect spot: a Watertown bistro known for its good food and relaxed atmosphere, but not so expensive as to make Dulcie feel she was being bought.

'So, what do you think of the wine?' He'd poured the last of the rosé into her glass. 'I'm game for another bottle. Or we can try something different.'

Dulcie sipped the light, fruity wine and tried to look serious. 'Summery. Fresh.' She licked her lips. 'I'm getting a sense of strawberries and—' She broke out in a laugh. 'I'm sorry, Luke. I think I've probably had enough.'

'Me, too, I guess.' He refilled her water glass. 'But some dessert might help soak it up!'

'Well . . .' She hesitated. Stacia did not have a roll around her middle.

'Split something?' He smiled a wicked smile. 'I'll take the half with the calories.'

'You're on! But, would you excuse me?' Face flushed from the wine, Dulcie needed the walk as much as the restroom. What was going on here? Was he being so friendly because he didn't see her as a romantic option? That line about calories had a buddy-buddy feel to it. Or was he just so sure of her? A small spark of anger rose up. 'If he thinks that I'm *just* a poor grad student . . .'

The flush of a toilet broke into her thoughts and brought her back to earth. It was a date. He was being nice. She wasn't even sure if she liked him, right?

A minute later, looking at herself in the ladies' room mirror, she couldn't tell. At least her hair was behaving, responding to the humid night with curls rather than frizz. And those long hours indoors had kept the freckles in check. She smiled. Nothing between her teeth, so she let the smile broaden into a real grin as she walked back to the table. There she found Luke staring off into space.

'Luke, is anything wrong?'

'What? Oh, I'm sorry.' He turned back toward her, his face sad. 'I just saw one of Tim's friends with a woman. His fiancé, I think. And it made me think of – well—' He sighed.

Dulcie reached out to take his hand. 'I'm sorry. It must be so hard.'

He tried to smile, and failed, but covered her hand with his own. 'It's just so odd. I mean, the timing. Maybe Tim would've been like that eventually. Settled down. Happy. Successful.'

'Well, he was trying.' She couldn't see it, but to say so at this point would be unkind. 'I mean, he was getting tutored and everything.'

'Yeah, he really liked her, too; said she was smart.' Plus, thought Dulcie, he was probably screwing her. That was often a bonus in a tutor. 'You know, when I think of it, he might have turned out all right. As funny as it sounds, he did like smart women, you know.'

'Tim?' She bit her lip. The deceased boor was Luke's brother, not hers.

'Well, he was impressed by you, and I know he thought his tutor was really smart.'

'And Alana?' That slipped out. Maybe he hadn't heard.

But Luke sighed. 'Yeah, well. Her pedigree was right. But, ring or not, I don't think he'd have gone through with a wedding. He'd even ratcheted up the "dumb blonde" jokes, talked about trading her in for a smart brunette.'

Maybe Luisa had stood a chance. Dulcie sighed. All in all, she was probably better off with Bruce. But Luke was still talking. 'I had the feeling there was someone he hadn't told anyone about. Some woman who mattered to him, and now we'll never meet.'

Dulcie thought of the young tutor. She was so innocent that Dulcie had assumed she'd been duped; used by the callous rich boy. But maybe he'd seen the earnest young student inside that lush body. Maybe he had cared, or would have, if he'd only had time. Just then, their dessert arrived, a berry tart dusted with sugar. Luke pulled off the mint sprig garnish and made to put it behind his ear. Dulcie couldn't help laughing at his silliness, and the serious subjects were left far behind.

Twenty-Eight

Sunday brought no solution to Dulcie's confusion, but at least it spared her a hangover. Whether to prolong their date, or to sober them both up, Luke had suggested that they walk a bit after leaving the restaurant. Although they'd driven up into Watertown, he'd shown her they were still on the Charles, and the view from the nearby bridge was beautiful, all lights and shimmering reflection.

'Rather like Paris,' he'd said, reaching over to touch her hair.

'Or Portland.' Her response was automatic, and not entirely accurate. But something about the romantic setting made her timid, and wry was a good fallback defense.

'That's right. You're from the Pacific Northwest.' He took the hint and turned back toward the river. 'Did you grow up in Portland?'

It was Dulcie's turn to sigh then. This was always the moment she dreaded, explaining her unconventional family dynamics to someone from a more normal background. 'Not exactly,' she stalled, wondering where to begin. Then she realized that she knew more dirt about Luke's family than she did about anyone's except maybe Suze. So why not share?

'So my dad's still in India. At least, last we heard. And my mother is living "on the land", back in the collective.' Fifteen minutes later, she had all the worst points sketched out.

'Cool!' He'd actually laughed when Dulcie had told him about the yurt. 'You really are a self-made woman, aren't you, Dulcie Schwartz?'

Dulcie shrugged, flattered. 'To be honest, my mom – Lucy – is a good mother. I mean, she's nutty, but she loves me. And when I wanted to go East to school, she didn't stand in my way.'

He was looking at her. 'Do you know how rare that is? I hang out with so many spoiled brats. They complain when their folks don't give them everything, and here you are.' He reached out to take her hand, but she turned away, pulling herself up to the concrete balustrade.

'Here I am, learning the ways of the oppressors!' She'd meant it as a joke, but the moment the words were out of her lips, she regretted them. 'Sorry, I don't mean—'

'No, I know.' He reached to grab her wrap before it fell into the water. 'But I think it's time we called it a night.'

All things considered, she should have been content with the small goodnight peck at the door. But when she woke, she found herself lying in bed, staring at the light playing on the ceiling. Had she wanted more? Less? Was she taking this traditional female role-playing too far?

Enough. If she couldn't straighten out her love life, she could at least make progress on her thesis. And maybe her new awareness of feminine dilemmas would pay off. If she could only find a motive for Demetria, she'd be set. A quick shower, an iced latte, and a mixed berry muffin, and she was good to go. Tossing the paper cup into a trash barrel outside the library, she hopped up the granite stairs toward what really mattered in life.

'No laptop usage until further notice,' the guard said without looking up. 'Bag, please.' Signs taped along the walls reinforced the ban, marring the marble grandeur of the library entrance: 'Please keep laptops turned off'. For Dulcie, the notices only stirred up the ashes of her fury. But enough of that. Outside of Widener, the real world might hold sway, with confusing men and idiotic police. Inside was her realm. She opened her bag, empty of everything but her pad and some pens. After yesterday's breakthrough, she was eager to get started.

'Hey, Mona!' She waved at her friend. The librarian smiled and came over, standing on the other side of the electronic gate as Dulcie swiped her card and walked through.

'Well, look at you! Have you been having some fun?'

'Why? What?' Dulcie could feel the blush climbing up from her T-shirt collar. 'I don't know what you're talking about.'

Mona waved her objection away, her jewel-inset nails sparkling in the sunlight-flooded entry. 'You've got the look. You're in *love* . . .'

Dulcie laughed. 'Well, it's never that simple.' Her friend opened her mouth to protest, so she continued without a breath, 'But, even better, I think I've got a thesis topic nailed down.' Mona had heard enough of Dulcie's late-night anxieties to take this seriously.

'Well, good for you. At least something is nailed down here.' At Dulcie's puzzled look, she continued, 'They still haven't tracked that bug yet. We're back to paper and pencil until further notice. Why do you think I'm here, after the Saturday night I just had?' The librarian's voice rose as she spoke, and Dulcie saw her glancing around, gauging her audience.

'OK, you're going to have to spill.' Dulcie gave her friend a quick hug. 'Later this week, at Grendel's. But now, I think we've both got work to do.'

'Nothing I can say in this place, anyway.' Mona grinned back. 'I'd set off the fire alarms for sure.'

As Dulcie waited for the elevator, she suppressed a shiver. Mona's words reminded her that when the library had been renovated, the architects had installed a state-of-the-art fire suppression system. Weighing the risk of both fire and water to the three million plus books and untold manuscripts, maps, and what have you, they had opted to install a supersensitive alarm that actually analyzed air content, in order to avoid the sprinklers going off unnecessarily. At least, that was what the publicity material had led everyone to believe. But, according to grad student gossip, some of the rare books sections were protected by a different system. At the first sign of fire, the rumor said, airtight seals would close the doors and windows in the rooms with the rarest manuscripts – the vellums and papyri – and super-powered fans would suck out all the oxygen. That would extinguish a fire, all right. But woe betide any researcher trapped inside.

It would be a horrible death, Dulcie thought as the small elevator descended and the pit of her stomach rose from the rush. Although she was not sure she really believed the rumors. Nor, she reminded herself as the steel doors opened, did she usually spend time in the 'locked wards'. Once she got down to writing, sure, she'd want to work from primary sources; to see the letters written by the first readers of *The Ravages*. She'd also want to read the contemporary critics, so much livelier – and nastier – than the modern press. But these papers, thought Dulcie as she walked by the tall, metal cases, were comparatively modern. Two hundred years was nothing to Widener. This place was like a pyramid, with secrets buried that were older by far.

'Buried. Great.' Everything was creeping her out today. 'Maybe I should have drunk *more* last night.' She raised her voice slightly in defiance. Two aisles down, she heard someone clearing his throat.

'Sorry,' she called softly, absurdly reassured that someone else was down here on Level A with her. And with that she went to work.

She started with the basics, first. '*The Polite Lady*, yes, that's good.' She pulled the book from the shelf, marveling that a work that had first been printed in 1760 should be so accessible. Here, in her hands, was one of the definitive guides for behavior for the latter half of the eighteenth century. She pictured tea being poured, as well-trained servants looked on. But there was so much more, even then. *Letters on Female Education*, yes, she thought, that was another important book. For women were reading, women were *writing*; and even such 'improving' books would hold hints of that wider world of newspapers and novels and intellectual turmoil. Dulcie knew what she was looking for. Here she'd find the foundation for her thesis; the proof that, yes, the author of *The Ravages of Umbria* would be just as aware of what was expected, and what was silly, as any contemporary author. In here – she pulled another book, *Letters on the Improvement of the Mind* – Dulcie would find the model for Demetria, a simpering, two-faced traitor. Once she understood who the character was, *why* she turned on her friend would follow.

Arms loaded, Dulcie retreated to the aisle's end. Around the corner, she could see an empty carrel. She deposited her books, put her feet up, and began to read. Time slipped away. 'Critics and snobs, all of them,' she found herself muttering more than once. Who cared if the author of *A Sicilian Romance* had ever actually been to Sicily? Had Defoe ever been shipwrecked? Just because *The Ravages* was set in a fictional Umbria didn't mean the author wasn't smart. Maybe the mountains were a dramatic device.

A light went on nearby. The owner of the cleared throat, she figured. Soft footsteps faded and in a moment the light turned off. Where was she? Ah, the struggle between the rational 'Augustans' and the emotional 'Romanticists'. Well, that was what they were called once men got involved. Historically, she was getting ahead of herself. Gingerly – her right foot had fallen asleep – Dulcie pulled herself up. How long had she been sitting? Too long, she realized, as she managed to straighten out both legs and hobble back to where she'd originally pulled the book. No, she would have to go back earlier. The card at the edge of the stack said '1805–1845'. Humming softly, she crossed over to the earlier rack and then, for good measure, the one before. With a slight buzz, a light came on: 1745–1780. Yes, that would do.

'Wow!' Dulcie pulled a bound volume off the shelf: *The Public Ledger*, 1761–62. How often would she be reminded of what a treasure trove this library was? Somewhere, a few stacks away, a lighter footstep passed by, making Dulcie smile. At least she wasn't the only one worshipping here on a Sunday morning. She reached up for one more volume – just above her reach. *The Leedes Intelligencer.* Nope, not quite. Looking around for a stepstool, Dulcie saw that the neighboring aisles had gone dark. No stool, no bystanders. 'May Toth, the god of libraries, forgive me,' she whispered, putting her toes on the first level of bound volumes and hoisting herself up. Her fingers almost reached over the top. If she could move the leather-bound volume out just a fraction of an inch . . . 'There, I've—'

Dulcie jumped back just in time as the thick crimson tome fell to the floor with a thud. 'Sorry!' Her stage whisper wasn't answered, even by a cough, but Dulcie thought she heard footsteps hasten off. Ah, well, so she'd disturbed another denizen of the depths.

The book itself, once she'd retrieved it, seemed unharmed, although Dulcie could imagine the scolding Mona would give her if she knew. 'Well, she won't,' Dulcie said to herself as she carried the two books, each containing a year's worth of daily newspapers, back to her carrel.

There she stopped abruptly, surprised. 'What the hell?' Dulcie spoke at full volume. Nothing here made sense. The books that she'd neatly piled were pushed back, her pad was on the floor, and her bag had been opened and emptied. One pen was still rolling, until it came to rest by Dulcie's foot. 'What is going on here?' If someone had been looking for her wallet, he'd be disappointed. After paying for her muffin, Dulcie had tucked it into the back pocket of her jeans. But who had done this? Only another student would be this deep in the stacks. Maybe it had been an accident. Someone had stumbled. Maybe someone really needed a pencil.

She sighed and bent to gather her pens. There'd been no harm done, but the disruption was disturbing. For a moment, she thought of Lucy's dream. No, having her stuff messed up was bad enough. Nothing really dangerous could happen down here. Not with all the security up at the entrance. She straightened and dropped the pens in her bag – only to watch them fall down to the floor again. Opening her bag, Dulcie looked inside. This hadn't been a random bag toss: someone had sliced through the bottom of her messenger bag, and whatever had cut through the canvas had been sharp.

'Oh, this is crazy.' Dulcie's own voice sounded loud in her ears. Why would someone do this? She looked around. Although the day had begun sunny and hot, down here the only light came from the soft glow of the overhead fixture. Even the nearby stacks had gone dark.

She'd have to tell security, that was all there was to it. Sure, they'd think she was nuts, but someone else might not be so lucky. Someone else might leave a wallet in a bag or a jacket pocket. Dulcie vaguely recalled a news item about book thefts. No, the rare texts – and the vast majority of standard ones – were now microchipped to prevent them from walking out. It was personal property that was at risk.

So much for the day's work. She gathered up her pad and pens, sticking them in the undamaged outside pocket of her bag. The books she gathered up in her arms. She had too many to carry; she'd reshelve the bound volumes but the rest were coming with her. Air-conditioning or not, she'd get some work done today.

But after that invasion, that attack on her property, Dulcie no longer wanted to leave anything out of sight. Slinging the bag over her shoulder, she hefted all the books. Where were the newspapers from again? Yes, three over, down by the end. Putting the three volumes she wanted to check out on the floor, she found the slight space where *The Public Ledger* had rested and slid it back in. Up there, just above her head, the slot for *The Leedes Intelligencer* made a guilty gap.

Dulcie sighed, suddenly tired. But reshelving by staff could take days. Among the grad students, library etiquette mandated a different response. If you weren't using it, and if you had the sense to put it back properly, you ought to.

Dulcie looked around. No lights betrayed the presence of any other person, and so, as quietly as she could, she slipped off her flip-flops, climbed on to the edge of the lower shelf, and managed to lift the bound volume up to the top shelf. 'There!' She couldn't resist a triumphant whisper. With a gentle push, the book slid into place.

And then she heard it. Not quite an echo, but something. She froze, listening. Had she somehow pushed a book out, on the other side? No, the metal frame of the shelves kept each section secure. So, what . . .? Dulcie turned. Yes, it was a footstep. Someone was walking slowly down the aisles.

It was probably someone reading the cards, looking for a specific date. Dulcie kept her thoughts quiet, as she stepped down. But as she picked up her books from the floor, she grabbed her flip-flops, too. She couldn't have said why she preferred to be barefoot just then, but she did – and began to creep toward the entrance.

The footsteps followed. In the quiet of the library, Dulcie couldn't tell if they were one aisle over, or two, or even more. All she knew was that after each of her own steps, she heard another.

This was crazy. Why was she being so quiet? The overhead light announced her presence like a beacon. These were normal library hours. She had every right to be here. Of course, other people were here, too. She stood up straight. 'Hello?' Even her stage whisper sounded loud. There was no answer. Even the footsteps had stopped. '*Hello*?' She raised her voice, trying to hold it steady.

Nothing. Maybe she'd been hearing things. Maybe whoever it was had simply been looking for a book and had left. Maybe . . . She took two quick steps. Three soft footsteps followed after.

Maybe it was one of her friends, playing a game. But if this were a game, it was an awfully mean one. Plus, whoever had cut her bag had a weapon: a knife or razor, something sharp enough to slice through canvas. Dulcie looked around. There were no windows, of course, not this far down. Though, if she could get to the elevator or even the end of this row of stacks she had a vague memory of something – an alarm, an intercom, a way out.

She bolted, her bare feet slapping against the metal floor. As she ran, lights sprang on overhead. But she was almost at the elevator. She was almost—

A cart, loaded with books, flew in front of her, banging into the wall with a thud. Dulcie froze, her path temporarily blocked. The stacks grew quiet again and she inched forward. The cart was still, the aisle behind it empty. She could move it, roll it out of her way. But who had pushed it there, and why?

The cart was a message. Somebody knew where she stood; somebody didn't want her to leave. This wasn't random, the snatch and grab of an unwatched wallet. This was personal. Down here, in the bowels of Widener, she'd felt safe from attack, from strangers, from rape. Unless it wasn't a stranger. Unbidden, an image of her broken window sprang into Dulcie's mind. Maybe whoever it was hadn't found what he wanted on her laptop. Hadn't gotten whatever it was from Tim.

The footsteps were quiet, but still there. Someone was moving slowly and very, very carefully, but Dulcie heard him. At the far end of the tall shelf of books, someone was moving to box her in. Someone had shoved the cart, letting her know that she couldn't go in that direction, and now that someone was walking up to the edge of her aisle.

She looked up the row of books, the metal shelving lit by the soft overhead glow. Whoever it was out there knew she was here. But if she moved very slowly back, she could put another stack between herself and it – him. She could maybe back out, work around to the other elevator, or a fire alarm, and be free. Dulcie looked around for the familiar red boxes. That rumor about the fire suppression system couldn't be true, could it? Not that it mattered; there were none in sight.

She took a step. The light above her buzzed and flickered. How sensitive was the motion detector? Thinking back desperately to the days when she and Jonah had made out here, she remembered counting twenty – no, thirty – seconds before the lights went black. But how long before they turned on?

Another step back. The light flickered again, and the footsteps fell silent. Whoever was out there, he was waiting, Dulcie realized. He would head her off, trap her. And he was armed.

But she knew this library, and with a flash of anger, she hit on an idea. Crouching low, she darted back to the wall aisle and dashed a few feet. Sure enough, the next two aisles lit up – and by reaching out her hand, she got one more to react. The footsteps followed. Good! Let whoever was out there think she was running scared. She could wait him out.

Quickly, before the light could shut off, she returned to where the cart had cut her off. Pressed against the wall, Dulcie tried to steady her breathing. Twenty, twenty-one . . . She'd had no idea she was counting until the light snapped off. Thank you, Harry Elkins Widener! Dulcie closed her eyes in relief. She'd give it a few more minutes and then—

But the footsteps had stopped. She'd been following the soft pad of the shoes, hoping to hear them fade away, but they hadn't. They'd simply stopped, and she could too easily picture someone – a shadow – standing there, waiting. Either he'd figured out her ploy, or he was smart enough to know that no matter how she ran, he had her trapped. She was in a corner of the stacks, up against the outside wall. He stood between her and both the elevators and the stairwells. He was fast, and he had a knife. Dulcie took a deep breath. Smarts were what were called for here. Smarts – and a little help.

Where was her cell phone? She tried to envision it, to picture whether it had been taken from her bag or fallen to the floor. If it was still in the small inside pocket of her bag, she could reach in and flick it on. Sure, she'd be breaking library rules. But assault with a deadly weapon was against library policy, too.

Slowly as she could, she slid her right arm up the side of the bag. Smoothly as she could, she slid her hand inside, feeling for the telltale lump – and jumped when the metal phone hit the floor. It clattered once, but by instinct she'd reached for it, and that was enough. The lights flashed on with a buzz and the footsteps came running.

There was nothing for it. Dulcie shoved the cart back up the aisle in front of her and took off. The footsteps were catching up, on the other end of the stacks, between her and the elevators; between her and the emergency stairs. She'd have to cut through at some point. Dulcie started counting. How many aisles on Level A? Would he be able to pin her against one of the walls? Lights blazed on as she ran, each step marking her trail for her attacker. Could she outpace him?

'Damn!' She caught up short. In front of her was a wire cage – 'Elizabethan Texts. Special Permission Only'. She'd outraced her century, and looked around for a way out. Behind her all was lit up. To her right was the wall. To her left, somewhere, her attacker waited. Dare she double back? She turned. Eight aisles back, a light flickered out, then another. Her every movement was being tracked. She'd run into a corner. She was trapped.

Was that him? She saw a movement, six aisles back. Something low to the ground – a foot? A shadow? She heard the footsteps again, getting closer. There! No, it came from this end. A rat? Here, in Widener? Suddenly, a dark aisle lit up, and then another, and another. A small grey shape was dashing down the aisle away from Dulcie, darting into every stack as she herself had done to ignite the lights. It was Mr Grey, emblazoning the entire floor. She heard the human footsteps pause and stop. She heard them start to run – away from her, toward the light, toward the fleet figure of her phantom pet.

'Thank you, Mr Grey!' Dulcie mouthed her gratitude, all doubt gone. She could have yelled the words out loud, but saved her breath for that last dash toward the fire exit, into the stairwell, and up to daylight.

Twenty-Nine

The scene that greeted Dulcie was shocking in its normalcy. As she burst through the door, heads turned – but only because she nearly fell, sprawling out of the stairwell. Instead of darkness and panic, she looked around to light, polished marble, and several startled glances.

'Are you OK, Miss?' An elderly clerk left his cart to offer her a hand.

'Guard! Police!' Dulcie's breath came in gasps. 'Close the exits.'

The clerk stepped back and withdrew his hand. The look on his face made Dulcie wonder for a moment if she had begun speaking in tongues.

'I've been attacked!' With those magic words, she broke through.

'You poor dear!' The clerk moved forward again to support her, and from over by the entrance a blue-uniformed guard came running.

'Are you hurt? Lie down. I'm calling for an ambulance.' He pulled a walkie-talkie from his belt.

'No, no, I'm fine!' Dulcie freed herself from the clerk's supporting arm. 'But there was someone trying to trap me. He slashed my bag.' She held up the ruined messenger bag. As if to prove her point, a pen fell through it to clatter on the marble floor.

'Hang on. Cancel the bus.' The guard turned toward her and pulled out a pad. 'You saw this? You saw an intruder with a knife or some other sharp object? Can you describe him?'

'No.' Dulcie was catching her breath. Two more library staffers had come up, curious and concerned. 'I can't. I'm sorry.' Eight sets of eyes stared at her. Twelve, if you counted the glasses. 'I was looking for a book, and when I got back to the carrel, my bag had been slashed. Then, when I went to reshelve the book – I'm sorry, but I knew right where it came from.'

The clerk nodded his forgiveness.

'Anyway, I started hearing footsteps. And, well, someone was coming for me.'

The white-haired clerk raised his bushy eyebrows. His hands were now clasped in front of him. The guard stopped writing. 'And you knew someone was coming for you how?'

'By his footsteps. He was following me up the rows of stacks, trying to trap—' Dulcie stopped. She sounded hysterical, but she had to make her point. 'Somebody was there. Somebody slashed open my bag. I called out and nobody answered, but somebody was dogging me – at the very least.'

'Well, what we have here is vandalism and attempted theft, for sure. Did the perpetrator get anything? Wallet? iPod?' Dulcie shook her head. 'Well, I'll take a report and we'll post a warning. Do you want to pursue it further? I am authorized to call in the city police in cases of violence or threatened violence. This is your option as a member of the Harvard community.'

As her panic faded, Dulcie heard his voice. He was repeating something learned in a sensitivity seminar. He didn't believe her. She sighed. If a Harvard guard didn't, what were the chances a Cambridge cop would? They already thought she was off; attention-seeking. She closed her eyes and didn't realize she was swaying until she felt the old clerk's arms around her again.

'Are you OK, Miss? When was the last time you ate anything?' Other arms reached out to her, and she let them lower her to the cool stone floor.

'I . . . I had a muffin this morning.' She did feel dizzy, and hung her head down toward her lap.

'It's nearly three,' said the guard. 'I think you've had a scare and someone tried to rip you off. Would somebody get her a drink with some sugar in it, please? Orange juice perhaps?' Dulcie heard footsteps hurry off, heavy ones this time. 'And is there a friend we can call for you, or a room-mate, perhaps?'

Maybe I am losing it. Dulcie was sitting in the guard's office, drinking yet another glass of orange juice. Maybe I'm hearing things – footsteps, ghost cats. She'd already signed the Harvard Police form, letting the entire terrifying experience be filed away as an act of 'vandalism and/or attempted theft'.

'It's like someone tried to rip off my bicycle,' she muttered.

'Excuse me?' The guard looked up. He seemed to be taking a long time with his report, and Dulcie had a sinking feeling that whatever he was writing wasn't complimentary to her.

'Nothing. May I go now?' At least, with all the hubbub, the clerk had made the effort to check her books out for her. She now held them on her lap, along with her various pens, pad, and the mutilated bag, in a black garbage bag.

'Are you sure you feel well enough to be on your own?' He didn't like it, she could see. Dulcie had told him simply that she lived alone. To bring up Tim's murder, at this point, was just going to make more trouble.

'Yes.' She stood up. The world had stopped spinning. 'I'd really like to go home now.'

'OK, Ms Schwartz.' He stood up as well, either to see her out or to make sure she didn't topple over and injure herself on his watch. 'I'm sure we'll be in touch.'

'I'm sure.' Knowing that every eye was on her, Dulcie stepped carefully out through the electronic gate, past the huge glass doors and on to the granite steps. Only when she was halfway down did she dare put on her flip-flops once again. She really didn't need another incident in her life today.

'Suze, where are you?' She left another message for her errant friend. 'You wouldn't believe what's been going on. Call me.'

At least her door, when she arrived home, was locked shut. And if the living room window was still covered over by plywood, a stiff breeze fluttered the curtains in her bedroom. Her pretty sundress lay across the chair. Had her date with Luke been only last night? Leaving the dress on the chair, she leaned across it to open the window wider and walked down the narrow hall to open the windows in Tim's room – Suze's room – too. The cross breeze sang down the narrow hall, fluttering the papers on her desk. A storm was brewing, she'd seen the clouds skittering across the sky as she'd walked home, but the eaves overhanging this top floor would keep the rain from blowing in.

Dulcie lay down on her bed and smiled. Mr Grey had always hated this kind of weather; some combination of thunder and the pressure dropping had made him a little needy, a little on edge. Maybe she was thinking of him too much. Maybe she . . .

A rumble of thunder announced the beginning of the rain. Dulcie arranged her arm, moving it away from her side. She was just beginning to feel the pressure of paws, the kneading of her pet, when she fell asleep.

Thirty

Maybe it was the pressure of those paws. Maybe it was the memory of seeing her pet in the library. Maybe it was the conviction deep in her heart that the feline phantom had run interference, had possibly saved her life. Or maybe it was simply that she was finally beginning to work on something that could possibly result in a decent doctoral thesis. Dulcie didn't know why, but she woke feeling more confident than she had in ages. She wasn't going crazy, she told herself as she showered; or becoming Lucy, which might be worse, she reminded herself as she dressed. She simply had a feline spirit looking out for her. And that, she repeated to herself as she trotted to the T, made all the difference.

At least until she walked up to the Priority building, with its oversized glass entrance reflecting the light like gigantic dark glasses. 'This place will always give me the creeps,' she muttered, pushing the heavy metal door open in front of her. Thank God, the summer was almost over.

And so, it seemed, was her job. 'I'm sorry, Miss Schwartz.' The elderly guard looked at Dulcie's ID and pushed her opened bag back toward her. 'No work today.'

She pushed the bag back at him. It was her old purse, a leather satchel that was worn and peeling in the corners. But it was still open. He could still look through it, shabby or not.

'No, Miss Schwartz. There's no temp work today. All the data entry clerk typists are being sent home.'

'But . . .' This didn't make sense. The agency hadn't called her. She'd accepted the lousy new desk, and everything. 'But . . .' Dulcie looked into the wrinkled face of the old-timer. His eyes were a pale grey; the lashes, when he blinked at her, pure white. 'But I get paid by the hour!'

It might not matter to this old guy, but it was a cry from her heart. 'I'm sorry,' he repeated and blinked again. Stalemate.

'Come on, Dulcie!' A strong hand grabbed her arm and spun her around. Joanie, black sweater dress crossed by a chain belt, was leading her out. By her side, a skinny redhead provided a flash of contrasting colour.

'I don't understand.' The three were back out in the sunlight, the morning already getting hot. Joanie had let go of Dulcie's arm, but motioned for her to follow. Dulcie trotted to catch up.

'I need more coffee. Come on.' Joanie marched ahead.

'What's going on? Do you know?' Dulcie asked the lanky redhead.

'Just that you're really smart.' He really did have an endearing grin. 'And Joanie thinks you're being framed.'

'Great.' Dulcie stood still and closed her eyes, waiting for the world to catch up. 'Just great.'

'Hey, Joanie! Wait up!' Ricky waved and the black-clad Goth girl came trotting back.

'What's wrong? Dulcie, are you sick?'

'No.' Dulcie opened her eyes. Two pale faces stared into hers. 'I just want to know what's going on.'

'Well, number one, we're going to get paid.' Joanie marked off her first point on her finger. 'We're contracted. We showed up at the assignment. That's all the agency needs to know – and they'll hear it from me if they try to say otherwise. Number two, this whole mess is finally coming to a head.'

Dulcie looked at her, waiting for her to continue.

'OK, I don't know the details. Ricky?' She looked up at her tall companion. Dulcie did, too. He sighed, color appearing and disappearing almost as fast behind his freckles.

'This is worth my job.' Joanie stared at him. Dulcie waited for her to bat her eyelashes. She didn't. 'Well, OK, I already told *her* this anyway.' He jerked his head toward the diminutive dominatrix. 'They've traced it. Nobody is supposed to know yet, because they've not yet made the arrests, but they figured out where the bug went in and I think they know who put it there. I think it's all going to break loose tomorrow.'

'And we're supposed to come back for that?' Dulcie imagined those large guards coming for her, once again. 'We're supposed to be there?'

'Hey, we're still on the Priority payroll, more or less.' Joanie, deprived of coffee, pulled out a cigarette. 'And I wouldn't miss it for the world!'

It was all too much. Dulcie made her excuses – a headache, school work – and left the couple on the sidewalk.

'Don't forget to come in tomorrow for the fireworks!' Joanie called after her, as Dulcie sought the cool comfort of the subway. The train had emptied of its rush-hour commuters, and Dulcie had room to put her feet up as the car swayed on the track. Was she going to be arrested? Should she show up the next day? Had someone been out to get her specifically yesterday, or had the attack in the library just been random – a foiled purse snatcher making one more attempt? As the Central Square station approached, Dulcie realized that her head really did ache.

The whole thing really was too much. She needed to focus; to see if she could salvage some of that clarity about her thesis. Climbing up to the surface, she looked around. Not Widener, not today. Somewhere she could think, but with other people around.

The little bell on the coffee-house door sounded welcoming as she walked in and up to the bar. 'Iced coffee, please. Lots of cream.'

'Dulcie!' At the sound of her name, she looked up with a start. Luisa was standing right behind her. 'Sorry, did I startle you?'

'Crazy morning.' Dulcie tried to smile and motioned to the empty stool to her left. Maybe, if she played her cards right, she wouldn't have to do any relationship counseling today. 'You've been all patched up.' In truth, Luisa was beaming, but the heavy hair that fell over her face didn't hide the bandage on her forehead.

'Thanks. My chin is still sore.' She gingerly touched her face, and Dulcie could see the darkness of the bruise. 'And I've got this on, still.' She motioned to the bandage and turned to order a cappuccino

Dulcie waited till the barista had moved on. 'But you look happy. You've got a glow.'

Luisa blushed, the color surging up from her neck. 'It's – Bruce. I've told him everything. After – what happened – I felt I had to.' Her mug arrived and she bent over the foam, hiding her face.

'You mean, your fall on the steps?' Dulcie twirled her own glass between her hands; she couldn't bring herself to say 'accident'. 'Do you think that had something to do with Tim?'

The younger girl looked up and stared at the espresso machine, biting her lip. 'I don't know. I don't even remember really what happened. But the only reason I was there was because of his stupid computer. Oh!' She turned toward Dulcie. 'And because of me, you didn't get it, either! And you probably had a really good reason to want it!'

'It's OK, Luisa. It doesn't matter now.' If Tim had transferred some kind of files to Dulcie's own laptop, used her computer as a cat's paw, it was out of her hands anyway. The Cambridge police would probably find the virus on her own laptop – and the missing photo of Mr Grey was long gone. For a moment, the two drank their coffee in silence. Still, the old questions lingered in Dulcie's mind.

'So what were you looking for anyway, Luisa?' She thought of Alana. 'Were there – well – did Tim have pictures of you?'

'Oh, no!' Luisa's blush deepened and she looked down into her mug. 'Just emails that, you know, said things.'

Dulcie remembered the papers she and Luke had uncovered among Tim's stuff. They'd seemed so innocent. 'I think we found some printouts, when Luke and I were cleaning out Tim's room.' Maybe the girl wasn't a ditz, just young. Dulcie tried to make her voice gentle.

'He said he'd never print them out. They were—' she paused, 'private.' She seemed so distressed that Dulcie suspected she wasn't giving up the entire truth.

'So, no photos? Just for fun, between the two of you?'

Luisa looked up, right into Dulcie's eyes. 'No way. I don't think Tim was that sleazy. I liked him, you know. A lot.' She took a deep breath. 'But, well, I know guys like him. He was fun, really fun, to be with. And I think he always meant what he said, when he was saying it. I mean, I didn't find love letters or anything from anyone *else* on the computer. But photos? Nuh-uh. A girl has got to look out for herself. We don't live in some fairy tale, you know.' With that, she drained her mug and pushed off the stool. 'Well, gotta run!'

Dulcie, slightly stunned, watched as the young woman bounced toward the door. She turned to give Dulcie a jaunty wave, and Dulcie managed to raise her hand in return. As she did, she saw, up on a high shelf, a small round bowl.

'Hey, is that a new fish?'

The barista was wiping down the counter. 'No.' She looked up. 'That's Nemo, we brought him back the other day.'

'Wasn't he getting freaked out by the crowd?'

She shook her henna-red head. 'It was just one or two customers. Go figure, but the owner thought he'd try again. Something's changed. Nemo doesn't seem bothered anymore.'

Dulcie drained her glass and wondered. For all her apparent vulnerability, Luisa had a decent sense of self-protection – at least around men. Better than Dulcie had given her credit for. Looking like that, she probably had to. Whatever the reason, it seemed like maybe Luisa had done the right thing, coming clean to Bruce. Maybe it meant she wasn't in any danger anymore. Maybe that's why the Siamese fighting fish was now circling slowly, surveying the bar below. Unless, thought Dulcie with a chill that didn't come from her iced drink, the fish's relative composure meant something else. Luisa had gotten Bruce, and had gotten rid of Tim's computer. Maybe Nemo's new-found peace of mind was for Dulcie, letting her know that Luisa was no longer a threat.

What had Tim been into? The women, the computers, everything seemed to lead back to her sleazy room-mate, and he seemed capable of getting her into as much trouble dead as he could alive. And what had Luisa meant, when she had made that crack about 'fairy tales'? Dulcie's thoughts went back to her dinner with Luke – and to her own ambivalence about the law student. She had left the coffee-house and now found herself on Massachusetts Avenue, walking toward the university. Up ahead was the tree-lined street that housed the legal clinic. She could only hope Luke was working today. Dulcie needed answers.

'Hey there!' The smile that greeted her as she entered the tiny Colonial looked genuine, and Dulcie smiled back.

'Hi, Luke. I wasn't sure you'd be working today.' She felt herself beaming back up at him. Maybe her ambivalence had simply been cold feet. 'Do you have a minute?'

He held up the stack of papers he'd been carrying when she walked in. 'Just about. Come into my office. I've just got to finish up one thing.' She followed him into the tiny windowless room beneath the stairs. Papers were piled everywhere. 'Printouts,' said Luke, removing a file box from a chair. He sat in front of a terminal.

'Thanks.' Dulcie sat. 'I forgot – you've been erasing all the computer files.'

'Well, it's a little more complicated than that.' He was typing, distracted, and, for a moment, Dulcie bristled.

'Hey, just because I'm an English major, don't tell me—'

He cut in, looking up with both hands in the air. 'Sorry! Sorry! Believe me, after everything Stacia did for us, I've been cured of any gender bias about programming. That girl is a whiz.'

'So you've said.' Dulcie examined Luke's face. He had turned back toward his terminal, but she could see a slight flush – admiration, or something more. 'She's a business major, right?'

'Yeah, if you can call it that over at Miss Chivers. More like data processing.'

'That's so funny.' Dulcie sat back while Luke typed. Life was odd. Data entry was what Dulcie had been stuck doing at Priority. She hated it. Maybe she and Stacia would end up bonding – if they weren't competing for Luke's attention. Stacia had proved that she could be a good friend; look at all she was doing for Alana. Nor did the pretty brunette seem to be playing dumb for Luke, which was a point in her favor.

Except that she'd denied knowing much about computers to Dulcie. Was she being modest? But she knew that Dulcie was a doctoral candidate, a serious scholar. What was it Chris had said? 'Everybody has secrets; it's human nature.' But why play dumb to Dulcie? Unless she had it wrong.

'Luke, did Stacia ever try to deny how smart she was?'

Luke didn't even look up. 'Play the "just a girl" card? Nuh-uh. Not Stacia.' Luke hit 'return' and spun his chair around. 'But you can ask her yourself!'

As if on cue, the door swung open and Stacia walked in. Wearing jeans, cowboy boots and a tank-top with a rock band's logo, her silky hair tied back in a neat ponytail, she looked more casual than Dulcie had ever seen her, if you didn't count what looked like a diamond hanging from a thin chain around her neck. Even in this get-up, she was still drop-dead gorgeous, the jeweled pendant setting off her dark tan. 'Here's the July twenty-third batch.' She looked around for a place to put the latest bunch of files. Dulcie jumped up to take them.

'Hey!' Stacia's smile lit up her face and Dulcie made herself smile back.

'Dulcie just dropped by. Can you give us a few minutes?' Luke reached to take the papers. 'Documentation,' he explained, placing the pile on top of a waist-high stack. 'We're going to need it.'

Documentation? 'No, actually, please stay.' An idea was forming in Dulcie's head. She needed to talk it out – to uncover a truth. 'Stacia?' Dulcie motioned to the chair she'd just vacated. The slim brunette folded herself into it. 'Luke?' He sat, too.

Standing in front of them, Dulcie began to feel ridiculous. Was she in one of her own novels? Nobody here was faking the pedigree of a story. Nobody here had any reason to counterfeit paperwork. This was crazy. But nobody had any reason to conceal a true identity, either. Not here, not with her. She thought of the files she and Luke had found, what looked like computer coding. Had those been bits of emails, love notes between Luisa and Tim? Or had Dulcie been so caught up in her books, in her own fears and worries about her friendships, that she had missed the obvious? *Trust yourself*. The echo of Mr Grey sounded in her ear. *Trust what you hear in the voice*. What if he hadn't been talking only about literature, but about life?

'Stacia, you've been telling me you don't know much about computers.' The brunette waved one hand in the air, a dismissal of a trivial point. 'But Luke says you're a whiz, and always eager to help out – especially in clearing out files.'

She was warming to her topic. 'And, now, I was wondering. A lot of women will pretend they don't know something. They'll play "poor little me", but you've done the opposite of that. You don't seem to want me to know how much you know. But you've already made yourself invaluable to Luke.' Maybe this *was* jealousy speaking. Dulcie heard it in her own voice. Luke and Stacia did, too. Stacia sat up straighter, the hint of a smile playing on her face. Luke leaned toward the slim brunette, protectively, and Dulcie felt them uniting against her. She was being silly. She was outclassed. *Trust yourself.*

'Stacia, help me understand something here. I'm a bookworm, I know that. But you're no slouch intellectually, and we both know that beauty and brains are a potent combination.' Dulcie looked at the golden pair, so perfectly matched. 'It's gotten you in here, where you can alter the records.' Luke opened his mouth to protest. Dulcie raised her hand for quiet. 'And I think it got you in with Tim, too. Especially when he was short of funds. Were you, also? I think you weren't just Alana's friend, helping out. I think you were also a savvy business major. And, maybe, Tim's business partner, too. But why?'

Stacia opened her mouth to protest, but Dulcie kept on talking. The facts were coming together, the dates, the evidence. 'You've been involved with Tim and Alana from the beginning; you've been their best buddy – the friend who's always there, the one with computer expertise. And now you're running around like mad, trying to cover up. That's why you've stayed close to everyone.' She thought about Demetria, about the book's warning: 'spells most potent for their proximity'.

Stacia stood up and rolled her eyes, and even as she made a face Dulcie realized how much prettier the other woman was; how much slimmer and better dressed. But Dulcie had the thread of an idea, and she wasn't letting go. 'Wait just one minute, Stacia.' Dulcie stepped between the taller woman and the door. 'It all makes sense! That's why you kept pestering Luke about Tim's laptop.' Luisa had seen the computer, and Luisa had no illusions about Tim – no reason to lie. 'There were no photos of Alana on it. There were no photos of anyone. You wanted to erase something *you*'d put on that computer. The forensic techs were getting close to the source of the bug. Tim never had the brains to install a computer virus. But you do. And he needed money – he always needed money! Once he was into the Harvard system, he could charge anything he wanted. Change grades for people. Check out class placement. Get people off probation. As a B-school student, he had complete access, so why—?' Suddenly, she realized the truth. Stacia had turned her back and was making a point of looking at the bookshelves, but Dulcie no longer cared. 'Tim was on academic probation himself. That's why the tutoring and the worry. Did they threaten to cut off his computer access? Were they monitoring his usage? Is that why he needed to get on my laptop?' She paused. The problem with logic is that once it started rolling, it gained its own momentum.

'Stacia, did you steal my laptop?' Her voice had gone quiet, she knew. Both Luke and Stacia were so still, Dulcie thought they were holding their breath.

Stacia spun around and broke the silence with a snort. 'That's ridiculous! Steal your laptop? And besides, you got it back. I heard.'

'Not yet.' There was something else here, something Dulcie had to tease out.

'Oh?' Stacia grew quiet again, her perfect mouth set in an odd frown, and in the silence an awful thought began to grow. Stacia – her laptop – Stacia was a summer student, working at the clinic. She'd have a card for stack access.

'If you thought I had it back, if you'd thought I'd gotten my files back from Suze, all my files . . . Were you the one in Widener yesterday?'

'What?' Luke stood up, his voice raised in protest. 'Dulcie, I really think—'

'No, Luke.' She held up her hand for silence. 'Someone was stalking me yesterday. Someone sliced open my bag. I thought – the cops thought – someone was going for my wallet. But what if it was Stacia, and she was looking for my laptop? That would explain why she tried to corner me. Erasing the files wasn't enough. She must have figured that out. She needed to destroy my laptop before the Harvard cops confiscated it.' The next thought hit her like a thunderbolt. 'She already had Tim's. She snatched it when she pushed Luisa down the Widener steps!'

Stacia let out a wordless squeal of protest and tried to push past Dulcie. But to do so, she had to walk by Luke, too, in the tiny, cramped office, and he reached out to her, gently touching her arm to stop her.

'This is ridiculous.' He turned on Dulcie, his eyes blazing. 'You think everything is supposed to play out like in one of your books, all high drama.'

'Luke!' Maybe it was seeing him reach out to Stacia, reach out to defend the woman who might have attacked her. Maybe, just for a moment, she thought, He's right . . . I don't live in the real world. Whatever it was, that cry had been torn from her – a little wail, heartbroken. I've lived too much in my own head, she thought, for, well, for ever.

'I didn't mean—' With his other hand, he reached out to Dulcie. For a moment, that was all she wanted.

'You Worthington men!' Luke and Dulcie both turned, the moment broken. Stacia was inches from them both, but she was staring at Luke. 'You're all so *feckless.*'

'You mean "fickle".' And with that Dulcie got a hold of herself. Yes, she was a bookworm, and, yes, she spent a good part of her time in the library. But she loved those books not because they were full of adventure and romance – *not only*, a feline voice whispered in her ear – but because they were true to the human condition, revealing character as only art can. 'Feckless means worthless, and I don't think you mean that.'

Stacia collapsed back in the chair. Dulcie knelt at her feet, the better to peer up into her perfectly made-up face.

'Stacia? Was I right about the computer virus? Were you helping Tim? Was he paying you?'

'It wasn't about the *money*.' Tears were streaming down Stacia's tanned cheeks, but her voice was flat and angry. 'It was never about the money. I don't care about money, I never cared. *Tim* cared. He had to have his guitars, his nights out, his nice things.'

'You cared for him.' Dulcie looked closely at Stacia's dark lashes, the mascara flecked with gold. Everybody does have secrets, she realized. Maybe Stacia was driven by love. That mascara – hadn't her novels taught her anything about our essential nature? About secrets? 'You were sleeping with him.'

'I loved him! And he—' She gulped, the make-up on her face beginning to smear. 'He never loved Alana. She was just a blonde. Another *pretty thing*. I was his helpmate, his partner.'

'But the ring?' Dulcie leaned close. The anger was going out of Stacia's voice, the crying getting louder.

'I found it.' Dulcie nodded, she remembered the afternoon when the two friends had come over. But Stacia was still talking. 'I found it one day right after – after we had made love. I thought maybe it was for me. And Tim laughed.' Stacia put her hands up over her face. Dulcie didn't need to hear any more. She'd been right in the first place, that Tim had been done in by a woman scorned. She'd just had the wrong woman.

'You killed him, didn't you?' The dark head nodded. 'And you took the ring, until you realized that it implicated you. Then you brought it back and pretended to find it again?'

With a big sniff, Stacia looked up. Her make-up had streaked her tanned cheeks. 'I thought I could play him, that he was the one who would fall. I thought he'd see—' She collapsed, crying again, and hid her ruined face.

Don't underestimate the power of love, Dulcie. 'Not like this, Mr Grey,' she whispered, and Luke turned to her. 'It's nothing,' she said out loud. 'But I think it's time to call the police.'

Afterward, she and Luke sat on the little white house's front step. The street was empty now, the blue and white police cruisers gone.

'Do you think he ever loved her?' Luke sounded wistful. For Tim or for himself, Dulcie didn't know. But she shook her head. It seemed unlikely, and she was out of words. 'He did tell me he'd grown to appreciate smart women.'

His smile implied more, but Dulcie shrugged.

'I bet he was talking about Luisa,' she said. 'From what she's said, they had fun together.' And Luisa, Dulcie now knew, was also able to set boundaries. 'He might have meant to propose to her.'

'Maybe. I wonder, though.' He leaned in close. 'Do you think she meant to set you up?'

'As an easy scapegoat? A fallback fall girl? I don't know.' She kicked at a loose stone. 'Maybe it was just convenience. His university account was in jeopardy, and there I was. I don't know that she ever thought of me at all.'

'You were a rival, you know. With both the Worthington men.' She heard the soft mocking in his voice and looked up. 'Tim always did say he liked you.'

She looked over at Luke, into his blue eyes. His tan hadn't faded much, despite the long hours at the legal clinic. His hair, dirty blond with surfer's highlights, still hung boyishly into those baby blues.

'I've got to go, Luke.' She stood up and turned toward home. 'I've got to call a friend.'

Thirty-One

She couldn't call Chris right away. It seemed too – she couldn't place it – sudden. But once again, only Suze's voicemail answered when she tried that number. 'Suze, you wouldn't *believe* what's been going on here. Call me?'

Dulcie headed for the shower. The hot day – the emotional encounter – had left her feeling sweaty and slick. But when the phone rang, she jumped for it. 'Suze!'

'Uh, no.' It was Chris. She'd come to recognize his voice and found herself perversely pleased.

'Hey, Chris. Well, do I have a story for you!'

'Does it have wild adventures and windswept moors?'

'No, but it's got a happy ending!' She was dancing a little. Ah, well, he couldn't see her.

'Do you want to tell me about it over a pizza? It's two-for-one night at Pinocchio's.'

It wasn't Sonsie, but Harvard Square was a lot closer than Newbury Street. 'Sounds like heaven.' Life as a struggling academic wasn't entirely without its compensations. 'Meet you in forty-five?'

Running from the T the next morning, Dulcie was almost able to forget her earlier worries. Life was working out, wasn't it? She couldn't show up at her day job just to be arrested, could she? She'd still have a job – wouldn't she?

'Please let me in,' she whispered aloud as she shoved into the door. The elderly guard checked her bag without comment, and she raced for the elevators.

'Where you been?' Joanie stood at the back of the crowd that had gathered. Everyone seemed to be waiting for the elevator.

'I'm late, I know. I had the most wonderful—'

'Here they come!' Joanie grabbed her arm and pulled her to the front. 'Ricky told me about this.' By instinct, Dulcie pulled back. What if this were a set-up? What if *she* were the one being surrounded? As if to confirm her fears, the elevator opened and out came Sally Putnam, flanked by the same two guards who had escorted Dulcie out of the building such a short time ago.

'We are extremely disappointed in you.' Dulcie heard a voice behind her and jumped. A grey-haired man in a blue suit was speaking. 'We gave you our trust, our every confidence.'

There it was again. Trust. She took a breath in order to respond – and he walked past her. Taking Sally Putnam by the upper arm, he led her away from the elevator, and back through the crowd where, Dulcie could now see, two uniformed policemen waited. As if noticing them all for the first time, the suit turned back toward the crowd. 'There's nothing to see here. Please go back to your workstations.'

As the two uniformed policemen marched Sally Putnam out, Dulcie felt a hand on her own shoulder. Still spooked, she whirled around. There stood the blonder of the two security guards, looking like a refrigerator in a suit. She stepped back, knowing that flight was futile. But he was smiling.

'You don't remember me, do you?' She looked up at the square jaw, the thick neck, and shook her head. She'd remember a suit that large.

'English 10. My freshman year. You taught my section.' Dulcie racked her brain. Had there been a football player in one of her classes a few years ago? Those big conference courses drew all types. 'I wasn't there as much as I should have been.' He cleared his throat and had the grace to look embarrassed. 'But I remember you. You managed to make those Puritan sermons fun. Anyway, I'm here now.'

Dulcie nodded, a vague image of a younger, and possibly even bigger version of the blond refrigerator, his feet up on his desk, coming to mind. 'You're working as a guard?'

'Management trainee.' He shook his head. His neck was still as wide as his jaw. 'But they want us to learn the entire business, so I'm doing security this month.'

A light began to dawn. 'So, if you recognized me . . .'

'I just couldn't see you as the embezzling hacker type. For starters, I doubted you had the computer expertise. No offense.' He held up palms that could have doubled as dinner plates, and for the first time she saw the engraved Harvard ring on his right hand. 'But when you said your sweater had been stolen, I started thinking: what was a senior HR manager doing up in data entry?'

Dulcie smiled up at him. 'You know, after that sweater went missing, my mother told me, anyone who steals a sweater is capable of doing anything. I didn't believe her.'

'Smart woman, your mom. You must take after her.' While Dulcie was mulling over that bombshell, the guard reached out his meaty paw. 'I'm Ethan, by the way.'

'Dulcie Schwartz. But you know that.' They shook. His grip was surprisingly gentle. 'Hey, any chance I can look in her office? Maybe my sweater's still there.'

'You can't.' His smile became broader. 'But I can. Why don't you give me your number, and I'll let you know what I find.'

Nobody seemed to mind when Dulcie picked up her day's worth of files and took them back to her old workstation. But neither she nor Joanie got much work done as they caught each other up on their various adventures.

'Ricky told me something was up with the old Snake, but he'd have been fired if anything had leaked out,' Joanie confided. 'I was trying to tell you not to worry.'

'And all you did was spook me more.' Dulcie shook her head in disbelief.

'Well, you were being investigated for murder. And more computer hacking. Did they ever figure out how that virus got in?'

'It was the Duke virus. Chris knew that.' She liked saying his name. 'Tim probably got a copy from one of his old prep school buddies. But he needed Stacia to put it into the Harvard system. We still don't know why she used my computer – maybe she did want to implicate me. Maybe she just wanted to muddy the waters, so to speak. She says it was Tim's idea, so who knows?'

'Men.' Joanie rolled her chair closer. 'Maybe he was claiming you as his own. Marking you.'

'*Ew*.' Joanie could never know how distasteful that idea was. 'If he pissed anywhere . . .'

Joanie laughed. 'Hey, you seem to have it, girl. I noticed that big hunk downstairs chatting with you.'

'Oh, I'm taken, I think.' Dulcie thought back to the evening before. It had ended with a kiss, but she knew both she and Chris were looking forward to more.

'Hey, don't limit your options just yet. And there's still the pretty rich boy, too.'

'You should talk.' Dulcie had seen the way Joanie looked at Ricky. 'How long have you known Ricky?'

'A couple of weeks at least.' Joanie looked around. 'And besides, his red hair looks so good against black.'

With very little actual data entry, the day flew by, and Dulcie realized with regret that her tenure at Priority was coming to an end.

'Hey, two more weeks and I start classes.' They were walking to the elevators in a building that had gone unnaturally quiet.

'And that's a good thing?' Joanie was a student at UMass.

'Yeah,' said Dulcie, with assurance, 'it is. I've got a thesis to write.'

Life seemed to be repeating itself, therefore, when Dulcie walked up her own street and saw Helene sitting on the stoop, holding a very young black-and-white kitten.

'Hey, Helene, what's up?' She looked down the street. 'Is everything all right?'

'Not exactly, child.' Helene's broad face looked worried. In her hands, the tiny kitten squirmed to be set free.

'What's the problem?' Dulcie sat beside her neighbor and automatically reached out for the kitten. The feisty little beast batted at her hand. 'Little fighter!'

'It's this little girl, actually. My buddy Jackie adopted her last week. Just fell hard. But it turns out she's allergic and her boy has asthma. She's heart-broken, but she's got to give her up.'

'Oh, that's too bad.' The kitten was exploring Dulcie's shirt, attempting a claw-by-claw ascent. 'But this little gal's so young and cute, someone else will take her.'

Helen shook her head. 'They had an outbreak of distemper at the shelter and they're not accepting any new animals, not unless they're old enough to be vaccinated. It would be a death sentence, and so, well, I was wondering, would you be interested? Even if you could just foster her until she's old enough to get her shots.'

'Foster a kitten?' Dulcie could feel the minuscule claws through her shirt. The kitten was making headway – until it lost its grip and fell to her lap. 'Yeah, maybe I could do that.'

As Dulcie carried the kitten into her apartment, she could see her machine had flicked on. A familiar voice was leaving a message.

'Dulcie, I'm so sorry I've been out of touch. You wouldn't believe what's happened.'

'Suze?' Dulcie picked up. 'Is that you? It's been so long. Ow.' She detached the kitten from her chest and set it on the floor to explore. 'I caught a murderer.'

'I knew you would.' Suze sounded distracted. 'And I've got my own news, too.'

'OK, you first.' Dulcie knew her friend had to get something off her chest. Besides, she had to figure out a way to tell Suze about Chris.

'I'm in love!'

Dulcie stepped back in surprise – and narrowly missed the kitten. 'Whoa! Uh, I mean, that's great.' She hopped over to the chair. 'Who is he? And how did this happen?'

'Well, you remember how I was spending all those hours in the library?'

Dulcie made an appropriate noise and reached to pet the kitten.

'There was a systems analyst, you know, working with their computers, and he was really so helpful. His name is Ariano.'

'Ariano – oh! Sorry, I just got bit.' Dulcie withdrew her hand. She was going to have to get some cat toys. And a litter box. And cat food. And— 'Hey, Suze, you're not staying down there, are you? I really don't want to deal with another room-mate!'

Now it was Suze's turn to laugh. 'No way. One summer here was enough! But Ariano is transferring. He's got a job at Harvard.'

The next two weeks flew by, partly because Dulcie saw Chris almost every night. In addition to burritos, good coffee, and libraries, the two discovered a shared love of old movies. Including, thought Dulcie a bit smugly, the really romantic ones that Jonah had never liked. Even before the semester started, she'd found time to type up her notes, and her adviser was optimistic that '"Jealous Spirits": A New Reading of *The Ravages of Umbria*' would be publishable. Dulcie knew that soon she'd be spending hours on end back in the stacks, pulling out diaries and letters to support her claim that the unknown author had been leaving clues with both wit and language. But that was something to look forward to, rather than fear. The stacks were her own again, not an escape, but a scholar's cave, where ideas were born and nurtured.

Her one regret, as summer turned to fall, was that Mr Grey seemed to have disappeared.

'Maybe he was only there when I needed him,' she suggested to Suze one Sunday morning over coffee. It was a rare weekend morning when both women were alone, and a great chance to catch up.

'Maybe it was the fact that you needed him to be there.' Suze let the idea hang as she poured them both a refill. 'I mean, cats are strange beings. Maybe,' her voice grew soft, 'he just lives on in your heart.'

'Maybe.' The morning seemed a little dimmer after that, but just then the kitten started to climb up Dulcie's leg, demanding attention and just a bit of the butter from her toast.

'Do you think it was all in my mind?' she asked Chris later that day. It had taken a while for her to confess about her ghostly companion. But he'd taken it in his stride, pointing out that such a phantom feline would fit with her academic discipline. 'Do you think I made it all up?'

'You didn't make up the murder, and something helped you through that.' He reached for her. 'Something besides me, that is.'

Sunday nights were the quietest time for the computer labs, so Chris left soon after. Suze was downstairs watching *Mystery* on TV and Dulcie thought about joining her.

'Kitten, where are you?' She'd still not entirely taken to the idea of adopting the little tuxedo cat. But increasingly she was thinking it might be time, soon, to give up and grant the little animal her own name. She needed more friends in her life, the kind she could trust. 'Kitten?'

She heard a voice. Had Suze come upstairs? But no, this was a young voice, a girl's, and it was in the middle of a conversation.

I'm working at it, really! I'm using all four paws and purring as loud as I can.

I know you are, little one. The answering voice was male, adult, and very familiar. *She just takes time to come around to new ideas. She's a human, after all. And they can be very stubborn. But she'll learn, little one. She'll learn.*